WALKING

ALSO BY KIM KELLY

Black Diamonds

This Red Earth

The Blue Mile

Paper Daisies

Wild Chicory

Jewel Sea

Lady Bird & The Fox

Sunshine

WALKING

KIM KELLY

First published by Jazz Monkey Publications in 2020
This edition published in 2020 by Jazz Monkey Publications

Walking

EPUB: 9781925786699
POD: 9781925786705

Cover design: Alissa Dinallo
Cover image: Shutterstock montage; illustration creator unknown, c.1950;
the publisher seeks contact from original copyright holder
Author photograph: Dean Brownlee
Printing: IngramSpark

Publishing services provided by Critical Mass
www.critmassconsulting.com

for the fearlessly kind
for Liz

*Make a habit of two things –
to help, or at least, to do no harm.*

Hippocrates, *Epidemics I*

ONE

DR HUGO WINTER DEAD

Dr Hugo Jacob Winter, leading Sydney orthopaedic surgeon, died in his private hospital at Rushcutters Bay, on Wednesday, aged 75.

A reclusive man, he was largely unknown except by his fellow surgeons, eminent colleague, Dr E. A. Slade, said yesterday evening.

Dr Winter graduated in medicine at Berlin University, Germany, and practised in New Zealand before coming to Australia a few years prior to the First World War. He was debarred from joining the Australian Imperial Force because of his nationality.

The funeral and cremation took place at the Northern Suburbs Crematorium on Friday.

Sydney
November 16, 1948

LUCY BRYNNE

The papers print some rubbish, don't they? 'A reclusive man'? 'Largely unknown'? I can't imagine Dr Slade saying these things about Hugo to a news reporter. Surely he knew his colleague better than that.

I can't imagine it's been almost one week since Hugo left us.

I can't imagine this tiny scrap of half-wrong nothing will serve as his obituary. But it seems it will. Not even a mention of his passing at yesterday's or this morning's ward meeting at the hospital. No official notice posted by anyone from the British Medical Association, either. Have we all seen so much death and destruction that the loss of an extraordinary man is no tragedy today?

Grief slips through every nerve; I'm not sure that I can make my muscles move to get off the tram. I clench the newspaper in my fists, staring out at a blue-sky slice of dusk between the grimy terrace rows of Bayswater Road, where it's just another Tuesday, and no-one knows:

Dr Hugo Winter is dead.

The bell jangles for Rushcutters Bay and my legs know what to do: they know the way down Waratah Street to Aurora House – without which, without Hugo, these legs wouldn't be walking as they do. Without him, I wouldn't have a right leg at all to do the walking business with. I wouldn't be who I am, today, this minute, these feet upon this footpath, if it weren't for Hugo Winter.

Twenty years ago – twenty years and four months ago, to be more exact – I first saw this view of Hugo's clinic, its crisp, bright white façade, large sash windows all gazing north towards the harbour beyond the picket fence of a sports oval, framed by figs that sprawl across a foreshore park. I was seven, the dark, silky ends of my plaits tied off with slim rose satin bows, and I wasn't walking anywhere then. Seized with guilt and fear and loneliness, I was – despite the best efforts of the lady who brought me to Sydney on the train. *It won't be long now.* She held me tight on her lap in the taxi the rest of the way. I don't remember her name: someone lovely from the Lithgow Cripples Fund, she had beautiful red hair that kept slipping out from under her hat.

Hero. That's the word I would use in my obituary of the man who remade my leg, my life.

Outspoken. Impatient with fools. Unceasingly kind. Astonishingly generous. Firmly gentle. Gently firm. Dauntless.

I knew him as Doctor Hugo when I was small – Old Hugh Shoe in a laugh. I came to know him as my best friend when I returned at fourteen, orphaned and destitute: he and Jo, his glamorous, incomparably elegant Jo, took me into their home, managed to find me a place at this city's most prestigious school for girls, paid my way through to university matriculation, then looked after me throughout the following year, that mostly horrendous year of 1939, in which he completed his remaking of my tibia, once all my bones had fully grown. He was my mentor, always encouraging me to do more, to join the Army Medical Service by way of learning to swim at the deep end of physiotherapy if that's what I really wanted to do, and I did, and in May this year he just happened to nudge me with the full force of his enthusiasm into the rather choice position I have now at Sydney Hospital. It's impossible to calculate how much I owe him. How much he has meant to me.

Hugo Jacob Winter.

Orthopaedic surgeon.

Erstwhile thespian and terrible clarinetist. Consummate party-thrower at his impeccably stylish home on Darling Point.

Amateur naturalist. Social documentarian. Occasional Australian correspondent for *Der Welt Spiegel*. Author of two books: one on the New Zealand Maori, and one on the flora of coastal New South Wales; both set to the steady rhythm of his gait, hiking hill after hill. A mind that never stopped even, I'm sure, when he was asleep.

A loved man.

So very loved. Not only by me, not only by Jo and their real daughter Claire, but by the countless children he fixed over half a century of fixing them, and their parents. The sort of man you can't take shopping in town without being stopped by someone wanting to thank him, shake his hand. Again and again.

The fact of his absence stuns me at the front door of Aurora. Coronary artery disease, that common thief came for him – and he knew. I can see that now: the shortness of breath, the weariness, the excuses not to come to the pictures with me this past month or so, the making certain I was safely into a secure job with my army work winding up. He died here, in his clinic – somehow, he made sure of that, too.

'Lucy ...' Mrs B is striding up the central corridor as I grasp the iron curl of the stair-rail, and stop there on the bottom step, wordless for a moment with too much to say. We look at each other, Hugo's indispensable matron and I, history clattering between us like a stack of clipboards falling and falling to the floor. I am crushed; we both are. We've each had our hearts wrung out too many times to count, we are each tough ducks, but this blow is ... tougher than the pair of us combined. I am stunned all over again by the memory: the shrill ringing of the telephone, crashing up the corridor of the nurses' quarters and into my room at eleven pm last Wednesday night, *Lucy, Lucy – it's for you*. What? Then Mrs B on the line, her voice shaking: *Hugo. It's Hugo – he's gone.*

Her voice is steady as ever as she says to me now: 'There's no rush to get it all done, you know – the building won't be sold until after probate is sorted out. That's months away.'

'I know.' No rush to get his office sorted out is what she means, no rush to keep coming here every evening after work to do a bit more, as I did yesterday and as I am tonight; but: 'I'd rather get it done while I'm still half mad.'

She nods; she knows my need for doing, for keeping busy, when I'm mad, half or completely: Matron Marjorie Benson has been my nurse through the worst of horrendous, as well as my friend.

She says: 'Corned beef and mash tonight – shall I have a tray sent up?'

'Thanks.' I'll make an attempt at it: whatever comes out of Aurora's kitchen is always excellent; and I am a little too ragged from missing proper meals. I ask her, already moving up the stairs: 'Is there anyone you need me to see?'

She frowns under the thick wave of no-nonsense, steel-wool hair bobby-pinned across her brow: 'Absolutely not. Dr Adinov has everything in hand.'

Dr Adinov is not far off eighty; wonderful orthopaedist that he is, he's retired – unsuccessfully retired, but retired nevertheless. There are only three patients left here, none of them serious, none of them children, but they're all bed-bounds still waiting for beds elsewhere: two ruptured ligaments of the knee, one belonging to a rugby forward, the other a dancer; and a wealthy Mosman dowager with an old lumbar fusion that's caused an acute spondylitis in the vertebra above it, so painful and intractable she probably won't get out of bed again. There's probably some helpful thing I could do for one or all of them. I begin to make a mental note to see Dr Adinov about it – when? Perhaps I should phone – no. Mrs B is right to frown at me: I have too much to do as it is; a pile of reports waiting for me back at my desk at Sydney and —

Keep on up the stairs. He carried me up these stairs once, Hugo, when I was small and the lift had broken down. A storm was sweeping across the water and belting against the windows; I think I'd been down in the basement for an x-ray. I can smell the apron he always wore under his white coat: a rubber apron the colour of a faded cricket ball, a tradesman's apron, an artisan's apron.

A humble man for all the ferocity of his arrogance, his temper where the welfare of a patient was concerned.

How I will miss his eyes: warm black-coffee brown; sympathetic, curious and challenging, all at the same time. No photograph has ever shown him as he truly appeared: the light that burned and danced in him, constantly.

I open the door to his office and I know why I am really here: to be with him. I smile at the towers of paper that teeter and lean on every surface, including the floor. I don't want to touch any of it: this is his brain displayed; his world. He could find anything within a few seconds of anyone asking, although there seems to be no logical organisation among it all: old letters and musical programs, patient files and personal notebooks, tram tickets and x-rays; and above this glorious mess, along the two side walls, his cherished drawings and cards from the children are pinned on boards that reach to the ceiling – hundreds of them. I'll leave them until last, make up some keepsake albums full of them, for Jo. She will be too sad to look at them, possibly forever, but maybe she'll appreciate having these precious pieces of him somewhere near.

For the moment, though, I'll return to hunting for all things easy to identify and remove: newspapers for binning; copies of both the Australian and Hebrew medical journals, and their German equivalent, *Deutsches Ärzteblatt*, which I will donate as a job lot to the student library at Sydney; and copies of all the botanical and natural history publications Hugo subscribed to, which I will donate to the Mitchell Library up the road, to do with what they will.

Only now do I realise my right hand remains a fist around the *Evening News*. Anger streaks through me as I toss it at the binning box: how easily we discard what's truly important. Whole lives worth of immeasurable importance. Among all the things that Hugo did, the gifts he gave, the man he was, why did that reporter choose to mention, 'He was debarred from joining the Australian Imperial Force because of his nationality'? What does that even mean? That Hugo didn't march off soldiering in the First World War? What a surprise. What a bizarre detail to include from a life so rich. Why bother mentioning his passing at all if it's only worthy of such a desultory afterthought? Published six days after his death, four tiny paragraphs wedged between the shipping news and an advertisement for motor oil.

Perhaps someone made a complaint to the press at the oversight: there was a sizeable horde at the funeral service on Friday morning, people from all over the state, people who'd dropped everything at once to travel miles to be there, people who must have all contacted each other about the service, because it wasn't advertised – it didn't need to be. The chapel was crammed with people, scores more spilling out across the lawn, so many of his children who'd grown and flourished, so many friends, including a contingent of nuns from the Sisters of Charity, both a rabbi and a pastor saying words – beautiful words I could hardly hear, because I was too sad. I am too sad. I don't understand why there wasn't an entire edition of every newspaper in this city dedicated to the celebration of all he achieved.

But then I would think that, wouldn't I.

I adored him.

I always will.

HUGO WINTER

To a boy from the coal-slashed hills and factory mills of the Ruhr, Berlin seemed the centre of the universe: a place where art and science met – and tangoed in smoky bars, arguing about Marx until dawn, before making love in a laneway off the Unter den Linden. Hugo embraced every moment of university life there. He forgot, most days, that he was the son of a surly, conservative lace-maker and his cold, dismissive second wife, both of whom would have preferred he hadn't gone to university at all but stayed on in the Ruhr trading in lace and totting up the accounts, doing what an eldest son of a middle-road businessman from a middle-road town such as Hagen should do: follow his father. It was only owing to the open envy of others, telling Herr Winter how proud he must be to have such a brilliant son, that they let him go.

And go he did, three hundred miles east, as fast as the train would take him. Hugo rarely wrote home, except to his little sister, Irma, who received at least a letter a month from him. She was twelve years his junior and he missed her funny face; sometimes he missed his three brothers, too, Kurt, Ernst and Wil, but not often: he was far too busy learning the tango, arguing in smoky bars with fast-talking Berliners and craving the kiss of a girl called Karoline who would never look at him – because, said her friend Marie, he was too short and too Jewish. None of the other girls minded these failings; his autograph book – an essential student accoutrement in those most romantic Belle Époque days – was full of sweet love notes from all sorts of young ladies. He read them often, and reminded himself that while he was not tall, he was strong, solidly built, confident in his physique. As for the other – religion – he didn't much care; it was mostly merely a necessary word on a form for him and, more vaguely, good for business, or might be when he discovered what business he would do.

Having always scored highly in mathematics and physics, Hugo had assumed during his schooldays that he would go into engineering in some way, perhaps build bridges and factories, but he'd enrolled in medicine when the time came because those high scores said he should. He hadn't thought about it in any depth: he was too busy learning – everything. New ideas, new theories, new mechanical inventions, drew his fascination more than any kiss might, and in the German university pool of the late nineteenth century, the first years of one's degree were devoted to just that: everything. Young people were encouraged to try on all hats before finally deciding on the one that fit, and that's how, in Hugo's first year, in 1891, he managed to study the English language, political philosophy, immunology, anatomy and the clarinet all in one go: because he could.

'You must continue with medicine,' his anatomy professor said in the middle of his second year, partly as a joke in response to hearing him play the clarinet one afternoon in a café near the School of Surgery, but mostly because of his perfect understanding of the body and all its functions. 'You should think about orthopaedic medicine. There is a lecture you must attend on Tuesday evening.'

He almost didn't go to that lecture; there'd been a play he wanted to see with his friends, Schiller's *Kabale und Liebe* – or *Intrigue and Love*, as it was in English. But he'd seen the play before, in both languages, and he didn't know all that much about orthopaedics. Bone-setting, wasn't it? Not much to it, he'd presumed: either the bone repaired itself with the assistance of splinting or surgery, or it didn't; and if infection or necrosis set in, the bone was excised, limbs amputated, before death ensued. One of his friends, Friedrich, had slipped on an icy step only a few weeks earlier, breaking his arm at the wrist, and Hugo had been more concerned Friedrich would miss an excursion to Prague they'd had planned – cheapest to go in the frozen month of January. At that stage, he was far more interested in the infections and diseases that attacked the skeleton – tuberculosis, infantile paralysis, rickets – and it had never occurred to him that the deformities caused by them or other abnormalities could be fixed.

Inside the lecture theatre, his professor beckoned him to the front row, where he sat fixed to his seat for the next two hours as a young surgeon from Leipzig told of a revolutionary approach to correcting such structural faults as club feet, congenital hip dislocation and curvature of the spine by stretching and manipulating the body into its proper alignment during childhood. This was the theory of an Austrian surgeon by the name of Adolf Lorenz, who performed these wonders without the cutting of any flesh.

'Impossible!' so most in the room that night declared. 'Ridiculous!'

'What do you think?' Hugo asked his professor afterwards, as they walked through the thick snow outside.

'I think it is genius,' the professor replied. 'It also works. I visited the Lorenz clinic in Vienna, last year. No child should ever be crippled by these rectifiable problems.' And then he told Hugo again: 'You should think about orthopaedics.'

'Why me?' Hugo asked him.

And the professor said: 'There are two things an orthopaedist needs – physical strength and intellectual daring. You have them both.'

The thrill of the compliment didn't last long, though. When he returned to his family in Hagen that next summer break and told his father he was contemplating orthopaedic medicine, his stepmother interrupted: 'The fortune your father is spending on your education and you want to be a bone-setter? Why not tell him you want to be a blacksmith instead?'

It was true that bone-setting was not a highly regarded specialty in those days – it would be three years yet before Röntgen's discovery of the x-ray at Würzburg would change all that, much to the benefit of limbs like Friedrich's arm, which had had to endure some painful guessing until it was put right. It was also true that every time Hugo looked at the tight, hard face of his stepmother, he remembered his longing for his own mother. He was only four when she died, giving birth to his brother Kurt, and he knew virtually nothing of her apart from that – a fact that made up his mind now. He said nothing more to anyone about it, but his course was set: he would put away that thought of orthopaedics and do something even worse, even less respectable – he would specialise in gynaecology. He would devote his strength and his intellect to mothers, to spite the one that showed him no love.

'No! Don't go!' His little sister Irma dragged on his coat-sleeve. 'Don't go back to Berlin before the holiday is ended,' her little funny face begged him.

But he said: 'I have to go.' He held her in his arms and danced her up the hall: 'One summer soon, I will take you with me to Berlin and teach you to tango.'

That would never happen. Five years he spent at completing his undergraduate studies and establishing his gynaecological specialty, taking up his first job at an obstetrics clinic down in Munich, and discovering that, among his many talents, he was pathologically obsessive about his work. Once the responsibility for the lives of all these women settled upon his broad shoulders, he could never seem to justify taking any time to get away for more than a few days, and Hagen, over three hundred miles north, was always a trip too far. The process of gaining a woman's trust, when she was at her most vulnerable, was not something that could be picked up and put down at will. He was obsessive in his learning, too. He learned enormous amounts about the strength of the so-called weaker sex; if he was fond of women before, he became somewhat in awe of them now. He learned a lot about joy as well, about that most sublime reward of life itself. And he learned a lot about loss, when things didn't go as planned. He learned how much life could be saved by the simple act of washing one's hands – and how reluctant his elders were to grasp this not-so-extraordinary innovation.

None of it could prevent or prepare him for the loss of Irma, though. *Your sister has died from Scarlet Fever,* the telegram from his father said, such simple words, such a hammer-smash to his heart. She was two weeks from turning twelve years old, and Hugo had not seen her since she had turned eleven. The new doll that he had bought her sat on the desk in his apartment, unposted. Shame pounded at him that he had not intended going home to celebrate her birthday this time; that he would never teach her to dance.

In that strange way grief has of pushing us where we need to go, Hugo packed his bags and returned to Berlin, thinking he would resume study in immunology, prove that the bacterium streptococcus had killed his sister, but it was his old anatomy professor who got to him first: 'Immunology will make you insane looking for needles in haystacks. Go into orthopaedics, you can rescue the lives of ten children a day. You can do it *now*.' So that is what Hugo would do: if he couldn't see his little Irma again, he would spend the rest of his life obsessively fixing other children, so that they might walk – so that they might dance.

For the next decade, Hugo did nothing else at all: no women, no bars, no theatre but a surgical one – and that one was a hundred miles south of Berlin in the city of Dresden, in what had quickly become the best orthopaedic clinic in Germany. He quickly became one of the best orthopaedic specialists in all of Europe, and possibly the world. He was thirty-four years old. There was nothing he wouldn't do for a crippled child; if the deformity or the injury was beyond fixing, he would at least make it more bearable, more workable. He straightened what was crooked, he pieced together what had shattered, and, as if by some magic or perhaps incredible luck, he never ever amputated, not so much as a fingertip: if a limb was in danger, he always found a way to rescue it.

He learned a lot about the business of compassion there at the clinic in Dresden. In those days, Dresden was arguably the most beautiful city in the Reich, gracious buildings strung along the River Elbe like jewels, its suburbs and spacious parks all studies in the marriage of art and science as it should ideally be in everyday living. An astoundingly wealthy city, at its centre. But that's not where most of Hugo's children came from: they were the sons and daughters of factory workers and miners from outside the gleaming hub. They were children for whom a disabling affliction could mean worse than a life of ordinary poverty: it meant begging on the street and, inevitably, a life cut short because of it. Fortunately for them, the civic-minded Dresdners didn't like the idea of fixable children going about unfixed – that was bad for Empire, as much as it was aesthetically displeasing; it was also cruel – and so they provided funds from their deep pockets to accommodate them at the clinic and to pay for Hugo's fixing genius.

To make up any shortfall in funds, the clinic extracted exorbitant fees from those who could pay: medical students from America eager to learn every new trick; politicians and their sore backs; military mishaps; bankers and their skiing snaps; high heels and ice skates yielding valuable crops of summer and winter ankle sprains. 'I think we must admit you overnight, Madam, to be safe and sure.' Hugo became adept at playing the game. He wanted his children to have the best equipment, swimming baths, gymnasium, the most up-to-date technology, and there was only one way to make that happen, a way Hugo would also stick with for the rest of his life: robbing the rich just enough to finance treatment of the poor.

Naturally, as Hugo's reputation grew, so too did his number of Jewish patients, who'd travel from all over the globe to see him – from Amsterdam, Budapest, Barcelona, London, even from Palestine. But it was one from New

Zealand who would change his course again and irrevocably, in the autumn of 1907.

Moe Frankel was a grain merchant from Christchurch who was returning to Prussia and his native Poland to visit his elderly mother, but also to explore the possibility of having his knee repaired while he was in Europe, the joint having been crushed several years earlier when he was knocked down and run over by a dray at the docks. An eccentric character, always on the move, he told Hugo at the clinic: 'I have a week spare.'

Hugo laughed: 'It will take months.' And he wasn't playing any game about it: 'First, I would have to reconstruct the kneecap. Second, I would need to take some muscle from the back of your knee and transplant it to the front, attaching it with wire. Finally, but crucially, I would then have to try to repair the damaged tendons as well. It's very complex, and the injury is so old, I couldn't guarantee these operations would restore function. I must be honest, I can't promise a successful result for you at all.'

'Oh,' said Moe Frankel, as if he hadn't heard half of what had been said to him. 'Well, could you come back to New Zealand with me?'

Hugo laughed again: 'No. I'm quite busy here.'

'Oh.' Moe Frankel shrugged and sighed. 'That's a shame. We don't have anything near to an orthopaedist in New Zealand.'

'No-one at all?' Hugo's interest was piqued.

'No,' Moe Frankel replied. 'There's a clever chap at the Children's Hospital in Melbourne we send the youngsters over to when we can, but Australia is a long way to go for treatment. Other than that, there are the usual unhelpful dunderheads who say no to everything.'

Hugo frowned at the idea of there being a place in the world, a civilised place, where there was no orthopaedist.

Then Moe Frankel made the offer that couldn't be refused: 'A thousand pounds, Herr Doktor. Come back to New Zealand with me for six months and I'll give you a thousand pounds – more, if we can raise the money to have you do some teaching at the hospitals. I can arrange a tour.'

Hugo laughed his loudest at that. He wasn't sure of the exchange rate between goldmarks and pounds, but that was a lot of money. In a flash of inspiration he saw himself setting up his own private clinic on his return, perhaps in Berlin.

He told Moe Frankel: 'All right. Six months.'

It would end up being four years. As predicted, Hugo couldn't work a miracle on Moe's knee, but he eased the pain and improved the movement in it enough that Moe bellowed his praises all over the North and South Islands on that initial tour, which in turn brought such a flood of people, mostly children, to his door that he couldn't leave. He set up a makeshift clinic in Christchurch instead, in the front room of his rented house, and travelled all over the islands whenever he could.

Something of his youth returned to him there: an excitement for new learning, a reinvigoration in the crispness of the air and the bright, wild blue of the Pacific Ocean. He particularly enjoyed any opportunity to be among the Maori people, studying their powerful physiques, their formidable athleticism and superiority on the rugby field; their striking ceremonial war dances; their hymn-like love songs and lullabies. He wrote many articles about New Zealand for *Der Welt Spiegel*, his old university friend, Friedrich, being the foreign news editor at that paper by then. In lively detail, Hugo described the majesty of the alps, the colonial quaintness of the cities, and marvelled at the surprisingly progressive politics throughout – a kind of sensible socialism under which women were allowed to vote and children didn't tend to starve. He made good comedy, too, from the lack of anything resembling champagne or theatre or orthopaedists, but all things said, he had a wonderful time.

So wonderful and so busy, he didn't really hear the rumblings of discontent coming from the medical establishment. 'Quack.' 'Upstart.' 'Charlatan.' 'Rude and pretentious little shit.' He'd heard all the German equivalents over the years anyway. That the hospitals in New Zealand weren't overly eager to have him demonstrate his techniques – on the grafting of tissue and bone, on massage and manipulation, on splinting and exercise, on anything – didn't bother him, either. It had taken five or so years for all these theories to be accepted in his homeland, and not universally; it would take as long for them to be accepted here. Surely these advances would be accepted eventually, though – when people saw the proof. When they saw the children grow into healthy adults.

It was a disappointment to have passed on so little knowledge to so few while he was there, but it was time – beyond time – for him to go. He was almost thirty-eight years old: he had to return to Germany, get on with his career. Already there had been new developments in fixation pins and x-radiographic imagery in his absence; he had to get home.

But the evening before he had planned to book his passage, he went to dinner at Moe's house, as he often did, and this time, among Moe's small though invariably interesting collection of guests, Hugo would meet a young woman from Sydney, the daughter of a very successful biscuit manufacturer to whom Moe sold a great deal of wheat. A young woman by the name of Joanna Levine, who was in Christchurch visiting her aunt and cousins.

Perhaps that crisp New Zealand air had replenished and repaired something deep in his heart that had been broken since Irma's death; perhaps it was just the right time for him to fall in love, that day, a Sunday, April 9, 1911.

For Hugo Winter fell in love with Joanna Levine not so much at first sight, but with the back of her head, the gloss of her dark hair luxuriantly coiled beneath its silver combs, before she even turned around there in the drawing room to smile at him: 'Good evening, Dr Winter, isn't it?'

Like him, she was short and Jewish, but that's about where the similarities ended. She was fourteen years younger than him, she was breathtakingly beautiful – so beautiful he was momentarily lost for words. Only a brief moment, though, before he was having to counsel himself to shut up and play this one game very carefully.

'So, Dr Winter, you're about to leave for Germany, I hear?' she asked him a little later, across the salmon bisque.

And he replied: 'I had been but I find my ship is suddenly delayed.'

She blushed, and if he'd fallen in love an hour ago, he was from this second irretrievably devoted. Joanna Levine was not the sort given to blushing. She was sophisticated, cultured, but unassuming, aware of her beauty and expert at its accentuation, and yet aware, too, of its superficiality. She was the woman at the party who made others feel welcome, the one who spoke in questions that drew out the light from those around her. She played the piano, sang like a lark, and laughed like one too, with a sharpness of wit that never cut another. She loved music and her Persian cats, three of them whom she'd named Socrates, Plato and Aristotle; she loved plants and flowers and walking. She was the woman for him.

Not a man given to wasting time, he didn't waste any now: within a fortnight, he invited her to picnic alone with him at Godley Head and there, as they walked together above the clifftops looking out to sea, he asked her with no other embellishment than the bright, wild blue before them: 'Would you possibly consider marrying me?'

'Hm.' She pressed her dainty fingers to her lips, thinking; she'd felt he might ask but it seemed too soon, too much a whirl. For all that her parents would approve of every dot of him, she wasn't sure. But she matched him for speaking the truth; she told him: 'I don't know that I could marry a surgeon, up to his elbows in blood every day. I'm afraid I tend to be a little squeamish.'

He laughed: 'I'm not asking you to be my theatre nurse. I won't bring any blood home, I promise.'

'Hm.' She smiled; such a glorious smile. Then she said, more seriously: 'There's one other thing.'

'What is it?' he asked her. 'Whatever it is you want, Jo, I'll give it to you – anything.'

She sighed, supposing this would end the affair: 'I'm a Sydney girl, Hugo. All my friends, all my family are there, or here in Christchurch. I know it probably seems perverse, parochial, even silly, but I don't want to go to Europe. I don't want to live in Germany, or anywhere but my home.'

'Oh.' Hugo sighed too, but with relief. Whatever thought he'd had of establishing his own clinic in Berlin, it flew away on that April breeze. 'We shall make our home in your home then, my darling. We shall make our life together in Sydney.' He swept his hand across the Pacific, across the world: 'We can do anything we like.'

And so it was that Joanna Levine became Hugo Winter's wife, all blessings bestowed at the Great Synagogue in her sparkling city of Sydney. Their celebrations were made under the grand chandeliers of the Emerald Room in the Australia Hotel, making Hugo Winter the happiest man on earth – not to mention that by mutually beneficial coincidence he'd stepped straight into a job at St Vincent's Hospital, in Darlinghurst, almost identical to the job he'd left in Dresden, where he could be both practising surgeon and teacher, and continue to treat the poor for free.

Just a week before the wedding, he'd picked up the keys of the house he'd bought for his Jo, the smallest house on the best street in one of the most expensive suburbs, Darling Point, where the city glittered day and night across the harbour. The most beautiful harbour. The most darling wife. And now, after they'd been cheered away from their lavish reception, he carried her across the threshold of their new home, their new life, and he taught her to tango there.

ELIOT SLADE

He hated Hugo Winter before he'd even met him, because that was the jealous, unsettled cast of Eliot Slade. He hated every other doctor who achieved any success. He hated his own father especially: Sir Alfred Slade had been, up until his recent retirement, President of the Sydney chapter of the British Medical Association, Chief Medical Officer to the Department of Health, internationally respected hydrotherapist noted for his theory on the therapeutic benefits of saltwater bathing, and was also, by all accounts, a pretty good bloke to share a beer with at the pub. It's no easy thing to be the mediocre only son of such an accomplished, well-regarded man; there are two ways one might go: into admiration, or into antipathy. Eliot Slade made a hard habit of choosing the latter.

Of course, he could have chosen not to follow his father into medicine; he could have chosen to take his lack of imagination somewhere it might have been better appreciated, perhaps into property law or insurance or right-wing politics, but he didn't; he couldn't. He was insatiably compelled into contest against those with whom he couldn't compete, and in doing so was driven to win by sabotage – by tripping up or belittling his perceived opponent in some way. Besides, although thus far only a lowly assistant to the head house surgeon at Sydney Hospital, he was already deeply attracted to the power of wielding the blade: the life in his hands, the unquestioning veneration from patients and lesser colleagues, the gratification that came from snarling at anaesthetists, barking at nurses – he was eager for it all. He was shaping up as just competent enough not to be a liability for the hospital board, and well-practised enough at blame-shifting to deal with any adverse situation he might himself create. He was also by now, at the age of twenty-nine, atrophied enough in his spirit that he wasn't much affected whenever a patient died: 'Oh dear. Bad luck.'

When it came to Hugo Winter, however, Eliot Slade's capacity for hatred took a darker turn. To begin with, Winter was a foreigner, a Continental, a Hebrew one at that, and Slade had convinced himself of the racial inferiority of every non-British specimen. This in itself was perhaps not remarkable: most doctors more or less agreed with these ideas, the sole notable exception being Sir Alfred, who was quietly but adamantly opposed, in strictest scientific terms, to the whole idea of race. In the son's opinion, though, the only way one such as Winter might make his mark on medicine was by sleight of hand, fakery or thieving from the work of others.

Furthermore, Winter had married Jo Levine. Being a Hebrew herself, Jo was in no way a prospect for Slade, but that didn't stop him from desiring her. Most healthy men would desire a woman like her, and as their social circles often intersected within the small upper set of Sydney, Slade had opportunity to desire her often. He had gone through school with one of her cousins, Edwin Glass, who was now a fast and hungry junior barrister with a leading firm – a smart arse, as far as Slade was concerned, but an inextricably well-connected one. When Glass told him at their last old boys' dinner that Jo was to marry a German orthopaedist, Slade almost choked on his cognac: how dare she? How dare she marry anyone.

But worst of all, Winter had been appointed as an honorary surgeon at St Vincent's, and within a month of being there, the word about town was that his techniques were going to revolutionise orthopaedic treatment in Australia. Testimonials drifted across the Tasman Sea from New Zealand: it was true, they said, the orthopaedist Hugo Winter made crippled children walk – children of whom accepted wisdom had said, 'No, never. Impossible.' He cured them completely, they said. He slipped young bones back into their rightful places as if he were fixing dolls, dozens every week, and for the most part he did it without cutting the flesh.

'I'd like to see that,' Slade scoffed to the head house surgeon during one such discussion over a game of snooker at the Empire Hotel, the medicos' watering hole of preference.

'Well, isn't that fortunate,' his superior replied, potting the black for the match: 'I'm sending you across to St Vincent's tomorrow afternoon to observe him in action.'

It would be fair to say that Eliot Slade did not attend this demonstration with an enquiring mind. The small lecture theatre was crammed with doctors and nurses both, from all over the city, and the atmosphere was alive with anticipation. Slade sniffed the air, discerning only ingrained odours of carbolic acid, chloroform and, he imagined, Catholicism. He supposed the Irish nuns who ran this hospital were up to something illegal, as the Irish generally were.

When Winter entered, Slade did not see him for who he was; he looked like a butcher in his rubber apron and with the sleeves of his gown rolled to the elbows; he was all blunt edges, stocky, and held himself like a wharf labourer ready for a brawl. The first thing Slade thought was: I can't believe Jo Levine married that.

'Good afternoon, ladies and gentlemen,' Winter addressed his audience with clipped and barely accented English. 'Today, I will demonstrate the closed reduction of the congenitally dislocated hip of a five-year-old girl. The dislocation is unilateral, affecting only the femur of the left leg, with no serious bone or ligament damage observed at this time. The discrepancy in leg length caused by the abnormality is presently two and one quarter inches. Unless corrected, this will lead to a worsening of the dislocation and discrepancy, and thereafter significant and permanent incapacity.'

The child was wheeled in upon a table, anaesthetised. Winter grasped her small, pale leg and, indeed, with astonishing ease, slid the head of the femur into the hip socket as if she were a doll; he spoke all the while to his audience, describing the manipulation he had performed and the reasoning and expectations behind the application of the plaster splint he next applied with his assistant, but Slade wasn't really listening to any of it. He took some cursory notes for his report: *six months minimum, x-ray, flexion testing and reapplication of splint at monthly intervals, yearly examination to adulthood.*

Winter went on and on. 'If, after this treatment, the hip reverts to its state of dislocation, open surgical correction will be required, as it will for most children above this age, where too much damage to the joint has already occurred. I invite all of you here today to follow the case of this patient, an interesting case because, for her, the result might go either way. Please, before you leave, record your name and address with my assistant so that I might keep you informed.'

And then, with a nod to suggest he was finished, he left the theatre, wheeling away the child himself.

This is a sham, thought Slade: it has to be. The man is an egoist, a sideshow performer. Once that plaster cast is removed, that child's hip will slip back out of its socket as easily as it went in. Six months or more waiting for this result? A failure for which he's already made excuses. What's he playing at? Slade wondered and quickly presumed this Winter was simply an ordinary orthopaedic braggart making a noise to drum up custom. He returned to the house surgeon at Sydney Hospital and said: 'That was a load of hogwash.'

He hadn't bothered putting his name on Winter's list to be kept abreast of the girl's progress. A few months later, when Winter opened private rooms on Macquarie Street, that esteemed strip of all manner of medical specialty that ran down the hill from Sydney Hospital and past the Botanic Gardens towards the harbour, Slade thought he had the rub of it: surely this was evidence that Winter was a cheat merely wanting to get the well-heeled and desperate through the door of his own clinic, to charge them a fortune for nothing but pain and disappointment.

Slade said as much to his colleagues: 'Those poor un-fortunate children he pretends to treat are pawns for his greed.' As if Slade himself cared about the kiddies. 'What else should one expect of a Jew?' He dropped that rhetorical into every mention of the man and this was the barb that stuck in the minds of any who were sceptical. A Jew might be a clever man, even a good man, but his motives were always open to question.

It was almost a full year later, in the September of 1912, that Slade finally received an update on that little girl and her hip. He'd been lunching with a colleague from Royal North Shore Hospital, angling for a promotion to house surgeon there, when a girl skipped past them in the street, holding her mother's hand.

'By God, that's wonderful, isn't it?' The colleague smiled at them as they went by.

And Slade asked him: 'What's wonderful?'

'That girl,' he said. 'The one Winter treated, you know, the closed reduction of the hip dislocation. You were there, weren't you? At the demonstration? Wouldn't have believed it if I hadn't seen it with my own eyes.'

And Slade lied: 'Oh *that*. Yes, well, two schools of thought about it, so I've heard. A fluke says one, he could never repeat it, and the other says it wasn't a deformity to begin with – the girl fell down some stairs at home, poor mite, so of course he fixed it. Anyone could have.'

'Hm.' The colleague frowned with two schools of doubt: was Slade having him on, or was Winter having them all on? Who could tell?

Slade didn't get offered the promotion at North Shore, but he didn't take that news as badly as he might have. He went to the house surgeon at Sydney Hospital instead and said: 'I've decided I want to specialise in orthopaedics.'

'Oh?' The house surgeon couldn't hide his surprise: orthopaedics was hardly weighted with the status he was sure the young man sought. As it was, he'd hoped Slade would get bored one day soon with the grind of general surgery, the appendectomies, tonsillectomies, the endless lancing of boils and stitching up of drunks. He'd hoped Slade would gravitate to something safer for everyone, like cardiology or urology physician, emphasis on physician – keep him away from sharp implements. Not that anyone would be so bold as to say such a thing to Sir Alfred's son. The house surgeon said now: 'I'll have a word with the Chief then, see what might be arranged.'

'Thank you,' said Slade and he smiled, for something resembling passion had begun to bloom in his heart: a passion for getting the better of Hugo Winter, for hunting out a way to trip him up, to tear him down. To win.

TWO

LUCY BRYNNE

'Is everything all right, Miss Brynne?' Dr Slade asks me outside Dr Oxley's office, as we wait for our morning meeting to begin – Alasdair Slade, the son, that is, or Slade the Lesser, as he refers to himself, being the junior ortho registrar here. He's as sweet as the father is sour, and his question is genuine: he's been the only one on the ward to have shown any concern at the news of Hugo's death; but then, I suppose that's because Alasdair Slade is the only one I've mentioned it to, having had to tell someone I wasn't able to come in to work last Thursday and Friday, and having sought him out specifically because he's the nicest of the bunch by far.

'Yes, I'm all right. Thank you,' I reply, still not really all right, still unable to sleep properly with a constant and overwhelming feeling that I've forgotten something important – such as Hugo, as if I might have left him on a tram. But at this particular moment, I'm still wincing a little at the x-ray on the viewing box, on the wall behind Alasdair Slade's face, inside Dr Oxley's office: the bulb's not switched on, doesn't need to be to show the nasty spiral fracture on the film, jagged and horribly displaced, about three inches under the proximal head of a tibia that has seen better days, an old callus above the ankle suggesting previous misadventure. There's not much that makes me wince, apart from such a woeful shinbone; a sensation of light bursting through my knees, the sharp scratch of a branch slipping through my hand. Although I'm sure I'm about to find out at this morning's ward meeting, I ask: 'Who belongs to that?'

'Fellow brought in yesterday evening,' says Alasdair Slade, frowning intently. 'The Greater is making him a special case, going to knock it together himself.'

'Good to hear,' I say, not a job for anyone who doesn't know precisely what they're doing, and I ask of this patient, already considering his therapy over what will no doubt be a long haul to come: 'An elderly man, I take it?'

'No.' Alasdair Slade continues to frown at the film. 'Twenty-nine-year-old motor mechanic, lost his footing as he stepped down off the running board of a lorry – a stationary lorry. He slipped on a spanner, apparently. Unlucky.'

'I'll say.' How does one do *that* stepping off the side of a lorry, slipping or not – a drop of what, a couple of feet? He deserves a prize. I look at the x-ray again: there's something not quite right about the callus of that old injury, either, an angulation coming from it, as though the break there was not properly set. Whatever it is, that is a mess of a leg, and I'm interrupted at the wonder now by the others arriving: Dr Oxley himself, our senior orthopaedic registrar, whom I most directly assist; and, following him, Dr McVeigh, our resident recently begun his specialisation; then there's Matron Moorefield, keeping a deferential two paces behind. All of them, apart from Alasdair Slade, continue to regard me as some kind of uninvited guest, despite my having been here almost six months, and having been employed as an orthopaedic specialist myself. I'm still finding the civilian medical system a bit of a baffle, having really only known Hugo's idiosyncratic way of running a hospital or the clear lines and regimentation of the army at Prince of Wales Repat – where, in the end, I held the rank of sergeant in the Australian Army Women's Medical Service, with a dozen or so physios, masseuses and nurses in training under me at any one time, where my opinion was considered and my dedication respected as a matter of course.

Here and now, Dr Oxley, who always appears faintly annoyed at having to bother with humanity at all, ticks us through the beds – eleven of them – four in women's, seven in men's, two discharges, one admission and not a lot other than that today but the run-of-the-mill schedule of who must have what done and when, and the expected outpatients list, as far as that can ever be known. No mention of what I'm to do with the tibial catastrophe still glaring at me from the box on the wall.

I dare: 'The new admission – ah, any requirements?'

'Requirements?' Dr Oxley doesn't meet my eye, rarely does: 'I'm certain the patient has many but none that involve you at this time.'

I'm overweary enough this morning to throw that one back at him: 'Forgive me, but just to clarify, doctor. You don't want me to see to it that the most serious patient on the ward is able to manage adequately? No preliminary assessment? No specific monitoring?'

'Not at this time, no. Thank you for allowing me to repeat it, Miss Brynne. Dr Slade senior is attending to this patient personally and has not, as yet, given any instruction.' Slight curl of the lip: Dr Oxley, I suspect, is a bit personally annoyed with Chief Orthopaedic Surgeon Greater Slade for this lack of instruction. I hope he's not suggesting this fracture has been without instruction at all since yesterday evening.

I ask: 'When is he going to operate on it?' Because I need to know, for my planning of treatment; and because the thought of even a moment's neglect here is unacceptable, I unleash upon my superior all of Hugo's influence upon me: 'That fracture should have been reduced as a matter of urgency last night. Was it?'

Silence. The clock ticks around a full fifteen seconds of contempt. I should return to my room, go back to my bed, and knock myself out with a fistful of barbiturate before I get the sack. But I get stone-walled instead. Dr Oxley snatches the x-ray film from the viewing box and leaves, closing his office door as he goes; Matron Moorefield clicks her tongue, the only distinct sound she's made all meeting apart from, 'Yes, doctor,' and follows him down the corridor, with Dr McVeigh.

'Well,' says Alasdair Slade. 'Hm.'

I groan – at myself. A woman can't get away with any outburst like that, not in this place full of men who've done things their way unquestioned for centuries; a woman, an inconsequential physiotherapist, neither doctor or nurse, can't get away with presuming to have looked at an x-ray – what an impertinence. Why did Hugo insist I apply for this job at all? I'm lost here at Sydney. Yes, it's *the* hospital to work at, but it's also a hospital so old-fashioned that unqualified, volunteer masseuses still range the wards providing 'comfort'; I'm not sure the board wants to change that. I don't think the doctors here will ever consider me a fellow professional – someone with something essential to offer a patient, someone in possession of a skill.

And Alasdair Slade is now asking me: 'How about you let me take you out to lunch today?'

'Lunch?' Oh dear God, no. This may well be nothing other than a friendly gesture, a consolation for the awful week I'm having, but I can't be certain it's not something more, and I don't want to give him the slightest nudge in that sort of direction. He really is a sweet man; he's conscientious and diligent in his work; and his tall handsomeness is all very pleasing to look at – those suntanned, yacht-club lines at the corners of his eyes combined with the soft hazel kindness in them. He will make some girl very happy one day, but I am well and truly not that girl. I fell in love with a doctor once, four years ago – thoracic surgeon. Twenty-three and still naïve, I was; he went off to New Guinea and he didn't come home to me, because he found someone else over there. I spent the rest of the war and beyond obliterating his name from memory and caring for those who did come home to me – in bits. I tell lovely Alasdair Slade: 'I have a dreadful stack of paperwork to do – thank you, but I won't be having lunch for the rest of the year.' Please perish the thought in the meantime.

He only smiles, kinder still: 'If you change your mind …'

I am absolutely sure I won't. 'Better get on with business, hadn't we?' I give him a brisk smile as I rush away, heading down the corridor towards the stairs, to Outpatients and the arthritic shoulder of Mrs Tomlinson who'll be waiting for me in one of the cubicles there. Besides, Alasdair is my ultimate departmental boss's son. I'm sure Slade the Greater is a wonderful surgeon; why wouldn't he be? Like his father before him, he's president of the Sydney chapter of the British Medical Association, he's on the hospital board, medical royalty, probably walks on water, too. I don't know much about Eliot Slade other than by formidable reputation, hardly ever see him, but more than intuition tells me he would not approve of his son having lunch with a physiotherapist who also happens to be, at the end of every day, nobody but the orphaned daughter of an alcoholic coalminer. I might be lost in this job, but I do need to make an effort not to lose it altogether. Hugo is not around to rescue me again; Jo will be leaving soon, too, to join Claire and her husband in New York, when she's ready to make that move, to be with her daughter. This job then is, quite practically, all I have.

I put my head down to it, get caught up in Outpatients with an unscheduled gait assessment, then get called over to Casualty for an ambulance-case: a forty-seven-year-old male, wrenched his neck in a car accident, in terrible spasm; spend most of my time trying not to argue with the straight-out-of-school resident there that I'm not going to manipulate that neck until it's had an x-ray; ask a nurse to get patient some aspirin; do my best to calm the man's escalating panic until they wheel him off. It's almost midday before I've seen anyone on the ward, and all morning the shudder of light along my shins has continued to try to push me over, displaced worry snagging at my sleeve for that mechanic's fracture, and deep memory of the pain that belongs to me alone. Grief is not a still or silent thing; it leaps and soars and plunges like a terror-struck bird crying out behind every smile, every word. Every step. I know it's not only the loss of Hugo I'm grieving but every burning hurt, because that's what fresh grief does, too: returns it all to you anew.

Which is why, when I reach the men's section of the ward, I look for him first: the mechanic. But he's not here. Six beds filled, seven empty, one missing, and Dr McVeigh is inspecting number three's dressing: a Mr Parker, smashed elbow Saturday night, motorcycle, drunk, almost killed his girlfriend, very lucky that honorary surgeon Professor Charlesworth was around the corner having dinner at the Emerald Room and sober enough to save your arm, is the way that story goes. One that will leave a lasting scar – as it should.

I ask Dr McVeigh: 'How's the movement in the hand?'

'It'll get there,' he says. 'I'll check with Dr Oxley, but I don't see why you couldn't start working it tomorrow, move him along to Outpatients.'

I smile at young and foolish Mr Parker: 'I'll be working you hard.' And I ask Dr McVeigh: 'Is the new admission in theatre now?'

'Ah, yes,' he replies, distracted by his note-taking. 'Lesser assisting Greater. They're going to wire it.'

'Oh? Goodo.' Don't say what I'm thinking: wiring that mess will mean it takes an eternity to heal – it needs a plate and screws. Not my business.

I stare at the vase of flowers on the central table of this long white room, as if I might quieten the frantic bird inside me, here in the pretty pinks and mauves of the Women's Auxiliary decorations committee. I'm not an orthopaedic surgeon; never going to be. I'm not only a woman and therefore debarred, I'm too slight; I've had a hard enough time since graduation convincing others I have the strength for physio, until they see me at it. Holding a man up is ten percent strength, ten percent technique and eighty percent smile. Let a soldier think you might go out with him when he's fit enough, he'll get fit twice as fast – and once he gets there he's so pleased with himself, he'll happily ask someone else out when you say you're busy. But the war is over, isn't it? It's 1948 – three years over. Perhaps my war should be over, too; perhaps I should find something else to do. A different challenge. Children's orthopaedics, maybe? I would be better needed there; perhaps better appreciated as well. The polio epidemic is not abating – it's getting worse. But I don't know if I'm suited to working with children; I don't know if I could take on the pain of innocents, deal with the infliction of it necessary for healing; I don't know if I have Hugo's strength of heart. What I do know is that I shouldn't be standing in the middle of the ward as though I might have left my brain at the bottom of a floral arrangement.

'Bella, will you work me hard today?' Mr Donatelli teases sotto voce from bed number two behind me. He's a brawny Haymarket wholesale fruiterer whose lumbago has laid him out after carrying one too many crates of bananas, and teasing me makes him forget his worries for five minutes: he's fretting about having to leave his business in the hands of his spoilt and lazy sons, and fretting he won't be able to get to his daughter's wedding next week, because this pain in his back is becoming more stubborn than he is. He's very proud of his medical insurance, though, that he's paid his Hospitals Contribution Fund religiously, he's no shirker, and don't call him a New Australian – his father settled here, in Newtown, in 1889.

'My day wouldn't be complete without punishing you, Mr Donatelli,' I tell him, and as I exercise his heavy, hardworking legs, massage the calluses on his feet, I wouldn't be anywhere else. I'm good at this. He tells me the Prime Minister, Ben Chifley, is going to ruin the country with his National Health Act and Medical Benefits Scheme. 'We can't afford it,' he says. 'All the immigrants coming from the war, with all their problems, who's going to pay for it? The trade unions?' I don't tell him I think the standardisation of the health system is a bloody good idea, along with entrenching equal care for rich and poor. I tell Mr Donatelli: 'Don't worry, the British Medical Association isn't going to let Mr Chifley ruin anything. They're the toughest union in this country – they'll make sure you're overcharged wherever possible for the rest of your days.' Mr Donatelli laughs so hard at that it's another level of exercise in itself, and I laugh, too – you have to.

Then I hear the creak of bed wheels behind me, in-coming, but I don't turn my head. I continue to chat with Mr Donatelli, longer than I should; he tells me more about his daughter's wedding plans; I tell him again I'm sure he's going to get to the church on time, as I would tell anyone, because there's no better way to guarantee a delay in healing than by encouraging a patient to become depressed or anxious. I wait until I hear the squeak of the orderlies' rubber soles stride away, before I leave Mr Donatelli and cross the room, to have a quick look at the new patient.

He's still asleep. Sun-bleached streaks through thick, light brown hair, he looks like a hundred young men I've seen asleep: washed out, about to wake up, strung up in a fracture bed, and possibly soon to express a few sentiments no-one will remind him about later. Left leg splinted on a Böhler frame, as to be expected, but I wonder at the distal traction weight, suspended from the foot; doesn't look heavy enough for that leg; that size of man. But then I don't know how they've used the wire inside, do I. Not my business. I'm sure the Greater Slade doesn't need me to query it, as I would routinely query such things in the controlled mayhem of a military ward, where mistakes are made if queries aren't, simply because of volume. It's not the same at Sydney, I must remind myself again and again until I get it through: don't say anything to anyone. I say, 'Good afternoon,' to the ward sister who's come in to observe him, someone new whose name has not yet lodged. She says, 'Good afternoon, Miss Brynne.' Just go and get some belated lunch, will you.

And yet I stop at Matron Moorefield's desk, which sits in the corridor between the ward sections, and I pick up the file that's been left there. Of course, it's his. Bed seven. *James J. Cleary (Jim).* He lives in Maroubra, seaside suburb; next of kin noted as mother in Canowindra – country boy originally, I suppose. *Mechanic, Heavy Vehicle Automotive Service & Repairs, Ultimo.*

That's as far as I get before Matron Moorefield interrupts: 'What are you doing with that file, Miss Brynne?'

'Reading the notes on bed seven.' My grief needing to know two things: the whole story behind that leg, and if it is going to be all right. Neither of which I am going to find in this as yet slim manila folder; I put it back on her desk.

'I'm sure you have better things to do than read notes that are of no concern to you.' Matron Moorefield expertly purses her lips and whips the folder into the file draw at her side as she sits down to resume her guard post, two first-year nurses looking on over armfuls of fresh laundry destined for the women's section across the way. 'Dr Oxley will give you instruction when he deems it appropriate to do so.'

Don't say anything, Lucy. When doctor deems it appropriate? What about as patient requires? Patient who is going to need my careful and considerable attention to see to it that a broken leg is the only unfortunate condition he must suffer while he's here. Hypostatic pneumonia, anyone? Compression of the peroneal nerve that feels not so much like pins and needles as knives and forks? How about a nice bedsore? Sudden death by thrombosis? Do not say a word. I say: 'Goodo.' At the same moment our Mr Cleary groans, loudly, obviously not well on waking, common reaction; resist interfering; not yet my patient. 'I'll leave you to it.' Definitely not my job to clean that up.

I churn through most of a vegemite sandwich from the canteen and a less than optimal chunk of the typing I have to do – Dr Oxley's always taking precedence over my own, so that my reports are always weeks behind. I don't get back to the men's section for the rest of the day, spending most of what's left of the afternoon with eighty-three-year-old Mrs Stevenson in the gymnasium, taking her fragile, arthritic hip for a very slow walk and then having a few minutes of fun doing her hair, chatting about her grandchildren, how much she's looking forward to their Saturday visit.

I count down the last few minutes until the end of my workday, and I fly out for the tram, for Aurora House, for Hugo's office, to be with him there once more.

HUGO WINTER

There are sound reasons why doctors should generally be prevented from getting anywhere near a loved one in medical distress.

'Please, Hugo, stop worrying,' Jo begged him at the threshold of St Margaret's Maternity Hospital, in the throes of rapidly progressing labour: 'Please. Your face is making me think something terrible is going to happen. Please go away.'

'We'll take good care of Mrs Winter, don't you worry, doctor.' The sister at Admissions smirked.

Hugo sat rigid with fear on the hard wooden bench seat, his experience in gynaecology and obstetrics useless to him now. He was just an ordinary man worried something terrible was going to happen to his wife. It was three am, and a quiet night at that, no-one else waiting there with him – only the clock on the wall, and it tormented him. Despite having delivered more than a hundred babies himself, he couldn't help asking that old self, the universe and every second: what's taking so long? Unlike an ordinary man, his mind ran through every possible complication – in every terrible detail.

But there were none. Claire Miriam Winter was born at three minutes past seven on January 9, 1913, perfectly healthy, perfectly formed, and Jo was so radiant with joy, Hugo cried on seeing her.

'Oh silly,' Jo said: 'I love you.'

He kissed his beautiful wife, his darling Jo, he kissed the baby, too – relieved to see that while she had his darkish skin, this seemed to be all she'd inherited from him – and then, like an ordinary man, he went around the corner to the pub and downed a whisky before heading back to work. He virtually danced up the street towards the city centre and the patients that were waiting for him at his Macquarie Street rooms. He couldn't stop laughing all that day.

He smiled at the wrist of the tennis player he was treating, the joint inflamed and painful at the thumb: 'I'm sorry, I suspect this is not going to be good news for you.'

'Well, you look happy about it,' the tennis player said, a bit upset, as he'd only yesterday returned from competing at the Australasian Championships in New Zealand, where he'd been unexpectedly beaten after an ungainly fall on the court. He said to Hugo, wryly resigned, 'I suppose this is going to cost me an arm and a leg, is it?'

'Forgive me, please.' Hugo smiled more sympathetically then, both for the possible costs of repairing this wrist to a tennis-playing standard and for his inappropriate smiling. 'My wife gave birth to our first baby this morning. A little girl. I've been made quite stupid by it all.'

'Oh!' The tennis player smiled now, too: 'Well then, I say congratulations to you.'

'Thank you, thank you very much,' said Hugo, but he wouldn't be making any reduction in his fee. The tennis player was from a wealthy family, and Hugo needed their cash and that of all others like them in order to continue treating his children for free – at his private practice here, as well as at St Vincent's Hospital. He also needed to pay for the recent renovations and extensions on the Darling Point house – well-appointed it might be, but it had been a bit of an old wreck inside, as well as tiny.

Hugo was a busy man, and so consumed by that busyness, he didn't hear the shift in tone from his critics, the shift in nastiness from 'charlatan' to 'mad man'. Blind conservatism at all the major public hospitals in Sydney, and from the British Medical Association itself, ensured none would accept that the dislocated hips and club feet of children could be treated by non-surgical means. They would not accept, either, the fixing of bones with the stainless-steel pinning wires newly invented by Kirschner in Greifswald – a wire Hugo would use on the tennis player's unfortunately fragmented scaphoid, because it was the most effective way by far that such a difficult fracture could be got to heal. They had their ways, the old guard, and they were sticking to them, even if it meant crippled children were left only slightly less crippled by their methods, and only then if the families of those children had the money to pay or the funds somehow otherwise raised. Hugo had no time for these backward-facing attitudes. And yet, despite the evidence glaring at him, despite these past eighteen months of his work being increasingly derided or ignored, he believed that the establishment would come around, if he persisted. If he got on with the job, did the right thing, the best thing by those who needed it done most, all would be well.

He was bent over a golfer's twisted knee, a typical tear of the meniscus medialis, the day he thought he heard a chicken clucking out in his waiting room – thought his ears were playing tricks until it squawked so distinctly, he had to dash away from his patient to look. But he found there was, in fact, a chicken in the waiting room – two of them, in a cage on the floor by his nurse's desk.

'What are these?' he asked her.

'Chickens.' She smiled. 'Mr Jones brought them in – little William's father. He said he couldn't bear the thought of you going unpaid.'

Hugo laughed until he cried at that one – and so did Jo, when he brought them home for her. The cats were not impressed, though, neither would their neighbours be, and so the chickens were donated to the sisters at St Vincent's.

'Oh my goodness.' Jo was so proud of her husband and all his kindness, that a poor man would give him chickens, but she was worried for him now, too. She felt the shifts against him; she heard the worst from her cousin Edwin Glass. Socially intelligent always, she knew where these vile snipes and condemnations were coming from at their very bottom: fear and jealousy.

So, Jo applied her own skills to what she knew would work best: she threw a party, afternoon cocktails and canapes, and she invited everyone from the Sydney chapter of the BMA; she invited every orthopaedic specialist on the New South Wales register as well. She would make them see that the Winters were simply generous people. She knew her husband could be rude and impatient at his work – she'd heard he regularly snapped at the registrar at St Vincent's, the orderlies too, put all manner of noses out of joint at demonstrations with his abrupt way of answering questions, letting his displeasure show if he had to repeat something or if someone in some other way wasted his precious time. This was Hugo at work, though. Hugo at home was a different creature: he sang, he danced, he drank too much and frightened the cats with his clarinet. Whenever he rocked baby Claire in his arms, he rocked the whole world with his love. He was wonderful: she would make them see.

She didn't. She couldn't.

Most of the BMA lot who came stood around stiff as corpses in her bright drawing room, their wives too, making such a show of boredom and discomfort it would have been less insulting had they not bothered to show up at all.

She watched as that one called Eliot Slade picked up a cucumber sandwich, looking at it as if to inspect it for maggots. A tall man, smoothly put together, he'd have been attractive if his mouth wasn't turned down as though he were significantly and permanently revolted at all he saw. He was young, thirty-one, the same age as cousin Edwin, living a charmed life, littered with silver spoons of every shape and size. What made him so unhappy? she wondered.

But not for long. Less than an hour later, she overheard him discussing her husband's Robin Hood approach to public health funding. 'Resources must be spent on those who can benefit most from the investment, and the lower orders can't look after themselves as it is, so what's the point?' he said, drawing on his cigarette, outside on the verandah.

The colleague he was speaking to replied: 'I rather agree. If they're going to be crippled in some way anyway and not contributing to society but instead a drain on it, then it's best those cases are left untreated in the first place. Certainly left out of the public system. If the charities can afford to help them, well and good, but we can't. The budget is finite for us – of course there are always going to be losers.'

'Quite right,' said Eliot Slade. 'If Winter's vanity compels him to get about like some misguided, self-proclaimed messiah for these losers, then that's not our problem, either.'

Losers. As a new mother, still breastfeeding baby Claire, and still tender in all ways for it, tears stung Joanna Winter's eyes. How could two grown men, intelligent and privileged, speak like that about children, and such awfully disadvantaged ones at that? These men, so many of them, had private rooms on Macquarie Street, too – they made bags and bags of money. Their personal budgets weren't finite but ballooning. And they questioned her husband's motives, calling him a vain messiah for losers out of one side of their mouths and greedy out of the other. Hypocrites. She wanted to push them all out of her house right now, and never see any of them again, but Jo being Jo, she wouldn't do any such thing.

She smiled and laughed all through those two hideous, self-inflicted hours. She watched her husband having a fine old time with the one and only friend he'd made so far in the medical realm, a fellow called Zlotkowsky, general house surgeon out at Marrickville District, a working-class area. Dr Zlotkowsky was of like mind, a boisterous Pole with whom Hugo enjoyed arguing about everything and nothing. She watched them enjoying one too many schnapps on this occasion, Hugo slapping his thigh in time with the string quartet's Beethoven selections, and shouting, 'Allegro! Allegro! Come on!' whenever they played too sedately, shouting with joyful enthusiasm. Looking like the mad man they said he was.

And when it was all over, with the last of the guests gone, he grinned at her sleepily: 'That went well, my darling, didn't it?'

How could he be so dense? she wondered.

But he wasn't dense, she knew. It simply didn't occur to him that his peers – his fellow surgeons and physicians, all men who had made oaths to heal and do no harm – might really be so deliberately mean and self-interested. This wasn't so much a virtue on Hugo's part; it was the way his brain was made – made for science, for looking forward. Made to give.

She put her arms around his neck and told him: 'You were wonderful. You always are.'

ELIOT SLADE

The most terrible of arguments, if eloquently and confidently expressed, can appear to have merit, and when put forward by a man of high status and influence, it can sound very much like the truth.

In the March of 1913, Eliot Slade wrote and delivered one such argument to the Sydney BMA, within a dissertation on the incidence of infantile paralysis acquired by poliomyelitis. In his paper, he showed that the disease was affecting the children of the middle and upper classes in relatively greater numbers and more severely than it did the poor, and he deduced that this was occurring because the poor lived in such filthy conditions that many of them must have developed a natural immunity to the virus. Had it been further explored, such an insight into the behaviour of polio could have been crucial in the fight against this steadily rising scourge, but for Slade it was merely a statistical detail supporting his conclusion that 'children from good homes' were, therefore, the most needy orthopaedic patients under the age of twelve, and that, as much as possible, public hospital beds should be held over for them.

It wasn't all about the money for Eliot Slade. It was about social order and the hygienic maintenance of the British peoples, the strengthening of their sturdy stock. Eugenic theory, with its principles of racial and societal purity, was becoming popular in medical circles. But it was also about the money, as nice, white children from good homes more often than not had parents who would mortgage those homes to save their progeny; they would pay any price, and they tended to keep their insurances up to date, too, which also meant hospitals could earn more per bed – good for all, unless you were poor. Although that polio paper of Slade's would disappear from sight in the mid-1940s when Nazism had exposed the putrid depths of these bogus claims of inferiority based on race, at the time, thirty years prior, it was applauded, and so was Eliot Slade.

At last, he was stepping out of his father's long and illustrious shadow, moving up the ladder in his own right. He quickly achieved the approval of his peers as an orthopaedist, despite comparatively limited surgical experience. He could deftly snip the Achilles tendon of a child afflicted with polio; he could amputate a leg at the hip with the quick-thinking competence required to preserve life. But he hadn't done any reconstructive surgery at all. These surgeries tended to be painstaking, lengthy, requiring a care and focus upon the needs of another that didn't come naturally to Slade. Reconstructive surgeries also required courage: the guts to risk your reputation on a patient who might end up the worse for your attempt to make things better.

But no matter. Eliot Slade was on his way now to the top of his trade – that was guaranteed. Whatever disappointment his father, Sir Alfred, might have felt at his son's embrace of pseudo-scientific eugenics claptrap, or his so undeserving rise, it was disguised by the old man's descent into senile dementia, which slowly but surely robbed him of speech. Whatever Slade's mother thought, didn't matter, not in the slightest: she was a woman, for a start, and she openly worshipped her husband, always the only man in the room; she'd never expressed an opinion of her own anyway – not that her son ever heard. She'd never given him what he wanted, although he couldn't have said exactly what that was, but no matter there, either. His parents had given him enough of what was needed – social and racial breeding that ensured he could do as he pleased.

That he took pleasure from nothing never occurred to Eliot Slade. He marked out his life in lists of achievements, conquests, winnings, takings, and this year's list included two main necessities for further professional advancement: obtaining his own rooms on Macquarie Street, and obtaining a wife.

The first was easy and a marvel of convenience: he took up his father's old rooms, which happened to be three doors down the hill from Winter's, and with a harbour view. As Sir Alfred had been predominantly a hydrotherapist, these rooms just happened to come with three bathing chambers as well, which gave the son a sterling and non-surgical little orthopaedic sideline: take an hour's float in a salt bath for your sciatica, five pounds a go – thank you.

The second necessity – the wife – wasn't much more difficult to come by, and she'd bring with her a lot more than five pounds a go.

Audrey McRae-Browne was twenty-one, and coolly mature for her young years. Tall and slim and dazzlingly fair, by his side, she and Slade looked very much the pair. A pair that could well have passed as an Adam and Eve for Nietzsche's super-species – at least on the surface of things. She knew the score, her place in this most ancient of trades: marriage. Second youngest daughter of a vastly wealthy family of pastoralists and bankers, her pedigree was her sole worth. She'd sized up Slade in an instant: she knew he wasn't a good man, but she was young enough not to care. She was young enough to believe it really didn't matter who or what he was, as long as his status and money gave her a life that her pedigree and purity implied she should have.

They married at St Andrew's Cathedral, in the high bride season of early spring, the bass notes of the grand organ there shuddering through her bones as a harbinger of all that was to come.

Their reception was held at that most fashionable of venues, the Emerald Room of the Australia Hotel, the groom's eyes glittering not with love but with success. Audrey knew that, too. She knew the eight courses on the menu, and the attendance of photographers from three newspapers, were more important to him than she was. She knew he didn't love her – he barely looked at her – but she could not have known then how profoundly she would come to regret saying 'I do' to those unloving eyes.

They stayed that night in the hotel's most opulent wedding suite, and there he forced himself onto her unbidden. He tore at her nightdress, he tore at her deep within; he hurt her in a shocking and dreadful way; and when she cried out, he pressed his fist against her throat and said: 'Be still.' She closed her eyes, waiting for him to finish his violence. There wasn't anything else she could do; not then; and not for all of the seven nights of their requisite honeymoon in the picturesque Southern Highlands that followed.

Slade had purchased a harbourside home at Point Piper for them, less than a mile to the east of Darling Point and twice the size of Winter's house. He'd finally made it, he'd achieved his necessities, and when he took Audrey home to that house, he defiled her there, too.

She shouted now: 'Please! You are hurting me.'

He slapped her mouth: 'Be silent.'

Their home was full of silence, and stillness. There would be no music there.

That first year was the worst year as Audrey strove to find herself, her peace, her life within his vicious rhythms. He complained after six months, in the March of 1914, that no pregnancy had resulted – for his desire to have a child was next on his list. She consulted several doctors to appease him, all of them men, and none could advise her to do anything but wait and become accustomed to the use of vaseline. She did, and it helped a little with the pain.

Then, in the April, at last it seemed a pregnancy had come. Audrey was so typically ill it couldn't have been anything else but a baby on the way. She was thrilled, not least because he now left her alone. Her breasts swelled and she softened in all her features. For eleven blessed weeks she allowed herself to hope that he would soften, too. But it wasn't to be. The baby didn't hold. Audrey howled with the savagery of this pain: the double pain of the miscarriage contractions and the dread of what her husband would do to punish her now.

'What have you done?' He shook her. 'You must have done something. Don't think for a moment you can get away with this.'

'I didn't do anything – I promise you. Please.'

He slapped her mouth: 'Shut up.'

And it started all over again.

She prayed every day for a pregnancy; he continued to demand and demand one. Neither of them understood the way terror can work upon the body, shutting down auxiliary functions to concentrate on survival. She even tried to love him. She thought perhaps it might have been her resistance to him that was preventing a baby from settling inside her. Perhaps if she gave herself to him with some tenderness in her heart, a baby might be more willing to stay – more willing to belong to her.

To her surprise, Eliot seemed to respond. He seemed gentler with her somehow. She let herself hope that the softening might have begun. It hadn't. She didn't know he'd only been diverted by the war that was about to come crashing down upon the world.

On August 5, 1914, as news filtered through to Sydney that Germany had invaded Belgium, forcing Britain's hand to defend any assault on France, Eliot Slade found another desire to slake, another match to win: Hugo Winter was a German; he would be an enemy of the British Empire now. Slade would have him struck off the medical register. He would have him deported. Why? Because he could; because it was achievable; because he saw Winter's popularity with both rich and poor growing by the numbers who would come and go from his door. Because the man was a Jew.

'I've heard him speak of the supremacy of the Reich,' Slade told the president of the British Medical Association.

'I've heard him declare himself in favour of the invasion,' he told the board of St Vincent's Hospital.

'I've heard him say a war with Britain is the only answer,' he told the New South Wales Police.

He would devote himself to Hugo Winter's destruction, and he would not relent until it was done.

THREE

LUCY BRYNNE

'It's late, Lucy – go home,' Mrs B calls up the stairs, keys clinking.

'Won't be too long now,' I call back. It's after eight – I'll go at half-past. I want to get to the bottom of this last pile of papers in front of me; then, I'll have sorted everything in the office except the filing cabinets, which are, as contradiction prefers it, mostly empty. They can wait until tomorrow, with the children's cards and drawings on the pinboards, which I will take with me, although I'm not sure how ... there'll be too many of them to carry on the tram.

I look behind me at the boxes I've made up already: the various journals, patient files, hospital files, accounting files, unidentified x-rays, correspondence medical, correspondence academic, correspondence miscellaneous, correspondence personal, ephemera medical and personal, and, unsurprisingly, very little rubbish. When it's all done, I think I will be able to grieve in some steady way; I won't need to come here, where it swirls and stabs; I won't sit in his leather desk chair wanting him to give me one last swift and crushing embrace.

But I do need to be here, inside this emptying out of Aurora House. The last three patients left today; the cook and the housekeeper have gone, too, found places elsewhere. All that's left to do is to organise the remaining contents in such a way that they can be auctioned off or donated to charity, eventually: the beds, the equipment, the linen, the artworks, the crockery, every cupboard, every lamp, from the children's ward on this upper floor to the comfortable private rooms downstairs on the ground level, and then the operating theatre, the plaster room, the x-ray room below, three different storerooms in the basement as well. The whole thing is almost as big as Sydney Hospital's orthopaedic department ... so much stuff. So much of me. All up, I spent almost a year inside these walls: my file is more than an inch thick and dull, dull reading, except for a photograph I found of me and Hugo in the pool out the back: I look like a skinned rabbit, such a tiny child I was, compared to Hugo's brickish solidity; I remember my right front tooth was wobbly; I remember the safety of Hugo's hands holding me in the water as he told me, 'Run, run, run,' building up my muscles. This is my goodbye, I suppose, not only to Hugo but to so much of the past that has made me. My long prayer of gratitude.

Under yet another couple of well-thumbed German medical journals, I find a curious collection of pages whose history I couldn't begin to know: hand-written and illustrated on lined foolscap, they look like home-made theatre bills, but as they're written in German, too, I don't recognise anything in them except the name Herr Doktor Winter, listed in the cast of characters for these plays or whatever they are. They look old. He must have done a fair bit of amateur performing in his younger years – a whole world of it I'll never know.

Wonderful and terribly sad at once, these teasing glimpses. You can never quite know someone, can you; no matter how much you love a person, there's always more to the story. I think I'll put these theatrical bits and pieces in a keepsake album as well, for Jo, though she doesn't read German, either. There's something of his true spirit in them, a sense of fun always at the ready to cheer a glum face.

As I move them to one side, I see the next thick and beaten-up file beneath is titled simply, 'Jo', a pencilled hieroglyph to his greatest love of all. I almost don't want to open it, this too-intimate piece of him, but of course I do.

My dearest Hugo,

Oh? They're letters from Jo herself.

How are you – truly? I do hope you're well and happy enough. I shouldn't say it, but the distance between us, small as it may be, is a stretching of my soul that aches more and more with each day. I see the curve of your eyebrows in little Claire's when she smiles and I have to turn away from her so that she can't see my tears.

What an awful burden for me to send you, even if it's true. I've written again to the BMA and to Edwin in Egypt, too, to see if there's anything we can do, but –

'Lucy. What are you doing?'

I know the voice, but I almost jump up from the chair and out the window at it.

'Dr Adinov —' I see Hugo's friend and colleague there in the doorway, a fellow brick, seventy-eight years of age but still with that set of an old-school orthopaedist: built for wrestling wayward bones against uncooperative sinews with his bare hands. 'I could ask the same of you,' I tell him: 'You just about scared me out of my wits.'

'I'm sorry, my dear,' he replies. 'I was downstairs making an inventory of the surgical instruments I wish to pilfer – I mean, commit to the archives.' And even that smile still has a heavy Russian accent. Every time I see him, I remember with startling clarity the first time I ever did: when he came to look at my leg, when I was that little rabbit: stern face, cold hands, flash of a gold ring – he scared me then, too. But he's one of the best, or was. He says: 'You look exhausted. Come on – I'll drive you back to the hospital.'

Suddenly, with the adrenaline of that fright passing, loosening all my tight strings, this is an offer I can't knock back. I say: 'Thanks. You're right. I am exhausted.'

I close the file. I shouldn't be reading Jo's letters anyway. But intrigue at what might have separated them when Claire was small makes me slip the whole thing into my satchel. I want to know; I want every last glimpse of Hugo I can get.

'You are doing some study?' Dr Adinov asks as we leave, looking at my satchel.

'Hm.' Guilt writhes around my stomach, at the letters.

He nods and says as we take the stairs: 'You should go back to university. You'll be a very good doctor.'

'Ha.' There's an echo through emptiness. 'You know there's only one area of medicine that interests me and I'll never be permitted to practise it.'

Dr Adinov grunts at this sorry truth and, out the door, into the night, he says: 'Surgery isn't everything. Be an orthopaedic physician instead.'

'There's no such thing.' I yawn.

'Be the first.' He grunts again as if it might be a reasonable suggestion.

'Oh yes.' I laugh as he opens the car door for me: 'I can see how that might work. I shall make diagnoses of orthopaedic problems and have surgeons ignore me. That's called being a physiotherapist, isn't it?'

He laughs, too; and then, getting in beside me, he says: 'You are quite correct, Lucy. But as a physician you'll get paid more.'

I shrug, far too exhausted to think about any of it.

He turns on the engine and adds: 'If you change your mind, I will support you so that you might return to university.'

I'm glad it's dark and his attention is now focussed on driving, so that he can't see or say anything about my furious blinking: I am extraordinarily blessed; clearly, Hugo was, too, to have such a friend who could so quickly and efficiently pick up the baton of badgering me to go back to school, to get 'properly qualified'.

I change the subject: 'How's Jo? Have you seen her?'

'Yes,' he says: 'I called in on her again this morning. She is overtaken by it, pretending she's all right. She will be all right, but she's asked that we leave her to herself for a while. Give her another week or two.'

I imagine her curled up on the sofa in the lounge room, curled around their wedding photograph, curled around the telephone, talking with Claire in New York, forcing herself to look forward to the baby due in March, her first and longed for grandchild, a little light in her dark: I hope so. And I'm stricken again myself at the cruelty of this contradiction: that Hugo will never meet his grandchild.

The city is a bright clutter of bulbs tossed out from the pubs and clubs at the top of the Cross, all swallowed up in the thick, black shadows of Hyde Park and Hospital Road, then flaring again in red fluorescent signs that say 'CASUALTY' and 'AMBU-LANCE'. This is where I live: suddenly a sad fact, too. One day perhaps I might stop living in a hospital, but I'm not sure I'm ready yet, never mind that I haven't had time to find myself a decent flat somewhere – at least, somewhere I can afford.

'Good night, Lucy, my dear. Get some sleep.' Dr Adinov leaves me on the footpath and speeds off, backtracking his way home to Bondi.

I look up at the hospital again: such an institution, grand sandstone edifice facing the medical mile of Macquarie Street, a place of prestige for every doctor, nurse and student, it's been here in some shape or form for more than a hundred and fifty years – since the First Fleet convicts set up a tent. Behind me, the newest building is made of solid concrete, comprising five floors of specialty wards and theatres rising above Admissions and Enquiries, triage and emergency surgery; it's called the Pavilion, simply and imperatively, as though it showcases nothing but the best of the best. I glance over my shoulder in the general direction of the orthopaedic ward: I really should be grateful for the privilege of working there, but I'm not. Across the central courtyard, bronze swans and brolgas frown down on me from their elegant fountain, and I quicken my pace, darting up into the Nightingale Wing, two flights. I should be grateful I have a room in this most beautiful building, with its medieval-princess window arches and fancy brickwork, grateful I have a room in these nurses' quarters at all, when most have been farmed out into the old offices of the Government Statistician's building three blocks away, where there's more space but not so much style.

Right now, though, I'm only grateful my room-mate, Elvia Hewson, is on night duty for the rest of the month, so that I can be alone. Elvia's a great girl, a theatre sister, ex-navy from Eastern Suburbs Memorial, and likewise shouldn't be living here, as if we're still in-barracks; we've had a few nights out on the gin together wondering when and how we'll make our break into real life. But tonight, I don't want to do anything else but take Jo's letters to bed and hold Hugo to my heart inside them.

Too tired to even bother washing the day from my face, I peel off girdle and stockings, drag bra out from under my slip, and that'll do. I turn on the lamp and get into bed, where I open the folder on my knees and lose a few moments among the graceful loops and lines of Jo's handwriting, not quite reading any of the words ... Until an envelope drops down onto my lap from behind this first letter and I see the address written there.

TO: Dr H. J. Winter
East Compound
Liverpool Concentration Camp
New South Wales

Concentration camp? I'm confused. Concentration camps don't belong in Australia. I look at the date of the letter: it's a little smudged, but I think it says August 15, 1915. It still doesn't make sense. I hunt through Jo's words now for clues as to what this might mean; and I find an answer over the page.

How can I not be worried? For goodness' sake, a German sailor has been shot at the camp – I read about the Coroner's judgement in the paper, calling it a 'justifiable homicide'. You say you are in with the businessmen and other officer-class types and being all very decently looked after, but you are still a prisoner of war. The injustice makes me weep more than anything. I weep with infuriation.

Hugo was interned during the First World War? I don't believe it. My God, I don't believe it. But here, in all Jo's words – in letter after letter – I see it's true.

So, I'm not in the shiniest of moods as I make my way to the morning ward meeting. I've had maybe three hours' sleep, tossing and turning; laceratingly wrung out now, and I'm angry. I want to know how long Hugo was made to suffer imprisonment, how long it was before he saw Jo and Claire again, but the letters give no indication: they stop a year later, August 1916, in the midst of a further appeal for his release. Why was he locked up at all? Simply for being German, apparently, and for not having lived in Australia long enough to be naturalised as a British subject. Plenty of Germans had a hard time of it, in both wars – but such a plainly decent man as Hugo? Something doesn't quite add up. And why would that scrap of a newspaper obituary have said that he was 'debarred from joining the Australian Imperial Force', when he was actually interned in a concentration camp? I want to know what happened, really. I want to ask Jo, but I can hardly crash through her sadness with this, a piece of the past she would probably prefer to forget. And how would I begin anyway? *Excuse me, I've just been reading your most intimate correspondence …*

'Good morning, Miss Brynne,' Alasdair Slade smiles his pleasant good-morning smile outside Dr Oxley's office.

I nod at him, just. I don't know how I'm going to get through today. What is today? Thursday – isn't it?

'Your first priority until further notice is bed seven, Miss Brynne,' Dr Oxley tells me.

Bed seven. Mr Cleary. Jim. Lorry mechanic. I'd forgotten about him.

'Draw up a full assessment of the patient as a matter of urgency, relevant history, immediate and longer-term plan, and commence two-hourly monitoring and remedial massage – I don't have to tell you what to do,' Dr Oxley tells the clipboard he's holding, but then he looks up at me directly, right into my eyes. 'Report to me on Mr Cleary – report only to me.' Then he tells Matron Moorefield: 'See to it that Miss Brynne is not called away unnecessarily. Send a junior doctor if Outpatients or anyone else requires unscheduled orthopaedic physio. Is that understood?' He hands Mr Cleary's chart to me.

I would enjoy a moment of vindication at this, the first time my expertise has been acknowledged since I began work here, but I'm too rattled and bleary to appreciate it.

And Dr McVeigh is complaining: 'I need Miss Brynne to take Mrs Stevenson to the gymnasium again this afternoon.'

'You'll have to do it yourself,' Dr Oxley says.

Wow. Dr McVeigh gives me an uncomprehending glare; I give myself a stethoscope from the cabinet behind him and, now on the job, I'm awake. And I'm remembering Mr Cleary's x-ray: shudder.

Down the corridor and through the open doors of the men's section, I'm trying to find a good-morning smile for him, stifling a yawn at the fresh lemon gladdies in the central floral arrangement, when Matron Moorefield stops me, hissing a whisper: 'Don't get ideas above yourself, Miss Brynne. Remember whose patient this is – Dr Slade the senior, chief of orthopaedic surgery at this hospital. I will inform you if Dr Oxley's instructions are superseded by his own. Is that clear?'

It's becoming clear that some sort of war has erupted behind closed doors; nothing to do with me. I tell Matron: 'I will do what's best for the patient.'

She says, for the whole ward to hear: 'You will do as you are told.'

Don't say anything. Don't say another word. I keep on my way and, down the far end of the room, here's a sleepy-eyed Mr Cleary, watching as I near. 'Well, good morning there,' I say to him.

And he smiles: 'Bad day?'

I'm not sure if he's referring to my lack of smile or Matron's dressing down just now, but he immediately gets a laugh from me. 'Bad day, all right,' I reply. 'Probably not as bad as yours, though.'

'Hm.' He closes his eyes, slow with the morphine, I suppose.

I tell him: 'I'm Miss Brynne. Your physiotherapist. We're going to be spending quite a lot of time together for the next little while.'

'Lucky me.' He smiles again, resigned and slightly apprehensive, and I like him already.

'You might not always feel so lucky.' I flirt automatically around the warning. 'Might change your mind about me in the next five minutes, actually, when I get you to sit up.' I look at the chart notes: last morphine six am. Good, he's not too knocked out. To test that, I ask him: 'What's the J for in James J. Cleary? What's your middle name?'

'Julian.' He opens his eyes fully; they're blue, a deep blue. 'Thanks Mum.' The smile broadens and he says: 'So there you go – nothing's embarrassing after that.'

'Goodo.' It takes me a little too long to break the gaze. If I was still at the repat, at Prince of Wales, I'd be palming this charmer off to another physio, preferably a male one; but there isn't another specialist orthopaedic physio in this building. I turn away to get the extra couple of pillows I'll need from the cupboard at the top of the room, pushing aside the flicker of attraction as I go. I'm exhausted, and exhaustion distorts brain function more dangerously than any pair of blue eyes can. Mr Cleary requires my care and attention, not my appraisal of his masculine appeal.

'All right, James Julian.' I put the pillows down beside him as I return. 'Get ready to change your world view.' I pull up the head frame on the bed: 'Quick game's a good game. How's that?'

'Fine,' he says, and he seems so; no flinch, no grunt, no groan.

'Well done.' Test that again: 'Can you sit forward a little and I'll put some more pillows behind you?'

He does and no trouble there, either. He says: 'Thanks.'

'My pleasure,' I reply, glancing away. 'Now, I'm just going to listen to your chest.' I unbutton the hospital-issue pyjama shirt; it's only a body, another body; a very nice body; one that no doubt has a girlfriend, not that it's any of my business; mind on the job. And it certainly is when I see the faded scar running down the midline of his abdomen, under the sternum, about six inches long, too neat to be anything but an old surgical wound: 'What happened here? Did you have an operation?'

'Don't worry about that,' he says, too quickly.

'I'm not worried about it, Mr Cleary,' I assure him, 'but it would be helpful to know what happened. Among the many other joys we'll share today, I need to take down an understanding of any medical history that might help with your treatment.' I guess, from what I saw on the x-ray yesterday: 'You've broken that leg before as well, would that be right?'

There's a darker, sharper flash of apprehension in his eyes at that, a look I've seen a hundred times or more before: he's either a returned serviceman of some description or he's been through some other awful wringer, something he'd rather not discuss.

I understand that; I try a tack I've taken a few times before, too: 'I know how you feel.'

'Do you?' That makes him smile again – doubtfully.

'I know something about it …' I step around the end of the bed and grab one of the screens from the back wall, wheeling it across for privacy – and to avoid giving Mr Donatelli a heart attack if he wakes up in the middle of my show. 'Much more embarrassing than "Julian",' I say to Mr Cleary, as I lift up my skirt, snap off my garter fastenings and roll my stocking down for the passion-killer: 'See?' The main scar on my leg, down the centre, is always such a startling, stubborn purple against my fair skin, and my shin is misshapen once you're really looking at it. 'A lot of orthopaedic trickery has gone into the making of this masterpiece,' I explain: 'Three operations in all, two bone grafts, hardware installed and removed. And a lot of time in bed, strung up as you are now.'

'What happened?' he asks, instantly concerned; a nice man.

I tell him: 'I fell out of a tree, when I was seven years old. A saga that continued until I was eighteen.' I let him see as much of that awfulness as my own eyes can impart. I'd lost my mother a few months before; my father had moved us from mine to mine, from Corrimal to Lithgow, to a town I didn't know, a school I didn't know, a yard full of enormous trees I didn't know. The terrifying fall that never goes away; the doctor at Lithgow Hospital telling my father it would be kinder to take the leg off; the fear and guilt in all the lines of my poor father's face; the very long road to rescue. None of which Mr Cleary needs to hear about; I pull up my stocking again and add only: 'I know it's not much fun. It was a similar fracture to the one you've achieved here, in fact. So, you tell me – what happened to you? What caused the original injury?'

'Hm.' He pauses; deep blue eyes taking their time to trust mine, before he tells me: 'I fell out of the sky.'

'Oh?' I'm not sure if this is more banter, another deflection.

He gives me another long, wary pause, before he answers: 'Yeah. Over Germany. Twenty-third of February 1945. I came down in a paddock, not a very smooth landing.' He speaks calmly but I can see the pulse racing in his neck, as he goes on: 'The doctor who looked after me was very good. He didn't speak much English, apart from being able to apologise a lot that he couldn't do better with my leg. He couldn't take an x-ray – he didn't have a hospital. His hospital at Wiesbaden had been bombed, guess who by.' He gives me half a beat for that guess, and a nod: 'Yeah. The place was a disaster area, and so was I. A month later, the Americans arrive, and I'm handed over to the Red Cross. I get home, and I'm fine. Very happy every day to know that I'm alive. Only wish I could find that doctor to thank him.'

'All right,' I say. 'You win the good story contest. I take it the doctor in Wiesbaden wasn't able to send along records with you?'

'No.' He frowns at my lame joke, and at the hard time he's had. 'All I know is that this German doctor saved my life. He took out my spleen, to stop me from bleeding to death. He did it in his house – or someone's house, I don't know. I don't even know what his name was. But yeah, he did the best he could with my leg, which was fine until I fell the wrong way on it, on Tuesday afternoon.'

I catch a trace of his upset in that, and I don't want to make it worse, but I've got to keep on with the job at hand, ask him: 'Do you know if there was a discrepancy in the lengths of your legs? One leg shorter than the other?'

'Yeah,' he says, as I'm jotting all this down: 'Two and a half inches.'

'That's significant.' Only a fraction less than mine was. There would probably have been some bone loss, I suppose, but now I'm remembering the odd angulation above the ankle I saw on the x-ray as well – which might explain how awkward fall has resulted in present mess. It wasn't set correctly, leaving a weakness, some kind of fault line waiting to crack and give way.

'It was fine,' he insists, as if insisting will make it so.

'It's not now,' I say, still scribbling notes.

'No.' He sighs, and I feel more than hear the worry in that.

I look up and see it, too, the worry behind those blue eyes, and I tell him in the gentlest, firmest terms: 'It's my job and everyone else's at this hospital to try to make sure it's fine this time.'

Right, that's enough staring into his eyes; I place the ends of the stethoscope in my ears. 'Deep breath, please.' Good. 'And again.' All good, all clear. 'And turn a little to your left, so I can get to your back.' All good there, too, and no intolerable pain as he leans that way, either.

But as he settles back down onto the pillows, I'm met with those eyes again. This is going to be a tough one. Occupational hazard, bound to happen if you hang around young men. Not as though I haven't had to ignore these kinds of feelings once or twice before. It's just that, this time, I seem to recognise – don't be ridiculous. All I recognise here is that I'm off my head with sleep deprivation and grief. Hugo …

Hugo would be appalled at my lack of focus. I button up Mr Cleary's shirt and start making my observations: the wound dressings appear clean, splinting comfortable, and nowhere too constrictive; no unusual swelling at the toes, good colour, good temperature to the touch; no tightness or heat at the back of the thigh; no angry redness at the incision for the Steinmann pin in the heel. I'm concerned still that the weight of the traction might be insufficient – call it intuition or too close a feel for this anatomy, but I don't think eight pounds is enough. How much does he weigh? *12 stone approx*, it says in the notes, but I'm guessing he might weigh more than that. He's fitter than the norm: right calf muscle is a specimen. I can only go by my experience of caring for such legs in the past, and that tells me twenty pounds at least would seem more appropriate, to keep this kind of complex fracture in continuous extension, keep its pieces well in place. I must mention it to Dr Oxley, and it doesn't matter if I'm wrong to do so – I might learn something about the wiring that's been done. Other than that, though, all looks as fine as it can be, at this point in proceedings.

I tell Mr Cleary: 'You're a champion patient so far. But starting now, and at two-hourly intervals throughout today, you're looking at a few gruelling bouts of massage therapy. Think you can handle it?'

His smile returns but the worry is still there.

And worry being the enemy of wellness, I have to make it clear: 'I also lend these ears of mine for free. If there's anything concerning you, anything at all, you can tell me.

Best to get it out, get it sorted, in the interests of getting you back on your feet.'

'Do you know how long that might take?' he asks me – the impossible question. 'When do you think I'll get out of here?'

'Not for me to say,' I tell him. I'm not going to give him the news that I've never seen a fracture like this treated in such a slow and conservative way get out of bed in under three months; or that he probably won't be walking on it for more like six; but he does need to be prepared, especially for enemy number two: boredom. 'It'll possibly be a while. Better to suppose maybe a few months rather than a few weeks, and hope that I'm wrong.'

'Right,' he says; that's a blow, naturally; good to get it out of the way.

'Don't fret too much,' I say. 'I'll be here to annoy you pretty much every day.' And then I drop the flip act to ask: 'Is everything all right with work and family? Need anyone to make any telephone calls that might not have already been made?'

'No. Everything's fine.'

It's not. He stares up at the ceiling fan, and I feel his worry gathering like a cloud. I begin the massage on his right foot, where the long, deep muscles attached at the arch are like all roads leading to Rome. It'd be good if these muscles could tell me a bit more precisely if he's depressed or anxious, or both, and how badly. Strictly speaking, it's not my job to know, but it helps to get a sense of what's going on upstairs for any patient; in the case of ex-services personnel, it can be even more important, not only to physical treatment and wellbeing, but to practicalities like getting applications into the Department of Repatriation for pensions or other assistance. The Department can be very unkind and unwilling to listen where emotional injuries are involved. I need Mr

Cleary to know how sincerely I will listen to him, and so I shift the chat back towards sensitive territory: 'Tell me if I'm testing the friendship, please, but I'm interested. What made you join the air force?'

'Aeroplanes,' he says, and he doesn't seem reluctant to answer; he's looking at the sling that holds his knee in counter traction, following the monkey ropes up to the bar above. 'I was at uni, second year of engineering, and when I went home that Christmas in 1939, my dad, in his wisdom, read my mind and said, "Better the RAAF than the trenches, son. Stay out of the mud. Don't do what I did last time. It'll be safer up there."' He looks at me, over at the end of the bed, and his regret is matter-of-fact. 'I took the safety seriously. I was a flight engineer, with the RAF Commonwealth squadrons. Big aeroplanes under Bomber Command. I wasn't there for the thrills – not once the reality sank in. I wasn't a lair.'

I nod to let him know I believe him. Everyone alive knows how 'safe' British Bomber Command was – highest number of casualties anywhere, even if they did win the war in Europe. One in three Australians who flew were killed, so I've heard. The friends he must have lost. I've never met anyone who came through the war via that route, though, and I wonder at what a university-educated ex-RAAF flight engineer is doing working on motor lorries now, but this might be a question too far for the moment; perhaps he likes lorries, good for him; or perhaps he likes that they're not aeroplanes.

'Don't let anyone tell you you're not good at this,' he says, closing his eyes as I work my thumb along the lateral edge of his Achilles, and then he asks me a question: 'Did you go overseas, too?'

'No.' A small, harsh laugh for that old disappointment. 'I didn't pass the medical examination, for obvious reasons.

They said I couldn't run in a fire, as if I wouldn't give it a red-hot go – as if I can't. I finished my science degree instead, majoring in physiology and biochemistry, with a postgrad diploma in physiotherapy.' Another small laugh listening to myself: what am I doing? Trying to impress him with my academic credentials, or the chip on my shoulder? 'Anyway, then I spent the rest of the war at Prince of Wales Repatriation, at Randwick, as a therapist there. Where did you come through repat?'

'Richmond air base,' he says, quickly, and I've hit a nerve again: he's begun tapping the side of the mattress, his right hand beating out a soft but persistent thud. 'I was only there long enough to get passed fit to work. The RAAF needed an automotive engineer for the road transport depot, vehicles coming in from everywhere with demobilisation, getting sold off and all that, and I needed something to get on with.'

I get on with the massage; he stops tapping. I wonder if he might have been offered correction of that leg at Richmond, told it should be reset, but there was a queue – or he refused, which would be perfectly understandable. Why would you voluntarily submit to being laid up when you'd just got going again? No need to underline it if not having done it has recently become a further regret.

A minute or so later, when I've got that calf muscle of his in my palm and I'm thinking, wow, this is a decent hunk of flesh, he says: 'There is something on my mind. It'll probably sound a bit stupid, though.'

'I doubt it,' I say.

And he tells me, finally: 'It's my dog. I'm worried about my dog.'

'Your dog?'

'Yeah,' he explains: 'My neighbour, Mrs Nichol, she's really good to me, she'll look out for him, but she's got her hands full, and, well, Mum and Dad'll come and pick him up, but it's a busy time, right between shearing and harvest, and it might be hard for them to get to Sydney. They're out at Canowindra, two hundred miles away. It's not a big deal, it's …'

A big deal. 'I'll make sure your dog's all right.' While I'm off my head and you're stealing my heart. 'What's his name?'

'Mate.'

'Mate?'

'Yeah.' Big, broad smile: he's very fond of his dog. 'We got him as a pup, eleven years ago, but he was too much of an idiot to be of any use on the farm. Too dopey. Mum kept him as a pet, but he's always been mine. When I got settled, when I got my place out at Maroubra, I brought him with me. He's my mate.'

'I'm sure he is.' Just as I'm sure I'm on my way to Maroubra at some stage today to check on a dog.

I take the tram out eight miles along the sandy-edged roads south of the city and walk from the terminus up to his house, a neat little semi-detached cottage sitting high on the rise above the rocks, above the beach. Dark brick, white window frames, blue sky, blue sea.

There's a motorcycle beyond the side gate for me to trip over; another motorcycle disembowelled under the shelter of the back patio.

'Oh, hello there, love.' The neighbour, Mrs Nichol, I presume, pops her head over the back fence; must have heard the screech of the gate as I came through it. 'If you're lookin' for Jim, he's not in. He's up at the hospital, in town, had a dreadful accident at work. Rory came around and told me yesterday.'

Who Rory might be, I don't know, apart from a two-legged mate. I tell her: 'I'm looking for his dog. I said I'd check on him.'

'Aren't you a good girl,' says Mrs Nichol. 'I've got Mate over here with us. A beautiful old dog, he is. Have a look for yourself.'

I peer over the fence and Mate is indeed there: a blue heeler cattle dog, paws up on the wood palings, saying hello, too, tail wagging, pink tongue lolling out of a distinctly dopey smile. There are three, four, no, five children as well – a couple swinging on the clothesline. One littlest girl is running around in circles with a laundry basket on her head. Hands full, I'll say. Children and seagulls shriek and zoom about the yard like one creature.

'The kids love him,' Mrs Nichol says. 'And they don't mind Mate, either.' She laughs, coarse and warm. 'Are you Carol?'

'No.' I smile over the thump of this reality. Of course, he has a Carol. Possibly has a Margaret and a Jenny, too. 'I'm from the hospital, checking on the dog and picking up a few things for J– him. For Mr Cleary.'

'Oh, aren't you a darlin',' says Mrs Nichol. 'How's he goin' up there?'

'He'll be fine,' I tell her, and he really does seem to be: hasn't had any morphine all day; said he doesn't like the feeling of being drugged, the drowsiness; doesn't seem to need it anyway, though, and I don't think he's faking stoic. But brief four pm conference with Dr Oxley an hour ago is spinning around in my head: he flatly said the traction weighting is to stay as it is, and he wouldn't tell me why. I'm sure he knows what he's doing, just as I'm sure my judgement is off kilter in every way possible, but each time I see that weight hanging from that foot, I think, no, it's not right. I asked to look at the post-operative x-rays, to see the wiring in there for myself, satisfy myself of my wrong judgement, but Dr Oxley only groaned at me: 'I don't have time to be chasing around x-rays you don't need to see.' Oh, but I do. How can I set a longer-term plan for the patient if I can't see what's been done to him? How will I be able to decide which exercise will be beneficial, harmful, painful, if I don't have all the information? I need to know how well that fracture is coming together. Why isn't it routine that I'm given a patient's x-rays full stop? Is it a disregard for physiotherapy? For women? Me? All three?

I find the key under the mat where J– Mr Cleary told me it would be, and I let myself in the back door. A surfboard leans diagonally along the kitchen's side wall like a giant timber fish pointing down the hall. And is that a drum kit I see in the room beyond? It is, and it lures me in to find a bookcase filled with more records than books: jazz, jive, jump blues, swing; Louis Armstrong, Cab Calloway, Benny Goodman; Louis Jordan's 'Ain't Nobody Here But Us Chickens' laughs at me from the arm of a pleasantly worn easy chair – I love that funny song. Stop snooping. Can't help it. Besides, it's research – on how people live in real life. The great whopping HMV radiogram and well-stocked drinks cabinet suggest there might have been a few late-night chickens around here. The next room is more sedate, though, a lounge, snug but stylish, with a jade velvet sofa – yes, he must have a girlfriend, somewhere. And I must stop snooping.

His toothbrush and razor are easily located in the bathroom, everything's so neat and tidy. Don't look at his bed in the front room – yes, it's a big double bed. Go straight to the wardrobe for the t-shirts he's requested. My God, look at that ocean view out the picture window. And how many suit jackets are in this wardrobe? Three, no, four; and what looks like two dozen shirts and three racks hung with ties. The man has more clothes than I do. You can't pick people, can you? I've spent approximately three hours in all small-talking with him today – about motors, grain harvesting, Sydney university days, how bad the campus cafeteria was, as well as present practicalities such as unfavourite things to do in bed and how best to do them – and I would never have guessed he fancied a tie. Or jazz.

Then I glimpse his very smart dress shoes in the bottom of the wardrobe, the left heel stacked as much as vanity will allow. If Hugo were here, we'd be discussing the means of reducing this length discrepancy. I hope the surgeons at Sydney are discussing it now. Maybe this is what the closed-doors war is all about: Greater Slade and Dr Oxley, Professor Charlesworth, too, perhaps they're tussling over what approach they might take to further surgery; perhaps they're deliberately delaying it. Maybe they're waiting for the worst of the usual swelling to settle down; or maybe there's been some damage to the surrounding muscle tissue and it needs resting first. They can't possibly be planning to put him through months of skeletal traction without addressing the underlying problem – surely.

'Hooroo then, darlin',' Mrs Nichol waves me off as I wander out again: 'Give Jim our best, won't you? We think a lot of him around here.'

I wave back distractedly, 'Will do,' thinking I should talk to Dr Adinov, have him stick his nose in, see if he can find out what's going on. But I discard the idea when memory tells me Dr Anton Adinov probably hasn't had anything to do with Sydney Hospital in my lifetime. He was once, long ago, an honorary surgeon at Sydney himself, but he resigned his position there in a disgusted rage over something or other – probably someone not washing their hands properly. I remember Hugo laughing about his friend's ability to hold a grudge. I can hear him laughing now. I'm so frayed, I can't think straight, taking the steep steps back down onto the footpath now and noting what a trial it will be for Jim to take them on crutches. Mr Cleary: this man I don't know, who has so much of my attention I'm compiling an outpatient's plan for him months in advance, when I can't possibly know what he might need, or how things will go with his leg in the meantime. What's going on inside me? I want to click my heels and go home, but I don't have a home to go to.

Close my eyes on the return tram back into town, and I can hear the hum of my brain – making that sound electrical wiring does just before it shorts. Thoughts swoop through and away in rapid succession: traction weights and pulleys, the rush of the air all around me, blue sky through branches, falling and falling, Mr Donatelli's need to be seen by the podiatrist tomorrow, Jim Cleary's dog wagging his tail, the drawings and cards from Hugo's children I'm yet to collect, the albums for them I'm yet to buy, Jo's lonely bewilderment at the funeral service, the unwashed smalls stashed in the bottom drawer by my pathetic little bed at Nightingale, barbed wire running around the fence of an internment camp. Blackout is imminent, but not before I've returned to the ward.

I'm there by six-thirty – in plenty of time for my last scheduled check-through that all is well with Mr Cleary before I let him have a good long sleep. When I get to him, though, it seems he's already asleep. But no, he's not; he turns his head and says: 'Hello.'

Someone's lowered the head frame and made him lie down. Why?

I ask him: 'Are you tired?'

'Not really, no. Hungry.'

'That's good. But why are you lying down?'

'I don't know.' He shrugs. 'A nurse came in after you last left and said it was time I had a rest.'

'Did she.' That would be under Matron Moorefield's instructions, and that would be nothing but a petty interference. I'm glad Matron Moorfield is not here, well past the finish of day shift, and the night matron, Matron Willis, is too lovely a person for me to shout at. My temper is too, too tired for games. I reach behind my patient and yank up the frame, probably a bit too furiously: 'I'm sorry.'

'It's fine.'

No, it's not. 'It's a bit hard eating dinner lying flat on your back.' It's hard enough having to do everything in bed. I take a count-to-ten breath, go and retrieve extra pillows; find a smile: 'More importantly, I can report that your dog is happily in the care of your neighbour. Gave me a big dopey grin – Mate, that is, not the neighbour. She's a good sort, isn't she, Mrs Nichol? All those children …' I take his t-shirts out of my satchel and put them in the bedside drawer; shaving case on top, in easy reach.

'Thanks,' he says, watching me. 'Thanks for everything today.'

'That's all right,' I tell him, getting on with it, taking up his right foot: 'I haven't finished with you quite yet. You haven't had any sudden pain or cramping in the last few hours?' I ask him for the fifth time today.

'No. All good.' He wriggles the toes of his left foot as well as he's able, and then he says: 'I really do appreciate the trouble you've gone to, Miss Brynne. I can see how busy you are. None of my mates know what day of the week it is until Friday, and even then, not one of them would remember to bring me anything except a beer. I owe you a big favour.' The toes of the foot in my hand curl around over my fingers, as if saying thanks again.

'You don't owe me anything.' My words are automatic, but right here, right now, it all catches up with me, tears of confusion, hurt, grief, anger, all streaming out at once, before I can put his foot back down and leave.

'Hey,' he says. 'If you want to talk about it, I've got nothing else to do.'

He makes me laugh; I put his foot back on the bed, wipe my eyes with my handkerchief: 'How's that for embarrassing?'

'Yeah, well,' he raises an eyebrow, 'there are worse things, aren't there.'

We both laugh at that, for what we each know too well; and I say: 'Yeah.'

'So, are you going to tell me?' he asks. 'If you don't, I'll lie awake wondering.'

'All right.' I tell him the very worst of it: 'I lost a friend last week. A very important friend, a man who was like a father to me. And I'm lost without him.' I can't say anymore. I mouth the words, *I'm sorry*, as I try to pull it all back in.

Jim Cleary says nothing; he holds out his hand, and I take it.

His grip is as sure as it is silent, and when I've got myself under control, I tell him: 'There's the big favour returned. I needed that. Thank you.'

'Don't worry about it.' He smiles; every kind of kindness in that smile. He presses his thumb gently, firmly into the back of my hand before he lets it go: 'Have dinner with me?'

I shouldn't. I absolutely shouldn't, but … 'Well, it's not like I've got a better offer.'

That smile. 'What's your name?'

'Lucy.' Here I am, breaking the cardinal rule – not only of general medical ethics but my own. Let's make it official: 'Lucinda Jane.'

'Beautiful,' he says with those deep blue, caring eyes, and I don't care about anything else, not tonight. I need a friend, and I want this one.

I get a vegemite sandwich from the canteen downstairs; he gets a decent slab of shepherd's pie when the dinner trolley comes around. Mr Donatelli winks at me through the gloaming and the gladdie blooms as I take a chair from the central table: 'I see nothing, bella – nothing.' I wink back at him, but there's nothing much to see.

Just me and Jim Cleary, talking over a chipped enamel bed tray under the buzz of the ceiling fan, talking as though we've known each other forever; perhaps in some strange way we have. Like meeting like, but the differences are as fascinating as those things we share. He plays the drums in a dance band most Friday and Saturday nights, at a club up in the Cross; I'm so dull and swotty by comparison. He organises his work schedule around surfing conditions, rising early and knocking off at three whenever he can, but he owns that little cottage by the sea, at least the percentage that's not owned by the bank. And no, there is no Carol – that's Rory's new girl. He has good mates, yeah, great mates, but Sundays, he usually goes for a motorcycle ride on his own. Where? Anywhere. I don't tell him I'm not a fan of motorcycles, or that I might be persuaded to change my mind, for the right fool, one day.

I don't leave him until after eight, and when I fall into my bed, I'm still talking to him. I talk to him in my sleep. The best sleep I've had in weeks. No – years.

HUGO WINTER

It was over the breakfast-table newspapers that Hugo learned of the rapidly escalating events in Europe, the talk of war, and the first thing he did on the formal declaration of it was to present himself for military service at Victoria Barracks, which lay a mere two-mile stroll from his home in Sydney. This enthusiasm wasn't entirely driven by love for his newly adopted Empire and country. Although he had no personal experience of war, he knew that the unleashing of it always brought an upsurge in orthopaedic cases, and he was eager both to help and to learn from this one. He also felt the Kaiser needed a good kicking for the invasion of Belgium. Yes, Britain was guilty of imperial muscling around, bullying Germany over shipping lanes and trade, but jumping at rifles was not the way. Hugo felt that the worst of German arrogance – with which he easily identified – should be sent back inside its lines. For the greater good of all, for peace to prevail.

He thought all along that Germany could not possibly win at this game.

He did not know that the armed forces of his homeland would dig in for the next four years – four years of epic, suicidal obstinacy. He did not know that this war, which would become known as the Great War, would kill seventeen million soldiers and civilians across all sides and wound a further twenty million. That was one hell of a surgical load – one that no-one saw coming.

Except perhaps the ever-prescient Jo. She could not have known the future or guessed at its details, but she knew that something tremendously awful was about to unfold – for her husband. And she was prepared to pitch her own battle over it, too.

'You didn't think it appropriate to discuss your plans for enlistment with me first, before offering yourself to the army?' It wasn't unusual for Hugo to go off along his own track without bothering to consult with her. He could disappear for hours and hours, walking, lost in his thoughts; he could disappear to a conference in Melbourne for a whole week, only informing her as he was rushing out the door. He could make a surprise purchase of a motorcar, 'for convenience, my darling', and then conveniently bring home a darling surprise child in need of care for a few days, saving the parents from an unexpected hospital cost. But this was different; this was not in any way amusing or endearing. This would change their lives.

'Jo, please. Consider my position,' he said. 'I don't want anyone to think that I might not be a loyal supporter of Britain. I don't want anyone to think I am an enemy.'

'Hugo.' Jo's argument against it was just as reasonable: 'It looks like you want to return to Europe – as the enemy within.' Then, within her anger, she challenged him: 'Do you want to return? Do you want to go back to Germany? Is that what is really in your heart?' She suspected the persistent refusal of so many of his colleagues to accept or respect his techniques must be getting to him, after these last few years of it; she thought maybe that would be enough to make him want to return to the hospitals and universities where his skills and knowledge would be valued.

But she was wrong about that. Opposition had never concerned her husband – he was not capable of understanding the stupidity of others, much less his own. Moreover, he remained always too busy to consider these things with any depth.

He told his wife, shocked at her accusation: 'No. I would never willingly leave you – what are you saying?'

'Hugo!' Her anger spilled into distress: 'Leaving me – us – is precisely what you have offered to do. Your daughter is not even two years old and you have offered to leave her, for an unknown place, for an unknown length of time. You have barrelled your way into an army barracks looking like a German spy.'

Hugo sighed. Surely she was overreacting.

She wasn't. She was perfectly right.

The wheels of injustice moved slowly, though. First, there was a knock on the door from the police, half a dozen of them, wanting to search the house, neighbours all over Darling Point wondering what was going on. Then, there was a raid on his Macquarie Street surgery in the middle of a busy Thursday morning, patients in the waiting room all aghast at the uniformed men marching in and out. Whispers grew louder, bolder; appointments were inexplicably cancelled at both the clinic and St Vincent's Hospital; colleagues who had been friendly, now distanced themselves; neighbours would no longer acknowledge them in the street. A police motorcar would regularly putter past their drive, headlamps sweeping across the stained-glass panels of the front door and down the hall.

'Let me remain here,' Hugo did not ask the police but told them, in his customary way of telling, during the second raid on their home, which occurred a little after midnight on February 3, 1915. 'Let me work for the army. I have so much in the way of surgical skill and knowledge to give to the Australian Imperial Force. I will offer this service for free, to show my allegiance to Britain. It would be a waste not to take advantage of all I might give.'

Of course, the senior policeman he was telling this to thought to himself: *Well, well, don't you have some big tickets on yourself, you high and mighty Hun.* But all he said to Hugo was what he'd come to say in the first place: 'Pack a bag, Dr Winter. You're coming with us.'

'But you have no evidence that my husband has been in any way disloyal.' Sharp and straight as blades, Jo threw her words at the policeman as he stood there in the library, directing his men to empty the room of all its documents and any book written in German.

'Madam, we have all the evidence we require.' The policeman warned her: 'Do not attempt to obstruct this operation or you will be arrested, too.'

'Arrested?' Jo was unafraid of this threat to her – she was a Levine, daughter of one of the nation's favourite biscuit-makers, and quite possibly more Australian than the policeman in front of her. But Hugo, he wasn't so secure. 'You're arresting him?'

'Yes.'

She shook her head at the nonsense of it: 'You're arresting my husband for possession of medical magazines and books printed in German? That small book there – ' She pointed into the box at his feet. 'It's about plants. It's about Hugo recording his observations of all the plants he finds when he's walking along the beaches he enjoys visiting. Is that important information for a spy to gather?'

'It might be, if you are the German Navy wanting information on the coastal geography of New South Wales. Are you proficient in the German language, too, Mrs Winter?' The policeman stared at her, unmoved.

'No. But I wish I was,' she said, not backing down for a second. 'I wish I was proficient in a hundred languages so that I could tell you in every one of them that you are making a mistake.'

'Please, Jo.' Hugo tried to calm her, not trusting that the policeman wouldn't act on his threat to take her as well. 'I'll go with them now,' he said, 'then we'll talk to someone higher up the chain of command and we will fix the mistake. Don't worry, my darling. It will be all right.'

Of course, it wasn't. This seemingly indiscriminate persecution of Germans was happening all over the state of New South Wales, all over Australia, and even to Germans who had become naturalised subjects of the British Empire. In all, over the duration of the war, some four and a half thousand Germans would be imprisoned, or so the official figures would say. It was not, however, as indiscriminate as it at first appeared. There were Germans who outright declared allegiance to the Kaiser, and wished to be deported; there were Germans who were found in possession of actually incriminating literature; there were even a few spies caught in the act; then there were the innocents, perhaps the most famous of them being the beer baron Edmund Resch, whose rivals in the lager trade wanted to see him and his ever popular pilsener off the market for a spell.

And then there was Hugo.

He could not imagine that any of his own rivals would want to see this happen to him. He was in the business of transforming the futures of others for the better – the young, the crippled, the injured. He did not believe for a moment that his fellow doctors could be so petty in their professional jealousies or doubts in his abilities that they would prevent him from giving what he could of himself for the nation. In Hugo's mind, that was far too far-fetched.

But it didn't matter what Hugo thought. Far-fetched or not, he was, in fact, on his way to Darlinghurst Gaol, bail refused while the case against him was assembled. He had not made a fuss of any sort during the arrest; he had not even kissed his infant daughter Claire goodbye – why would he wake her up in the middle of the night when he was so convinced he'd be back home in a day or two? He could not have known that this missing kiss would become one of his greatest regrets, for he would not see Claire again until April 10, 1920 – five years, two months and seven days away.

Jo, meanwhile, went straight to her cousin Edwin Glass, the barrister, who lived only two suburbs away in Rose Bay. He'd know what to do – she hoped.

The first thing Edwin said to her was not encouraging: 'Reasoning with a police prosecutor is like talking to a boiled potato, but I'll try.' He did all he could, and as quickly as he could, too. Edwin had just taken up a commission as captain in the infantry and was due to leave for service overseas in eight weeks' time. He was busy in training, with his company, but he made every effort to gather counter evidence, to see if he could have the case dropped.

To begin with, he obtained the names of those who had adversely testified against Hugo by affidavit: all nineteen of them were doctors; all of them detailed supposed instances of Hugo's disloyalty and un-British character – 'the man boasts of German superiority', 'he mixes only with other foreigners', 'no-one has ever seen him join in any toast to the King', 'he attracts the lower classes to his clinic, poisoning vulnerable minds with Marxist doctrine'. The whole denunciation seemed so bleedingly false to Edwin, a hand so overplayed and spiteful, he couldn't grasp what might be driving it, until one name loomed out at him from all the rest. A name he knew: E. A. Slade.

'That chap is a card-carrying prick – diabolical,' Edwin told Hugo when he visited him at the gaol. 'We were at school together. Trust me, Eliot Slade would make a good hard case for Freud. Is there anything you might have done to make him, or any of this lot, so set against you? Anything that we could use to prove their claims are malicious?'

All Hugo could think of was what he knew to be the truth: 'Only the fact that I am more successful than any of them, in terms of my patients' results.'

'Hm.' Edwin couldn't do much with that. No magistrate would believe that members of the medical fraternity could behave in such a childish and despicable way. The word of doctors was sacrosanct and, in this time of war and heightened emotion, was unlikely to be questioned unless some vexatiousness or error of judgement could be demonstrated. Edwin scratched his head: 'Why do you have to be such a good stick, Hugo? Why couldn't you have had an affair with one of their wives?'

The two men laughed about it, hollowly: tall, dashing Edwin in his khaki tunic and slouch hat, about to risk all for his country, and Hugo, stocky and stuck, beginning to look scruffy in a shirt he'd been wearing now for almost a week – when he should have been serving, too, with the Medical Corps.

On bidding Edwin farewell, Hugo embraced him, more concerned for his cousin-in-law, his friend, than for himself. 'Well, at least no-one will be trying to shoot me while I'm here,' Hugo assured him: 'Whatever defence you manage to put together, it will be good enough – thank you. However it goes, I'll be all right. We'll be all right.'

Edwin was fairly convinced by this time that the case against Hugo would go through; internment would be inevitable. But there was one thing left he could do. He wrote to Colonel John Monash, the highest serving officer he knew, commander of the 4th Infantry Brigade, presently in Egypt. The man was a civil engineer in his civvies, as well as a fellow lawyer, and they'd met each other a few times when Edwin had been down in Melbourne last year, chasing one of the young lady friends of the Colonel's daughter, Bertha. The chase didn't work out, but he did share a few whiskies with Colonel Monash in commiseration. He would ask him now to write to the Department of Army about Hugo's case. The Colonel hadn't met Hugo in person, but everyone in the Jewish community knew of the doctor and his work. He was also married to Aaron Levine's daughter Jo – in terms of a character reference, that spoke for itself. Edwin was sure the Colonel wouldn't mind, if he had the time, if the letter got to him before the brigade was called to action.

No-one could have known then that Colonel Monash would finish the war as Lieutenant-General, commander of the entire Australian Corps, a man whose leadership and battle nous would see him celebrated as among those who smashed the Hindenburg Line in the blood-drenched September of 1918, forcing the ultimate surrender of Germany. Back in 1915, he was merely commander of the reserve forces who would bring up the rear at Gallipoli; he was merely another Jew the establishment didn't like, even if, or maybe because, his soldiers loved him. There was a campaign then and all through the war to see that Monash would not progress, but here was a man whose character was stamped with an even more robust form of German arrogance – for he was of the Prussian breed. And so there, in his tent in Egypt, as he waited for orders from British High Command, orders that would bring Australia fully into the fray, Colonel Monash found a few moments to pen a decent letter for a fellow Hebrew and a distinguished, worthy one at that.

Unfortunately, it didn't reach Sydney in time to prevent Hugo being photographed and fingerprinted as prisoner number 3576A and thenceforth removed to Liverpool Concentration Camp, a patch of muddy, tick-infested scrubland twenty-five miles southwest of Sydney, on July 31, 1915, with all requests to see his wife and child denied. Hugo didn't argue. He thought it would be safest for Jo and Claire if he kept his mouth shut, did as he was told. He was safe, too, more or less, or so he thought, while he stayed shut-up there: he wasn't being slaughtered on a distant beach in the Dardanelles, as so many were. It was only when he received the letter from the British Medical Association a few days later, telling him he'd been struck off the register, that he shed a tear – not with self-pity, but with bewilderment.

He couldn't understand it. Sure, he wasn't the easiest man to get along with on the job – he wasn't so stupid he couldn't see that he was occasionally brusque and snappish with the slow – but who would take things this far? Who would so badly want to prevent him from practising? That fellow Slade? Although the name rang a faint bell, Hugo wouldn't have known the man if he'd fallen over him in the street. He was utterly mystified as to why *anyone* would want to so thoroughly annihilate his reputation and his work.

Why? The question tormented him.
Why?
Why?
Why?

ELIOT SLADE

Hatred, once entrenched, has little need for reason. Like a fox who takes a chicken not because he must eat but for the thrill of the kill, desire for blood overruns all sense, and then, no matter how many chickens he gets, he'll never have enough of them. In the same vein, Eliot Slade could not content himself with having had Winter so comprehensively dishonoured and put away. Instead, disappointment rankled that deportation orders could not be immediately arranged – damn the war for this delay.

Slade needed a new objective, and found it in a sudden appetite for service, deciding to enlist in the Medical Corps himself. Of course, this move wasn't prompted by any courageous or patriotic impulse to care for the wounded. The Allied attack on the Turks and the Germans at Gallipoli was proving to be a bit of a disaster – it was the last place Slade would want to be – but he'd seen the elevation in status of those doctors who had joined up. He anticipated that the experience would accelerate his career in ways no other posting or position might. A little glory got overseas: yes, that was attractive. Besides, he'd not travelled much, and here was the opportunity to gad about with all expenses paid. He also hoped to get away from his sullen, barren wife for a while: he was finding Audrey so tiresome, so boring, he might as well have been screwing a cadaver.

'How long have you had difficulty with your breathing?' the enlistment doctor asked him at his examination for the corps.

'Never had difficulty breathing,' Slade replied, unconcerned at the question.

'But I can hear the rasp in your lungs,' the doctor said. 'What's the history with it? Bronchitis? Asthma? TB?'

'TB.' He couldn't lie about it – there'd be several x-rays and a file somewhere in Sydney Hospital to say he'd had tuberculosis, 1905, confined to a sanatorium in the Blue Mountains for the second half of that year, missed his final undergraduate exams. 'But I completely recovered.'

'Not quite, it appears.' The enlistment doctor frowned sympathetically. 'Sorry, you can't serve overseas. Once the lungs are weakened in this way, there is always a susceptibility that remains. Too great a risk to send you off only to have you fall ill yourself.'

Slade was enraged but he kept it all contained. This old damage to his lungs wasn't what incensed him – it was the thwarting. It was having been told no, he couldn't go; told he couldn't wear that diggers' uniform and all the admiration it inspired. And why? Because some filthy patient gave him TB on one of his first student rounds in Casualty. He stood, adjusted his tie; he wasn't going to beg.

'Plenty of doctors required at home, you know,' the one in front of him said. 'There'll be repatriation needs soon, and even sooner than that, if you're interested, there's a vacancy about to open up at the Royal Alexandra – honorary ortho.'

'Thanks for the nod,' he replied and then he left. He wouldn't be putting his hand up for repatriation work: no kudos there, so far removed from the action. He wouldn't be looking into that honorary ortho vacancy, either, solid position as it may be: the Alexandra was a children's hospital, out towards Parramatta, a place where city poor met rural poor and they were all deformed – he'd rather send himself to Liverpool Concentration Camp.

He stayed put at Sydney Hospital then, where at least a modicum of distinction could be preserved, and where, as the luck of war would have it, the plum position of senior orthopaedic registrar became available soon enough. The chief surgeon at the time wasn't exactly spoiled for choice, with half the nation's best and brightest lately called away, so Slade just about walked into the job, and its substantial teaching load. Still yet to perform any difficult and delicate reconstructive surgery himself, he focussed his students' minds instead on the basics of limb removal, tendon severing and joint fusion, surgeries that, while they had their place, would always leave patients with some degree of disability. His resistance to learning the latest and much improved techniques lay, of course, in both an absence of natural talent and fanatical resentment of Hugo Winter's, but he justified his approaches with remarkable ease – for the most part, emphasising the savings in costs that came from treating patients by the most expedient means.

When one of his Sydney University students queried, 'But isn't it more effective for the infant club foot to be gradually stretched and splinted rather than surgically cut at the tendons?' Slade dismissed the idea as asinine. He told the class that science did not support theories invented by egotistical pretenders who gave no consideration to the unnecessary burden hospitals would endure by children lining up to have plaster casts changed every five seconds. 'A complete waste of orthopaedic resources,' he spat the words out with disgust, and made a note to fail that student. There was no-one but the oldest guard of orthopaedic conservatism left at the university to stop him – and that they certainly wouldn't do. To a man, they heartily approved.

In fact, while the most advanced medical thinkers were off ducking bullets and dodging trench fever, Eliot Slade was promoted to Vice President of the Sydney chapter of the BMA. A meteoric rise for one who had begun with so little promise, and such an elevation in power he was now ideally placed to not merely influence policy but to personally quash every appeal against Winter's imprisonment and deregistration.

The first of these appeals Slade received on behalf of the association came from Jo – Jo Levine, as he still thought of her. She implored the BMA to reinstate her husband and help clear his name, attaching a letter from some high-up military fellow, and saying that some government official or other had undertaken to look into the case seriously if the BMA would retract their evidence. *Surely the unconditional support from Colonel Monash proves beyond doubt the fine character of my husband,* she pleaded, and in perceiving her desperation, Slade only smiled to himself at the thought she must be regretting the marriage these days. The endorsement from Monash was, however, glowing indeed:

Hugo Winter is a surgeon held in the highest esteem in Australia and throughout the world. There is no question that the man is a patriot, a loyal subject of the British Crown and devoted to his adopted country. He has offered his medical services to the nation on at least two occasions that I am aware. Who does it serve that this doctor should remain in gaol? We need him over here.

But it didn't take much detective work for Slade to discredit every word.

'Monash is a Jew,' he told the association at their next meeting, during which the appeal was to be considered – and a handful were by this time beginning to question the heavy-handedness of their attack on this fellow whose record of clinical achievement was, on reflection, rather impressive. 'It goes without saying that a Jew will stand up for another Jew,' Slade pulled them back his way: 'They all do that – stick together. You can't believe what a Jew might say in defence of another Jew. By definition, it will be a perversion of the truth.'

The gathering nodded as one, the appeal was rejected unanimously, and the meeting moved on to other business: a further unanimous decision not to give in to wage rises demanded by domestic staff at public hospitals; and hearty agreement on the matter of pushing for a general increase in specialists' salaries. The business out of the way, Slade treated his colleagues to a paper he had written arguing against the new medical 'fad', as he called it, of grafting bone to restore length and structural integrity after injury or to correct deformities – again, a waste of time, as far as Slade was concerned. Bones could not be chopped out from one part of a patient and transplanted into another part with long-term success; if the bone did take, it would never mend sufficiently or be strong enough; the bone would break eventually. Slade provided no corroborating data for these assertions, and he ignored absolutely the news of much successful experimentation that had been coming in from the Medical Corps on the front lines. Nothing was going to stop him from loud-hailing his ever increasingly outdated views in journals and any lecture hall that would have him – because they were views with which the old men of the medical establishment vehemently agreed.

The wheel was turning very certainly Slade's way: he would be chief orthopaedic surgeon of this hospital one day; he would be president of the BMA within the next two years. He would be the one to set best surgical practice in this state.

He would be a father, too, in the shorter term, so it would seem, for his wife had become pregnant again, after all this time.

Audrey had become somehow inured to his violence; never accepting of it in her heart, but her body gave in to it, as bodies under siege eventually do. Hers found a way to hold onto this child, and she was thrilled – not least because, again and mercifully, it meant he would leave her be.

She held her swelling belly lovingly, imagining it to be a precious seed pod, guarding and growing the blossom of new life. A miracle, this life, all life, springing forth even in the most hostile of places.

He caught her once, when she was about seven months along, gazing at her form in the mirror of her dressing room and wondering at her child in there.

'Close the door or cover yourself,' he said, walking past, on his way through the bedroom to his own wardrobe.

Her maid, Jessie, who was in there with her, making some alterations to her skirts, pretended she hadn't heard the master's words; she told her mistress: 'I've never seen a prettier mother than you, Mrs Slade.'

And Audrey pretended she hadn't heard this kindness, such was her isolation, such was the complexity of her shame.

She gave birth to a baby boy, Alasdair, on September 3, 1916, crying out in the quiet of her harbourside home, crying out as the war raged on at the Battle of the Somme. Fields in faraway Pozières were now ploughed deep with the blood of Australia, but this boy – her boy – was safe in her arms and splendid in every way. He was beautiful.

She fed him at her breast herself that very first day of his life, her world rocking sweetly as she smiled and smiled and smiled.

'Don't do that in front of me again,' said Slade to his wife when he came into the room that night to inspect the child.

'Do what?' She was unsure as to how she could possibly have offended him this time.

'Don't have the child suckling on you like that,' he told her. 'It's revolting. You look like a fat sow.'

She was so full of joy and wonder, she laughed and forgot to hold her tongue: 'Why are you a doctor at all if you hate people and their bodies so much?'

He smacked her mouth; he startled his newborn son, causing him to bleat in fright; and then he told them both: 'Shut up.'

FOUR

LUCY BRYNNE

Jim Cleary and I are walking down to George Street together, heading for the harbour or the pictures, I'm not sure
which, because I'm dreaming. Obviously, I'm dreaming, but
now he catches the toe of his shoe on a crack in the footpath
and stumbles beside me, and the dream seems horribly real as
I try to catch him up by the arm but can't. He's too heavy. As
though I'm looking through a fluoroscope, I see inside his leg
and all the bones are crumbling.

What?

I wake up in the dark but it's not dark – the blind is closed
so the sun doesn't wake Elvia, snoring softly there in her bed
across the room. What's the time? I pick up my little clock,
and almost drop it again when I see it's a few ticks after six-
thirty. Evidently, I sleepwalked into bed so soundly last night,
I forgot to set my alarm. I'm supposed to be on the ward at
seven, monitoring priority patient.

Jim Cleary.

Thoughts race through exclamations – *Oh no! Oh wow!
Oh really?* – as I throw myself under the shower in the block

across the corridor, not waiting for the water to heat up – *Good morning!* Back in my room, scrabbling as quietly as I can for wayward hair pins, I hear the squeak of laundry-trolley wheels trundling along outside and remember last week's uniform didn't make it to Friday pick-up because I wasn't here – I was with Jo, being useless on the day of the funeral. Hugo … Push past the wave of loss; the breathtaking crash against that beach; the cry of my frightened bird. I don't have time. I can't miss uniform laundry today and risk ending up caught short, so I dive into my cupboard to find relevant blouses and skirt, before skittering out the door.

'Just in time.' I smile at the laundry lady as she nears, taking my bag full of uniform over to her rather than hanging it on the door handle for collection.

An older woman, careworn, she stops and sighs, but smiles when she recognises mine and wags a finger at me: 'Lucky.' I think she has a soft spot for me because I don't wear a nurse's uniform, with all those starched collars and cuffs and aprons that must triple the work every Friday. Right at this second, though, she's got me bailed up with a reckoning squint: 'You all right, dear?'

'Yes.' I could exclaim that I've just slept ten hours straight for the first time in who knows when, but I don't think laundry lady is asking about my sparkle; I look down to check I'm actually dressed, see that I am, and ask her: 'Why?'

'There's been a word of concern.' She nods, as if she receives intelligence via some higher power. 'Mrs Tunnidge down at the canteen said she doesn't know how you live off vegemite sandwiches alone – a girl who works as hard as you do.' She gives me a meaningful stare, and I think I'm being offered help should it be needed.

'Oh …' I'm so touched. I don't know Mrs Tunnidge – there are at least half a dozen different ladies in the canteen, and dinner ladies, tea ladies, all over this four-hundred-bed hospital – and I don't know the name of the woman talking to me, but it's sunshine on my shoulders that anyone in this place has any concern for me at all. It's also not a little bit mortifying that my dietary deficiencies have been noted. 'Don't worry about me,' I assure her: 'I'm just a vegemite addict, and we're all working too hard, aren't we?'

'That there is the truth, dear.' The laundry lady nods again, going on her way, take-it-or-leave-it generosity trailing in her wake, and making me remember the truth of where I come from: people who know what it means to want despite hard work. *Daddy, it's all right – don't cry.* And I definitely don't have time for that; I press those memories down, down into my empty belly, and run for the stairs. A small girl running, that's who I am, and as I run across the courtyard, a further truth occurs: the real reason I'm dragging my heels over leaving the boarding-cloister of Nightingale is because I'm so institutionalised I don't know how to be a proper independent adult in the outside world. I don't even know how to operate the staff washing machine without assistance. The truth is: real life has too many complications and I'm too busy to figure out any of it.

Up the central stairs of the Pavilion, I keep running, telling myself now there's no way I'm going to make Jim Cleary a complication. He's very attractive, very lovely, I'm sure we're going to be great friends, but first and foremost, he's my patient; I was only a bit insane yesterday, for all good reasons. Jo's letters come rushing back to me, of Hugo's internment, and again I can't believe it: anyone who can see me run would see where Hugo's singular allegiance lay – in orthopaedic wizardry. Halfway up this third and final flight of where I need to be, I decide I'm going to go through all of his correspondence at Aurora to see if I can find out any more about it, a thought which prompts a little panic at not having packed or picked up the children's cards and drawings yet – I don't want them hanging about there at risk of being accidentally tossed out. I'll need someone with a car to help me move them, though – but who? Dr Adinov? Yes, I'm sure he wouldn't mind. I'll call him when I get a chance sometime today.

'Good morning, Mr Donatelli,' I whisper at his sleepy wave as I enter the men's section of the ward, and note two other admissions have arrived overnight, but there's only one man I'm here to see.

'Good morning, Mr Cleary.' And my heart flutters so crazily on sight, I should hand in my resignation and be done with it. I am made of butterflies as he turns his head and sees me.

'Hello,' he says, but he doesn't return my smile; I suppose he's not quite awake.

'How are you, James Julian?' I ask him, sparkling. Another day together, how will I cope? Pretty well, I'd say. 'Did you have a good night?'

'Not the best,' he admits, and he does look a little pale as I turn on the light above the bed. Butterflies vanish instantly.

'What's the grief?' I ask him.

'Every time I sneeze,' he says, and it looks like it hurts him even to speak. 'I've got a cold coming on.'

I can hear it; he has a quiet, raspy sort of voice anyway, but this is a croak. 'Hm. Annoying.' I frown in sympathy, and at the unfortunately all-too-common occurrence: come to hospital and get sicker than you were when you were wheeled in. I ask him: 'How bad is the pain when you sneeze?'

'Not nice.'

I take that as excruciating. 'Where is it? In your shin or all over your leg?'

'All over.'

'Hm.' The first thing I think, again: that traction is not heavy enough; it's not keeping the muscles from contracting, the splint is not keeping the fracture from moving, which could suggest a problem with the fixation inside, with the wires that are meant to be holding the bone together.

He sneezes now: trying not to; failing, violently. 'F— there,' he croaks, trying not to swear.

This is not normal two days after surgery; Dr Oxley will have to do something about it now. I touch Jim's forehead with the back of my hand: warm but not too hot. Find the thermometer in my pocket, shake it, shove it under his tongue, wait for it to tell me he doesn't have much of a fever at least: only slightly up at a hundred and one degrees.

Ask him: 'Have you mentioned this to any of the nursing staff? Have you had any pain relief yet?'

'No.' He's still obviously inside the sharpest of the pain as it is, trying to breathe through it: 'I thought it would pass, but it hasn't. I did tell that older one half an hour ago when she came in to open the blinds. She said, "You've broken your leg, it's going to hurt for a while."'

How very pleasant of you, Matron Moorefield, mother of compassion.

I tell him: 'I'll request some morphine for you now.' And I'm on my way. Apart from considering this from the patient's perspective, I can't do my job with him in that amount of pain.

Matron Moorefield tells me at her desk: 'It will have to wait until Dr Oxley arrives to assess the need.'

'It can't wait.' I dig in. Let me break your leg and see how you like it. 'The need is now.'

She presses her lips together and shakes her head, as if I might not know whether I've been played by a dope addict or not.

'I'll sign for it.' Alasdair Slade is behind me, already writing out the instruction.

'Thank you.' I smile, and mean it. Matron will not argue with Lesser Slade: worships him as son of the chief. Goodo. I say to him: 'You're early today.' Thank God.

He says: 'Yes. Hm.'

Awkward few moments of silence during which I think he's going to have another go at asking me to have lunch with him; but he doesn't. He says: 'You're doing a very good job with Mr Cleary. Keep it up.'

What a strange thing to say. I haven't really done anything yet with Mr Cleary apart from keep his circulation lively, and establish that, yes, I am more than likely developing an inappropriate relationship with him. Perhaps Alasdair Slade is only making a point to Matron that I'm the boss where Mr Cleary's concerned, I don't know; I don't think any more about his comment.

I help Jim Cleary raise his head off the pillow long enough to take the tablets, my hand still at the back of his neck as he says: 'I wish we'd met some other way.'

He sneezes again; it's very hard work. I tell him: 'Don't worry about it. I'm glad I'm here.'

'Dr Oxley, please, can I have a word?' I linger after the morning meeting. 'Mr Cleary's pain, it's … Please, can you review the traction and the splinting? In my experience, it's —'

'Yes, yes, noted.' He dismisses me with a flick of the wrist, index finger pointing the way out.

But I have to press: 'It's urgent. He's double the pneumonia risk now and I can't do anything about it by way of exercise. I can't sit him up in this state.'

'Yes.' He looks at me directly, and he looks harried rather than irritated: 'Steps are being taken.'

'This morning?'

'Yes, Miss Brynne. This morning. If you will allow me.'

I return to Jim with a big box of tissues, but he's gone back to sleep now, drug-induced. There's not a lot more that I can do.

Nothing much for me to do on the ward all round. The men's section is empty except for those two new admissions at the other end of the room: a cracked patella in bed one and a dislocated clavicle in three, neither of whom need me for the time being. Dear Mr Donatelli has been taken to his podiatrist appointment, to have his poor old hardworking feet looked at, see if some better footwear might help with his back – then he's going home, because it's miraculous what a few days' rest can do. Over in the women's section, the three sets of bunions there are looking after themselves, hobbling about happily enough, and entertaining Mrs Stevenson as they all swap crochet patterns and discuss the birth of Prince Charles. Orthopaedics is like that, like so many specialties are: either dozy lulls or mad storms.

I look out of the window, beyond Jim's bed: great view of the cream-painted brick wall of the Pathology building; it's a slightly nauseating shade of cream, too, like a wedding cake left out in the sun. He's going to be moved from this ward soon, though, so Alasdair mentioned in the meeting, off to a 'special case' private room on the fifth floor, when one becomes available. It'll be a better view up there, but I hope our Mr Cleary's medical insurance is in order – it's going to cost a fair bit. Repat might assist, if the original injury can be shown to have been a cause, and I'm already filling out the form in my head, making a note to Dr Oxley, requesting a letter in support, if it comes to that. Let's say a little prayer for every ex-services individual who doesn't have an advocate to help sort these things out.

The cracked patella in bed one lights another cigarette, as two orderlies amble in with their calm detachment, seen everything before breakfast: 'Bed seven, Mr Cleary. That's him, yeah?' one of them asks me almost rhetorically.

'Yeah.' I nod; and smile, glad that Dr Oxley has acted so quickly, whatever that action might be. 'Where are you taking him?'

'X-ray.'

I could follow them, make a nuisance of myself trying to catch a glimpse, but I'll go and attack my paperwork monster instead, take advantage of the quiet. My desk is also a good place to loiter, being tucked around a dead-end corner from Dr Oxley's office, where I'll be able to hear him come back. I find a couple of extra files have been stacked on the already teetering in-tray: more scribblings from Dr Oxley for me to decipher. Mr Donatelli's discharge notes for the attention of his GP, detailing psychosomatic factors suspected as the base of his idiopathic back pain: *Encourage him to relax, take up smoking or a hobby*. I'd like to add: *Suggest his lazy sons work a bit harder and send him on a holiday occasionally*. Then there's Mrs Stevenson's not very good prognosis: she's too old to attempt emplacement of an artificial hip; only worth the risk on the young. Sad, although not unexpected. But the good news is, I type my way to the bottom of the file pile for the first time in almost three months – including all my own.

It's now a few ticks after one pm, just over four hours passed. Dr Oxley hasn't returned; I knock on his door to confirm it. Wander back over to the ward; my patient hasn't returned, either. I wonder if they've found a problem other than the obvious ones. Spontaneous crumbling? Highly doubtful, but that dream I had this morning returns to make my shoulders shiver. I don't bother asking Matron Moorefield what's going on.

I go back to my room at Nightingale to get some change for the phone, to make that call to Dr Adinov that's been rattling around the back of my mind, and when I open the door, I find Elvia is awake, eating peanut-butter toast in bed with her book, platinum curls a merry mess on her head.

She gives me half a glance: 'What are you doing here, slacker?'

Mostly for her amusement, I reply: 'Oh, you know, just searching for the professional judgement I seem to have lost in falling for a patient.'

'You are joking.' She looks up from her book.

'No, I don't think so.' If I'm honest, I'd have to admit I'm even starting to fret a bit, but I'm not going to say that much to Elve.

She's incredulous enough as it is, laughing: 'Who?'

'Nasty fracture, left tib, blue eyes.' I laugh at myself, fingers plucking pennies from my coin jar. 'It's pretty bad all round.'

'Hm.' She frowns. 'I think I saw that one come in – Tuesday night? Young guy, fell off a lorry or something?'

'That's the one.' I nod; and a little butterfly flits back through my chest, saying, *Yeah*. 'But he didn't have surgery until Wednesday morning.'

'I know.' She's still frowning. 'Oxley and Slade the Greater Fascist were arguing about it for ages.'

I knew it; I know it. 'What were they arguing about?'

'Wasn't really listening.' She thinks on it for a second. 'Something about how they were going to fix it, what hardware to use, then they waited for Professor Charlesworth to turn up, more arguing, someone slamming a door. It was a busy night. I hardly looked at the guy, except to notice how quiet he was – you know that way some get, suddenly finding themselves out the back of Casualty with no trousers on, so quiet you can hear them thinking, *How the fuck did this happen?*' Because no-one knows swearing like an ex-navy theatre sister previously specialised in the care of Americans. Her wry smile asks: 'But is he falling for you, too?'

'Maybe.' Is he? I don't know. I hope so, though he might be a bit too sick for it today. I'm incredulous that I'm thinking any of this.

'Aw, Luce. That's terrible.' Elve scrunches her nose, delighted at the terribleness.

'Been a good week …' I trail a wave as I leave her, heading back down the corridor for the wall phone at the top of the stairs, trying to remember why I need to call Dr Adinov – yes, boxes, drawings, cards, Aurora – before I throw a couple of coins in the slot.

'Adinov.' He answers as though he's offended by the interruption, but he always says his name like that; when I was a child, I used to think he was growling, 'Had enough!'

'Hello, favourite Russian.'

'Lucy! Hello, my dear. What can I do for you?'

The burst of warmth is like a battery charge. I ask him: 'Would you be able to help me pick up some things from Aurora?'

'Of course – when?'

Good question. I won't knock off before seven pm tonight or tomorrow night, long days filled with possibly increased needs of unwell priority patient; I'll need an hour or more in Hugo's office, too, I guess. I suggest: 'Sunday? Maybe mid-morning?'

'This would suit me well,' Dr Adinov replies. 'I'll come and collect you at ten am. No, make that ten-thirty. I am slower at my swimming these days.' He laps the length of Bondi Beach every morning, just about never fail: that's how you get to be so strong and fit at seventy-eight.

I pause, my thoughts slipping into the tiny black holes of the mouthpiece. I want to ask him what he'd do with Jim Cleary's fracture, be reassured of my own logic, my under-standing of the anatomy and physics involved, the sense of my purely medical concerns, but I don't say anything. The problem is being sorted as we speak. Surely.

'Lucy?'

'Yes. Sorry.' I snap to. 'I'll see you then – I'll be waiting outside Casualty from ten-thirty.'

He pauses now, before he says: 'If you ever need to talk to me about anything, I am always here for you, you know that, don't you, Lucy?'

'I know. Thank you.' Thank you more than I can say. 'See you Sunday. I've got to go.' Go before emotions surge again.

Go and return to the ward to find Dr Oxley looking for me there, waiting at Matron's desk: 'Where have you been?'

Of course. I was fifteen minutes, if that. I lie: 'Getting something to eat.' I haven't bloody well eaten anything yet. Matron Moorefield's eyelids quiver in disdain, as though I might have been caught sneaking off to make a personal phone call.

Dr Oxley's not interested in where I've been; he says, to matron, stiffly: 'Mr Cleary will be more comfortable now.' Not a suggestion but a fact. Then an abrupt jut of the chin I interpret as instruction to follow him. I do: all the way back to his office, where he closes the door behind us, voice low and fierce: 'If there is any further issue with Mr Cleary's condition or treatment, any issue at all regarding him, come straight to me. In the interim, you are to resume and maintain the close monitoring of this patient until I personally tell you to stop.'

'Are you concerned about anything in particular?' I have to ask. Agreeable as I am to be so compelled to stick fast to Mr Cleary, and all day Sunday if it comes to it, I have a feeling I'm being used in this conflict between ortho chieftains. I also need to know if there's something I should specifically be looking out for.

Dr Oxley keeps it vague: 'Anything at all that concerns you, concerns me.'

I dare: 'Can I know what's been done just now? I won't tell anyone you've told me anything.' How mad that sounds. 'I only want the best result for Mr Cleary. I don't want to cause any trouble.'

'No, you don't want to do that,' he seethes, wearily, but he tells me: 'The distal weight has been increased to seventeen pounds.' That sounds like a hard-fought not much. Seventeen pounds instead of twenty or more? Don't ask, don't but in. 'Other than that, things are ... what they are. The wound is good, there's no sign of infection, and Alasd– Dr Slade, the registrar, has applied a cast incorporating counter-traction points and pin, hip to toe, solid as Gibraltar. If Mr Cleary can't sneeze comfortably now, I want to know about it – immediately.'

'Of course,' I say and go on my way, not terrifically thrilled at having the senior registrar take me into his confidence like this. I suspect he has the same concerns I do: that he would approach things differently if it was his decision. But this is what we've got, so let's make the best of it.

When I get back to the ward, priority patient has not yet fully roused from the anaesthetic, and caretaker nurse is fussing about him and the monkey ropes with an arrangement of sheets.

I ask her: 'Please, don't bother with that too much. I'm only going to take it all up again in a minute.'

She looks appalled at the idea: 'But it's visiting hours soon. He must be tidy.'

Oh, dear Lord: can't have a patient not tucked in to within an inch of his life for visiting hours, whether he's expecting visitors or not. All across the entire hospital, nurses everywhere will be covering up and tidying up the public wards and thoroughfares for the show: two until four, Monday, Wednesday, Friday, Saturday and Sunday, except Christmas Day, apparently, when it's extended to ten until six. Wow. How is one supposed to get well on that? Have another cigarette. The nurse – a nervous third-year, keen to be seen to be perfect – keeps at her tucking-in, and knocks her elbow quite vigorously into the bottom upright of the traction frame, shaking the overhead pulleys. I flinch for her and Jim both, but it doesn't wake him.

She takes his blood pressure and, when she's finished, I lift the head frame of the bed a notch, and ask her: 'Could you please get me another pillow?' since she's returning the gauge to the cupboard anyway.

Appalled again.

'Don't worry,' I assure her: 'I won't tell Matron you helped me.'

'All right.' She scuttles over with a pillow, half petrified. No wonder such a number drop out of nursing before they even get this far.

I tell her: 'You can leave him with me now.' I give her a smile: 'If anything terrible happens, you know who to blame.'

She doesn't smile back, but she scuttles off. Maybe there's something in all that starch that makes the spirit brittle, too?

'You going to wake up?' I ask Jim, as I listen to his chest: steady heart, clear lungs. And then a groan. 'Welcome back.'

He opens his eyes and I'm shocked at the blue, shocked at wanting to touch his face. I'm not going to.

Ask him: 'How are you feeling? Any nausea?' I have a sick bowl at the ready. 'Lean towards me if you do.'

He shakes his head; croaks: 'No.' Closes his eyes: 'Chucking up on you was going to be my next move, too.'

I laugh as I fall and fall: 'Wouldn't matter if you did, you know.'

'It might matter to me,' he says, and then he sneezes – one of the loudest and most forceful sneezes I've ever heard. The whole bed shakes.

I ask him: 'How was that?'

'Nowhere near as bad as it was before.'

'Good.'

'Can I have a tissue, please?' He looks at his leg, which looks so much worse for all that it feels better; mutters: 'F— Christ.'

I pass him the tissue box: 'You poor thing.'

Grunts and blows his nose, makes an attempt at a smile: 'I couldn't have planned this one better if I tried.'

I'm not exactly sure what he means by that, but here, in his eyes, and in mine, a new truth is irrefutable: we're in this together.

'Jimmy?' A woman emerges from behind the gladdies on the central table. A trim figure in a neat, beige-and-white spotted frock, her voguish bob greying decorously, she has the same blue eyes – pretty on a woman.

'Hello, Mum.' A different kind of groan from her son.

'What have you done this time?' She gives him a kiss on the cheek, and then gives me a nod of acknowledgement as I move away to the end of the bed to stand guard by the distal weight. She's not the dowdy bush wife I might have expected; her pearls, her watch, her wedding rings, her shoes: they are well-off sort of farmers; her vowels are crisp and polished, with a hint of a lilt I can't pick. 'Did you fall off that motorcycle?' she's asking him.

'No.' Grunt. 'Didn't Rory tell you what happened?'

'Yes, he did, and I didn't believe him.' Mum's not silly, even if she's sadly wrong in this instance; she looks over at me and says: 'This one is my worry child. You'll have one of them one day, dear, and you'll know you're alive. Harum scarum, can't stop still.'

'I'm stopped now, aren't I.' Grunt.

'How long will you have to be here?' She pushes his hair to the side, the way that mothers do, tidying up her child even though he's twenty-nine; the way that mothers have of giving me a moment of envy, because I don't have any memory of my own mother at all.

He shrugs: 'Who knows?'

I tell them both: 'The doctors should have a better idea of time in a week or two, when they see how it's all healing.'

Mrs Cleary bites her lip, looking at the frame, the ropes, the cast; shakes her head: 'Jimmy.' She says: 'Your father will be here on Sunday, with the ute. We'll take the dog home with us then. I was hoping we'd take you, too.'

He blows his nose, annoyed, no doubt with everything: 'What were you going to do, throw me in the back with Mate?'

'No. I was going to catch the train, myself – the same way I got here last night, stopping with Betty in Roseville, thanks for asking. And you've got a head cold as well.' She clicks her tongue and looks over at me again: 'This one gets a head cold three times a year now. I don't know what the Germans did to him, to send him back like this.'

'Mum.' He warns her off the subject.

'Three head colds a year?' I can't help asking Mrs Cleary.

'Catches anything going,' she says. 'He never used to.'

'Hm.' I file that one away under anecdotal evidence that the spleen plays some part in the body's defences; not that a doctor will have a conversation about it, especially not a thoracic one: to them, if the function of a body part is unknown, then it has no function. I think I will keep a close eye on this head cold.

'What do you think it means, dear, all these head colds?'

I can only tell Mrs Cleary: 'I don't know. At least, not beyond this present one adding a bit of extra discomfort.'

'Oh …' She turns back to her son and touches his face; I want to touch his face, the stubble on his jaw. I should leave them alone; I'm sure his leg is safe with her.

'Jim – mate.' Another face appears above the floral display, big grin, slicked back quiff, long legs loping over, tall and thin, a way about him that suggests he is a mobile, one-man nightclub. I think I'll stay right where I am. He says: 'Jeez, that is a job, all right.'

'Rory – keep your distance.' Jim puts up his hands and I don't know if it's in mock defence or genuine, but I'm ready: it never ceases to astonish me how many people think it might be fun to pull on a traction rope. Jim says to him: 'I don't suppose you told Mum it was your spanner I slipped on?'

'G'day, Mrs Cleary.' Rory is giving her a kiss. 'It was, in fact, my spanner he slipped on.'

'You two …' Mrs Cleary clicks her tongue again, but with some kind of affectionate exasperation, and all of a sudden this far corner of the ward lights up with the bright chatter of people who love each other. I want to know these people. I eavesdrop openly and learn that Rory's a country boy, too, from Gunnedah, that they're having a bumper wool clip over that way, and that Jim and Rory aren't workmates – they're partners in the lorry-servicing business, and it's a busy business.

'You'll have to put someone else on.' Jim seems pragmatic enough about it. 'I can't see how you're going to get it all done without help.'

'Can you afford it?' Mum asks both of them, in a way that suggests she's got a chequebook in her handbag, and that maybe things like medical insurance and inadequate Repat pensions aren't among her worries.

'Everything's under control.' Rory seems to brush off the whole idea of concern, as if it's a foreign concept to him. 'I don't know what we're going to do for a drummer tomorrow night, though. I can't get anyone.'

A grunt that sounds like this one hurts: 'You'll find someone.'

'Not anyone halfway up to it,' Rory is quick to reassure.

But Jim sneezes again, gale-force, and I have to step in: 'How's the pain?'

'It's fine,' he says, and I believe him, more or less, but I can see he's tired, past it. Today has been an ordeal.

I round it up with Rory: 'Perhaps tomorrow might be a better day for a longer visit?'

'Oh. Right,' he says, sympathy quick, too, and genuine, and maybe a bit guilt-tinged as regards that spanner. 'I'll come back tomorrow, then. Don't you worry about anything,' he tells his mate; a tender press of fist to shoulder: 'Don't you worry about anything at all.'

'You do look wrecked,' his mother says, in a way that suggests she might have said it a few times before. 'I'll come back tomorrow, too. You need to rest.' His eyes are already closed as she kisses him again, whispering a fond: 'Behave yourself.' Then she smiles at me as she turns to leave: 'Look after him for me, will you, please?' Words lightly spoken but her deep blue eyes are full of worry.

'I'll look after him,' I promise her, as she goes; words I've spoken a thousand times, but this time, it's … not normal.

I look at him dozing, and I baulk now at what's happening here. I can't be his physiotherapist. It's not right. But there isn't an alternative. I can't abandon him to – what? The conscientious care of the doctors in this place? Or one of the general physios from downstairs, who are all jolly nice and probably all right but none of them qualified as I am? There is no choice but to get on with it, and to administer care above all else. Do the worst first: in this case, that will be the muscles in the top of his thigh; I didn't have to go so near his groin yesterday; unavoidable today because of the cast. I pull a screen across and turn down the sheet at his waist; place my hand on the top of his hip, firm, gentle, confident, delivering words from the usual script: 'Don't panic. I'm not going to look at anything I don't need to see.'

A sleepy laugh: 'You should get paid danger money just in case.'

A line I've never heard before and, my own smile joining his once more, this all seems completely reasonable. I work the plait of muscles under my fingertips, imagining the way they run through the leg towards the injury, the way they contract and relax, the way they move when we walk.

He winces at the pressure I'm applying to his upper thigh, and I distract him by asking about his family; he tells me he's the middle child of five, three sisters, all married, and a much older brother, John, ten years older, who's on the land with their mum and dad, and will take the reins of the property one day. 'I'm the spare wheel,' he says, as I move away to check the toes of his left foot. 'But I've never been that interested in farming, never planned to stay in Canowindra or anywhere out bush. I like being near the ocean.'

That glimpse of long-held worry in his mother's eyes returns to me and I ask him: 'Did your brother go off overseas, too?'

'No.' Half-laugh, half-groan; blows his nose, breaks my heart. 'Dad was happy we didn't both go. Someone had to stay at home and keep producing fleece and food for the nation anyway, didn't they? John would say I'd do anything to get out of helping at harvest time. But things were a bit cooler than that between me and him afterwards, when I came back. I wasn't the same kid that left. We don't know how to take each other anymore.'

That's sad, and not uncommon; war builds all kinds of invisible walls, but I don't need to say that. I take up his right foot and ask him instead: 'What about Rory?'

'Oh yeah.' He sighs with the rub and a whole lot of history: 'We've done every stupid thing together since schooldays, including the air force. But he stayed on the ground, in maintenance and then training other engineers, didn't leave England. I had to beg him regularly not to put his name on the flight list: he is a lair. But I think he had it the worse, in a way, waiting to know … you know. He didn't know where I was for almost six months. Well, he thought I was dead, like the others. It was pretty good to see his dopey face again. First thing he said when he saw me was, "You've got to meet these blokes I've been jamming with – we're looking for a drummer. How's that for lucky?" like nothing had happened in between.'

I'm going to hear what happened to the 'others' one day, but not today; I'm going to hear this band one day, too. 'What instrument does Rory play?' I have to ask.

'Sax,' he smiles, that lovely, broad smile.

'Of course, he does.' I laugh, turning my attention to his Achilles tendon. 'What else would a lair play?'

'He's pretty good,' Jim says, but I hear something strained in it that makes me look up again. He's looking at his broken leg and there's pain in his eyes as he says: 'I don't know how I'm going to cop all this without music.'

My heart really does snap a string now; I'm no musician, but I know this kind of pain myself: *How the hell am I going to get through this?* And there's nothing I can do right now to bring any music to him. There's no music allowed on any of the public wards, rationale being that not everyone has the same taste and it could be disturbing for the very ill. Hugo had music of some sort going every day – the gramophone, concerts, and shows for the children – something musically joyful every single day. At Prince of Wales Repat, too, it wasn't unusual for a singalong to get raucous and not for a lady's ears as the men entertained each other. My heart says, I think I don't want to work here anymore, where it's all right to smoke a cigarette and make everyone share it, but not all right to sing. If it wasn't for Jim Cleary, I think I might just walk out the door, today.

And that's why I lay it out for him now: 'Well, music or not, I think we both know you won't be copping it alone, hm?'

'Hm?' He blinks; I fall into his deep blue ocean.

'Hm.' I perch beside him on the bed. No-one can see us here behind the screen.

I touch his face; he touches mine; and here it is: Us. Begun.

We kiss, softly, briefly, and the only thing that's not normal about it is that I've never felt like this before. I don't care about anything but this kiss. And I don't care if I catch his cold.

'I don't know how you're copping the romance,' he says, Thursday morning, almost a fortnight later, as I'm checking over the back of his hips for any redness, any sign of a pressure wound threatening. 'I usually wait a bit before showing a woman this much of my arse.'

I love him; I love his arse; I tell him: 'Romance is overrated but your arse is all right.'

'If you say so.' He smiles like a picture of shiniest male health as he settles back on the pillows, a window full of sunrise at his shoulder, lighting the gold threads in his hair. Nothing wrong with him, except a leg waiting on news of yesterday's x-ray – but he's already going insane. Moved last Monday, he has a private-room view across the fig-dotted lawns of the Domain, and visiting hours up here of nine till nine. He has a portable radio set and headphones, so he can turn the music up if he wants to. I got him a job, fixing any gadgets that can be found to keep him busy: two surgical drills, three blood-pressure gauges and a radio belonging to one of the orderlies, so far. He has his wonderful family taking it in turns to travel two hundred miles from Canowindra and surrounds to Sydney to keep him company during a busy harvest: sisters, cousins, aunties, all bringing extra butter because it's still under rationing, and because Jim likes it spread an inch thick on anything that's butterable. He has mates who turn up of an evening with a bottle of beer and a deck of cards. He gets a kiss from me every spare moment I can be here with him, too. But none of this compensates for not being able to get out of bed, for that screaming, deep-bone boredom of it, around and around the routines of breakfast, lunch, dinner, washing and abluting, having the sheets changed under you, your bodily functions measured and inspected – that last, thankfully, never by me.

It's a particular kind of madness: like being submerged in aspic and simultaneously having your brain attacked by personality-eating bacteria. Or that's how being stuck in traction felt for me, nine years ago, or yesterday if I let that memory overwhelm – one I won't share with him, to avoid giving him any distraction he doesn't need. As it is, he's developed quite an abnormal fascination with his blood pressure and pulse rate: must know what it is every time it's taken. When I asked him why, he said, *I don't know. Never thought about it before. It's interesting, I suppose.* Hm.

'Lucy …' He says now, and I love the way my name sounds inside the low notes of his voice, a voice that's always thoughtful and slightly hoarse.

'Hm?' I sit down on the chair beside him, trying not to think about my own insane day ahead: although I don't have to be anywhere for half an hour yet, after the morning meeting, I have a crazy outpatients schedule, nine on the ward, and a couple of special cases who need me a lot more than Jim does now: a factory worker from Pyrmont, Mr

O'Reilly, whose right arm was eaten up to the elbow by a canning machine, so that he has to relearn how to do everything left-handed; and a young woman called Janina Shaw, who is having a mighty battle with herself in facing the reality that she'll likely never walk again after a horse-riding fall – none of which I'll share with Jim, either, as he certainly doesn't need the second-hand stress. As it is, I've missed hearing the question he asked me two seconds ago: 'I'm sorry, what did you say?'

His eyes laugh at me for a long moment before he replies: 'I asked you, have you ever been in love before?'

'Oh.' There's a question, but I don't mind telling him the truth of it: 'Yes, but I'm not sure I'd call it love these days. It was a few years ago – thoracic surgeon, quite a bit older and not a very pleasant person, as I would come to realise. He took care to remind me at every opportunity that he was above me in every way, then he left for New Guinea and took up with one of the nurses over there. Cured me of romance.' The double-leg amputee I was trying to coax away from the edge of the abyss at the time helped, too; fun days at the Repat; fun days feeling kicked in the guts. But I make fun of it now for Jim: 'I didn't even get a Dear Lucinda letter. Found out the hard way on the grapevine.'

'That makes him an idiot, then.' Jim squints a little in contempt for my betrayer, and that's all the romance I'll ever need.

I tell him to make it clear: 'So, I'm damaged goods.'

He shakes his head: 'No, you're not.' As if his opinion decides it; wouldn't that be nice.

I ask him: 'What about you? How many women have you robbed of their innocence?'

'None.' He gives this one an outright laugh, and something darker: 'Don't get me wrong – there've been girls, a few. But nothing that ever went anywhere. I was too young when I left to know what I was doing and then, afterwards, I didn't know who I was for a while. Does that make sense?'

'Yes.' It does, very much. There are thousands of men and women all over the country who've had their sense of themselves blown up and blown away, leaving them lost, angry, aching. I ask him: 'Do you know who you are now?'

'I know that I'm in love with you,' he says, plain and serious. 'You're a very special person, Lucy Brynne. I just wish this wasn't happening here.'

'Oh well,' I say, butterflies exploding everywhere. 'Look on the bright side. If it wasn't happening here, we probably wouldn't have even gone on our second date yet. We might have gone to the wrong film or the wrong restaurant and not seen each other again at all, after some petty disagreement over Brussels sprouts or some stupid thing.'

He reaches out for my hand and I take it, linking my thumb around his, as he says: 'I'm so in love with you, I haven't had time to understand it yet, and time is something I'm not short of.'

Time stops, I can't breathe, and my natural streak of scepticism says nothing to challenge those clichés, or even whisper that only bedbound psychosis could have caused his declaration. Because I know he loves me; I feel it through his skin, every time and every way I touch him. I know this is the man I will marry.

I'm so caught up, I don't hear the knock at the door, or perhaps there wasn't one, but Dr Oxley is suddenly standing at the end of the bed and by some feline reflex I've sprung up and exclaimed: 'Oh, good morning, Doctor!'

He smirks. I've never seen the man smile before. With eyes closed, he tells me: 'I'm not at all interested, Miss Brynne, as long as you do your job.' And then he looks at me directly:

'But it is good that you are here, so that we might discuss this together.' I don't suppose it's an accident he's dropped in then, thinking he might find me with Jim at this hour – the whole hospital has probably worked out who my favourite patient is – and I'm already bracing for what this might be about, in terms of radiographic results, before he says: 'Unfortunately, there's been no significant healing in the bone as yet. Disappointing but not so unusual. Sometimes there is a slow start to these things. We'll review it again in a further four weeks to see what's happening, but you should be prepared for quite a long stay.'

'How long is a long stay?' Jim asks, and I wish I could block out the answer.

'It's difficult to say.' Dr Oxley looks somehow as disappointed as Jim does. Disappointed and something else – worried? 'But I must say that, at this stage, as things stand, it would seem prudent to suppose about twelve weeks or so, although I must also emphasise how difficult this is to predict. It's a waiting game, I'm afraid. Not the best news, but not the worst. These things happen.'

'Three months,' says Jim: 'Right.'

Wrong. This is what we've been working with: the wrong approach. I knew it. This is rubbish. This is not right.

I tell Dr Oxley: 'I need to speak with you in private.'

'I'm sure you will.' He slides his eyes out the door. 'But that will have to wait, too, for another time.'

'No, it won't.' I've never been so rude: 'I want to talk to you now. It'll only take two minutes. Or I can wait at your office door all day until you make time.'

I make my way there, thumping down the stairs; he follows me, growling at my ear: 'Don't you dare speak to me like that in front of a patient.'

Too late. I mutter back at him: 'I'm sorry I was so rude but I think you know as well as I do that the situation for Mr Cleary is not acceptable. I want to see yesterday's x-ray. I want to see all the x-rays.'

'No.'

'All right, then I'll leave. I resign. Effective immediately.' Leave you with a full house and no specialist physio who routinely does twice the therapeutic and outpatients work your junior registrar and resident do put together.

He knows it; in his office, he finds the latest x-ray on his desk, clips it to the viewing box on the wall, switches it on. The dark, jagged lines of the fracture are clear inside the cross hatch of wires holding it together; it doesn't look wrong; it looks old-fashioned, outdated. And not yet begun healing. It also shows how pronounced the angulation is, from the original, badly set break.

'Why?' I ask the film. 'Why do things this way?'

'What would you do?' Dr Oxley asks me, and it sounds like he actually wants to know.

I answer him: 'I'd use a vitallium plate and screws, a long plate, and I'd wedge in an iliac graft by osteotomy here, above this old callus, to realign the bone. I'd have him home next week, non-ambulatory cast for eight to twelve weeks, and then, all being well, a walking cast for a further six to eight. That would be the most efficient path to healing, and kinder on the patient. I wouldn't have him cooped up out of the sunshine and the fresh air, making body and spirit weaker with every day.' Stretching and flexing and throwing sandbags at each other across a room isn't a substitute for proper exercise. It's bloody hopeless, long term.

'I agree with you.' Dr Oxley shocks me, ripping the film from the box. 'But I would prefer to use a Küntscher nail – smaller incisions, faster recovery. Nothing like that is going to happen, though, until after Christmas – in four weeks. If there hasn't been sufficient healing by then, the approach will be reviewed. But do not speak to the patient about any of this, please. Far *kinder* that he be able to plan for the least desirable possibility.' I nod at the hard and tricky truth of kindness, and he adds: 'The severity of the fracture has necessitated a great deal of caution. The present delay could be explained by something as simple as the temporary effect of a head cold – impossible to know. It could merely be the course of the trauma itself. It's only been two weeks. Next month's x-ray could show a very different picture, much improved. I know you know these things.'

'Hm.' I do, and in ways I wish I didn't. I wish I didn't know this could go the other way and drag on for a year.

'You should know, too, that everyone wants the best outcome for Mr Cleary here.'

Of course, they do; and I'm not going to do anyone any good by getting about impersonating Hugo. Who do I think I am? I haven't seen a Küntscher nail used before; I'm not exactly sure what one is, apart from the most recent development in hardware, something Hugo and Dr Adinov discussed over schnapps. I feel like a fool now.

'Miss Brynne.' Dr Oxley is not treating me like a fool; he says: 'I understand your emotions have got the better of you this morning. I am no ogre – I really do understand. And you must understand that I do not wish to lose you – I had to go to a great deal of trouble to get a dedicated physio on this ward in the first place and I am pleased to have got one of your calibre – but if you ever speak to me like that again, I will not only sack you, I will have you banned from the hospital. You will not see Mr Cleary at all.'

'Understood.' And fair enough, too.

'The best you can do for your patient is to try to make sure he stays as fit and well as possible, and optimistic that a good result will be achieved eventually. And it will.'

I know that. I apologise: 'I'm sorry, I truly am. I won't do this again.'

'No, you won't.' Dr Oxley's chin juts in the direction of *now get out of my office*; but he smirks again: *silly girl*.

I go back up to Jim; he's tapping the edge of the mattress, tapping out the beat of endless waiting; bemused, asking me: 'What was that about?'

'Me being overinvolved with my patient. And then getting into trouble with my boss for being rude. I just don't want you to be stuck here that long, either.'

'I'm fine.' Not his most convincing smile; it's such a tough blow. Yes, there are plenty of people in this hospital, in this world, suffering far more, but suffering is what it is to the sufferer, nothing more, nothing less. He says: 'I should have done something about my leg before this, and maybe it wouldn't have been so bad.'

So, I was probably right there, too: he was offered a correction, probably from the RAAF Repat, and didn't take it. Don't encourage the regret. I tell him: 'It doesn't quite work like that. You could have had a perfectly good leg and still had the same freakish break.' However unlikely. 'It is what it is. Besides, if it wasn't what it is right now, you wouldn't have met me.'

'I'm paying a high price for it, aren't I.'

'A premium.' But I have to ask him: 'You haven't had any trouble with bones healing before, apart from present leg, have you?'

'No, I don't think so.' Then he shakes his head at some other thought: 'Well, when I was sixteen, I busted the same wrist twice in the one summer, but that was my fault.'

'How did you manage that?' I must know; must be a good tale for him to have avoided mentioning this in already eventful medical history.

He shakes his head again at whatever he's remembering, bites his lip over the laugh, embarrassed: 'We used to backflip down off this ladder on an old grain silo in town, see how high up you could do it from – there's not much else to do in Canowindra. First day home for the school holidays – crack. Then I went and did the exact same thing again, but a more thorough job of it, the day before I was due to get back on the train to Sydney. Mum threw me and my bags on that train anyway, straight from the hospital – not amused. I wasn't too popular at school, either. I missed the whole of the rest of the cricket season, not that it made much difference, as we always got thrashed anyway, but I was the only one who could bowl with half a chance of taking a wicket. Grim statistics, that season of 1935–36. Even Rory called me an idiot – every morning, as he had to help me get dressed.'

'That's pretty funny,' I say, and it is. 'Was the girl impressed?' I guess there must have been a girl involved somewhere in this.

But he shakes his head yet again: 'No. Worse than that. This kid I went to primary school with reckoned I couldn't do it, reckoned I'd got citified, gone soft. What I didn't realise was how much I'd grown since the last time I'd done it – probably half a stone and four inches. Can't believe I miscalculated that badly – *twice*. I was always top at Maths, too.'

'Congratulations.' As if there's nothing fundamentally wrong with the idea of deliberately and pointlessly launching yourself from a height in the first place. Who'd be a mother of sons? A mother of anyone. But maybe there is a hint of a problem here, too, bones that take a leisurely approach to healing; maybe not. Hopefully not. I ask him: 'Where was the break?' He points to the place on the radius, about two inches back from the joint: typical. And there's no outward sign that it ever occurred; I should know – I do enjoy looking at these forearms. I remind him now: 'Well, however reckless you might have been at sixteen, this present leg is definitely not your fault.'

'I don't know about that.' There's a look behind his eyes I don't like; a look of pain that's all emotional, all things we haven't spoken of, yet.

'I *do* know about that,' I tell him, but it's two seconds to eight: 'I've got to go.'

'I can't do it, Miss Brynne. I can't.' This will be the story of Janina Shaw's life if she doesn't take a turn off this road. She is not quite nineteen, and was a promising equestrian until she came off her horse badly two months ago; the spinal injury has been stabilised and she's in no pain now, except for the torment of not being able to feel her legs: paralysis from the waist down and every distressing thing that comes with that. I'd like to offer her a miracle, but in lieu, I'm trying to encourage her to pull herself up in the bed by the overhead bar, so that she can sit up on her own.

'You can do this,' I tell her firmly, gently, mostly firmly. 'You can do this because you have to, and you need to. If you don't, you won't be able to exercise properly, and if you don't exercise, you won't improve.' The prognosis is dire, but no prognosis is ever a reason to stop trying.

'I can't.' She begins to cry. This is why she's here, at Sydney. The expensive private hospital that dealt with her original admission and surgery has turfed her out with the notes 'nothing more we can do' and 'disturbing other patients', and the expensive private physiotherapist her parents want to employ for her won't take her on until she's 'compliant'. Janina is my last patient for the day, and I'm so tired I could tell her she'll end up in an expensive but absolutely horrible nursing home if she's not careful.

'Janina, please. You must try. Let me help you.'

She cries so hard, I'm sure Jim must be able to hear her three doors down. Spinal patients, any patients requiring intensive therapeutic care, should have their own wards, not be shoved about the city like this, being told they're too difficult. If I was in Janina's position, I might be inconsolable, too. No-one knows how well they'll cope or not, until they're lying in that bed.

I try another tack: 'Tell me why, Janina. Why don't you want to sit up?'

'I'm too frightened,' she says, and her eyes are spilling and spilling with it. Of course, everything must be frightening for her right now, especially the grief.

'I know you're frightened,' I tell her. 'But I also know you're very brave.' No platitude: the girl was a steeplechase champion, jumping over fences – you couldn't pay me to get on a horse. I grasp the bar above her, to show her how secure it is. 'You can do this.'

'But I'll fall.' She looks up at it, as if it's Mount Everest. Because it is, at the moment. 'I'll fall backwards and hit my head.'

'I won't let you fall,' I assure her. I can't know what her injury really feels like, but I'm sure she's not bunging this on: her balance is probably scrambled; her faith in reality, too. 'Let's do it together?' I don't let her answer before I've slipped my arm beneath her shoulders with the lie: 'I've got to knock off in ten minutes and I'll be in trouble if I haven't got you sitting up today.'

Remorse in small doses can be handy: she reaches for the bar and pulls herself up quite easily, with hardly any help from me. 'See? See how strong you are?' I give her shoulders a squeeze, then she cries again, and I hold her in my arms, because compassion can never be overdosed – if only we had limitless time. I make a little time for Janina Shaw: I don't let her go until she's finished this bout, until she whispers: 'I'm sorry. I'm all right now.' And I whisper back: 'Don't be sorry. You've just sat up, job well done, doesn't matter how you got there.' Then I move away, so that she's sitting on her own, holding herself there with her hands on the bed, and I tell her: 'Now that you've done it, keep doing it, pull yourself up once every ten minutes or so, if you can. I'll show you some more tricks tomorrow. You've got to build up your stomach muscles and your arms. Will you do that?'

'Yes.' She doesn't smile, but she's won the day.

And I'm completely whacked. By the time I've gone back downstairs to my desk and typed up some of my notes from today, and some of Dr Oxley's, too, I'm sleepwalking as I drag myself upstairs again to Jim.

'Lucy, why don't you go to bed early?' he says as I drift in yawning. 'You don't need to hang around with me every night.'

'I've hardly seen you all day,' I whine. 'Besides, we haven't done your exercises yet.'

'I'll throw sandbags at Rory – he'll be here after work, and you can miss out on a chat about Bedford carburettors.' Jim holds out his hand and pulls me to him as though we might dance. 'Don't worry,' he whispers sweet everythings, 'I'll still be here tomorrow.'

Oh, he can make me laugh, but guilt shoots through my knees at the thought of not staying with him until nine, until the night nurse comes to take last obs and pretend there's nothing unusual about that physio from orthopaedics hanging around up here night after night. It's an irrational guilt that I'm somehow leaving him lonely, as I was when I'd been in this same stuck state. But he's not lonely – is he? How can anyone know another's loneliness, though? Shut up, brain. I'm in love, unlikely, sudden, mixed-up love: not a lot is rational.

'You're incredible,' he says, holding me to his solid chest, his steady heart. 'But you don't have to be so incredible all the time, not for me. You work hard enough. Please, go to bed.'

'All right.' I sleepwalk out inside this goodnight kiss, with him calling after me: 'Don't forget to eat.' Only two weeks, and he knows me so well.

I have every intention of eating, though: up in Nightingale, I pinch four slices of Elve's bread from the kitchenette for vegemite toast and take the plate to bed with a cup of tea. But I won't be going to straight to sleep. To wind down, I take out one of the boxes from under my bed, one of the three that Dr Adinov helped me fetch last Sunday; I want to be with Hugo in the children's drawings and cards, fill another album for the present I'm making for Jo – I'm up to number eight now, and almost finished the lot, good job for an insomniac.

The first one I pick up shouts *DOCTOR HUGO* over a yellow crayon sun-face that's wearing his round spectacles – those specs dating it at somewhere post-1935. And I burst into tears: tears I didn't shed with Janina, tears I didn't share with Jim, tears of tiredness and missing Hugo, tears of old pains and lonelinesses I'd rather forget. Then a flash of childish anger: that Jim's leg is not healing as I want it to. That it's not fair. And that's enough of that.

I take out the box of Hugo's personal correspondence instead, to look again for him less sentimentally there. I haven't found anything else about his internment yet, but whatever I find is usually entertaining or interesting in some way: letters from the Sisters of Charity at St Vincent's, letters from the Hebrew Friendly Society, from the Maori Rugby League Club, from fellow amateur botanists discussing shrubs. Letters from all kinds of people who admired and respected him.

Tonight, I pick a random letter from the unnamed file on top, and I'm delighted to see it's from one Anton Adinov, dated March 13, 1921. A letter as old as me, grumping Russianly at some issue of surgical incompetence from the first paragraph, and I think this one will send me off to sleep very nicely, thank you.

Until I read the words: *That imbecile Slade – he shouldn't be allowed to slice roast beef.*

And I won't be getting too much sleep now.

HUGO WINTER

There was not much time for self-pity or despair. The concentration camp at Liverpool, when Hugo first arrived there that winter in 1915, was a squalid morass upon which leaky canvas tents sat in rows – some thousand tents in all, to begin with, and never enough blankets or firewood for stoves to keep away the cold. Never enough food, either, to keep body and mind whole. Everyone was sick – with colds, flu, gastroenteritis. And everyone, no matter their circumstances, was furious, which meant, if you weren't sick, you had hurt yourself or someone else by violence. Hugo was the sole doctor at the camp: he did not have time to scratch his head from the moment he set foot in the place. So much for the BMA debarring him from practice.

'I need a dedicated place for medical procedures,' he told one of the dull-eyed guards, when he'd made his assessments of all that would be needed that first week. 'I must have supplies. You can't expect all these men to exist here with no doctor, no treatment of illness, no treatment of wounds.'

The guard shrugged. To be fair, he was only a guard, and not a very intelligent one at that. He was also unaware the authorities had no intention of providing adequate medical care for the prisoners. Acting purely on the essential wartime need of harnessing as much public fear and loathing for the enemy as possible, and as quickly as possible, the authorities hadn't thought that far ahead.

Hugo said: 'These men are still human beings. Some of them aren't even the enemy by any interpretation of the word.' Shopkeepers, farmers, men with German surnames who were British citizens with all the correct paperwork, but with a neighbour or a colleague who had accused them of treason and treachery; men who had not had a trial or magistrate's hearing, no dealings with any police except the ones who had arrested them without warning and thrown them behind barbed wire here; men whose wives had no idea where they'd gone. As far as Hugo knew, there were about two dozen of such absolute innocents amid this general confusion of outcasts, and they made him feel slightly less hard done by – at least Jo knew where he was.

The guard shrugged again: 'I dunno anything about all that.'

'All right,' said Hugo, with remarkable patience, given his usual capacity for letting fly at any kind of stupidity that threatened the welfare of others; or perhaps not so remarkable, given that this young guard was holding a rifle, and given that, just before Hugo's arrival at the camp, one of the German sailors, a man called Max Arndt, was shot dead for 'mutinous conduct', whatever that might have meant. 'Hm. Yes.' Hugo smiled as congenially as he could at the boy with the gun. 'What I will do is draw up a list of what is required, with a letter to your superior, for you to hand on to him. You could do that, couldn't you?'

'Ah. Yeah,' said the guard. 'I can do that.'

'Good, good, thank you.' But, for the purposes of requesting approximate quantities of supplies, Hugo had to ask: 'How many men are in the camp at present?'

The guard looked around at the shambles that surrounded them, the filth and the mud, and he said: 'Dunno.'

'Does anyone know?'

'Dunno.'

'Never mind. It's all right.' It was unbelievably wrong. 'I'll make a good guess on my own.'

Making his way back from the guards' small wooden barracks to the tent he shared with an insufferably smug, Reich-loving fleece agent called Gustav Brenner, another skirmish broke out among the rows: another sailor losing his temper, and the sailors here – men who had simply been caught at the wrong port at the wrong time – were not only the most furious, they were, by and large, the most fervently nationalistic of all the inmates. They were, in fact, dangerous and needed to be locked up – away from everyone else. Nevertheless, if one of them needed a broken nose set or a split forehead stitched, Hugo Winter would see to it; he would leave no man without whatever care he could provide. He was as neutral as Belgium, and as overrun.

In his letter to the camp commander – to whomever it might have concerned – he pointed out that too many inmate deaths would probably not be acceptable to the public, or, therefore, to the government in the long run. He pointed out, too, that an outbreak of typhoid or cholera could affect the surrounding population of Liverpool, and that no-one could ever tell how devastating such an event might be. But he received no response.

Nothing happened until almost two weeks later, when a young man of twenty, Christofer Schmidt, an apprenticed stonemason from Erskineville via Bremen, fell through the canvas flap of Hugo's tent, doubled over in agony, his appendix burst, septicaemia already well along the way to claiming him. He died that night but not before his tortured screams stopped the hearts and the tongues and the minds of every man who heard him.

It was then that Hugo went off his head, marching up to the guards' barracks to thunder at them all: 'Murderers! You have killed a blameless boy. You condemned him to die in unimaginable suffering.'

Nothing was said in reply: no admissions, no apologies, no instructions; but almost everything he'd asked for in the way of supplies appeared over the next few days.

Not that this made life much easier for anyone; it only meant that no-one died – for a while.

In the following April, 1916, another young prisoner was killed: Paul Albrecht, a sailor, but a quiet boy, aged twenty-one. He had gone mad with what all the prisoners called 'barbed wire disease', desperate to escape his confines, desperate for news, desperate to be anywhere but this endless hell, where he was regularly assaulted and taunted by his own countrymen for being *schwul* – homosexual. What did the Australian guards do then when he was found between the inner and outer fences of the camp, his face and arms bleeding from the barbs, as he tried to break out? They put him in the compound they had newly created for the worst of the criminals in the camp, a place they called Sing Sing. Hugo would never discover the truth of what happened, but that night they put young Paul in Sing Sing, he was shot in the head – at close range. Hugo was called to witness the mess of it himself; helpless to do anything but shout: 'Get him to a hospital, for God's sake!' Pointless as that was. Pointless as the coronial inquest a week later was, too, quickly and quietly declaring the action lawful, 'the execution of a duty'.

The execution of a boy ... Hugo wrote several letters of complaint about it: to the Coroner, the Premier, the Prime Minister and the Minister for the Army, so furious himself now, he did not care about the consequences.

What world is this, that a boy barely old enough to know himself can be thrown in prison without trial, sent mad and then shot in the head? Without his mother even being allowed to know where he is! How can Australia claim itself to be a civilised nation in doing this? How is this not considered to be a black stain, a stain of innocent blood, on the soul of the British Empire?

Ask he might, but each of his letters was promptly destroyed on receipt – not that he knew that then.

At the time, all he could do was wait for a response – one that he was sure was going to be brutal. He was not surprised then when two guards came for him in the middle of the night, shouting: 'Number 3576A – get up! Pack your belongings!' Not unreasonably, he thought perhaps he was going to Sing Sing to be shot in the head.

He asked them: 'May I write a brief note to my wife?' Of course, he hadn't written about any of these terrible things in all his letters to Jo; he wrote only of how ironically busy he was, how bored he was without her and little Claire, and how generally well he was being treated – lines he always included in the hope that they would ensure the letters would be approved of by the guards and posted to her. Now, most of all, he wanted to tell her how much he loved her and their daughter; he wanted to tell her in some subtle, gentle way that this was goodbye. He hoped she would be pleased that he had stood up; he hoped she would come to understand why it was that he just couldn't keep his stupid mouth shut.

But the answer he received was: 'No. There is no time for that.'

They didn't take him to Sing Sing, though; they took him to Liverpool Railway Station instead, and then, on arriving at Sydney's Woolloomooloo wharves, they bundled him onto a steamer bound for a different camp, up the coast – he could have waved to Jo from the deck as the steamer chugged by their harbourside home on its way out through the heads. The camp he was going to was located at a place called Trial Bay, he was told, and he already knew a little of the area, three hundred miles to the north, having hiked its rugged, rocky promontory at Laggers Point with Jo a couple of years before. *Oh look, another wide, white shell-strewn beach with pounding surf,* he could still hear her cheerful sarcasm at taking in the view as they'd walked along; she'd been tired, newly pregnant at the time.

'Lucky you,' said the guard escorting him.

'Lucky?'

'Where you're going is a holiday resort compared to where you've been. You were never supposed to have gone to Liverpool – right? There was a mix up with the paperwork – right?'

'Right,' he supposed.

As the steamer pushed out between the harbour heads and met the deep blue swell of the Pacific, Hugo heaved the contents of his stomach overboard. What game was being played with him – with everyone? The relief, the grief, the sorrow and the longing, all ensured that he was ill, and wretchedly, for the rest of the trip.

'I've never been seasick before,' he said to the sea, wiping his mouth with his handkerchief, as they rounded the hook-shaped point at the entrance of Trial Bay.

'Sure.' The guard flicked his cigarette into the water. 'That's what they all say.'

The solid stone gaol atop the promontory was indeed a different story, though, and the place where Hugo would have been sent if a certain voice from the BMA hadn't been so loud in suggesting he was a spy. A gaol to which he might never have been transferred if Jo hadn't worked so hard to get him out of Liverpool, taking her pleas in person to the Governor-General, with little Claire on her hip – not that Hugo was aware of any of that then. Then, he was only strangely thrilled to be able to write to her of how embarrassingly sick he'd been on the ship, and how truly comfortable Trial Bay Internment Camp was.

Here, he enjoyed a private room, crisply white-washed inside the old stone walls of what had once been an actual prison, built the previous century with the idealistic intention of actually reforming prisoners, before being abandoned as too kind and too costly. Here, he could ramble the promontory as if free, he could walk the broad stretch of beach to the west that Jo had so admired, up and down, up and down. There was even a tennis court. This was the place where the German consuls were housed, the lawyers, the academics and patrician business-types, with lesser ranks scattered across the grassy grounds in neat wooden huts. A place where the inmates expected a play or a musical recital every Friday and Saturday night, and so entertained each other well.

The only theatre Hugo was involved with there was of a dramatic kind: Cafe Fledermaus, it was sardonically dubbed, and they performed all manner of shows from self-penned satires, to Schiller, to Strauss. He even borrowed a clarinet one evening and appalled them all for old times' sake. He was one of three doctors at this camp – the others being a general practitioner and a neurologist – and there wasn't all that much to do medically. An ache. A pain. A heart palpitation. An ankle sprained.

Most dramatically, one young man, Rick Bauer, a gold miner from Western Australia via Frankfurt, threatened to throw himself onto the rocks one glary summer afternoon in January 1917, a day so oppressive with humidity it was bound to send someone over the edge. '*Wann wird es enden?*' the young man shouted and shouted. '*Wann wird es enden?*' When will it end? He stood there holding his head as though he had every intention of ripping it off his shoulders and hurling it into the waves. Hugo would never know if he saved young Rick Bauer's life that day or had simply made a show of himself tackling him to the ground and pinning him there with the weight of his chest, his fist against the young man's chin, telling him: 'Don't let them win. Don't let them win.' Hugo was so frightened by the idea of giving up, giving in to the invisible generals that kept them here, he held the young man under his fist until he heard him beg: 'Please, I can't breathe.'

The neurologist clapped, 'Well played,' and lit a cigar. Then they all went fishing on the beach.

There were jellyfish stings, countless cuts and scrapes, and, the following summer, a sad end to a cardiac case that could have happened anywhere. The only other remarkable occurrence was a raid on all rooms at the discovery of wireless equipment under one of the boards of the dining hall – give a group of Germans access to jam tins and a pair of nail scissors and they'll engineer some useful thing. There was no ill-purpose in it, though: they just wanted to hear word from home; they just wanted to *be* home.

So did Hugo, but home for him was Sydney. Australia. This land beneath his feet. If pressed, he would confess he was originally from Hagen; he would say he hoped his younger brothers, Kurt, Ernst and Wil, weren't stupid enough to have joined the Kaiser's army, but supposed that they had, not least to escape from lace-making and their parents. He couldn't know any news of his family, not during the war, but he didn't write to them anyway. His last letter was years ago, telling his father of his marriage and new address; the reply he received wished no future happiness or congratulation, relaying only criticism that he hadn't included any information on the respectability of Jo's family lineage. Hugo did not respond. He'd had nothing else to say, and hadn't done, not really, in the two decades since his little sister Irma's death: the day his family ties, slim from the beginning, had seemed to snap and contract irreparably, leaving in Hugo a wound dug along such stubborn and conflicting veins of shame and resentment he would never see the full extent of it. All he ever wanted to see, in any notion of family, was the little girl who danced in his dreams to the beat of his heart.

Jo and Claire, they were his girls today. His truest home. Jo wrote and wrote, trying to give him every glimpse of Claire she could, and he lived from letter to letter. Pages and pages of baby's babbling and toddling about, too soon talking and running, and then a special liking for the word 'Yuck!'; making a first friend at nursery school; going to her first proper birthday party. How could she be four years old? And then five?

And then he received the letter telling him that Jo's beloved cousin Edwin had died in France, at the Battle of Amiens. *A great advance for the Allies, so I have heard,* she wrote: *But they have killed a sparkling part of me. I have such terrible, angry thoughts I barely recognise myself.*

Hugo wept then; he cried for a very long time.

Why?

What was all this for? Why were the people who made these decisions on their lives such a fistful of unforgivable pricks?

ELIOT SLADE

At the end of the war, in November 1918, almost as soon as the last of the guns had fallen silent across the bloodied, battered lands of Europe and Palestine, it became apparent to Eliot Slade that he had a problem on his hands. Scores of surgeons were returning home to Australia and bringing with them all they'd learned overseas: life-and-limb-saving splinting techniques, the internal and external fixation of fractures of all kinds thought previously to be impossible cases; there had been huge advances in wound care, infection control and pain management; and, most difficult for Slade, a plethora of knowledge on reconstructive surgery had been gained, most particularly on the grafting of muscles and tendons and bone.

Of course, Slade had spent so much of his war at home decrying the whole idea of the graft as a fantasy, but now, even the BMA in London were excited about what it could all mean for humanity. In other words, the old guard around the globe collectively panicked in one great scramble to get itself up to speed. Many older surgeons thought it best to retire, but Slade didn't have that option: he was only thirty-five.

It wouldn't look good. If he was going to progress beyond senior orthopaedic registrar, he had to know how to perform all these newfangled whatevers.

He'd never used an electric bone-drill, he'd never placed a traction pin or wired a break. He had no desire to become wonderfully proficient or the best at any of these things, but he had to be able to do it all. He'd already decided he'd further specialise in arthrodesis, in fusions of the spine and other joints, permanent immobilisations; this was surgery sophisticated enough to further his career, see to it that he would be chief surgeon one day, but not so exacting as the surgeries required for restoring function and mobility. Whatever he did, the first thing he knew he had to learn was to graft a damned piece of bone from one part of a body to another. A little easier said than done.

He had to do it without acknowledgement of his previous attitude towards grafting, and he had to do it as discreetly as possible, because he could not admit to his ignorance. The first was relatively easy: doctors, like politicians and economists, do not make mistakes; they simply change their minds as new information comes to light. But the second was trickier: he had to choose patients whose injuries or deformities were severe enough that he could either bury or amputate the evidence of any failure.

As the troops came home in their thousands, there were plenty of patients to choose from – some one hundred and fifty thousand of them, all in all. Although so many advances had been made in medicine throughout that first war, the sheer scale of numbers meant that many men returned incompletely or poorly healed of their injuries. Some of the worst of these cases involved long bones that had been badly damaged by shrapnel or bullet wounds and then by subsequent infection; cases which, a few years earlier, would have meant getting rid of the limb altogether or keeping it permanently splinted. These men couldn't get on with things either way, their wounded arm or leg or multiples of them keeping them in a state of delicate, and often painful, incapacity.

When the case of one Arthur Pembury presented itself, Slade saw straightaway that this man couldn't have been a more ideal candidate. A lowly ex-corporal and before that an ex-carpenter, both of his legs had been machine-gunned below the level of his knees but the bones inside each of them were sufficiently healthy enough for reconstruction to be attempted; the man was desperate enough, too, to give it a go, to get out of his wheelchair, to stop the unceasing pain.

Slade smiled at the man: 'If in the end the bones turn out to have been damaged beyond repair, then I'll take the legs off and we'll get you up and walking on prostheses in no time.'

'Just do it,' said Arthur Pembury, just about beyond caring.

Now, Slade had done eleven grafts by this time, each time taking the graft required from the fibula – that slim bone which, with the tibia, comprises the lower leg. He'd had varying success at it, if the seven amputations and two deaths were subtracted from the count. But in the case of Arthur Pembury, his fibulas were not in a state to withstand any harvesting, certainly not the amount that would be required for this surgery. Slade would have to take the graft from the iliac crest of the pelvis, that great knuckle of bone which comprises the hip.

It was a disaster, not so much for Arthur Pembury, but for Slade himself, who didn't realise that, by this time, his work, and his failures, had come to the attention of one of his colleagues. That colleague was Anton Adinov, a private orthopaedic specialist who was also, these days, honorary emergency surgeon at Sydney Hospital – a stablemate of Slade's, and a superior one at that. Adinov had arrived on the scene at the end of 1917, but because the man was a Russian, a Berlin-trained refugee from the communist revolution, whose practice at Waverley was already making a name for itself in bone-realignment and joint reconstruction, Slade hadn't paid him any attention at all.

'What have you done to that man Pembury?' Anton Adinov challenged him only a matter of hours after the surgery. Having heard that Slade was on a big job, and having heard, too, that Slade was rather slipshod, he'd thought, in the interests of the patient, he should look over the case unsolicited – and was dismayed at the x-ray images he saw when he made his own fluoroscopic examinations.

And Slade knew at that moment, there in the corridor outside the surgical ward, he'd been caught out.

'I will tell you what you have done,' said Anton Adinov: 'You have taken too much bone from the hip, so that when he wakes up and moves there will be risk that one or several of the arteries within the pelvis will rupture and he will bleed to death. All that excessive harvesting and by some mystery the graft you have made in the left tibia is insufficient – unlikely to thrive. What did you do? Throw half of it away? Drop it on the floor? As well, the drill holes in the right look like a child has made an attempt at fixation. Your patient is going to wake up in the midst of a nightmare of suffering that no-one except you should be subjected to. You are an imbecile.'

The two men stared at each other for some moments before Anton Adinov continued: 'See to it that the patient is completely, immediately immobilised and I will make the necessary corrections when it is safe to do so. If you don't comply with my direction, I will personally ensure that you are sued for medical negligence. I will fund this man's case.'

Slade ordered one of the junior registrars to apply the plaster cast, so that he himself couldn't be blamed if anything went wrong from that point onwards; then he made himself scarce for the next few days, feigning a stomach upset, waiting, planning for all eventualities, wanting to slit Adinov's throat.

Despite all expectations, things would turn out quite well for Arthur Pembury: he got his legs back, not quite the way they were before the war but good enough, as far as he was concerned. Anton Adinov could not let Slade get away with it, though. He encouraged Pembury to sue anyway, for the first botched surgery and all that it had cost him in time and money and pain. The chances of the case being successful were slim – Adinov hadn't been in Sydney all that long but long enough to know that attempting to sue a member of the establishment was pointless, especially as the man hadn't lost his life or his legs. What Adinov really wanted to do was bring Slade's incompetence to the attention of all.

And it worked. This negligence case would stall Slade's hospital career for a decade to come. Surprisingly, it would also cost Slade more than £580 in compensation – for, despite the odds, in the general climate of sympathy for returned servicemen, Pembury actually won.

It meant, too, however, that Anton Adinov himself was forced to resign his honorary position, incensed and shocked that the hospital board had not even once considered sacking Slade. Adinov continued to observe him from afar, though, and from within the workings of the BMA. He was curious as to how the British medical establishment, albeit in this sunny, often slow outpost, could have elected one such as Slade to the position of chapter president. A remorseless impostor – a back-alley butcher in a three-piece suit.

At the BMA's quarterly meeting of June 1919, he watched Slade attack some former, absent colleague, a man called Winter, a German orthopaedist who'd been interned and was still yet in prison, seven months after the end of the war. The excitement of Slade, his enthusiasm for denouncing a fellow doctor, was sickening.

'Winter must be deported now,' Slade instructed the meeting. Apparently, an appeal to have Winter's deregistration overturned had been received, and, with it, some sort of request for professional support to try to have him released. 'The war might be over but that doesn't mean the treacherous Hun gets off the charge,' Slade went on: 'He remains an enemy. He must go back where he came from. We have enough doctors here. We don't need any non-British traitors among us. All agreed?'

All of them agreed, 'Aye,' even a couple of young graduates who probably didn't even know who this man Winter was.

Anton Adinov stood up and left; he never went back to another BMA meeting; he never went back to Sydney Hospital, either. He wasn't sure he'd come to the right country: while the Bolsheviks in Australia were tamer than the Russian equivalent, the bourgeois class here seemed not only lazier and more bigoted, but its professionals appeared to be deficient in the basics of professionalism. He dropped out of the public medical system entirely. Adinov was unsure then if he could even live in Sydney itself at all.

Slade was never unsure of anything. He refused to give up his campaign against Hugo Winter, the Pembury negligence case having only hardened his hatred further, if that were at all possible. He would never again attempt a graft on a complex fracture; for the sake of his career, he had to leave the surgical heroism up to better, braver men. Despite his lack of interest in anything like surgical excellence, that cut him. And as impotence breeds insanity, anything that cut him was somehow Hugo Winter's fault. That shitty little upstart Kraut. Slade hated the man as if he'd invented bone-grafting himself.

Hatred was striking a few new lows for Slade at home as well. Audrey was pregnant again and even fatter with it this time. Oh, he left her alone these days, all right: he couldn't stand the sight of her; couldn't stand being in the same room, watching her worship the baby, Alasdair, as if the child were more important than him. He began an affair then, with one of the technical assistants down in the x-ray department; bought her flowers and caressed her gently, kissed her as he'd never done his wife. Why? Because the girl showed him respect, she was obedient. Her name was Shelagh and he called her She. She was no-one. And he made sure Audrey could smell her perfume on his clothes.

FIVE

LUCY BRYNNE

'Adinov,' he answers the phone with his usual growl.

'It's Lucy.' It's also not quite half past six in the morning; I couldn't wait any longer to call. 'I'm sorry about the hour.'

'No need to apologise, my dear.' He chuckles. 'Old men don't sleep, not if they've got any conscience. Is everything all right?'

'Yes,' I say, and obviously it's not: 'No. I – this is an odd one. I've been reading Hugo's correspondence, some personal correspondence. That sounds terrible, doesn't it?'

'No. Not at all.' I can hear him smiling; I'd told him the files in that box were ancient patient files I wanted to look through for medical interest, not private letters that are none of my business. 'What did you read?' he asks me. 'What's on your mind?'

'A letter from you, to Hugo, written in 1921.' I try to keep my voice hushed so that it doesn't travel under every nurse's door along this floor. 'You were telling him about Dr Slade, Eliot Slade – a negligence case.'

'Oh *that*. Ha!' He laughs, loud, rough. 'That man, if he can be called a man – I wanted to kill him. I know precisely the letter you mean. Hugo and I were exchanging notes, getting to know each other and where our paths had crossed. He was in the process of setting up Aurora at the time.'

I imagine these two men in their forties exchanging notes even though they lived less than five miles away from each other; people don't do that sort of thing anymore, show that kind of courtesy. Two blunt hard-heads politely sizing each other up. I ask him what I have to know: 'The negligence, the surgical errors, with that patient, Mr Pembury – was it really so bad?'

'Of course, it was so bad.' I imagine Dr Adinov flicking his hand at the Bondi surf, gold ring flashing in the sunrise. 'Slade is a public liability, always has been. What disgraceful thing has he done now to worry you? I thought that imbecile had all but given away his butchery these past few years – isn't he only a specialty figurehead these days?'

'I don't know much about him. I —'

'What's he done?' Dr Adinov talks over me, old anger swiftly lit: 'Has he ruined someone's knee? Nicked a spinal cord?'

'What?' As if he's been known to do these things often.

'Oh yes, Slade has managed quite a few *errors* over the years. All surgery carries risk, but he should come with an official warning. He does not care who he harms. Unfortunate that one can't be sued for being a c— cold-blooded narcissist. But tell me, he's not worrying you in any untoward way, is he, Lucy?' He says that last as though he's about to get in the car.

'No.' Thank God, no; I don't seem to get pestered by doctors here, as some do. 'I'm sure he doesn't even know my name.' My heart races ahead, telling me over and over that Dr Slade has made a mistake on Jim's leg; but my head insists, no, I've seen the x-ray and the wiring looks like a textbook sketch: it's not wrong, it's only not what I want it to be. I tell Dr Adinov: 'I'm all right. I'm worried about a patient —'

'What is worrying you about this patient?'

'Oh …' A door opens behind me, someone getting up and heading for the showers; I don't turn around. I feel suddenly foolish, standing here on the phone in my nightdress, possibly making a habit of overreacting. Break down some quick facts: Dr Adinov clearly does not like Dr Slade; Dr Slade made a bad mistake on a new technique almost thirty years ago, wouldn't be the first or last surgeon to do something like that; you don't get to be chief ortho by developing a reputation as a public liability, though; so, Dr Adinov must be exaggerating, displaying one of his famous grudges. Overriding fact: surgeons are temperamental, nuts, all of them – they have to be, to find the arrogance and guts to do their job. Worst fact: I've lost too much sleep over this because I'm ridiculously fixated on the patient in question. I tell Dr Adinov: 'I'm not worried about anything terrible. It's just a particular fracture, complicated … Um.' Ask him the other thing I have to know: 'What exactly is a Küntscher nail?'

'Slade doesn't want to have a go at *that*, does he?' Dr Adinov barks, and I'm sure everyone in this building heard it.

'No.' I keep my voice low, hunching around the phone. 'Quite the opposite, I think. Dr Slade is being too conservative. It's Dr Oxley who wants to use the Küntscher nail, on the patient I'm worried about.'

'I see.' Dr Adinov explains: 'It's a nail, hammered into the medullary cavity of long bones – down through the marrow. Becoming very popular in Europe but a slow start here, as usual. Lucy, what's really worrying you? I love to hear from you, any time, any time at all, but no-one calls at dawn to talk about Küntscher nails unless there's a problem. You're causing me to worry now, too.'

'Hm.' I don't know what to say for myself.

'Lucy?'

I admit: 'I might have lost a little clinical perspective with this one.'

'Oh?'

'Hm.'

'Oh …' I can hear him smiling again as he makes his correct guess: 'The patient is a young man.'

'Yes.'

He laughs, so warm the sound slips around my shoulders: 'It happens.'

I laugh, too, embarrassed, and I don't know what else. 'Yes. And it's pretty bad.' Another couple of doors open behind me; I should get off the phone and get ready for the day myself. 'I might tell you all about it on Sunday, if you promise not to make too much fun of me,' I say. We'll be going to have a cup of tea with Jo then, at last, and I'm just as confused and in conflict at the thought of that: hoping I won't cry; hoping she doesn't feel obliged to see me; hoping she's not upset that I haven't called – when Dr Adinov made it perfectly clear she needed a little time alone. But I'm making a habit of muddle-headed panic, too, asking Dr Adinov now: 'Do you think I should bring the albums for Jo? Do you think it's the right time for that? Or should I wait?'

'Lucy.' Dr Adinov's concern seems to radiate through the brick wall I'm staring at: 'It sounds to me like you're worrying about everything. Jo will be so touched you thought to make up those albums for her at all – you must know this. She wants to see you. She would not have telephoned me to arrange our visit if she didn't want us to come. She's much better, really. But are you all right, really? Are you looking after yourself?'

'No. Possibly not, really.' I'm possibly mostly on the phone to Dr Adinov right now because, really: 'I miss Hugo so much, I don't know what I'm doing.'

'I do, too, Lucy.' He lets me hear his sadness. 'I do, too.'

Because it's normal to grieve; and there's no such thing as normal in grieving. I know this as well. It's not normal to fall in love at the same time, though, is it?

I'm not about to ask Dr Adinov his opinion on this; I get off the phone and get dressed. And by the time I'm crossing the courtyard for the Pavilion, I'm half convinced mourning has caused me to fantasise Jim Cleary, or the most compelling elements of him, at least. I think I'm going to marry him, do I? I'm so not myself I'm having one of those desperate, tacky hospital flings with a wounded serviceman, and just can't see it. I can hear myself saying to one of my nurses at the Repat: *You think you're Hemingway's dutiful lover? Remember how that story ends – and stop it. All you're doing is ruining your reputation.* My reputation is all I've got; and this job. I can't afford to throw away either of them on – what?

This sensation of tiny wings flitting against the soles of my feet the last few steps to his door; his face, smiling as he turns to see me: 'Not you again. I'm going to have to make a complaint to management about this.'

Tapping the edge of the mattress with his thumb. Waiting.

Waiting for this kiss.

Sunday morning, and the kiss is longer, as if I've never left him alone for a few hours before. I don't want to leave him at all, and it's not because of any other reason than that I want to be with him. Kissing him, and trying not to kiss him too long.

As I pull away, he says, 'I like your dress,' tracing a finger through the erratic pattern of crimson and white speckles on the sleeve and down the bodice. Every cell inside me swells with desire, wonderful, yearning desire; a promise that all this waiting will be worth it.

'Enjoy the sunshine out there, won't you.' He gives me an envious frown, and even that's all right. No, it's not fair that I can go out and he can't, but that's what this is, for now. It's not medically sensible that he's prevented from getting some more of this sunshine into his bones, but that's nothing except my opinion, and this is not forever, only until Christmas, or soon enough after. It's amazing how all right things can seem after a decent sleep-in – someone should make a study of it.

'Don't you look sweet in your civvies.' Jim's Aunt Betty arrives with the compliment and a bag full of butter and fruit. She's ex-forces, too, went overseas with the Australian Army Nursing Service in the first war; she has the same broad smile as Jim's, a smile that makes all of this unquestionably real, and above board: I'm his physio, not his doctor or his nurse; she'd know the difference in intimacies and responsibilities, and if it doesn't bother her enough to mention any of it or raise an eyebrow, how can it bother me?

'Thank you.' I smile down at my one good summer frock as if I'm sixteen, as if I ever smiled like this back then. 'I was just on my way out,' I say. 'See you later.' I wave to Jim, and his eyes assure me, *You'll be fine*, because I've told him, a couple of times, I'm a bit nervous about today, seeing Jo.

He calls after me as I go: 'Yeah, don't spare a thought for me, here all on my own, with Aunt Betty.' Because Betty, apparently, has never let a silly thing like a personal relationship interfere with her nursing.

I laugh down the stairs. How could I not love him? He seems to see me, and want me, as I am, and that makes me certain somehow. If I'd met him on some night out with Elve, at a cafe or a bar or something, I'm not sure I'd have looked twice at those 'come here' blue eyes; I'd have found a reason to reject him, to avoid the risk. I'd have said he was too manly – I can hear myself saying exactly that.

'How beautiful you are today, my dear.' Dr Adinov is waiting for me on Hospital Road with his car, his big black Dodge, parked in the no-parking area, and I even feel a bit beautiful, too. Maybe that's the strangest thing of all.

Still, my nerves jump and spin as we collect the two boxes full of albums from where I've left them in the foyer of Nightingale, so that I can hardly hear our small talk about the weather and this morning's surf. Once we're away, though, Dr Adinov shouts, 'Lunatic!' at another motorist innocently nudging out of a driveway, and I know where I am: in good company. Along the streets that wind east towards Darling Point, familiarity settles in, and I want to see Jo.

I see the house first, two stories of ivory stucco sprawling down the steep bluff towards a private wharf, and I can hear Hugo declaring, as he often did, what a bargain it was when he'd purchased it: *A wild and tiny colonial bungalow with a leaking roof and rising damp. But it was so romantic, wasn't it, Jo?* It would be worth a fortune now. I suppose it will go up for sale soon, too – don't think about that.

Jo is giving us a wave from the side patio. Even from a distance, and even at sixty years of age, *she* is beautiful, astonishingly beautiful, all grace, walking towards me as I get out of the car.

'Lucy, darling.' She kisses my cheek and presses my hand, and I don't know what I was nervous about, except that I've always felt a little out of place in her presence. That's me and Jo. Everything about her is so perfect: her dress is dark navy, not a confrontation of black; her only pieces of jewellery are her wedding band and the marcasite J brooch Hugo bought her for her fiftieth birthday; even the way her hair is silvering in fine, subtle streaks seems a statement of style and good taste. 'How are you?'

'Oh, muddling along,' I reply, and force myself to ask: 'How are you?'

She shrugs and pulls a face as though she's fed up with herself; takes me by the arm. 'Come and sit around the back, on the terrace. Hannah has made her poppyseed cake, which you must eat at least half of.' A gentle squeeze above my elbow, a suggestion that I've got too thin lately, and it's true. She looks over her shoulder at Dr Adinov, bringing both boxes down from the car: 'Anton, what have you got there?'

My cheeks flush as I tell her: 'The children's drawings and cards from the office, I put them in some albums, some old theatre bills as well. I thought you might like to keep them.'

'Oh.' She squeezes my arm once more as we walk. 'Thank you. Thank you so much. You're such a thoughtful, considerate girl – but you always have been.' She turns back to Dr Adinov again: 'Could you put them in the lounge, please? Just in the door will do, thanks.'

My hand clasps the back of hers, our arms a tight mesh holding all things in: she can't bear to see them, and that's all right. It wasn't the point that she look at them, but that she have them, and they are here now. Boxes full of Hugo;

I suppose she will take them to New York, and not look at them there, too.

We untangle arms at the glass table on the terrace and as soon as I've sat down, Hugo's dog, a lanky Irish setter called Rudy von Red Hound the Second, slowly ambles over for a pat. I rub one of his silky ears, before he slouches at my feet, heavy across my toes: he's devastated. Don't think about Hugo sitting here, reading the paper, pretending he couldn't hear Rudy whining and bouncing about, desperate for a run: *What are you trying to say, old friend?* I look away at the view of the harbour: the city tumbles like rubble through trees towards the blue, north and south, either side of the bridge; and yet here, it's constant, permanent tranquillity. This place, this house, was my home for four and a half years, from August 1935, when I arrived even thinner than I am at the moment, until I left to take up scholarship digs at the university in February 1940; but it's never truly been my home. Every room is a photographic spread for *Home Beautiful*, but it's more than a home for me, maybe: a monument to gratitude.

'Have you made your travel plans?' Dr Adinov asks Jo as he joins us.

'Yes,' she says. 'January the tenth. I want to try to get to Claire before the baby comes, of course. The estate won't be sorted out until March or perhaps April – but I'm not waiting for that. Anton, would you mind keeping an eye on the solicitors, make sure everything is done properly?'

'Anything you need, anything at all,' he assures, just as he will take Rudy with him as well, when she leaves.

We have tea; we chat about everything and nothing; we laugh for a stupidly long time when Rudy inevitably farts like a freight train under the table. I have a second helping of poppyseed cake, mostly to occupy my fidgety hands, and also because it's delicious, but on realising this might be the last time I get to taste it, I wander up the back steps into the kitchen and tell Hannah, the housekeeper: 'This is the best cake I've ever eaten, you know.' She is all old-world roundness inside the up-to-date atomic lines in here, patting my cheeks with her plump hands: 'Darlink, you must eat more.' There's nothing subtle about Hannah; she cuts a fat chunk from the roll and wraps it in a paper napkin: 'Here, take some with you.' I smile, 'Thanks,' thinking this'll be a treat to share with Jim this afternoon, but when I return to the terrace, Jo frowns at the parcel of cake I'm holding: 'Yes. It's time for me to give you something, too.'

I sit back down; I don't want Jo to give me anything. But she's already got up to go and get it from inside, whatever it is. I pat the dog, determined not to cry; and she comes back with a small envelope.

'Lucy.' She places it on the table in front of me. 'I don't want you to open it here, and I don't want to discuss it ever. Hugo and I decided this a long time ago, but it's not in the will – because of Claire, you know how sensitive she can be.' Yes, about me; Claire, eight years my senior, has never approved of her father's generosity where I'm concerned, and that's always been all right with me – I'm just the stray. And Jo is saying: 'I want you to take it to the bank and have it cashed straightaway into your account before the solicitors settle everything. Marjorie and all the staff at Aurora will be receiving a little something, too, but this, for you, is a different matter – and it's in no way a reflection of how much you were valued by him, how much you meant to him. He wanted you to have something to be going on with – that's what this is for.'

I fold the envelope into the pocket of my dress, hoping I remember to take it out before I toss it in the laundry, and hoping I forget about it. This business end of goodbye hurts too much. 'Thank you.'

And at that slight but unstoppable quaver in my voice, Jo has had enough: 'I think I'm going to have to excuse myself, I'm sorry. I've got another headache just begun to pound.'

No, you don't, but I quite agree. I want to take my cake and my cheque and run away, too. I hug her quickly: 'See you soon.'

'When you have time, Lucy darling.' A glancing kiss; too, too tender. 'I know how busy you are.'

Back in the car, I'm still trying to keep the spill at bay, as Dr Adinov starts the engine, saying: 'Don't keep me in suspense – what's in the envelope?'

'Dr Adinov.' I don't know if I laugh or groan; dizzy. 'I'm not opening it now.' It's probably a hundred pounds; bizarrely, I think it'll be enough so that I won't have to scrimp on a nice twenty-guinea wedding gown and some decent new smalls; more realistically, perhaps it'll get me started with furniture for a flat, bond and phone and gas and whatnot.

He says: 'You should stop calling me Dr Adinov all the time. You make me feel older than I am. Call me Anton – we're friends, aren't we?'

'Yes, we are. Anton.' That does feel good; somehow right.

He glances at me as he drives: 'A friend would tell friend what is in that envelope.'

'Oh – you …' I take it out of my pocket and I see what game he's playing: making me laugh properly. I ease the envelope open and look at the note, a simple slip of white card paper-clipped in front of whatever the cheque is, Hugo's distinctively scratched-out scrawl upon it; handwriting that

Jo complained about in her letters to him: *I can hardly read your writing at times. What do you call this style of script? Babylonian Chicken's Feet?* Too true. I can read this lot clearly enough, though:

> *Make an investment in yourself, Lucy. You are worth ten men in brains and courage. You were the strongest, most determined little girl I ever knew. You are an extraordinary young woman. My admiration and love go with you always,*

> *Hugo*

That is everything to me. I don't want anything else.

'Stop your whimpering and tell me how much it is,' says my friend, Anton.

I flip up the note and see – *what?*

'What?' He glances over again at my gasp.

'It's too much,' I tell the figure on the cheque. Read it again ten times: 'It's a thousand pounds.' That sort of investment is the purchase of a small house, my own little cottage somewhere. It's my future secured. No wonder Jo doesn't want Claire to know: this is far too much.

'It's a good amount, Lucy,' says Anton Adinov. 'Hugo wanted you to go back to university, complete your medical qualifications – here is the opportunity.'

'This is a lot more than university fees.'

'Yes, it is,' he agrees, and then suggests: 'Perhaps he was thinking you might want to have your own clinic one day.'

It sounds as though they might have discussed it. News to me, though. I don't know what sort of a clinic I might ever have. I'm never going to be an orthopaedic surgeon – I don't have the biceps, and maybe I don't have quite the level of insanity required, either, to drill and bolt and hammer bones. What else could I do? Appoint myself the first ever non-surgical orthopaedic physician? Or first princess of unicorns? But then, I suppose perhaps I could have my own physio practice – that's an idea – a practice where I could spend as much time with a patient post-surgery or post-injury as *they* require. Like that guy Janina's parents are employing to help her at home – I'm so pleased that's going ahead for her, she's been such a champ the past few days, she'll probably go home next week. That private physio will be charging the Shaws something like twenty guineas per month, and he's only got the same qualifications I have: Bachelor of Science, Diploma in Physiotherapy. I wouldn't need to go back to university to set up that sort of a shop. I could do it right now.

'Be a physiotherapist and be a physician,' Dr Adinov, Anton, says, as if he's read my mind. 'Full medical qualifications will give you some clout. Think about it. Yes, the Macquarie Street men's club can still call you a quack and dismiss your opinion, they can say whatever they like, but you'll be a doctor. You'll be able to do more for your patients.'

I fold up the cheque and put it back in my pocket. 'Yes, I'll think about it.' I nod, even as the chip on my shoulder whispers: *People like you don't become doctors. You're just a woman. Just a little half-starved stray.* Shut up. But I'm already putting it off, telling Anton: 'I'll think about it when we're all a little less heartbroken.'

'Heartbroken,' he growls over the steering wheel at the Sunday-empty centre of the city. 'Don't wait for your heart to heal, or you'll never get anything done.'

No. My heartbreaks crowd in with the evidence: my mother is a door slammed shut; my father is slumped at the table in our boarding house room, cold and grey; a patient has gone unexpectedly in his bed, several not come back from theatre; a guy called Rob Norton with blue eyes and lines as good as anyone's has hanged himself in the shower block at the Repat; one of my nurses is telling me in the mess, *Oh gosh, sorry, didn't you know about Ken and Sandra? They got married in Darwin*. And, here, Hugo. Heartbreak doesn't stop for you to catch your breath. It's an H-bomb dropped in the middle of Hyde Park that no-one but you can see.

'My wife died in 1903,' Anton drops his own right now. 'Forty-five years and I still can't believe it. We were so happy, all before the world went to the sh— doghouse of war and revolution. Some mornings when I wake up and see that I am not in St Petersburg, it can still take me by the throat. I still want it all back – my house, my streets, my cafes, my clinic. My wife, Irena. It was puerperal fever and the baby died with her, my son. I didn't think I would ever recover. And guess what.' He throws me a wise, ironic smile: 'I have never recovered. As they say, life goes on. Loss walks hand in hand with love. And Hugo expects you to go back to university.'

'I know.' But I'm scared I'm not good enough, that I won't make the grade in real life. I'm glad we're turning into Hospital Road now and this conversation is nearly over.

But Anton Adinov isn't finished: 'Hugo had his own challenges, believe me. He didn't like to talk about it, but since he's no longer here to object, I'll tell you. Professionally, he had the hardest time of anyone I've ever known. He was called every name under the sun, shut out from the BMA, shunned – colleagues would cross the street to avoid acknowledging his existence. During the first war, he was even interned. Did you know that?'

'No.' I shake my head with the lie; I'm not about to confess I've read those letters of Jo's; but I have to know: 'Why? Why was he interned?'

'They said he was a German spy.' Anton grunts with disgust. 'But the truth is, they wanted to get rid of him. They wanted him out because he was the best, and they couldn't stand the thought of the best not being one of them.'

'Who is they?'

'Slade.' Anton says that name with such revulsion, the sound of it is chilling enough. 'Not on his own, of course,' he adds with no less contempt, 'but Slade drove the campaign, as president of the BMA. I arrived in the middle of it, as they were attempting to have him deported, after the war.'

Oh my God. I'd always supposed Hugo wasn't fond of the BMA because he hated going to meetings, hated any bureaucracy. But *they* put him in the concentration camp? Dr Slade did? 'I don't understand.' I have to ask again: 'But why?' Why would any doctor do that to another doctor?

'I told you, because Hugo was the best.' Anton sighs, pulling up at the kerb outside the ambulance station. 'Because he was Jewish, German and the best. The BMA didn't need further reason. Slade, on the other hand – if you ever discover the reason why that man is such a piece of — such a destructive maniac, then you might win a Nobel Prize for forensic psychiatry.'

'Wow.' That's not surgical rivalry – that's scandalous.

'Yes, wow. But the point is, Lucy, they didn't win against him. No-one wins against one like Hugo, no matter how they might try. No-one beats a real doctor. So, when you think you're too small and it's all too hard, think about that.' He turns off the engine and I stare ahead at the Sunday-busy hospital throng, visitors everywhere.

It's impossible to know people, isn't it? Impossible.

'Lucy?'

'What? Pardon?'

He chuckles: 'I said, you're not getting away without telling me about this patient of yours, the young man, and the associated loss of clinical perspective.'

'Oh?' Instant rush of joy at the thought of him; I look down at the napkin-wrapped cake in my lap, and I'm mad with it. Mad for him.

'Oh dear,' Anton laughs. 'Does he have a name?'

'Jim. James. Jim Cleary.' It scatters out of me. 'Lorry mechanic, engineer, actually, among other things.'

'Not that far removed from an orthopaedist then.' Anton has to make that joke, but he's not making fun of me. 'What's the damage?'

I tell him: 'Spiral fracture, left tib, nasty displacement, and complicated by a previous injury. It's not unlike mine was, needs straightening out, but at present it's languishing in traction, wired, and not surprisingly a little delayed in healing. It's only been just over two weeks, though, and Dr Oxley will review it in another four, for further surgery, maybe, using the Küntscher nail I mentioned.' But I'm now recalling anew that litany of Dr Slade's incompetence Anton barked down the phone on Friday morning, and I have to ask him: 'Is Dr Oxley good enough for the job?'

'Yes.' Anton nods, carefully. 'I believe David Oxley is excellent.' He gives it some more thought and then says: 'If you are worried about anything, medically, call me straightaway. If you're not happy with the treatment, I will take him.'

'Take him as a patient?' I'm not sure I heard that correctly. Dr Adinov, Anton, doesn't have a hospital of his own anymore to take a patient to – he sold up St Christopher's back in March on his 'retirement', and it's now a day nursery with a seesaw and sandpit in the yard. 'It'd be a bit difficult to arrange the transfer, wouldn't it?'

'Difficult is a word only cowards know.' Anton brushes off the idea with a wink. 'But seriously, if you need me to, I'll sort something out.'

I hug him: 'Thank you.' Everything is strange. But everything is all right, too.

Christmas Eve, ten past eight, and we're playing backgammon, again. I'm winning 172 games to 169 over the long count; Jim keeps impeccable score in his head, as well as move-by-move memory of each game played, to go with complete and completely useless history of blood-pressure readings. We're listening to ABC Radio 2, a comedy script about a family whose festive table is heading for a bunfight – not terribly funny, but it's not Bing Crosby or Carols by Candlelight. I yawn, he yawns; he yawns, I yawn. He grits his teeth with another cramp: 'Jesus.'

After six weeks of not being able to move as it should, muscles wasting, atrophying with lack of use, his hip is in rebellion. I remember what that's like: when you're lying down, it feels as though the head of your femur might detach from your pelvis at any moment; when you sit up, it feels as though it'll drive a hole through the socket; and the cramps, whenever they come, are inescapable.

I wheel the tray away from the bed; he says: 'Don't knock those pieces out of place – I've made plans to beat you.'

'Don't worry, I won't knock them.' As if you won't remember exactly where each piece was. I move the tray over by the chest of drawers behind me, turn off the irritating, pointless radio, and then reach under the small of his back to try to relieve this odd tension that comes from slackness. After a while, I feel the spinal tendons relax against my wrist: 'Is that better?'

'Yeah, it is, thanks.' He hauls up a smile, but it's not better. It's incredibly boring. He looks at me with the silent plea: *When is this going to end?* Hopefully next week. Monday would be good: x-ray day. Wish I could say that to him.

He looks over at all the Christmas cards sitting on top of the chest of drawers, and then he frowns, a pained sort of frown that makes me think the cramp is back; I'm about to suggest I go and get a heat lamp for it, but he shakes his head: 'I just remembered that I meant to send Mrs Nichol something for the kids, for the holidays – she'll be missing the money she usually gets from doing my washing. Can't believe I forgot.'

'I'm sure she understands.' You're lovely.

'I know she would.' His disproportionate remorse plays all my strings at once. 'She's on her own,' he shakes his head again, 'with a million things to do, and she manages to send me a card. But I've got all this time and I didn't think of her.'

'Time runs differently in here,' I remind him. It does: brain bugs.

'Can you take her something from me during the week?' he asks. 'Please?'

'Of course, I will.' I'd do anything, anything at all; I tell him. 'While I'm there, we'll gossip about your greasy overalls and your smelly socks and what a selfish man you are.'

He smiles, properly, deeply, so lovely: 'My socks never smell.'

'I'm sure they don't.' Wouldn't care if they did.

What's going on inside his head? I wonder, as he keeps on smiling and smiling at me. 'Hm?' I perch beside him on the edge of the bed and he tucks a strand of my hair behind my ear.

'I didn't want to ask you this here,' he says, and already I'm a bundle of sparkling foreverness. 'I wanted to wait until I could go shopping, you know, jewellery-shop shopping, but since it's Christmas, maybe you can give me a break and say yes anyway.' Here it is: 'Will you marry me, Lucy? Lucinda Jane? Not in the immediate future, obviously.'

I tell him with everything: 'You know I will.'

'That's a relief.' He bites his lip as if there might have been a chance I'd say no; laughing, folding me into his chest: 'Right, so let's pretend we make passionate love at this point.'

'That's what we're doing, isn't it?'

I'm listening to his heartbeat charging, and as far as I'm concerned, we've made love a hundred times. But yeah, it's going to be more than wonderful when we really, really do. One day.

'How romantic!' His middle sister Lizzie shouts – the loudest. This tiny room is filled with his family, just the immediate family, all shouting congratulations and Merry Christmas, not because they're shouters but because there are so many of them: Mum, Dad, brother John, sisters Fran, Lizzie and Maryanne, brother's wife Kate, sisters' husbands Pete One, Pete Two and Bill, various children, ten of them – no, eleven. Small niece, Wendy, aged almost eight, throws her skinny arms around my hips as though I've never belonged anywhere else: 'Can I be a bridesmaid?'

'Of course, you can.' You have no front teeth: you are adorable: you can be anything you like.

The dog under the bed, smuggled in inside a laundry trolley, whacks his tail enthusiastically into the back of my knees. I couldn't abide him staying outside all alone, tied up on the tray of a ute, could I. And he doesn't bark once.

Until Rory arrives with champagne, almost breaking the window with the cork, and toasting me: 'Good thing she said yes.'

I look at Jim: 'You planned this?'

'I might have.'

'You sly thing.' I see what he's done: he didn't want this Christmas to be boring for his family.

Rory kisses us both and has to run: it's an eight-hour drive to Gunnedah: 'You've made me late for lunch.'

'Can't do anything without putting on a show, can you, Jimmy.' I hear his brother behind me, a patronising and resentful undertone. He'll turn around and go back to Canowindra this afternoon, on his own, leaving the wife and kids, because someone's got to look after the farm, and be sour about it. 'Girl doesn't know what she's agreed to.'

Jim says nothing to that; he's holding out his hands for Maryanne's new baby.

'I'd say there's no better way to get to know someone than in here.' His father, also called John, is beside me and between his sons. My father-in-love-to-be is permanently, quietly worried: about his lambs, his wheat, his whole life limping from one war to the next. His old-soldier eyes tell me he knows what it means to be cared for, and to be vulnerable. 'Welcome to chaos, Lucy.'

'Oh, I am so pleased, so glad.' His mother grips my hand as though I might stop her boy from ever being hurt again.

That's not going to happen; but I will love him as if it could be true. As if I could do anything more than try to keep his nephew-monkeys from climbing up the traction frame.

'Is there a dog in here …?' It's a matron I don't know, taking the special casers Christmas Day shift, and I don't know if she's naughty or nice.

'Dog?'

Lizzie starts barking and the children all start barking, too, and matron smiles; she's nice: 'Please do try to make an effort to keep the noise to an ordinary festive level.'

'Oh, all right. We'll try.'

Nah. We don't. Today is too wonderful. I'm too full of fizz.

Not a great deal to celebrate on Monday, however: long-awaited x-ray is almost identical to the last. Still no apparent reason for it: no infection, no deterioration, no problem with blood supply. No nothing. The dark translucence of the twisted rift remains just as it was. 'Why?'

Dr Oxley shrugs. Ultimately, bones don't need a reason to fail to unite. My own will tell you that; my right tib has written a PhD on the subject entitled, *Prolonged Traction is Rubbish*. Compared to the alternatives anyway, and here is only more evidence.

But this is not all bad news: Dr Oxley will absolutely have to do something about it now.

I ask him: 'Will you graft into the fracture as well, to get it moving?'

'Yes.' But he looks concerned, still examining the x-ray himself.

'There's no other problem, is there?' I ask him.

'No.' But there is – I can see it somehow written on his face.

'Do you want me to get Mr Cleary's medical records from Canowindra Hospital, check if there's anything in the notes about delayed union, with that schoolboy break?' It's the only thing I can think of that might provide a useful clue.

'No.' Dr Oxley knows very well what he's looking at, and he's not saying anything about it to me.

'What should I tell Mr Cleary?' I'd quite like to share the compensatory joy that at least there'll be no more traction soon.

'Tell him nothing, for the moment.' Dr Oxley switches from concern back to his charming self, snapping at me: 'It's Christmas–New Year week. I can hardly book a theatre for it this afternoon.'

Obviously not; skeleton staff all round. Dr Oxley's left hand is reaching for the telephone, his right pointing my way out.

'Well, cheerio then,' I say. And I pretend to leave him to it, thumping my way down the floorboards. But as soon as I hear him close his door, I skitter back to listen in to whatever call it is he's making.

His words are calm and cold: 'I ordered the hardware months ago, in May – you know that. Yes, from Germany, from the manufacturer in Kiel. What does it matter where they're made? We must have these nails as a matter of course. I can't conscionably allow this situation with Mr Cleary to continue, no, and I'm not asking you to come back from your holiday to do it. I intend to do it myself – next Tuesday – yes, Tuesday the fourth.'

Bloody good idea. I presume he's conferring with the Greater Slade Maniac himself. Couldn't be Professor Charlesworth – he's gone to Hawaii on a cruise, and doesn't have anything to do with admin things like hardware supplies.

'Sack me?' Dr Oxley laughs, caustically. 'What for? Not being an irresponsible —' A pause. 'Yes, I am considering the reputation of this hospital, couldn't be more firmly at the front of my mind. I'm very aware of my own reputation, too, and I can't —'

He slams down the phone with a highly audible: 'Fuck off.'

Hm. Surgeons: nuts. Orthopaedists: probably more nuts than the average. Hugo would often say that both the o's in orthopaedics stand for obsession; he'd say, too, that doctors have to do terrible things sometimes in order to do good. He'd delight in detailing the example of Fritz Steinmann, the guy who invented the traction pin: he used to hang cadavers from the trees in his back yard and fire his rifle at them in order to observe the effects of gunshot trauma on the bones; but equally, Steinmann was so devoted to his live patients, he wouldn't leave his hospital grounds for months on end, until a crisis of healing was over.

Whatever's going on here is not so noble. It sounds like a game of schoolboy trumps, of who's got the biggest scalpel.

I will give Dr Oxley until Tuesday – eight more days – and then I'll be calling Anton to get Jim out of here. Hang my own reputation on the way out.

HUGO WINTER

*T**he appeal against internment is rejected. Deportation proceedings will commence forthwith.*

Jo sent Hugo the letter from the Federal Solicitor-General's Department. *I am at the end of my sanity,* she wrote. *What do they want, really?*

His wife didn't have to tell him of her suspicions there: the authorities wanted to make her so confused and exhausted with despair and frustration that she would give up. Authority must be relentlessly unhelpful to those it does not wish to help.

> *They have never been able to produce the slightest piece of evidence against you – because you have never done anything to harm another in the entire world. The war has been over nine months and still they won't let you come home? Is this what Edwin gave his life for?*
>
> *Darling, Hugo. I'm so sorry to burden you further with these thoughts of mine, but you must know that*

*my anger has found new clarity today – you must know
I will keep fighting for your release. You will not be
deported. You will be coming home.*

Hugo wasn't too certain of that. As he sat there in the doorway of his hut, he looked out at the prison as if it were a symbol of the slowly dying world. He was back in Liverpool Concentration Camp, the place deserted except for one hundred and thirty-two remainders, those who continued to appeal their cases against deportation. There were some diplomats who had no desire to return to a defeated Germany; there were some Lutheran pastors who had made Australia the home of their mission; there were many others who, like Hugo, had married Australians and could not justify dragging their non-German families back across the globe to a home that was not home anymore. Here, was hell's limbo. And it hadn't changed much, except that the rows and rows of canvas tents had been replaced with lines and lines of huts – not so much an improvement as a more efficient means of torture, for they baked their inmates in summer and froze them in winter.

It was the end of winter now, August 1919. Hugo tried to imagine what might be happening in Germany, and every imagining gave him cause to shiver. He'd never gone around shouting it, but he was proud in many ways of his own Germanness, his character that could have come from no other place on earth; he was proud most of all to have enjoyed the benefits of a German education, the intellectual rigour, the enthusiasm; but pride here was the double-edged sword: Germany wasn't going to cope well with losing. The Treaty of Versailles and all its conditions, designed to impoverish and punish in every way, could only lead to further disaster.

In his mind, he saw millions of soldiers and sailors belting each other on the streets of Berlin, desperate for someone to blame. He wasn't far wrong, of course; it wouldn't take long for that anger to find its target elsewhere and more specifically in communists and socialists, in Romany gypsies and, most devastatingly, in Jews. All betrayers of the Reich. Hugo could not have known what the future would bring, but he knew enough of the past to guess: the double-edged extremes of German determination were generosity of spirit and base ruthlessness. He wasn't taking Jo and Claire into that, not for five minutes, possibly not ever.

He wasn't going back to Hagen, that was the only absolute certainty. He'd received a letter from his brother Ernst in June telling him that the rest of the family was dead: their father had died peacefully in his bed in 1915, two days after his seventieth birthday, their mother, Hugo's stepmother, the year after that, of an ulcerated stomach; Kurt had been killed at the Third Battle of Flanders and Wil at sea when his ship went down. It was a polite letter, mostly requesting that Hugo refrain from making any claim on the family business: *As you are a doctor and have never shown an interest in the lace factory, please consider that it is all I have and my sole livelihood.* It might as well have been a stranger asking him if he could get past in the street. Ernst was a stranger; and Hugo hadn't found the words to write back to him yet. What could he say? *Don't worry, I'd rather die too, than be a lace-maker in Hagen.*

But how was he going to prevent his deportation from happening in the first place? If the camp guards marched him onto a ship, that would be it. He tried to imagine accepting this fate. He would leave Jo and Claire here, and, after a time, try to return to Australia. When? How? Where would he go in the meantime? America? Argentina? These thoughts threatened to unravel him – to the point where he thought the kinder and more honourable thing to do might be to divorce Jo, to let her, and his daughter, have a happier life without him. And every time he thought this thought he was violently sick.

What Hugo also didn't know, though, was that this dainty, doughty wife of his was preparing to speak to someone quite a bit higher up the chain of command: John Monash – now General Sir John Monash. He was due to arrive in Melbourne a day or two after Hanukkah, at the end of December, and so Jo decided she'd happen to be there herself, visiting friends, hoping for a word with the great man. What she didn't know was just how great a man John Monash had become: proclaimed 'Australia's Greatest General', knighted on the battlefield by King George V, crowds flocked to St Kilda pier to catch a glimpse of him. The establishment might not have liked Jewish upstarts, but ordinary Australians showed they could not have cared less about his religion or how German he was: to them, Monash had won the war, and he'd put Australia on the map. He was only too pleased to meet Jo Winter as well, at a private reception a few days later, although he was not so pleased at what she had to say.

'*Deport* him?' The General was indignant that the letter in support of Hugo Winter he'd written more than four years ago had meant nothing to the government, but at the same time he was not enormously surprised. He narrowed his eyes, the lines of his weather-bronzed face creased in deliberation: 'Leave it with me, Mrs Winter. I'll see what I can do.'

Jo stayed quiet about her back-room plea, not wanting to get Hugo's hopes up, as she waited to see what might come of it.

As Hugo waited, and waited, too, ever more despondently.

Until, some four months later, on April 10, 1920, two guards stormed into his hut at dawn: 'Number 3576A! Wake up! Get up!'

'What's happening?' He stood to attention straightaway, alert; he hadn't been asleep.

'You're leaving,' said one of the guards, going through the drawer of his small desk.

'Where am I going?' he asked, expecting this would be it, a train to Sydney, a ship to Hamburg. He would take it with dignity.

But, to his surprise, the guard replied: 'Campbelltown police station.'

'Why?' Campbelltown was a dairying district ten or so miles further south.

'You're being released.'

His knees almost gave way.

The guards continued to search his hut, taking anything and everything that looked as though it might have been correspondence or writing of any kind. Hugo had to try very hard not to laugh – with joy and with derision. What did they think they were doing confiscating his letters and notebooks? How petty and senseless for them to suppose they might rob him of the facts of his experience this way. What were they trying to do – steal history? He didn't care what they did. He was going home! He wouldn't discover for a further five years that they didn't quite rob the lot – a bundle of letters from Jo, from that first year at Liverpool Concentration Camp, remained in the bottom of his medical bag, in the leather correspondence envelope there. He'd never meant to conceal them but to keep them safe on the journey to Trial Bay. Authority is an ass, was what he thought that day, and every day for the rest of his life afterwards.

'Hugo!' Jo was waiting for him behind the picket fence of Campbelltown police station and he didn't take the sight of her with any dignity at all. He wept against her cheek, her neck, gulping in the scent of her perfume. He held her so tightly there under the tin-roofed verandah he might have crushed her ribs.

And she didn't mind; she whispered in his ear: 'We won.'

'You won,' he cried.

It had been a battle that even Australia's greatest general had had difficulty fighting. The initial telephone messages Sir John Monash left with the Solicitor-General's office had gone unreturned, then the telegram he sent received no reply, forcing him to resort to turning up unannounced, with the threat of making a public fuss unless something was done. And even then, there'd been a delay, while every official involved panicked over how they were going to handle the innocent doctor's release. How were they going to justify his internment – and such a lengthy internment – to begin with? Of course, in the end, they decided they wouldn't justify it at all. Winter would be released because authority had changed its mind. Authority also had the advantage of that mad chap, Eliot Slade, who was prepared to speak to the press.

'BMA MAINTAIN WINTER MUST BE DEPORTED,' the headlines in the Sydney papers said, curiously timed to coincide with his release. What was the medical authority attempting to do by this? Destroy his reputation again before he'd had a chance to rebuild it? Let them try, Hugo felt the challenge as a bolt of lightning in his chest. Let them try to humiliate him – he did not know the meaning of the word anymore. The BMA could collectively throw itself into the sea for all he cared.

He had more important things to do. He had a little girl to meet: his darling daughter Claire.

But time, especially for children, holds a cruelty in its double edge: while its boundless valleys can erase pain, it can also misplace all other memory. Claire was seven years old; her father was a man she didn't know. His broad, strong hands and shoulders were shapes she didn't know. His smell, his laughter, his smile, everything about him was foreign, except for the olive skin they shared. When her mother exclaimed, 'Your lovely papa is home!' Claire looked at him and said, 'Hello,' wondering whether they would be having jelly and ice-cream after lunch.

'Give her some time to adjust,' Jo consoled him, but Hugo and Claire would never be close. The authorities, who had failed in so many ways, managed to rob him successfully in this one.

And it hurt. It didn't matter that Claire herself had a natural reserve, an aloofness to her character that would see her keep all others at a little distance throughout her entire life; it didn't matter that she'd possibly inherited that from her father as well. Hugo took it as rejection. It hurt more than any slight he'd ever known. It sharpened all his old memories of his little sister, Irma, too, of how close they'd been, dancing and laughing up the hall in Hagen. It returned to him all the searing guilt he carried at having been too busy for her, too wrapped up in his adventures in Berlin, and his oh-so-important work; the ton-weight of grief he still carted around in his heart for Irma every day, whether he remembered her or not.

So, he did what he knew how to do best in the face of any pain: he got himself busy all over again.

With the help of his father-in-law, Aaron Levine, he began searching immediately for a suitable property he might use as a private hospital. If the establishment wouldn't bring him back into the fold, he'd go his own way – and he'd do it in a big way. Within only a few days, he and Aaron found a stately old mansion at Rushcutters Bay, a small palace built around 1860 and long abandoned, the broken dream of some fellow whose history truly had seemed to have disappeared, except for a whisper he'd struck it lucky on the goldfields. The building was comprised of two stories and a cavernous basement; two long reception halls downstairs would be ideal for dividing into rooms for patients prepared to pay, while another huge hall that ran almost the length of the building upstairs, would become his children's ward. Dilapidated it might have been, but it was bright and airy, all its large front windows looking out across a cricketing green to that most soothing of views: Sydney Harbour. Aurora, he'd call it, for it faced the dawn. The promise of new light every day. Incredibly, it was only a stone's throw away from his home as well. It could not have been more perfect. It was as though the place had been made for his purpose, and had been waiting for him to arrive. Perhaps most importantly, it also came with just over half an acre of land, which Aaron Levine could sell off to recoup his losses if Hugo's dream broke, too.

This land, this 'rambling garden', as the estate agent had called it, was so overgrown with roses and blackberries it was a jungle of thorns, and Hugo made it his first job: he hacked at it and hacked at it like a wounded prince. Then he lead-lined a section of the basement for his x-ray room; he fitted out his operating theatre and plaster room with the most attractive tiles and taps so that no-one small or grown would ever be frightened there; he even put in a hydraulic lift, and a sixteen-yard-long swimming pool. Madness! He didn't even have one patient yet. But he wasn't worried. He would make this place, Aurora House, the most successful orthopaedic clinic in Australia.

And that's exactly what he did – at speed.

ELIOT SLADE

'Perhaps you should drop it now.' Eliot Slade received some quiet, unsolicited advice from a colleague one evening after a BMA meeting, a fellow returned from the trenches of Flanders. 'You're beginning to seem a little unhinged about it. Who is this Winter that we should be so bothered about him?'

Slade scoffed at the man: 'I suppose you're all right with a German going after your job now, are you?'

The fellow scoffed back: 'There's enough ortho reconstruction work in this country to keep me in tweed and tears for a lifetime, old cock – and I'm a bit bored with waging war.'

Slade would ensure this surgeon never got work at Sydney Hospital ever again.

He took his campaign against Hugo Winter all the way to the floor of the federal parliament, in Melbourne, as it was in those days. He found the ear of a Nationalist MP from a conservative, no-foreigners-here Sydney seat, an ex-serviceman called Marr whose war against the Hun would never end, and whose own belief in racial discrimination would have him passionately declaring that the truth of crimes committed against Aboriginal people in the creation of Australia must be suppressed because such unfortunate facts might damage the legal veracity of the White Australia Policy. This was the man Slade now urged to go after Winter in the House of Representatives, to throw the question directly at their Nationalist Prime Minister: 'Why has the government not deported the German, Hugo Winter, a native of Munich, and a known enemy of our country?'

But, notwithstanding that Winter was no more an enemy than he ever was a native of Munich, the answer, and its consequence, didn't unfold quite as planned. Slade had thought that this question would force the Prime Minister to state on the record that the case of Winter would be further investigated – a promise he could then be held to in all future lobbying. Slade thought if anyone would be on his side it would be Prime Minister Hughes: Billy Hughes was the nation's top jingo and Kraut despiser, having been among the most vociferous at the Paris Peace Conference for the punishment of Germany, demanding that the Treaty of Versailles should send that country right off the map for the next several millennia. Slade thought if anyone was going to punish Winter, Billy Hughes would do the job with alacrity. That didn't happen, though.

For Hughes – a populist, political whore before he was ever anything else – had already been approached from the other side. The Solicitor-General had brought the case of Winter before him several months earlier, and while Hughes was quite deaf, often missing half of whatever was said to him, he could lip-read the name General Monash at fifty paces and had caught the gist that his favourite soldier was considering making a noise should the good doctor continue to be wrongfully persecuted. 'Why do we have him locked up at all?' Hughes had asked and the S-G had distilled it to its basic fact: 'The BMA don't like him.' Hughes knew union bullying when he saw it; he told the S-G: 'Get the man out of there.' And thus it was done. But now the question was being raised in the House, Hughes sought to be informed more fully.

'Why does Monash support the fellow?' Hughes had asked the S-G that very morning before the House of Reps Question Time.

'It's not Monash alone who supports him,' the S-G had replied. 'Winter is an altruist, most famous for treating crippled children from poor families. He cures their ailments and does it for free. His wife – who is the businessman Aaron Levine's daughter – is prepared to take depositions from each of the families involved. So, we'll have Monash and a small army of kiddies marching on us. Wicket could get sticky.'

Now, there were two things here that had made up Hughes' mind instantly. First, he had a little daughter at home himself, Helen, his only child, and he worshipped the ground she skipped upon, every golden curl on her sweet head. Second, Hughes was a socialist at heart: a Labor man before he split the Labor Party over conscription and went on to reinvent himself as a Nationalist – a twist that perpetually confused everyone around him – it remained that any man who worked for the good of the many was all right by this PM.

So, when the unwitting Marr asked his question, his back straightened with bigotry and certainty, Hughes stood and said: 'Dr Winter has not been deported and will not be deported because he possesses skills of surgery and muscular manipulation that have made and will make an important contribution to the nation. There is no evidence against him to convince me that he is an enemy of Australia. His lengthy internment was over-cautious on the part of this government, if necessary at the time, and it is high time now that this government allowed him to get back to his work – especially the life-transforming work he does with our precious children.'

Marr was just about blown out of his seat and on his feet once more, quite out of order: 'But Prime Minister, the deputation from the British Medical Association most vehemently disagrees. All of them most eminent medical men, they say there are British doctors who will do this work for the children of Australia.'

To which Hughes replied under his breath: 'Bullshit.' He said then to the House: 'I thank the honourable member for his question and refer to the answer already given.'

Slade was sent to a place beyond all fury when he heard the news. How could the Prime Minister have betrayed him this way? The answer Slade gave himself was that Hughes, a Welshman by genetic inheritance, must be of sub-normal intellect.

'Daddy! Daddy!' his son, Alasdair, interrupted his thoughts, calling up the hall as he was dressing for dinner that evening. 'Look at the aeroplane I made.'

The boy had only turned four a few months ago, but he'd made a toy aeroplane from a clothes peg, using a piece of cardboard for wings, with no help from Nanny or Mummy, and his excitement had got the better of him. He knew he shouldn't run into Daddy's private dressing room, but he did anyway. He was a very bright little boy, gold glinting in hazel eyes that greedily drank in the world around him, inventive and serious-minded, but prone to bursts of enthusiasm.

Slade looked down at the boy, annoyed at having to suspend the churn of his anger even for a second, and said: 'Get out.'

'But Daddy, see?'

'Get out.' Slade clipped him across the head with the back of his fingers, little more than a tap, really, as the boy had already begun to turn and run away again.

Oh, but it stung. How it stung. Alasdair raced down the hall to his mother, who was cuddling his baby sister Catherine over a storybook in the nursery. Mummy was soft, a shimmering fairy in her beaded evening gown, she always smelled of flowers and sadness, and he buried his face under the back of her arm because it was warm there.

'Alasdair, what are you doing?' She laughed a little, his head tickling against her ribs.

'Daddy doesn't like my aeroplane,' he said. 'I got a smack.'

'Daddy doesn't know the first thing about aeroplanes.' Audrey sighed over the muttering in her soul: *You rank bastard.* 'Why don't you sit down and paint the wings? When you're finished, I'd like to show your grandmothers this aeroplane, at dinner, show them how clever you are. Do you think that's a good idea, too?'

The last straw is often the smallest, isn't it? Audrey Slade née McRae-Browne was born and raised to be the property of a man and to be good at it – this was her sole purpose, apart from producing heirs. To this extent, the abuses she had received at her husband's hand, though unpleasant and often terrifying, were par for the course. She had learned to take it, as centuries of women before her had taken it: the rape, the brutality and belittling; the affair he was having with an x-ray assistant called Shelagh Kildare. The latter was an absurdity to Audrey: she knew he was trying to insult her and make her jealous – he'd made it so obvious, even leaving around receipts from jewellery purchases – but she felt nothing less than empathy for the poor girl. And she was only a girl – only nineteen. He got away with it, as he got away with everything, because of his wealth and privilege, and because he instilled fear in all around him. Everyone was frightened of him: his staff at the hospital, his staff at his Macquarie Street rooms, the staff here at home, the BMA, the hospital board – everyone. But she would not be frightened now.

For another few moments, she watched her beautiful little boy painting astoundingly accurate bullseyes on cardboard wings; then she handed baby Catherine, plump little lump of nearly one, to Nanny: 'I'll be back for that aeroplane.'

She found her husband pouring himself a cognac in the library; she said: 'Don't you ever do that to Alasdair again.'

'Do what?' Eliot Slade was quite honestly nonplussed.

'Don't you ever hit him again like that.' She moved further into the library towards him. 'He's your son. He was showing you something he made.'

'It's not for you to instruct me on how I must behave.' He shook his head and laughed.

'If you do it again, I will divorce you.' She would not be deterred, not now.

He laughed louder: 'No, you won't.' And, still seething from the news about Winter's reprieve, he closed his fist and punched her, backhanded, across the face: 'Shut up.'

Audrey fell heavily against the edge of the bookcase nearest, her bare shoulder taking the brunt, her cheek hot with the blow. She stood up to her husband: 'No. I'm not going to shut up. Not anymore.'

That night's dinner was a small family affair: both of their mothers would be there, but not their fathers – Audrey's was away on business and Sir Alfred was far too ill with dementia these days. Stepping in as elder gentleman, though, was the Slade family solicitor and old friend, Horace Daleforth.

'Audrey,' said her mother, sitting down at the table, 'you've got a red mark on your face.' She said it with some distaste, as though her daughter had been shabby at presenting herself.

'Do I?' Audrey pretended to ignore the comment, placing the little aeroplane in her mother's hand: 'Look what Alasdair made. I know I'm biased, but that boy takes my breath away – he's so dextrous, so quick.'

'Well. Yes.' Her mother looked down at it, not all that interested; not all that maternal herself. She handed Alasdair's aeroplane across the table to Lady Slade, Fiona, Eliot's mother, who doted on the little ones, and now declared: 'Oh my word, I see what you mean, Audrey. Did he really paint it himself? Oh, he'll make a fine, fine surgeon with that hand, won't he?'

Not if Audrey could help it; she pictured him asleep in his little bed upstairs, sweet-dreaming, and she wished for her son to have some gentle profession, something to match his nature. She looked up from the aeroplane and into her mother-in-law's happy eyes: such a nice woman. Sir Alfred was a nice man, too, or had been – by reputation, a good man. Good people. How had they made Eliot? What perversity, what lottery was that?

Her husband smashed his way into the conversation this very moment: 'You really should do something about your face. Go and put some powder on it.'

She looked at him: *No*. She knew the bruise was deepening in colour: she could feel it swelling; her shoulder still ached as well.

'What happened?' her mother-in-law asked, noticing the mark, too, just as Audrey turned her face.

Eliot spoke over her: 'She tripped in the nursery, fell against the chest of drawers.'

'No, I didn't.' Audrey looked at the lawyer, Horace Daleforth, and held his gaze: 'Eliot hit my face with his fist and I fell against one of the bookcases in the library.'

'Eliot!' his mother shrieked at him. 'What have you done?'

'Audrey.' The threat in his voice shot splinters of ice through her marrow. 'That is not what happened.'

'Yes, it is.' She would not take her eyes from Horace Daleforth: 'If he does it again, I will ask for a divorce. Will you help me, please?'

'Now, now, Audrey.' The old lawyer frowned in that circumspect yes-and-no way lawyers have, before saying: 'I think we can settle this here.' He turned that frown on Eliot Slade: 'If you beat your wife again, I will not only help her divorce you, I will make sure you suffer every personal humiliation for it. The law may allow you to wheedle out of a charge, but I will ensure you pay the penalty.'

'Oh, Eliot,' Audrey's own mother said, 'but you didn't mean it, not really, did you?'

'Of course not.' He feigned shame. 'An error of judgement, the pressures of responsibility, at the hospital, at the BMA. It won't happen again.'

And it wouldn't. Eliot Slade never laid another hand on wife or child: Audrey had him cornered there.

But the cruelty didn't stop, of course not. He simply found other means, other targets, elsewhere.

SIX

LUCY BRYNNE

The little girl starts to cry, quietly, holding her elbow protectively. Her name is Jilly, Jilly Wilson, her new rollerskates from Santa have resulted in a radial greenstick fracture so typical it might have come with the manufacturer's guarantee, and she's been an absolute trooper, until now. I immediately think there must be an issue with the cast I've applied; it's been almost a year since I've plastered anything, and never anything so delicate as this nine-year-old's arm, but Christmas–New Year staff shortages and associated onslaught of holiday disasters have meant I spent most of yesterday's Sunday and all of last night here in Casualty helping out as needed.

'What's wrong, sweetheart?' I ask her, my stomach knotting with empathy and concern. 'Tell me where it hurts.' She only hangs her head, tears beginning to overwhelm, sitting there on a too-big chair, her feet not quite touching the ground. I check her fingers again – no, the wrapping doesn't seem too tight – and I glance over at Alasdair Slade, who's talking to Jilly's mother. Try not to look too worried as I catch his eye: *We have a problem here.*

Alasdair takes a step back this way and crouches down to her. 'Now, this is no good, Jilly,' he says, sweetheart to sweetheart. 'You'll have to tell us what's upset you, so that we can make it better.'

She's trying so hard to be brave; trying so hard to keep her chin from crumpling again as she tells him: 'It's raining.'

Alasdair looks over his shoulder at me; I shrug – no idea.

'Yes, it's raining.' He nods at the window behind her. It is pelting with rain out there this morning. He treats the girl's mystifying anxiety with the utmost seriousness: 'Why is that upsetting you?'

'You told Mummy I mustn't get my arm wet.' She sniffs. 'What will happen if I can't keep the rain from getting on it?' Her eyes are enormous with fear.

'Oh?' Alasdair takes a moment to understand, and so do I, before he treats that fear with the utmost kindness, too: 'Nothing awful will happen, Jilly, not at all. If your cast gets wet, it might get loose and not be able to do its job well enough. All that would mean is you'll have to come back in and have a new one put on. But that would also mean waiting around for hours and hours again, and that would be very dull for you. I'm sure you have lots of other things you'd rather be doing than hanging about here, isn't that right?'

She smiles. He's a paediatric natural. When Jilly and her mother are gone back out into the world, and we're heading for the lift, I tell him so: 'You're very good with children.'

He smiles with the compliment; he really will make some lucky woman very happy one day. Even his uncertainty is appealing: 'You think so?'

'If Jilly is evidence, then yes.' I'm still shaking off the stress of her tears. 'I can't cope with the suffering of innocents – makes me want to cry, too.' Branches slipping through my fingers, the grass racing towards me; pain is the strangest place on earth. 'Or reach for the gin. I might like one right now.'

He laughs at that – bit early for a drink at a quarter to nine, Monday morning – and his eyes are twinkling, yacht-club wrinkles squinting at me as we step into the lift: 'I hear congratulations are in order. Is it true, you're engaged to Mr Cleary?'

I blush a thousand shades of love and embarrassment. 'It's not official yet, I …' I was hoping I could continue to get away without telling Dr Oxley for a few weeks yet, look after Jim myself post-surgery. I know he can't be my patient anymore, though; it doesn't look good, someone's bound to make a complaint. Favourite patient is one thing; fiancé is another. Some other arrangement will need to be made, and I'd rather not think about that.

'He's, um …' Alasdair seems to blush, too. 'Well, congratulations anyway.' And then he adds: 'I suppose the last x-ray was all right then, was it?'

The first alarm bell goes off in my head. 'No. Not all right. Still no union.' How could Alasdair not know that? I know he's been on his break with the sun on his face and the wind in his hair, but how could he not know that his father is in the thick of a stoush with Dr Oxley over it, especially when Alasdair himself assisted in the original surgery and there's a corrective round scheduled for tomorrow? But I don't ask – he's obviously been cut out of the communique for some reason; maybe it's just the time of year. There's only one doctor I need to speak to about it – Dr Oxley – who'll probably be annoyed we've missed the morning meeting. I need to speak to him anyway: Jim has to be told what's happening, give his consent, be prepared for this next round.

But when we get back to the ward, I find Matron Moorefield in Dr Oxley's office, and she seems to be tidying up his desk; alarm bell number two: no-one touches anything on Dr Oxley's desk. I ask her: 'Where is Dr Oxley?'

She looks at me as though I am a bucket of sick: 'Dr Oxley is not in. Dr McVeigh is in possession of today's schedule, should you find yourself unable to remember where you need to be.' Dr McVeigh is a resident, hardly begun his specialty – what the hell is going on?

'Where is Dr Oxley?' I repeat the question.

She smirks at me. She actually smirks: 'Dr Oxley has been suspended.'

'Suspended?' Alasdair says behind me: 'What for?'

Matron Moorefield blinks at him in surprise at his ignorance, too: 'I'm afraid I can't say, Dr Slade.'

'Can't say, or don't know?' Alasdair looks to be hearing his own alarm go off.

'I don't know,' says Matron.

'Right,' says Alasdair. 'Excuse me, please.' He strides off, back down the corridor towards the stairs, I imagine on his way to his father's office, which, like all the chiefs' offices, overlooks Macquarie Street from the Central Admin building, across the courtyard and another world away.

I stride off, too, but for a moment I don't know what I should do. Call Anton now? No. Surely, I need to get some sort of answer first on what is going on, before I throw the hospital into complete uproar by kidnapping a patient. I can hardly think: I haven't had any sleep – of course. Thanks, Santa.

I decide I'll go and see Jim first, before I do anything else. The sight of his face will settle my thoughts; besides, I need something to eat and he has a big bowl of fresh peaches up there, thanks, Aunt Betty. I'm not going to show him any panic, because I'm not panicking. There's no reason to panic. This will all be sorted out by this afternoon, I'm sure. Jim will be treated to a series of interesting surprises; he might even find it entertaining.

But when I get there, a doctor is with him; at a glance, from behind, it looks like Alasdair. Of course, it's the father. It's Slade the Maniac.

Every nerve I own shouts: *Get away from Jim – get away.* And at first, I can't hear what is being said to him.

Jim looks at me, and I can't read his expression at all, as Dr Slade turns and says: 'Not now, nurse.'

'Nurse?' The word slips out as the alarm rings ever louder: was that an automatic insult or does Dr Slade not know I'm a member of his staff? I'm obviously not a ward nurse, even at a glance, and while he'd probably have seen me less than a handful of times to grunt at, it's not as though there is more than one specialist orthopaedic physio in the entire hospital. I inform him of the more important fact: 'I'm Mr Cleary's fiancé. Anything you have to say to him, you can say to me. So, it's good timing I'm here, isn't it.' I'm not leaving this room.

'Oh?' Dr Slade stares at me, right into my eyes; stares down at me from his great height, as if he couldn't care less. 'I am explaining Mr Cleary's options in regard to his leg.'

'And what are Mr Cleary's options?' I ask.

'Well, Mr Cleary's leg is very badly damaged. Perhaps you might sit down.' He speaks in a way that intends to make me small; but I will not be made small; I will not sit down, either. Makes no difference to him. 'The bone is not healing,' he says. 'There are three options for further treatment. The first is to wait another six weeks to see if there is any improvement, and

I very much expect there won't be. The second is to attempt a complex installation of a long metal nail, which will be very expensive and, because the bone is of such poor quality, will likely only put off the inevitable. That brings us to option three, which is to take the leg off below the knee.'

'What did you say?' My eyes are saying: *You want to amputate a leg because of a delay in healing that you caused? You're not nuts – you should be in prison.*

He smiles; it's an oddly warm, even friendly smile: 'I understand, it's a big decision to make. But in my opinion, and with more than forty years of experience in these things, it is inevitable that the leg will have to go at some point. The sooner it goes, the sooner Mr Cleary can get on with his life. You don't have to make the decision today – I am prepared to wait the further six weeks, if you need that time to come to terms with it.'

You're prepared, are you? Goodo. I look at Jim: he's staring up at the ceiling fan.

'Thank you, Dr Slade,' I say.

But he's already walking away: 'I'll leave this with you.'

I close the door behind him and then I sit down on the bed beside Jim: 'It's not happening. That doctor doesn't know what he's talking about. Your leg will heal, eventually. It's being slow, that's all. There's no indication of any other problem. You're young and otherwise fit. It would be an absolute freak of nature if that bone doesn't heal. Please, believe me.'

He looks at me now and I can see clearly enough how tired and sore and past it he is: 'I'd like to believe you, Lucy, but you might be a bit prejudiced, mightn't you?'

'Yes, I am prejudiced – to the extent that if anyone tries to cut off your leg, I will cut off one of theirs first, with a blunt axe. I am prejudiced, madly, but this is my business and I know it well enough to know Dr Slade is wrong.' Even if that doctor has just sent in a few special brain bugs designed to make me doubt it: the bone is of 'poor quality', is it? Won't take hardware? How does he know? I tell Jim and myself: 'There's another doctor, an old friend of Hugo's, who is going to fix your leg. He's going to put that nail in it and straighten it, make it better in every way. It'll all be good, you'll see. By this afternoon, you'll be out of traction, out of here, and in a few days, you won't know yourself. This is what Dr Oxley planned to do all along, and I should have told you that, but there's been some sort of stupid power game going on behind the scenes. It's disgraceful. You shouldn't have had to listen to this rubbish about amputation. It's not happening. It doesn't need to happen.'

'Maybe it's time that it did happen.' He stares at the fan again; it spins around and around as the rain continues to beat down outside.

'What are you talking about?' I don't understand, except that, after seven weeks bedridden and with no other conceivable end in sight, I think he might have cracked.

After an age, he says: 'I should have lost my leg in Germany. I shouldn't be here at all.'

'No, don't say that,' I almost shout at him, but he has every right to say what he feels. I ask him: 'Why do you think you shouldn't be here?'

After another age, he says: 'You'd have to know what happened, over there, to know why.'

'I'm listening.' And making the first of my vows: to listen harder.

'I shouldn't have gone.' He's still talking to the ceiling fan. 'I'm the wrong personality. I've never hated anyone in my life. It sounds unbelievable, I know, but I didn't make the connection between dropping bombs and people dying until I was part of it.'

I don't say I understand, because I don't; but I do know there's a reason why the services prefer to recruit young men who haven't made those kinds of connections yet. I tell him only: 'I believe you.'

He shakes his head. 'You'd think I might have got a bit of anger going, you know, with the Blitz and then losing so many airmen, time after time, until I hardly knew anyone outside my own squadron anymore. But I could never be anything more than confused. Most of the time, I made the job all I thought about, and I was pretty good at that, getting the plane in the air and keeping it there. The noise up there is enough to make any other thought irrelevant. And the cold, in winter – I'd spend the whole eight-hours or so of every operation praying that none of the instruments would freeze, praying the heating wouldn't fail and the windows wouldn't ice up, trying to ignore the sound of bullets relentlessly hitting the plane, killing our bombardier when I looked over my shoulder, slicing a hole in the sleeve of my jacket, the plane ahead of ours exploding like a weird star, dropping out altogether. I'd keep watching the instruments, listening to the engines, listening for instructions from our navigator, from our pilot, always double-checking our pilot. And praying. Praying for me meant going over and over every calculation, every number in my head and on the panel in front of me; every check I did before taking off, our speed throughout, altitude, revs, fuel, oxygen, until that plane landed safely again. If I kept thinking about the numbers, everything would be all right, and death, if it came, would be quick – I wouldn't know about it.'

He turns his face away, looking out the window at the rain: 'Between operations I didn't do anything else except drink, a lot. Drink and dance. I went to bed with a lot of women, too, Englishwomen whose names I don't remember. It wasn't fun. I wasn't there – in my mind. I wanted to go home, all the time. I wanted the war to end. Everyone did. But for me, every single second of it was a grinding nightmare.'

He looks at me, finally, and he doesn't seem mad at all; just broken; and far too remorseful. I touch the back of his hand to tell him I don't care what he did to get through it.

But he cares; and he's got more to say: 'If I thought about the targets we were going to hit, I told myself, these are dots on a map, fuel depots or factories or whatever. If I thought about the people down there, I told myself, they'll all be sheltering from us. But that all changed, near the end, when we bombed Dresden. It was a night raid, and we were in the second wave, so I could see everything we were doing. The city beneath us was one big fire. That's what it looked like from eight thousand feet. That's all I could see: fire and blackness. I was freezing, so cold I couldn't keep my hands from shaking, but down there, they'd have been fried in their basements. Ordinary people, in their houses. I kept thinking about the dogs more than anything, though. How could a dog run from that? How many dogs were killed? When we got back to the airfield that dawn, I should have told our squadron leader I'd lost my guts, couldn't do it anymore, couldn't stop shaking, cop the shame, but a couple of other crews were breaking up with the same problem.

'So, ten days later, I was on another night raid, on a place called Pforzheim. It wasn't as big as Dresden in terms of the number of bombs dropped but the fire was the same. I kept trying to focus in on the numbers on the panel in front of me and the numbers in my mind, but I couldn't stop thinking about the pounding we were giving these people – thinking that it was too much, that it wasn't right. There was hardly any retaliation that night, that's how pounded they were. But then the job was done, we were heading back, and, like I usually did, I got up out of the cockpit to use the can at the back of the plane – just quickly, you know, before we got too high in altitude.'

No idea whatsoever, except that the sadness in his eyes says more than any of his words.

'The last thing anyone said to me was my pilot, giving a thumbs up, "All good. Okay." I was standing there at the can looking at the back of our rear-gunner in the dim light from my torch. I was thinking he must have been frozen onto the gun – it's the coldest, most exposed part of the plane, at the tail, on any night. I didn't realise we were losing altitude at first, didn't realise the engines had stopped, all four of them. I thought I was dizzy from standing up, from not wanting to be there, that maybe my ears had blocked, that maybe we'd lost oxygen too fast and I might have been about to pass out. Then there was yelling and screaming and our wireless operator grabbing for the door, trying to bail out, but there wasn't time – a Lancaster bomber is a heavy machine. About ten seconds, we had. I was too busy trying to hang onto the line of cabling pipe that was above me as we spun portside. I don't know why the plane came down. I'll never know why. But it'll always be my fault in here.' He knocks the heel of his hand against his forehead. 'It'll always be something I must have missed, something that happened when I got up for that piss. And my whole crew were killed because of it, all six of them.'

Not going to say don't blame yourself, darling. I take his hand in both of mine, and I can feel he's not here, but there, with this awful weight of guilt; looking at me but somewhere else.

He says: 'The tail split off from the main fuselage when we hit the ground, and I got thrown out. I couldn't see anything at first – it was the middle of the night. It was sleeting, I could feel the ice hitting my face. Then the fuel tanks went up somewhere behind me and I saw the paddock I was in had just been ploughed. I could see the rows, smell the fresh earth. Then, I don't know. It was a couple of weeks before anything began to make sense, before I understood where I was – in that house, in the countryside west of Wiesbaden, that was all bombed to blazes as well. I was in that much pain, Lucy, I thought my next breath was going to take me out. But this German doctor, this nice old bloke, is patting me on the shoulder, telling me I'm going to be all right, apologising that he didn't have more morphine. I couldn't have been his only patient, but he kept me safe there, out of harm's way, until the Americans rolled in. He looked after me, he made sure I lived, despite everything I'd done. So, you see, if I lose my leg now, it doesn't really matter. Maybe it's supposed to happen. Maybe it's the price I have to pay for being lucky. Maybe it's a good thing.'

Maybe you need to see a psychiatrist. I have to make this plain: 'Losing a leg is never a good thing.' It's hard work, it hurts; it's disabling, no matter how strong you are; I've seen that struggle enough times to have an opinion. 'No-one deserves it. And it's not happening to you.'

But he's not finished yet: 'I want to get out of here, get back to work. I have to do it the quickest way.'

Oh, I know you want that, but you're not going to get it by cutting off your leg. I tell him again: 'Everything will change today. Please trust that it's true. My friend Anton – Dr Anton Adinov – is going to fix your leg. He's one of the best there is.'

'How long is that going to take?' Jim asks me, because he can't take it anymore.

Tell him the truth: 'Couple of months.' Don't say maybe three or four, or that no-one can possibly know. 'I promise you, it will be worth it. You won't be trapped and strung up like this.'

'I can't spend that much more time off work.'

'Yes, you can.' Never mind that an amputation would take twice as long to deal with – never mind the string of all-too-common and hideous complications that might come with it.

'I can't afford it.'

'Yes, you can.' I can't believe he just said that. His little lorry-tinkering business with Rory made a net profit of more than £2000 last year – even split between them that's a junior doctor's salary each. I remind him: '*We* have plenty of money.' He knows we have Hugo's gift to me, too, which I haven't even begun to think about spending; he also knows his parents would give him anything. We are, on paper, extremely well set up. 'I'll sling you twenty quid.'

'You're not spending any of your money on me,' he says, because this is a conversation with someone who is so sore everywhere, he's lost his grip on reality.

I tell him: 'I'll spend my money on whatever I like. And an amputation is not on my list.'

He says: 'Would it change things between us?'

Tell him the truth: 'Physically? Not one bit. Mentally, I would have to have you committed to an institution for your own protection.'

But still he hasn't finished. 'I hate my leg,' he says, as if it's the only enemy he's ever known, and the heart of his confession: 'The pain has never really gone away, nearly four years of it – I've had enough. I roll my ankle all the time, it's like I've forgotten where my foot is in space and I put it down the wrong way. And if that's not giving me crap, my hip aches so much sometimes it keeps me awake all night, so I don't want to get out of bed in the morning. The whole thing drives me around the bend. I don't want it anymore.'

Don't ask him why he hasn't told me all this before. 'I'm sure it does drive you around the bend. I know it does. But your ankle rolls because your foot is not sitting at the end of your leg at the correct angle. You're an engineer, you know the principles – you wouldn't put a wheel on crooked, would you. It also probably means you've got some nerve damage, making it seem as though your foot is not where you think it is. And your hip aches because you've got one leg shorter than the other. These are the things Dr Adinov can make better – a lot better. Not reasons to amputate a leg that otherwise fairly successfully holds you up.' Pain, on the other hand, is its own load of crazy: 'How have you been dealing with it all this time, pain-wise?'

'I try not to think about it,' he says. 'Get up, keep moving, go for a surf, go for a ride, go for a run with Mate on the beach, jam with the band, drink, dance, work, fill up time. Tighten my bootlaces. Wear myself out. But here, all I can do is think about it.'

'I know …' Worst brain bugs ever. But this answer might also suggest the stresses that helped cause this present fracture to occur: he's flogged that leg so hard, I would bet it was broken somewhere before he fell off that lorry, for the more thorough job of it. What do you do for a sore leg? Go for a run. Wear it out. There's some old-fashioned masculine logic. Perhaps his leg has been too frightened to get better; perhaps that's not a facetious idea.

I ask him: 'Do you want something to settle your nerves? A tranquiliser – there's no harm at all in having one, to take the sting out of this.'

'Drugs to change my point of view?' He looks away again. 'No, thanks.'

I promise him again: 'I'm getting you out of here today, by this afternoon. You're going to have some more surgery, and then I'm going to look after you myself – at your house.' Because I'm not going to have any other job by the end of this day, either. Here's a way to catapult myself into real life. 'All right?'

He tells the rain: 'All right.' Not at all convinced.

'I'd better get going then, get it happening.' I kiss his turned-away cheek, and don't want to leave him in this state, but I've got to get him out of here, get him away from Dr Slade, so that creep can't get in his ear again.

I run out into the corridor, shivering hot and cold at the terrible power of doctors. A power to transform; a power to destroy. But why would Dr Slade want to amputate this leg? Try to be objective: why would anyone want to harm another in this way? It seems too far-fetched. But it seems that this is what he's set on doing. So unnecessarily, but so deliberately. What would have happened to Jim if I wasn't here? How many Jims have there been? But then again, maybe I am too prejudiced, to close to see – what?

Alasdair catches me, before I reach the stairs: 'Miss Brynne.'

He doesn't have to say a thing; I can see he knows his father's intentions, too: he looks both horrified and humiliated.

But still doubt drags and I have to ask him: 'Is there some other damage to the bone? Some deficiency? Is there something I don't know?'

Alasdair shakes his head: 'No. Mr Cleary's leg is only suffering from poor treatment.'

There, it's said. I tell him: 'Dr Anton Adinov will take him as a patient. I want the transfer to happen today.' A transfer to who knows where, but somewhere.

'Good.' Alasdair nods: 'I'll help you with the paperwork.'

'Thank you.' That's an unexpected generosity; an action, a risk, he should not have been forced to take.

He adds: 'I'll get Mr Cleary out of the rigging for you myself, have him ready to go in an hour or so.'

Because Alasdair Slade is going to hang his career on this, too.

I look around the confines of my room at Nightingale as I pack up my sparse belongings, waiting another five minutes for Anton to return from his swim and pick up the damn phone. After today, it dawns, I won't live in a hospital anymore.

I have a suitcase containing one good woollen suit, one good summer frock with matching bolero, one party frock, two winter skirts, two summer, half a dozen blouses, two sundresses, two pairs of bathers, and a ratty looking lot of smalls. One pair of sandals, one pair of patent leather court shoes, and two pairs of white leather tennis shoes – for work. Half a dozen books – all medical. I'm twenty-seven years old and, fraught as it is, it seems today – January 3, 1949 – my own war is finally over.

Cheerio, Elve – I begin to scribble out a note to my room-mate, who's still on her break with her family in Queensland, but I don't have time to think of anything else to say apart from, *It's all true – I've run off with him. See you soon.* And I will, sometime, for a very long-overdue gin or half a dozen. *Lucy x*

I carry my suitcase down to the foyer at the bottom of the stairs, race back up for the box of Hugo's personal correspondence I seem to have acquired on permanent loan, and then back up once more to try the phone again.

Ring, ring.

Come on. I've made a heavy load of promises this morning, all dependent upon you.

Ring, ring.

Please.

'Adinov.' He answers at last.

'Feel like stealing a patient this afternoon?' I ask him.

And he laughs: 'There I was wondering what I might do with myself today. I had a feeling you might call.'

Small but important matter for the paperwork: 'Where are we going to take him?' Anton is still a consulting surgeon for a couple of hospitals, St Luke's Private and Marrickville, occasionally called in to put car accidents back together, but we can't just turn up on a doorstep with a patient kidnapped from Sydney – from Dr Eliot Slade – can we?

Anton is unfazed, all business: 'We'll take him to Aurora, of course – not as though they have much of a patient list there at the moment, is it. It might take me a day to get organised, however.'

'No.' I panic. 'We need to go today – now. Not tomorrow.'

'Yes, yes,' he says, calm down, as though he does this sort of thing all the time. 'I will call Marjorie now, and she will make preparations – *now*. I meant I need a day to organise a surgical team – you know, that thing called an anaesthetist, and an assistant. Actually, I want to ask a young fellow to assist, nephew of an old friend of Hugo's – Zlotkowsky. Do you know him?'

'No.' Maybe the name; I don't know. I'm sure he'll be excellent.

'And will you be joining us at the table?' That's a serious question.

'Me? No, thank you.' Not that I haven't observed a few surgeries, mostly via Hugo – *Come and see the inside of a boxer's shoulder tonight, Lucy, if you're not doing anything else* – but I won't be observing this one: 'I don't love him that much.' I love him too much. 'See you out the front of Casualty at two pm?' It's a tick after eleven now. Only eleven? It seems as though days have passed; as though locked-up years have cracked open, altering the run of time.

'I'll be there, my dear. Don't worry, I'll be there, let's say, from one o'clock. I'll bring a book and wait for you.'

HUGO WINTER

The two surgeons met for the first time in the flesh at the end of March 1921. Anton Adinov had returned to Sydney from Berlin only a month earlier and, having heard that the new private hospital, Aurora House, had opened at Rushcutters Bay, he'd struck up a correspondence with the now increasingly famous Hugo Winter. After the Russian's last note, telling him of Slade's negligence and his own general loathing for the BMA, Hugo had to invite the fellow over to Darling Point to discuss it all further – and, more importantly, for a drink to cement the friendship.

'Berlin is no longer the city we knew,' Anton Adinov told Hugo. They had not shared the same barstools at university there, Anton being three years older, but they had walked in each other's footsteps. 'The begging in the streets, the untreated but treatable disability. So many young men ruined in all senses. It was difficult to see. Cheerless. Bitter. Anarchy. I had left Sydney thinking I couldn't live here, and now I don't think I can ever return to Europe.'

Hugo downed his second schnapps and shook his head, sorry for Berlin and still sore at those who had fought so hard to send him back there – to ruin him.

'But,' Anton shrugged, 'it remains that Berliners could never be quite so dull in thought, in art, as lacking in appreciation of any brilliance or ingenuity, as the professionals are here, hm?'

'I shut the dullness out.' Hugo shrugged back. 'That's all you can do. Keep the troglodytes from the door. You are always welcome to dine here with us, you know, have a drink with me and Jo, whenever you feel like it. We make an art of having a good time, all the time. Our world is small but always full of interesting castaways.'

That was a slight understatement. Hugo and Jo had taken to throwing fabulous parties on the harbour-view terrace of their home, in part to raise funds for the children's ward at Aurora House, but also to make clear to Sydney that the Winters weren't going anywhere and certainly not quietly.

'Thank you.' Anton very much appreciated the invitation. 'I may become a pest.' He was thoughtful for a moment before he said: 'I have an interesting patient, a fellow I've been treating for the past few years, a walking orthopaedic problem – wounded at the Somme, variously patched together. He's a preposterously talented artist – a painter, sculptor – German by heritage, but reticent as only an Australian can be. I've been trying to convince him he must go abroad, to the Academy in Dresden, actually.' The Russian rolled his eyes at the reticence – who wouldn't jump at the chance of studying at one of the world's most prestigious art schools? 'His problem. Anyway, his name is Ackerman, infuriating character, as only a friend of mine could ever be, keeps almost everyone from his door, but I think he and his wife might be interested in supporting your cause, at Aurora House. I might mention it to them, hm?'

'That would be wonderful, thank you,' said Hugo, genuinely touched anytime that anyone took an interest in his ambitions for Aurora. 'Can't have too many supporters.'

'You can't have him as a patient, though – he's mine,' Anton warned and the two surgeons smiled together for the beginning of what would become twenty-seven years of friendly rivalry, of sharing information and skills, now and again covering for each other if one was ill with cold or flu. They celebrated each other's victories, they commiserated as one over any failure; they drank a lot of schnapps and listened to a lot of Beethoven. Occasionally becoming extremely drunk, they laughed like little boys; sometimes they shed a few tears, too; and on one particularly messy evening they nearly ended Anton's career when he slipped and fell with glass in hand severing the main abductor muscle of his right and most necessary thumb – but Hugo fixed it.

Even their clinics were complementary, rather than directly competitive. Anton's hospital, St Christopher's, named so for those forced to travel, was a weatherboard ex-temperance hostel situated on a windswept ridgetop above Bondi Beach, and his work there focussed primarily on the reconstruction of traumatic injuries, patients mostly referred to him from St Luke's, an Anglican establishment which, coincidentally, lay barely two hundred yards up the hill from Aurora. Hugo's primary focus, in his rather grander hospital, would forever remain the children, whom he was insistent upon treating in comfort and style, many of them referred to him by the sisters of St Vincent's – the Catholics over in neighbouring Darlinghurst. In order to fund their respective charity cases, they both adhered to the Robin Hood method they'd individually always practised, sending big payers each other's way if either was overloaded, and building up a healthy clientele from the fertile orthopaedic ground surrounding them: the Sydney Stadium boxing arena, the Eastern Suburbs rugby league team, several private boys schools, two ballet schools, as well as the small but loyal Jewish and Russian communities, and the endless recommendations that flowed from all of the above.

But it was only Hugo who opened rooms once more on Macquarie Street, to remain under and indeed up the noses of those who had tried to destroy him. In fact, he waited for the right rooms to become available, which they did in 1925 – almost exactly across the road from Sydney Hospital, where the far edge of the North Wing shared a shady lane with the New South Wales Parliament House. He barely used these rooms, except for those big payers who expected to visit their doctor on Macquarie Street, as a matter not so much of maintaining confidence in his credentials, but of being able to say that he was 'my Macquarie Street surgeon' to their friends. It was far more important that Hugo himself knew, every day, that Eliot Slade and all the rest of the Sydney-based BMA would have to walk past his name on the plaque screwed on the brick wall outside the door.

Jo would laugh at him: 'That's a very expensive revenge, darling.'

'Worth it.' He would grin, and with reason as yet un-foreseen: it would soon become a handy tax deduction against the profits Aurora House would bring.

Profits which were helped along by a cheque he'd receive each December and each June from the man called Ackerman. Apart from being a reclusive artist and infuriating friend of Anton's, Daniel Ackerman was a wealthy industrialist from Lithgow, the coal town over the Blue Mountains; he was in his thirties, a mine owner who'd been a miner himself before the war, and took his socialism very seriously. The cheque would come with no note other than one line: *For the treatment and care of the children of Aurora House.* It was generous and a little larger every time it appeared, and Hugo ploughed every penny of it into his children's ward – never any expense spared on their care, their entertainment, anything and everything that would make time more bearable while they were confined there.

This continued until 1928, when he was approached by the newly formed Lithgow Cripples Fund with a request that he agree to an arrangement of care for the children of that district, so that they might come to him in Sydney as required. It was decided that all the mining lodges of the valley there would strike a one-shilling levy per month on each trade union member, so that no child in the district should ever suffer a remediable affliction of the body. Of course, Hugo wrote back telling them he'd be honoured to oblige. He would have said yes to any such organisation advocating for children, but he also had a natural sympathy for miners and their families. Having treated the children of so many workingmen in the clinic in Dresden, and having grown up as he had in the industrial Ruhr, he knew how hard those miners worked: the arduousness of their days at the coalface, the precarious rope they walked that could see them struck down by a debilitating injury themselves, one which they invariably could not afford to have properly treated, sending them and their children to the poor house.

He suspected the mysterious Daniel Ackerman was behind it somewhere, perhaps formalising the relationship via this fund; and he thought the personal cheques would stop. But they didn't.

Hugo asked Anton some years later: 'Why does he do this?'

But Anton could only shrug: 'No-one knows why Daniel does anything, not really – not even his wife. Don't bother asking.'

He never did; he would always presume this was simply one of the many ways returned soldiers give back something of life for all the death they have seen. Hugo never once met Daniel Ackerman, either, though he would meet Mrs Ackerman, his wife, Francine, that first year of the fund – 1928. A delightful woman, she would bring him his first patient from Lithgow: a little girl called Lucy Brynne.

ELIOT SLADE

By this time, for a growing majority of the medical establishment, Eliot Slade had become something of a joke, and an albatross at that, but one who could not be disparaged or cut loose in any overt way. No-one could say what they wanted to say: *Eliot Slade, shut up.* He was still Sir Alfred's son – and the fondly regarded, esteemed Sir Alfred was hanging on to life as though he intended to be a study in the will of the body to endure long past the capabilities of the mind.

Eliot Slade was also still a conniving bully. He had become accomplished at only one thing: the art of psychological manipulation. And, these days, he could use it to devastating effect. When opposition to his presidency of the Sydney chapter of the BMA arose – with the highly reasonable complaint that he had had the job now for more than a decade and perhaps it was time for someone else to have a go – he turned on the instigator of the move, threatening to report and expose his homosexuality. Another opponent was torn down by crude ridicule: the man had a stutter, and Slade mimicked it behind his back at every opportunity among his colleagues: 'Im-m-magine how he'd g-g-g-go g-g-g-etting anywhere w-w-w-with the m-m-m-minister for h-h-h-health?' He'd cultivated an almost cheerful, raffish smile to accompany his attacks, one that encouraged the nastiness in others, encouraged them to join in – and often enough there were just enough who did join in, which in turn encouraged Slade himself.

The hospital board was able to keep his surgical career idling at Senior Registrar, but he had just enough friends remaining there among the upper echelon, too – powerful ones, far too fond of Sir Alfred to believe the worst of his son. Half-demented elders in the Faculty of Medicine at Sydney University kept him with a teaching role – in, of course, limb removal and joint fusion. It could never be said that Slade was anything but workmanlike at either of these. In his wake he left scores of pain-wracked patients: stumps left with too much bone, not enough soft tissue to support weight; hips and knees in greater discomfort than they were before the surgery. They weren't his problem: he left them to his junior registrars, to the volunteer masseuses and the ever overworked prosthetists. But he had just enough success with just enough patients to balance things out; still a very handsome man then, in his prime, he could make a lady forget her sciatica at the touch of his hands in one of his warm and inviting Macquarie Street hydrotherapy baths: *Oh that Dr Slade, he worked a miracle on my back.* Oh yes, and he'd screw the good-looking ones, too.

Slade wasn't so dim that he didn't know he was being held back from further promotion. After almost nine years, he was still angry at having lost that negligence case against him, still convinced it was a conspiracy of foreigners to discredit him – *for one mistake.* For getting caught.

Barking irrational as it was, he still blamed Hugo Winter, denigrated him now as a radical who was pushing all other doctors to take risks that shouldn't be taken. But while there had been no abatement in his anger and hatred, Slade had become patient with his further ambitions: he'd ride it out, bide his time. If he stayed where he was long enough, he'd progress – to Chief House Surgeon or Chief of Orthopaedics, whichever came first, he didn't care.

In early 1928, he wrote a paper attempting to discredit the use of stainless-steel pinning wire for fixation of complexly displaced or splintered fractures. Again, as in all his papers, he had no compelling evidence to support his argument other than the lie that outdated modes of splinting, and the subsequent deformities caused by them, were preferable because, he wrote without any sense of irony or shame,

The surgery is dangerous to the patient, with risk of infection from the skeletal traction commonly involved and, therefore, exposes the hospital to complaints of malpractice.

The reality was, he hated the pinning wire because both Hugo Winter and Anton Adinov were now renowned experts at its use – masters of the precision drilling required, with scores of satisfied patients each to attest to the happy results.

The true men of science within the Sydney BMA wanted to tear out their hair in frustration that someone so patently stupid was their representative. Sure, Slade was a rabid advocate for ensuring the minister for health was too terrified to say no even to fee increases for public patients, but that hardly compensated for the taint by association – for the suspicion the reasonable had that Slade cared so little, and was so intellectually miniature, he'd bring down the whole profession without understanding what he was doing outside his own pathetic lusts and grievances.

There was a drift among some members towards the parties thrown at Winter's Darling Point home, where they could be seen to be supporting a children's charity, with their wives' diamonds spangling and their champagne glasses filled, when what they really wanted was advice on a patient, or a new technique, or word of any developments abroad – which Winter was always keen to share, as any true man of science would be: generous in the desire to see, and play a part in, the progress of ideas for the betterment of all.

Slade could never compete with that. He couldn't throw a party to save his life, for a start, and he'd never be invited to one at Winter's – not that he'd go if ever he was, he told himself. Into the ears of those who'd listen, he continued to whisper of Winter's greed: 'Look at him, putting on another show. A twenty-piece orchestra this time? Money might be better spent on the children, don't you think? He'd be no-one in Europe – that's why he dug his heels in to stay here. The grandstanding Jew.'

Audrey would hear of none of this, and not only because her husband barely spoke to her. These days, she was vice-president of the Women's Auxiliary, and in that capacity had gone to the Winters' one afternoon for tea and cake and a short seminar on the benefits of physical exercise for children, as well as to dare to satisfy her curiosity. She'd never met a lovelier couple than these two; Mrs Joanna Winter, in particular, warmly drew her in: 'Mrs Slade, so good to meet you at last.' A quick look between the two women: one apologising for her husband, the other assuring no judgement of the unlucky wife. The Winters made Audrey envious, oh yes, they did, for what they showed a marriage could be. A partnership. A dance. Indeed, an impromptu, sun-drenched tango across the terrace, laughing into each other's eyes.

'I forbid you to go there again,' said Slade, when he found out where she'd been, and she could have told him to shove his forbidding where it's darkest, but she didn't.

She couldn't, for there were now worse consequences than physical violence: his attacks upon the children – mostly on Alasdair – were an ever-present threat. He never left a mark, or none that could be seen, but he would get into Alasdair whenever he was in a mood to do so: quietly digging at him, chipping away at the boy's confidence each time the insults came. Whether it was at cricket or swimming or out on the water in the boat, his father would thump him down with a word: 'weak', 'lazy', 'thick in the head'. At twelve years of age, Alasdair topped his high school entrance exam, and his father responded with the smiling jibe: 'Must have been an easy paper.' The boy had won his place at the most academically competitive school in the city on merit rather than by money alone – as Slade well knew, having gone through there himself incapable of achieving more than an extraordinary feat of pedestrianism. Audrey couldn't afford to do anything to make life more difficult for Alasdair than it already was. She enrolled him in every extracurricular thing conceivable – piano lessons, scouts, orienteering in the Blue Mountains, chess club – she sent him to his grandmother, Lady Slade, in Rose Bay with all manner of errands, anything to keep him out of the house and away from his father as much as possible.

She told her husband: 'As you wish.' A refrain for his every command.

An empty man, a hollow man, Audrey often thought, almost sorry for him.

But he was never sorry. The day after Audrey had told him she'd gone to that Darling Point afternoon tea, Slade was walking between the hospital and his rooms on Macquarie Street, as he did almost daily, and as he did this time, he saw the sun flash on the brass plaques across the road, among them Hugo Winter's name, and it taunted him.

It sat in his gut like a splinter of bone, so that by the time he'd got to the top of the stairs and his surgery there, he was already reaching for the telephone. A fellow he'd gone to school with had recently been appointed assistant commissioner at the Federal Taxation Department: he'd have Winter investigated for tax fraud; have him audited. There would have to be dirt in those Aurora House accounts to hang him on – no Jew was ever honest with money, was he?

'Hello. Yes, Slade here. Eliot Slade. How are you?'

He was still convinced that he might yet win – something.

SEVEN

LUCY BRYNNE

But one more telephone call first, and a fistful of pennies for it. I take my little red address book out of the pocket of my skirt, find the number for the operator and wait for the trunk line to connect, long distance to Canowindra.

'Hello. Clearys.' Jim's mother, and the line's so sharp she could be next door.

'Mrs Cleary? Hello, it's Lucy.'

'Oh, Lucy.' She already sounds wary at my wariness; her crisp and polished vowels requesting I be direct: 'None of that "Mrs Cleary" with me, please. You call me Tess or Mum, whichever you'd prefer. What can I do for you?'

'Oh, nothing.' Nothing out of the ordinary: 'I'm just letting you know that Jim's moving to a different hospital this afternoon.'

'Why's that, dear?' Warier: what's happened?

Say it quickly: 'He needs to have another operation on his leg, but it has to be done elsewhere. We'll be at a private hospital. It's called Aurora House, big white building on Waratah Street, Rushcutters Bay, behind the cricket oval there – easy to find if you want to be here but don't feel you need to rush out. Everything's all right.'

'What operation?'

'The surgeon wants to make a correction, that's all. Do a better job of it.' I'm not telling you, two hundred miles away, that a mad, elderly Russian is going to drive a twelve-inch stainless steel nail down the centre of his shinbone, among other procedures. 'It'll be done tomorrow sometime, and in a week, hopefully less, he can go home. I can look after him myself then, in Maroubra, if you would approve of that.'

'Approve? You're two grown adults. Sounds like nobody's business but yours. Sounds like good news to me.' She brightens. 'I'll bet he's happy about it.'

'Hm.' I tell her to will it into being: 'It'll be a lot better than it was.'

'What do you mean, better than it was?' Mrs Cleary asks me, and I've got her instantly worried again. 'Hasn't it been all right all this time?'

'No, yes, it's all right. I only mean that it's given him a fair amount of trouble for a while, hasn't it, and it should be fixed now.' There's the plan.

'For a while? What trouble?' she asks me.

I think we're talking at cross-purposes and I'm confusing her. 'Trouble from the original injury,' I explain. 'When it was broken the first time, when the plane crashed.'

Silence; a gaping silence except for the faint crackle on the line; then: 'The plane crashed, did it?'

Oh no, I have hit some horrible nerve. 'I'm sorry. I …'

'Don't apologise, Lucy,' she says, and the lilt slips through the polish, that trace of a song that is, in fact, from Derry, in Northern Ireland. 'He's never talked to me about it – everything is always "fine, Mum". I'm left to guess, from the pieces of information we got from the RAAF, which wasn't much. He's never told me what they did to him over there, and he's never told me his leg gave him any trouble, laughs it off that he pays extra for shoes now, laughs it off if ever I ask about his health. He doesn't tell me anything anymore.'

'I'm so sorry,' I apologise again. 'Mrs Cleary – Tess ...' Can't call her Mum; can't call anyone Mum, and certainly not at this moment. 'I didn't want to upset you – that's the last thing I wanted to do.' Wish I could tell you my best guess: the reason he doesn't talk to you is because he's ashamed, and he shouldn't be.

'You haven't upset me.' She sighs, upset. 'If he's told you things about it, I'm glad he has. I'm so glad, so very glad he has you at all.' So much sadness in that. 'Will you telephone me again and let me know when it's done?' she asks. 'Let me know he's all right?'

'Of course, I will.' Don't cry: for every barb-strung wall that war has ever built. Don't have time, not today. Don't have enough pennies anyway.

The rain trumps us all for insanity, smashing upwards from the courtyard fountain, blinding me as I dash across Hospital Road, with my hand in the air to request that no cars run me over, please. My shoes are so sodden I make puddles up the stairs of the Pavilion as I run, running up these five floors to Jim as if running will prevent the sky from falling in. As if I'm frightened by all terrible things – because I am. I'm frightened that I am too small, too mad myself, to protect him.

The door of his room is shut when I get there, and I barge through it without knocking, as if there's a fire, as if Dr Slade will have returned. But it's Alasdair I see, where he said he would be, pliers in hand, twisting the pin out of Jim's now bare foot, and glancing up at me: 'Won't be long.' A nurse is standing beside him, a familiar face, though her name has slipped my mind; she smiles, and my knees turn to water with relief. Everything's all right; or it will be.

'Not hurting, is it?' Alasdair asks Jim.

'No.' He's looking at me, frowning: 'You're soaked.'

'Bit wet out there.' I pretend my heart isn't threatening to crash through my ribs, as I turn away in search of the fruit bowl, on top of the chest of drawers beside him: I pick up a peach and bite into it, forcing myself to eat, forcing normal, and not looking at the Steinmann pin coming out. It's not a painful procedure, Alasdair will have given him a local anaesthetic anyway, nothing more than an odd zinging of nerves around the heel, but it's all too close.

'No bleeding, looks good,' Alasdair is saying, and I keep eating this peach I can't taste, telling myself that we're doing the right thing. Of course, we are.

'I'll wrap this foot to a slab, shall I, Miss Brynne?' Alasdair is asking me.

For a second I don't know why he wants my opinion; then I realise he needs to know whether to bother setting Jim's foot comprehensively again or only basically, depending on how soon the surgery will be; I say, wiping peach juice from my chin with my handkerchief: 'Yes. Don't worry too much. Dr Adinov is making preparations for tomorrow.'

My head spins: I need something more substantial to eat; I'm barely in the room.

'The paperwork's there.' Alasdair nods over at the clipboard sitting on the bedside table. 'You can check over it, see that it's right, fill in the blanks.' He smiles at Jim, so that no-one would know what stress he must be feeling himself: 'Then you can sign it. Then you can go.'

Jim's stress is not so well concealed: 'Lucy, you're going to lose your job over this.'

'That's not relevant right now.' I pick up the clipboard, start filling out the transfer details.

'It's relevant to me. You can't just walk out.'

Watch me. 'I can, and I have every good reason to.'

'What about your other patients?'

Yes, there's a bit of a wrench, but there's no-one serious on the ward at the moment; no-one that can't be seen by a general physio: 'They'll survive. And maybe Admin will work out they need more staff.'

'I don't want you to do this. I don't want you to lose your job.'

'I'm doing what I want to do.' Terrifying and unfamiliar as this feeling is. And I'm not having an argument with you about it in front of Alasdair Slade and a nurse whose name I still can't remember – two people who are also risking their jobs, yes, for you. You'll be grateful soon when you grasp the fact that you're no longer strung up. I grasp the fact now that Alasdair Slade is so incredibly thoughtful, he's even taped down the little counter-traction hooks above Jim's knee so that they won't bother him. I glance over the rest of the form, can't see a thing. I hand it to Jim with my pen: 'Sign it there, down the bottom, please.'

I will stand here until you sign it.

He signs it, but the worry in his eyes as he hands it back makes me somehow ashamed, as if I'm forcing him to do this against his will. Because I am, I suppose. Ignore it: he's not in any fit state to be making his own decisions. Only a couple of hours ago he was about to agree to mutilation.

'I'm going to get a sandwich and a wheelchair,' I tell him. 'Would you like one? A sandwich, that is. You'll be having the latter whether you like it or not.'

'No, thanks,' he says, blank, beaten, sense of humour removed.

Some multilayered delirium takes me down to the canteen, where I begin eating my vegemite sandwich off the tray before I've paid for it. I eat the rest on my way to the wheelchair and trolley bay across the main lobby and down into the basement, breaking the no-eating-in-public-thoroughfares rule, hardly applicable to me today. I pass the orderlies' and ambulance-drivers' lunchroom, a crowded den of sweat and cigarette smoke, where some fifty men eat their meals, change and shower between shifts and are generally taken for granted, despite the very basic fact that this whole hospital would come to a screeching halt without them, and the rest of us would have no-one to come and scrape us off the ground when we fall down. Beyond them, I can hear the clanking of the surgical splint-maker, the guy who welds and bolts together frames and fracture beds and braces, and is completely invisible to everyone. I'm not going to miss this place. I'm not going to miss living in a hospital.

I start pushing a chair up to the lift, and once inside I close my eyes. Whatever happens, I'm going to sleep well tonight; I flicker in and out of sleep on this slow ride up. But once the floor-bell dings I snap to again, holding onto the thought that in a few short hours we'll be gone from here, oh yes, we will.

'Miss Brynne.' A voice behind me in the corridor; and I turn, thinking it's Alasdair, but it's not: it's Dr Slade. So, he *does* know my name? He knows who I am? That thought shudders up the back of my neck, cold and black. I don't answer him, and I don't stop walking. I am somewhere over the other side of fear, as he follows me. Has he been lurking about, waiting to bail me up? I do not want to know what he wants.

'Miss Brynne.'

I feel his hand grab the top of my left arm, tight.

I stop, and stare at his fingers.

'Miss Brynne.' He presses my name down into me from his great height. 'You might think you're very clever, but you are a very silly little girl.'

I look up at his face: he's all sneering, ugly anger now. I tell him: 'Get your hand off me.'

He digs his fingers hard into my flesh, just for a second, before he lets go. Of course, doctors can touch female staff however they like. I could scream out here all along this corridor and the report would say I provoked him. I'd be despatched with, so that he could go on his way. Happens too often – everywhere. Not happening with this little tough duck today.

He says: 'Your dear fiancé is crippled anyway. Why are you making things so much more difficult for him than they need to be?'

'Wow,' is all I can say to that, for the moment; the rain pelts and pelts on the roof above us, and I say it again: 'Wow.'

'Why can't you accept the reality, Miss Brynne? Won't you love him anymore if he's damaged? But then you haven't known him long, have you, and young love can be so fragile. Don't you think you should reconsider your haste here, for his sake?'

I don't think I've ever encountered a more damaged person than Eliot Slade. Anton was not exaggerating about him in any way. But he's pushed that button of doubt in me once more. I've only known Jim seven weeks – am I being too hasty? Am I only rushing at Jim because I'm lonely and scared and damaged, too? Because I'm not clever enough, I'm not good enough for anything so important as love? Am I wrong about his leg as well? God, no, is the answer to that last question and it's enough to push the rest away. I tell this hateful creature Slade: 'I'm not sure you're qualified to advise me on my personal affairs, Doctor. As for reality, I think your understanding of it, and everyone else's, are two very different stories.'

His eyebrows twitch; he seems perplexed, but not for more than a blink, before he says: 'Curious. You're a not a bad-looking thing, in your own way. What are you doing throwing yourself at this chap? Not as though he's a winning ticket. What are you making such a fuss for? He's just a mechanic.'

What? As though a mechanic doesn't have any business needing two legs; as though a mechanic isn't worth making a fuss for. As though a mechanic is ever *just* a mechanic. As though any ordinary working man is nothing to be bothered about. Although Slade is well over a foot taller than me, my revulsion for him and all he stands for suddenly makes me larger than he could ever be.

I clench my fist.

I tell him: 'What would I know? I'm just the daughter of a Welsh coalminer. Nobody.'

I want to bash the back of my fist across his jaw, but as I raise my hand, he catches it in his own.

I tell him: 'Get out of my way.'

He doesn't. He drops my fist, smiles, smug; my hand stings where it met his palm. He stands over me: 'You'll pay for that as well.'

I'm not backing down for any threat now; my own anger is too high. I say: 'What are you going to do? Put in me prison like you did Hugo Winter?'

Slade is stunned at that; I see he doesn't know of my connection to Hugo. So far above me, he could never imagine, never mind have heard that Hugo trained me before any university or hospital did. Hugo made me in so many ways, and Slade has no idea. For one excellent second, I wonder if this is what Hugo himself had planned by pushing for me to work here – a little cheerio from the great beyond.

'Oh yes,' I nod. 'I know all about you, Doctor. I know all about the mistakes you've made. The lives you've ruined. The trail of destruction you have left in your wake everywhere you go. We all know who should really be in prison, don't we?'

That was more than half a guess, but it does the job.

He says, softly, menacingly: 'Well, aren't you a nasty little surprise.' But the certainty has left him.

I start walking past him, gripping the handles of the chair in case my knees fail altogether.

He says, behind me: 'You'll never work at Sydney Hospital again – you'll never work at any Sydney hospital again.'

I throw the words over my shoulder: 'Break my heart.'

It's a long, long walk down this corridor back to Jim and, when I get there, it's rather a big effort to keep the shockwaves from him. So, I start packing his things, not that there's more than his travel-bag's worth to pack. It's a smart bag, this travel bag, tan leather; he has such solidly good taste in everything. He's such an amazing man, I don't know why he wants to marry me. Shut up. I check through all the drawers – wouldn't want to leave behind a card or a piece of my backgammon set. And what's this? A yo-yo – must belong to one of the kids.

'Lucy. Please …' he says from the bed, when Alasdair steps out to get some more tape for that foot. 'Please, can you slow down? Come here for a minute and be still?'

I can't; not yet. 'You don't have a dressing gown here, do you? I'll go and borrow one from the Women's Auxiliary now.'

'We'll have to make a run for it, so to speak.' I'm looking out at this ceaseless rain and looking at my watch again: it's three minutes past one; Anton will have arrived now outside Casualty, and it's about ten yards from building to kerb. 'We're going to get wet.'

'Well, you could test Jilly's theory.' Alasdair stands up from where he's been sitting by the door, reading the newspaper, tacitly making sure that we get away without any further interference. How this Slade could be the son of the other is a wonder for a later date. He gives Jim yet another apologetic smile: 'Or I could get my raincoat and throw it over you.'

Jim only nods: 'Thanks.' So blank it might seem rude, but I suppose his apprehension is dialled right up. So is mine – nearing maximum. What the hell am I doing to him? Me? Us?

On his way out, Alasdair steps back with the question: 'Do you need assistance with that transfer?' He points to the wheelchair.

And I take the opportunity to laugh: 'No, we should be all right. If you hear me shout for help, you'll know I've dropped him.'

Jim looks a little more lively at that idea, and a bit horrified: 'What are you doing?'

'Getting you out of bed and on the road.' A moment I've so looked forward to but didn't imagine it playing out quite as it is. 'Honestly, I've never let anyone fall.' I know what he's thinking; what they all think: she's far too flimsy for this. 'What we're going to do is put your right leg down on the floor. I'll keep your balance on the left and take care of your leg. Your job is to get that lovely arse of yours in that chair.'

He almost laughs at that but looks unsure, as well he might: despite the daily exercise regimen I've put him through, he has comparatively so little strength in arse and quadriceps this seems a mammoth challenge. And it is.

'Try not to think about it too much.' I put the chair in position, double-check the brake's on. 'Are you ready?'

'As I'll ever be,' he says, and I've been wanting to hold him all day, but not like this.

I'm still under his shoulder, still guiding his leg onto the rest, as he says: 'I'm sorry, Lucy. I'm sorry about this morning.' That hoarse edge to his voice abrading something in my soul. 'Blowing it out like a five-year-old, I shouldn't have carried on the way I did.'

'You don't have anything to apologise for.' I let the hold become a hug. I don't think many five-year-olds are called upon to fly screaming death machines, and then compelled in every way afterwards to pretend that nothing bad happened while you were there, because these days Britain is maybe a little embarrassed about the amount of irreplaceable medieval architecture it blew to pieces; I imagine Jim's voice is hoarse from yelling above the noise, the terror.

He says: 'I didn't mean to speak so sharply to you. I love you so much, please don't ever think otherwise.'

'Please be quiet again, or you might well make me cry.' I stand up and look away, too much yet to do.

Alasdair comes back and takes Jim down to the car, as I dash across to Nightingale for my suitcase and box of Hugo, the rain easing off a little at last. When I get to the car myself,

Jim is already in the backseat, and he's shaking Alasdair's hand goodbye.

We are here. Outside.

'My dear, you're too efficient – I didn't get to read one chapter of my book.' Anton is putting suitcase and box into the boot; then he's behind the wheel, smiling over his shoulder at Jim: when Anton Adinov smiles he always looks slightly threatening, a little too ready to wrestle with muscle and bone.

I slump into the front seat, my face in my hands as I force hysteria into a shout of joy: 'Oh! I can't believe we just did that.'

The clouds are clearing, silver-bellied over the water; two boys ride past on their bikes along the path that skirts the oval, one chasing the other under gulls that circle in hope of stray chips.

'I've never stayed in a hotel like this one before,' Jim says, enjoying the cool-warm harbour breeze through the open window.

'It's a bit posh, isn't it?' I reply, sitting on a chair beside the bed, and even this well-padded chair is a study in comfort. 'You're orthopaedic royalty now.' Such beautiful rooms downstairs; Jo has never changed the décor here, like she does at home – she's never needed to. Timelessly soothing mahogany and ivory, and best quality everything. Soft and heavy cotton quilts, stitched all over with daisy-wheels; a pattern of promised order and ordinariness I've lost and found my own mind inside several times, watching the way the shadows cast by the twelve square panes of the upper window frame moved across the stitches, hour by hour, through the days.

'If I'd known how good it would feel to lie on my side like this, I might have come sooner,' he says, happy again; himself again.

Such a simple pleasure to lie on your side, and how happy his happiness makes me, too. But I must warn him: 'Enjoy it while it lasts. You might feel a bit shabby after this operation tomorrow. Anton is going to do a graft as well, take a small piece of bone from your hip and —'

'Shush.' Half-laugh, half groan. 'The less I know, the better.'

'Aw. I'm sorry. You do need to know, though – your hip will probably hurt more than your leg. The pain won't last long, most likely, but it's a cracker.'

'And it'll be fine, whatever it is.' He smiles, deep blue smiling right into my weary bones. 'Really, it'll be fine.' He holds out his hand. 'Despite all my carry-on to the contrary, I do prefer having two legs, believe me.'

'I do.' I take his hand and make another vow: 'I'll always believe you. Except when you talk rubbish.'

He says: 'I don't know how you cop your job at all. The crap you must have to listen to.'

I nestle my face beside his on the pillow, nose to nose: 'Never worry about that, Jim. Seriously. I have plenty of crap of my own. You've got no idea.'

JIM CLEARY

I watch her fall asleep.

I know everything is random; no-one deserves whatever it is they get. It's pointless and stupid to think otherwise: you might as well be alive as dead. You don't get to choose option number one. But it's difficult not to think there's been a significant error in probability calculations somewhere, that's meant I've ended up with her.

That's meant she just walked out of her job because of me.

That she's just rescued me from myself, so I can lie here on my side.

That she's reopened some kind of door on life for me, or opened a new one for the first time, I don't know which. Both, most likely.

And I can't cop being lucky? What a tragic problem to have.

Whatever happens tomorrow, doesn't matter, does it, as long as I'm still here, and she is, too.

'You must be our Jim Cleary, are you?' An older woman comes into the room, grey-haired and curved everywhere. She smiles at Lucy; puts her hand on her shoulder, and says to me: 'I'm Mrs Benson, Marjorie Benson – Mrs B. I'll be taking care of you while you're here. Lucy might have the rest of the week off – what do you think?'

That's not really a question. I'm not sure who this Mrs B is except someone who worked with Lucy's Hugo; she was the matron here; someone from Lucy's world. I tell her: 'I think a week might be a bit cheap.'

'That's the idea, young man.' She smiles, but it seems she's taking some stock – of me. 'I hope you know what a wonderful girl this one is.'

'I hardly know her yet,' I tell this Mrs B. 'But I'll be taking care of her as well as she takes care of me, if that's what you're asking.'

'I am, I suppose.' Mrs B laughs. 'Forgive me. I know you're good for it. I know your Aunt Betty, in fact. We did our nurses' training together, many moons ago in 1916, served in Palestine together, too. So, all essential research on you and your credentials has been duly conducted.'

That is a laugh: Aunt Betty, Dad's sister, will have told her what I weighed as a baby and every minute of trouble I've caused my mother from that day onwards. 'There's no getting away with anything in a small country, is there.'

'Not in the long run, no.' Seems as though she's borne some witness to that, and she looks down at Lucy again. 'I'm rather fond of this girl. You'll only admire her more, the more you do get to know her.'

'I already know that much.' I look at her hand inside mine: hers might be remarkably smaller but it's the superior design. With her hands, she makes others feel stronger than they think they are. Wanting to know her: that's what this life, our life, will be about, for me.

'Would you like a cup of tea?' Mrs B asks, on her way back out.

'No, thanks.' I don't want to move and wake Lucy. I've never watched her sleep before.

I want to give her everything she needs. She'll never know how much she's done for me. I couldn't have got through the last seven weeks without her, not a chance: I'd have mentally disintegrated on day two. She reckons she's got my number on that, but I can do a lot worse than this morning's performance, even if it's only going on inside my head. She'll definitely never know any more about that, because I won't be sharing the load a second time. I don't want to give her further cause to change her mind.

The moment I first saw her, I thought we'd already met somewhere – I thought I must have asked her out before, maybe sometime during the war, but I knew a moment later that I hadn't. I'd have remembered her. Those big brown eyes, dark and bright, constantly busy, thinking, working, chatting, all at the same time. The way she touched my shoulder the next morning when I sneezed, pain off the scale, it's a touch that says you're not on your own, and I heard it even inside the creaking of those clamps on the bed frame that sounded more and more like rivets letting go on impact with every subsequent sneeze. The way she can laugh and sympathise as one complete emotion, one complete idea. I've never met anyone like her, and I don't need probability to tell me I never will again.

I'm not worried about this operation tomorrow. No, I'm not. Because I'm counting Lucy's eyelashes instead.

HUGO WINTER

'She's had such a rough time of it.' Mrs Ackerman took tea with Hugo downstairs in the reception room there, while the girl, Lucy Brynne, was upstairs, becoming acquainted with Marjorie Benson. A 'rough time' seemed about right judging from the x-rays alone: the original on admission to Lithgow Hospital showed a fracture caused by such a force of torsion the bone had been driven down into itself. But that one didn't trouble Hugo so much as the further two at the proximal heads of both the tibia and fibula, under the knee, and, most concerningly, the one above the knee at the end of the femur: these didn't look much by comparison, but unless they were stabilised, the joint would be compromised – she would be lame. It was not surprising the surgeon at Lithgow had initially thought there was no hope for this leg; it would be a test even for Hugo – and one he was keen to get to straightaway, as the injury was already more than a week old, carelessly set and incorrectly splinted.

But it was also important to him to find out as much about his young country patients as possible, for in his experience they were always the loneliest, particularly if they were poor, their parents unable to travel long distances or take time from work to visit their children often; occasionally, not at all.

'Her father, Gareth, isn't doing well.' Mrs Ackerman's clear blue eyes were wide with compassion. 'His wife, Enid, Lucy's mother, died only in May – and they'd only moved to the valley just after New Year, from Corrimal, near Wollongong, on the coast.'

'Yes, I know that coast,' said Hugo, thinking of its tough, low grasses clinging to wind-beaten dunes, as he rambled its long golden beaches. 'The father was a miner there, too?'

'Oh yes,' said Mrs Ackerman. 'But not for more than a few years. They'd emigrated from Wales in 1924, I think, when Lucy would have been about three, I suppose. This is all a little second-hand, but I understand Gareth was looking for a sunnier place to raise his family after the war. He served in the Welsh Regiment, met enough Australians in Turkey to make him think this'd be the place to go. Enid was never well, though. Several miscarriages and the final one carried her off – unstoppable haemorrhage, I believe.'

'Oh, rough indeed.' That thought sent Hugo back thirty years to Munich, watching helplessly as a young mother died the same way, bleeding out. Harrowing to see her fade before his eyes, and too quickly, nothing anyone could do. 'So, it's the father and daughter alone?' he asked. 'Lucy is an only child?'

'That's right. And quite clever, according to her teacher,' Mrs Ackerman replied. 'As well as quite naughty. Those two go together, don't they? I seem to have a couple of them at home myself – five, in fact. The story is, that's what got Lucy into trouble to begin with, this naughtiness, climbing the trees, out of bounds, at school. Some children go that way after a shock, don't they? Tear around a bit. Make a ruckus. Lucy is, as you would expect, fairly subdued now. She wasn't very talkative on the train. Very polite and very much in pain – such that it was requested I not take her by car, to avoid our juddery old mountain roads – but she didn't make a peep about it to me the whole way. I have one of those resolutely stoic types at home, too – rather larger and more difficult. I believe he signs the cheques.' Mrs Ackerman laughed, cheerful in that way of those who've honed cheerfulness into a weapon against despair. She added, to emphasise the point: 'Lucy's teacher says she has a very active mind, bright as a button, top of the class by a mile.'

Hugo nodded, taking it all in, asking: 'Will her father be able to visit often?'

'I'm not sure about that, I'm afraid.' Mrs Ackerman sighed. 'Mr Brynne, Gareth, can hardly look after himself at present. When he was told Lucy might lose the leg, he collapsed, apparently – inconsolable. Who can blame him? We have a new young surgeon at Lithgow, Sydney fellow, and he'd tried to calm the man by telling him an amputation would be less costly. Can you imagine?' Mrs Ackerman's eyes watered at the thought. 'Gareth is back at work now, not at our mine, but another, and he's barely hanging on – financially and spiritually. He's had a very rough time himself. A rough time for a long time.'

Hugo nodded again: 'Tell Gareth Brynne I will care for his daughter as if she is my own. I will do whatever it takes to make her leg better.'

'How are you feeling, Lucy?' Hugo asked her, a little while after she'd woken from the anaesthetic.

'Not very comfortable, thank you,' she said, and it was at that moment their minds met, the first inkling of a bond forged between fifty-five-year-old doctor and seven-year-old patient.

'Where does it hurt?' he asked; he always asked a child these questions first, to find out which was worse: the wound or wanting to be home, away from strangeness and fear.

'It doesn't hurt.' Lucy Brynne frowned at him, annoyed: 'I want to sit up and I can't.'

'Yes, well, I agree it's not comfortable to be unable to do the things you want to do.' He nodded, sympathetic. He'd been able to manipulate those most worrying fractures around the knee into a good position, but in order to ensure they stayed there, the whole leg would have to remain completely still, which meant a plaster splint extending from her toes to her chest. It would be three months before she could sit up. It would be a long road for Lucy Brynne. While Hugo had drilled a wire through the more spectacular mid-tibial fracture to hold it together well enough to heal, he could not use any traction for the best result – because the tension would displace those more difficult others. This meant that the leg would lose some length, and possibly require a correction later, when she was older, when her bones were fully grown, but he confidently promised her now: 'Your perseverance will be rewarded. If you can put up with all of this, and put up with me, one day not too far away, you'll be able to walk again. You'll be able to run and dance and play.'

Lucy sighed with her bundle of unspoken burdens and looked away: 'Do you have any books?'

'Books?' Hugo smiled. 'You can have as many books as you like.'

It took her about a week to read everything that could be found for her inside the walls of Aurora, after which Jo brought in a box of Claire's castoffs, piling them up on the bedside table where Lucy could reach them: colourful, illustrated works of May Gibbs and Beatrix Potter; at least a dozen editions each of the *Children's Treasury*, *Stories for Girls* and bits and pieces of other annuals.

'Thank you.' Lucy watched Jo Winter as any little girl watches a beautiful lady: in awe that such a person is possible, breathing in the rose-tinted scent of her, mesmerised by the glint of diamonds in a ring that morning as she made book after book appear. But Lucy's still fresh grief for her mother kept her from saying anything more than was necessary to show her appreciation. Lucy's mother had not been beautiful; she'd been gaunt and addled and at times quite terrifying, but Lucy had loved her as children love their mothers however they come; she'd needed her, and, cruelly, her mother had never been well enough to give her much but instructions on how to help. Now she wasn't there at all and Lucy was here, wondering if her father had had something to eat for breakfast; wondering if he'd had work on that day or was sitting alone by the fire, lost.

'She's an old soul,' Jo told Hugo at dinner that night. 'There's a lot going on behind those brave brown eyes.' Jo knew the difference between a little girl's reserve and a little girl's isolation; she'd marvelled often enough at her own daughter Claire's self-possession, her ability to please herself. 'Don't be deceived,' she told her husband: 'Lucy Brynne might well be the loneliest little girl I've ever met.'

Marjorie Benson had said a similar thing to him: that Lucy's lack of interest in conversation seemed more than ordinary shyness. She did not even care to talk to the other children in the ward, at the time there being four, two of them girls almost the same age and in quite similar predicaments, both with hip abnormalities, and they talked so much Marjorie often had to shush them so they didn't wake the infants at the other end of the room. Was Lucy concealing a physical pain? That was Hugo main worry. Children rarely did that sort of thing, or not for long – they didn't have the wherewithal – but this child was a little different from the outset. He thought he'd have a go himself at trying to get her chatting.

When he went to her the next day, she was reading, chin in her hands, lying prone on a nest of pillows, having been settled into that position by one of the nurses, as she couldn't turn herself. He sat down on a chair beside her, so she could see him easily, and asked her: 'Have you been enjoying all the books Mrs Winter brought you?'

'Oh, I suppose so,' she said, not looking up from the words, and then remembered her manners: 'Yes, thank you.'

'Have you found any of them interesting?' he asked.

'Not really. They're all the same after a while. Bad things happen and then there's a happy ending.' She sounded more like his fifteen-year-old daughter, more like Claire in all her teenaged disregard, than the small child she was: an odd contradiction of too bored and too busy.

His immediate inclination was to insist that life is, in fact, full of happy endings, but he suspected this patient hadn't experienced many yet, so he thought he'd try a circuitous route into her thoughts instead: 'If you could read any story today, any story in the world, what would it be about?'

She looked at him then, thinking on it for a moment, before she said: 'I want to know what's happening in my bones. I want to know what they're doing. Is that a story?'

'That's quite a story.' Hugo smiled: here was a conversation. He told her: 'Your bones are doing extraordinary things – they're healing.'

'How do they heal?' she asked him.

'Well, every bone is made up of millions of tiny cells, and when a bone is broken or injured in some way, special cells called osteoblasts charge into action to mend it.' He took his notebook and pencil out of his apron pocket and drew her a simple picture. 'But you see, each osteoblast is tiny, so it takes very, very many of them and a long time to complete their work.'

'Millions.' She gazed at his drawing, repeating the word as if to test its meaning, and then she blinked across at him in wonder: 'You mean bones heal by themselves?'

'Yes.' He was delighted by her quick intelligence and her curiosity. 'Your body is full of this magic. But for bones to heal, they need to be protected and treated very carefully, so that they can concentrate on their work. And that's the short version of the incredible story of what your bones are doing now. Would you like me to find you a book about bones?' In his office, he had a basic anatomy text with lots of illustrations he sometimes used for showing patients and parents what was what; perhaps she'd enjoy looking at that. Was she too young? It didn't matter; it wouldn't hurt to give it to her.

She nodded: 'Yes, please.' Lucy returned his smile now, and with relief. For the first time in what seemed to her like a thousand years, something finally made sense.

The book Doctor Hugo brought her held new worlds of revelation on every page, and she'd spend hours there most days, puzzling over the diagrams, studying the skeleton and musculature of the human body, its maps of the vascular and nervous systems; she'd spend hours looking at her own hand and imagining its workings, its layers of being beneath the skin.

And Hugo would watch her, intrigued that somehow here was a kindred spirit. Their conversations ranged around her reading: ligaments, cartilage, marrow, the interplay of flexor and extensor muscles around each joint, each bone.

'But how does thinking to do something get from the brain and down through all the nerves?' she asked him one day. 'How do we make ourselves move?'

'It's a mystery, a beautiful mystery.' Hugo shared all of her wonder. 'There's a theory that messages are conveyed from the brain throughout the body by some form of electricity, but the truth is, no-one knows how it happens. Perhaps one day you'll answer this question for the rest of us, hm?' He would scratch his head, happily baffled that this somewhat undersized seven-year-old was grappling with concepts that men spent whole careers ignoring.

What sudden, inexplicable joy she brought him.

Joy: there was no cure like it, and Hugo insisted there be as much of the stuff as possible in his hospital, for the power it seemed to bring to cells, to push them forth, to multiply.

Each second Sunday of the month, as had become his habit, he and the nursing staff would put on a pantomime for the children – warning any paying guests downstairs that there'd be all manner of screaming and stamping from above for an hour or two. He'd bring his dog, Rudy von Red Hound the First, up to the ward as well, to play the part of hyperactive Irish setter. Whether it was Snow White or Sleeping Beauty or Hansel and Gretel, these performances were invariably ridiculous, and Rudy von Red Hound was always the star, barking and grinning and bounding about, at the same sensing with some uncanny perception every gentleness required by his audience. But during the first of the shows Lucy saw – a retelling of 'The Old Woman Who Lived in a Shoe', with Doctor Hugo playing the leading lady – Rudy von Red Hound refused all invitations to make mayhem, preferring instead to stand with her, his snout upon the bed by her shoulder, their eyes engaged in conversation only the two of them would ever know.

This show descended towards its ludicrous conclusion, as all these shows did, with Doctor Hugo finding his clarinet somewhere unlikely – in this case, in the linen cupboard – and with the rest of the ensemble holding their hands over their ears, crying, 'No! Stop it!' as he tortured a tune – in this case, 'The Little Brown Jug', not that anyone could guess it.

'What did you think of my performance?' he asked Lucy afterwards, theatrically dabbing his brow, still wearing his Old Woman red velvet dress and garish blonde wig.

She frowned, and after a moment said, very tactfully, very seriously: 'You're good at lots of other things.'

He laughed a little every day for the rest of his life at that.

And every Sunday evening from then until she left Aurora, they'd have a round of backgammon there in the ward or, as the weather warmed, he'd take her onto the balcony in a reclining chair and let her beat him at the game out there. Or so he told himself. Hugo was a generous man but not quite so generous he could accept the number of times he was actually bested by a seven-year-old.

'Got you again, Old Hugh Shoe,' she'd say, wisecracking, making him wonder if he should pass her his pipe; making him sure he was going to have some difficulty accepting that, one day, she would have to leave.

Gareth Brynne was lean and lined, a handsome face made bereft of its flesh in the way of any man who works at hard labour and forgoes food for alcohol. His hands trembled this day not from want of a drink, though, but from the stress of being in the city, alone, overlaying all the worries and fears he held for his daughter, the clench of his stomach that had not abated all this long month since he'd last seen her.

'Lucy will be quite all right,' Hugo tried to convince him of this, preparing him for the sight of his little girl, explaining that her present incapacitation was all in aid of a good result: 'She's healing very well. I have every reason to hope she will be home with you before the end of the year.'

Both men swallowed hard at that. For Hugo, the end of the year was only three months away; for Gareth it was an eternity.

The miner said: 'I don't know how I can ever repay you, Doctor,' his accent a melancholy glissando across the globe from old South Wales.

'You don't ever have to repay me,' Hugo told him, knowing this did nothing for any man's pride. He gave him the more palatable facts: 'You've paid your Fund levies, I presume. Children are our future, are they not? I like the idea of investing in the future – and all the members of the Fund, as well as many others, feel the same way.'

Gareth nodded his acknowledgement that something had been said, but he only wanted to see his daughter now.

'Daddy!' The look on Lucy's face had Hugo swallowing his envy, but within a moment he'd resumed his concern: it was clear who was the more resilient of the two – and it wasn't Gareth.

'It's all right, Daddy,' he heard her say before he left them alone. 'I shouldn't have been in that tree. All the trouble I've caused. I'll never make you cry again.'

Gareth Brynne was still wiping his eyes when he left a few hours later to make the evening train. A defeated man, thought Hugo, for all that his daughter seemed indomitable.

Lucy was determined and diligent in all things: the school work her teacher sent her; every physical exercise Marjorie had her do; and once the last of the plaster splints was off she looked at her leg as she did any other puzzle: how was she going to make this work?

Anton Adinov had a look, too, as Hugo and he conferred.

'Hm,' said the Russian, clasping her leg where the callus bulged at her shin, and gentle as he was, she wasn't sure about him. He said, moving her knee: 'The joint is perfect, yes, but the rest … What's the difference in length?'

'Two and three-quarter inches,' Hugo replied: it was disappointing even if it wasn't unexpected; it was much more significant than he'd hoped.

Adinov made a face – one that frightened Lucy.

'What's wrong with my leg?' she asked.

'Nothing is wrong.' Hugo smiled. 'There will be a delay in that promise I made to you that you would soon run. You will have to have another operation when you're older, maybe sixteen or seventeen, when your bones are grown. Until then, there will be quite strict rules about what you can do and what you can't. There'll be no running or jumping, or things like that.'

'That's all right,' she told both men, chin up even though it was disappointing for her, too: 'I don't like running and jumping anyway.'

'And no rodeo riding, either.' That Dr Adinov shook his finger at her, and Lucy wanted to shrink away. She thought he might be joking, but she really couldn't be sure.

Whatever the case, she'd do as she was told. It took a month of further therapy, of bending and stretching and swimming, to satisfactorily unlock her knee, to have good boots fitted, the right one with a raised heel, and to learn to walk again, with strength enough to return home. She and Hugo would walk around the oval and along the foreshore path through Rushcutters Park, up the eastern arm of the bay; they talked about the Sydney Harbour Bridge and what it might look like across the view once the two halves of the great arch had met; they talked about what she might like to do when she grew up, and she said she'd like to be a nurse like Mrs B.

'Not a doctor?' Hugo asked, surprised by how much smaller she was out of bed.

And she said: 'Can girls be doctors?'

'Oh yes.' He told her: 'I want to hear that you've been working very hard at your studies when I see you again next year.' Once a year, he wanted to see her, and had written to the Fund to make certain that would be taken care of at the Lithgow end.

'Good luck then, Lucy,' he shook her little hand when it was time for her to leave, another pleasant lady from the Fund having come to collect her.

'Thank you, Doctor Hugo.' She waved from the window of the taxi. 'See you soon.'

He wanted to stop that taxi, grab her back, give her a hug, that crushing hug he was famous for among his inner circle of friends, and he would come to regret not having done so, for it would be seven years before he saw Lucy Brynne again.

Life went on, as it does.

Hugo received another letter from the Taxation Department – a second one – requesting an audit of the hospital accounts and, as was his custom with such things, he threw it in the waste-paper bin: 'Bureaucrats be damned.'

Lucy didn't appear for her appointment the following November of 1929, and so he wrote to the Fund, asking after her. Receiving no immediate response, he wrote to Mrs Ackerman just after New Year, only to be told by Anton a few days later that the family had gone abroad, to Germany; Daniel Ackerman was at last going to take up an offer of study at the Dresden Academy of Arts, spend some time in the ancestral homeland.

Hm. It was a heavy thought, but one Hugo had to face: like a few children from poorer families he'd treated in the past, perhaps Lucy had simply disappeared, swept along by whatever life decided for Gareth Brynne. Perhaps they weren't even in Lithgow anymore.

And he was right.

Lucy and Gareth had moved to Newcastle, a hundred miles north of Sydney, Gareth having needed a fresh start after letting his drinking interfere with his ability to work one too many times, burning his bridges in Lithgow. The myth of the alcoholic coalminer is just that: no-one wants a man who is a danger to himself and others working underground, and compassion doesn't enter into it. Grief and a decent war service record don't mean a thing. Safety is the issue here, and as they say in those circles, Gareth couldn't be trusted to shit unsupervised.

Despite the hardships of the gathering Great Depression, he rallied for a few years, securing a good job at the ever busy and familiarly named Cardiff Colliery, and keeping it long enough for Lucy to excel in her final year of primary education, upon which, at the age of eleven, she was offered a government bursary to attend high school – one of only three hundred bursaries in the state. Gareth was so, so proud of her, always stunned at where she might have got her brains, but during her first term at Newcastle Girls', he lost his job again. It wasn't his fault this time; the Depression was now so rough it was claiming the jobs of one in three men across the board. It was merely a matter of odds and it was enough to set off his drinking once more – his quietly determined, no-fuss, staring-into-the-fire obliteration.

Even still, they scraped through together for almost another two years, living off the bursary and charity. He never spent a penny of his daughter's money on alcohol: he'd get enough coin by odd jobs and rabbiting to buy himself cheap grog, and then metho, as his hopelessness wore on. Lucy made it to the end of Second Form, when the wheels finally fell off and she had to leave school to get a job – any job, to pay their boarding-house room rent, to keep them off the street. She found work at a poultry farm, packing eggs six mornings a week, at Wallsend three miles away. She was philosophical about it. It wasn't as though she was the only thirteen-and-a-half-year-old this sort of thing had happened to. By now, though, in the January of 1935, there was plenty of talk of the Depression turning around. Things would change. She'd get a better job; she'd go to night school. She'd get things done however she could. She'd try not to worry that her father wouldn't wake up one day; and she worried, too, that sometimes she wished he would quietly slip away, so she would never have to clean him up, or beg him to wake up, ever again.

There wasn't a morning she didn't wish for new boots, measured up properly by an orthopaedist. Several years now of wearing ordinary boots had given her quite a pronounced limp and an almost permanently aching hip. She never ran, she never jumped; it didn't matter what she did: some days the ache was so sharp she didn't want to walk to work. But she did. She had to.

Until one day, that next August, she returned to their Newcastle boarding-house room and, there at the table under the window, she found her father dead. Head on his arm, eyes staring down into nowhere. Cold, grey; not unkempt. Not there. By his elbow, their little black pot was full of baked beans that had never made it onto the kerosene stove.

It was a slow suicide but a suicide nevertheless. He left no note, no nothing at all. No word of the ghosts that had followed him here from the fly-blown crags of Gallipoli, and then from the Western Front, the mud and the blood that remained under his boots wherever he'd gone ever since; the shouting and the tears of the pointlessly dying, and dying, and dying, always in his ears. His dear Enid forever gripping his hand, gripping onto this life: 'Gary, please, I don't want to go.' He died a long and terrible death; he died of a heart broken one too many times.

Time froze and fell away, until Lucy could feel her feet in her own boots again. She went downstairs, to find their landlady, Mrs Innes, in the kitchen, and told her: 'My father has died.'

'Oh, you poor girl,' Mrs Innes cried, then threw up her hands in dismay: 'What's to be done about it!'

'I'll go and get the doctor,' Lucy said, for she knew by some vague memory that doctors had to be called to fill out forms for any such thing.

She walked out into the street, the dusk above the smoke-stacks of Newcastle turning every shade of amber and purple and pink – mad – and she didn't try to find any doctor at all. She kept walking for the train station and caught the 7.15 pm to Sydney.

A journey of more than three hours, it was, and she'd never remember a minute of it, such was her state of shock. She asked the ticket officer in the empty vault of Central how she might get to the Children's Hospital, Aurora House, at Rushcutters Bay, hoping it hadn't been some dream she'd dreamt long ago and far away. It wasn't; the ticket man knew it, as most ordinary people did – two quick trams and straight down Waratah Street, the stop before Sydney Stadium – and she was there on the doorstep just after eleven pm.

A woman, the night matron, answered her knock. 'Yes? Can I help you?'

'I hope so,' she said, so small there on the doorstep, though she was now fourteen. 'I need to see Doctor Hugo – Hugo Winter. That's his name, isn't it?'

'Yes, yes, that is Doctor. But he's not here, my dear,' the night matron said, not unkindly but more increasingly con-cerned by the second. 'It's very late. He's at home.'

'I'm sorry to disturb you,' said Lucy, in a daze.

'Come in, dear, come in.' The night matron took her by the arm. 'Come and sit inside. I'll call Doctor on the telephone. What's your name? I'll tell him you're here.'

'Lucy,' she said. 'Lucinda Jane Brynne.'

In less than five minutes, Hugo was there – he'd grabbed his coat by the door and run out to the car, in his slippers and pyjamas, he'd pushed the accelerator pedal to the floor around the bay.

'Lucy.'

She could only look up at him with those brave brown eyes, and he hugged her to him then; he would never let her go again. They sat there together on the sofa in the reception room while she cried silently into his chest; they sat there, and sat there, until she could speak to tell him what had happened, in all its small enormity.

'You're sending her *where*?' Claire was not happy at the idea her parents had decided to practically adopt this scrap of a thing, and now she was outraged that they were about to spend a fortune on the urchin's education at her own alma mater, the Sydney Church of England Girls Grammar School. She wasn't at all interested in who Lucy was, where she'd come from, or how much of a hand up she needed. Claire was twenty-two, with all of her father's natural arrogance and too little of his generosity.

'Claire.' Jo tried to warn her daughter not to take a step too far on this. Hugo didn't often lose his temper these days – he rarely had to deal with anyone who might provoke him, other than those in the Taxation Department who insisted on a yearly audit of all his accounts – and he'd never said a cross word to either his wife or his daughter before, ever, but Jo could see his blood beginning to boil, quietly, as he stared across the lounge room at Claire. 'Please, Claire,' Jo spoke softly to her: 'What harm can it do to you that we are helping someone who is so much in need of our help?'

'She's some little rat of a thing off the street – one out of thousands.' Claire was dismissive; a spoilt princess, left too long to please herself among the smart set, with their rounds of endless parties – lunch, tea, cocktails, dinner and a show, sleep until midday, do it all again tomorrow. She turned her own ice-cool temper on her father first: 'What is she, a new pet?'

'Claire!' Jo was the first to shout: 'Please. What are you saying?'

Hugo continued to stare at his daughter; this stranger to him. There was silence for a few moments, and then: 'If you don't like it, you can leave this house at once.'

'Exactly what I was going to suggest.' Claire's eyes glittered with her own vanity and certitude – her father was a crank, a loon, a social embarrassment among the upper-tens, Gentile and Jew alike. A maverick? A joke. She chose only to hear the worst of what those in her over-pampered circle said of him.

'Please.' Jo tried to step in again: she knew Claire would one day regret this – one day when she grew up, took on responsibilities of her own. Jo could see both sides: Claire had her shortcomings, yes, she was far too interested in money, but her father had been so rarely interested in her, always focussing his energies on other children, always around the bay at the hospital, or loudly drunk on the terrace entertaining benefactors, and whenever he did take time off, he went hiking along some desolate strand of beach up or down the coast that all looked the same even to Jo. 'You can't leave,' she told her daughter: 'Where would you go?'

'Melbourne,' said Claire, already leaving the room; she'd been planning another shopping trip with a friend anyway, and this time she'd simply stay.

'Good,' said her father. 'Pack your bags and get out.'

He glared at Jo: 'And don't you give her any money.'

Claire left that afternoon, and Jo slipped her twenty pounds, but that was all: she'd have to go her own way, take her own train, take whatever fall was coming to her. Yes,

Claire would be all right, whatever happened – she was old enough and selfish enough to look after herself. But Lucy was not; and, sitting in the guest bedroom across the hall with the dog, she would have heard just about every word of that spat.

'Don't worry about Claire,' Jo told Lucy's sad and fearful eyes, sitting beside her on the bed: 'She's only jealous right now that Hugo is so very fond of you. She'll come around.'

'I don't want to cause any trouble,' Lucy said.

'Trouble?' Jo smiled: 'Trouble sometimes needs to happen. That trouble there in the lounge – you didn't cause that. Claire and Hugo's trouble is for them to sort out.'

They never would sort it out, not entirely, not that anyone could have known that then. Then, Lucy put her head down and repaid the Winters with excellent academic scores in all subjects. The school started her in Third Form, despite the terms she'd missed, and she performed as though she hadn't skipped a beat. She didn't have much in the way of distraction from study: she wasn't allowed to play any sports or join in any dancing lessons; she spent that first term at her new school on crutches, with Hugo anxious for the inflammation in her hip to abate – and it did. She was such a little pixie wisp, she wasn't teased too badly by the other girls for her orthopaedic boots or physical limitations; in fact, her medical condition made the principal inclined to offer a partial scholarship. Of course, Lucy would meet a few snooty Claire types in the school yard – there were always those types anywhere, the ones who sniped, 'She must have cheated on that test,' or, 'You know she's an orphan, her real parents weren't anyone,' and the worst one, 'Tiny Miss Twist,' after Dickens' most pitiable waifs – but she met as many types that were more like her: studious girls who enjoyed doing the work, with thoughts of perhaps going to university one day, and they pushed each other on.

'What would you like to study?' Hugo asked her at the beginning of her final, matriculation year, hoping she'd say medicine, but she didn't.

'Um … science,' she replied, calculating that she had a greater chance of getting a full bursary for this lesser degree. The Winters couldn't possibly pay for her to go to university: Lucy did not expect any such thing, nor would she ever ask for it. And in any case, she'd probably fail at medicine; she supposed someone like her couldn't fluke it quite that far.

'What would you like to do with a degree in science?' Hugo asked her next.

'Um … I'm not sure. Maybe I'll see when I get there?'

He smiled; he remembered what that was like, not knowing, and she was only sixteen, seventeen in June. Plenty of time to make these big decisions and change her mind a thousand times before breakfast.

There was another big decision to make, however, and he made the suggestion now: 'After your final exams, how about I fix your leg?' He'd calculated it would be the right time to do it, Lucy having put on quite a growth spurt over the last summer that had taken her height up to a surprising five feet, three inches – a little under the average but not by much. He'd also thought if he got to it in the November, she would at last be ready to run and play whatever games she wished by the February, when the university term began – she would be ready to dance. Or near enough. He thought then, when it was done and she could wear pretty shoes, whatever shoes she liked, the spark of self-assurance she'd had when she was seven would come back again.

'If you think it's the right time, then so do I,' Lucy said, a bit nervous at the idea, but trusting Hugo in all things. To her, he hoisted the sun each morning before the rest of the world was awake.

But he wouldn't have her leg fixed by anything like February, or anything like 1939. For a start, he got a bad flu at the end of the November, one that put him right out for more than a fortnight – caught no doubt at the school farewell assembly while he was applauding the announcement of her honour prizes in mathematics and biology. He thought about asking Anton to step in, just to get it over with, but he wanted to do it himself – finish the job he'd begun – which would be delayed a further fortnight while he got on top of the backlog caused by the flu. It was Christmas Eve, then, before he'd get to Lucy, a time of holidays that, at least, didn't mean much to either of them.

'It'll be all right,' he said. 'You'll still have the cast on when you start your classes, perhaps for a month or so.' Probably more like two months, but he knew she'd be fine regardless – she'd endured far worse.

Lucy nodded; she'd do what she was told. If Hugo thought it was achievable, then it was. She was looking forward to joining the other science-minded girls at Sydney University, however it came: she'd won a scholarship to The Women's College, room and board paid.

Why things didn't work out that way would, like so many things, always remain a mystery – one that Hugo would carry like a pebble in his shoe for the rest of his days. Not a religious man in any way other than in his rituals of surgery, which involved the autoclave steaming of all instruments and fixation materials, the boiling and bleaching of all linen, as well as the near maniacal washing of hands for a minimum of fifteen minutes before any operation, he would never understand how it was that Lucy got the infection that would ultimately destroy the first bone graft, necessitating a second, and then a very slow process of healing afterwards, during which it seemed the bone was quite undecided about repair.

She never complained, but she suffered: there had been no other choice but to hold the leg in traction until there was sufficient healing, and that would take seven months in all. 'I'm sorry, Lucy,' became his refrain after every disappointing x-ray.

'I'm only sorry I couldn't begin university here at Aurora,' she'd say: 'I could have completed three degrees.' And four. And five. Some of her spark returned for the ordeal, or it tried to, her quips droll and dry – she couldn't bear that look of guilt in his eyes.

He spent as much time as he could with her every day, playing backgammon, chess, talking nonsense, talking science, bringing her books – on anatomy, astronomy, geology, pathology – and journals of all kinds.

'I will not fail you,' he told her, even as she cleaned his pieces off the board again. 'My promise to you is made of iron now, my girl.'

She shook her head: 'Nah. It's an alloy of cobalt, chromium and molybdenum' – the elements that made up the vitallium plate in her leg. And they laughed for far, far longer than the crack was worth. They held each other up.

She'd confide solely in Mrs B: 'I think I'm losing my mind.' On the worst of her days, she whispered: 'I don't know what's outside this hospital anymore. I don't know where I am. I don't know if Hugo and Jo are real, or if I dream them.'

'They're real.' Mrs B always spoke with calm, cut-through authority: 'I'm real, too, and I say it's time for your exercise.'

Some days, it had seemed only Mrs B's touch could make her believe that she really could endure this: her cool-warm hands relieving screaming muscles, silencing the cruel little voice inside her head that said she deserved nothing better than some form of distress. And it was there, in the touch of those hands, that Lucy found what she wanted to do at the other end of a science degree, when she got there: physical therapy. She wanted to learn how to bring this relief to others – not merely as a comfort, but as a measurable, clinical skill.

'Physiotherapy?' Hugo approved. It wasn't quite medicine, at least not formally, but a step in the right direction. He would encourage her in every way.

But still, he wouldn't have her walking unassisted all that long, long year. She spent most of the rest of it in a wheelchair, at Darling Point, waiting for those hesitant osteoblasts of hers to arrange themselves solidly enough around the wedge-shaped graft. Hugo would have nightmares about it. Should he take out the plate and start again, put her through another arduous surgery, or should he wait? If he continued to wait, would that invite another infection? Was it the vitallium itself? Was the bone having an adverse reaction to the metal? He'd been using these plates for the last three years, and neither he nor Anton had ever come across this problem before. The graft site in her pelvis had healed normally, *twice*, so why wasn't this?

'It is me?' he asked Anton at one point. 'Have I missed something?'

'Don't be an idiot,' said his friend. 'You couldn't miss a tram if you tried. Get her up and walking on it. It'll be all right.'

'I can't take that chance,' Hugo replied. If it fractured, if it failed, after all this time …

September 1939 and the world was at war again, but Hugo was interested in no battle other than the unfathomable one going on inside Lucy's leg.

A fellow from the Taxation Department telephoned in the October: 'Dr Winter, there appears to be a discrepancy in the receipts for —'

'Why don't you go and join the Gestapo. I hear they have vacancies.' He hung up; he'd give Lucy's leg one more month before deciding what to do. These ten, almost eleven months he had suffered, too, every day, with this dread of failing her – of all patients.

Fortunately, for his blood pressure, and for Lucy as well, the next x-ray was free of any trace of a shadow around the graft. 'You beauty!' he shouted the Australian vernacular for the best of all winnings.

'Really?' It was the one and only time that Lucy cried.

'Really.' He cut the cast off, placed her toes on the tops of his shoes and held her tightly as he danced her around the room. It would take several more patients and a research article in *Deutsches Ärzteblatt* for him to work out what he might have done differently: that was, get her up and walking on it earlier, at the twelve-week mark, to stimulate the bone growth. He'd been too conservative with her, after that second graft, too involved with his patient, too worried, to take the logical, sensible risk. Anton resisted telling him, 'I told you so,' because Hugo truly hadn't known, the way only rough experience can make a man know; the way only a true friend can assure with a hand at the back of the neck: 'You did the best thing you could do at the time. Idiot.'

Back in that December, though, after his painstaking removal of the screws and the plate, Hugo was yet to allow her to put her full weight on it, when Claire came home, unexpectedly, during Hanukkah – after an absence of four years and never much more than sparse, 'I'm fabulous' telephone calls to her mother in between.

Claire arrived with a man called Leon Kessler, whom she introduced as her fiancé, but as ever, Claire herself was the only person in the room. She practically ignored Lucy, 'Oh, hello,' glancing at her as if she'd expected nothing less than that the attention-seeking street rat would be in a wheelchair; she was offhand with her mother's questions about this sudden engagement, tossing them back with blithe queries of her own: 'Oh, yes, yes, time gets away, doesn't it?' and, 'I'll tell you all about it over lunch – oh, but can't we eat out on the terrace?'

'No.' Hugo stepped past her twittering. 'We'll eat in the dining room.' He was not in the mood for uninterrupted views, and the terrace from here was downstairs – a problem as yet for Lucy.

Once they'd sat down, his daughter leaned across the hastily festive table at him, stabbing a potato pancake with her fork: 'Did you know Jews trapped in Germany have now been forbidden from purchasing new clothes or even leather to mend their shoes? They're being deported to Poland and murdered. What are we doing about it, Papa? Nothing, it seems. Are you going to hold one of your famous fundraising dinners here for the refugees?'

Hugo sighed, and not least because Claire would use even this unfolding tragedy to score a point against him. Yes, it was true that Hanukkah meant little more to him than the opportunity to eat potato pancakes in greater quantities than he should, gorge himself unthinkingly on these traditional latkes that were piled on a platter between them, but he could never not be Jewish. It didn't work like that – and certainly not for the Nazis. The Jews of Europe were under siege; this was the deadly endgame set in motion by the Treaty of Versailles, as far as Hugo was concerned, a disaster that was gathering more and more force. The Ackermans had returned to Australia three years ago, in '36, telling Anton that the violence was too intolerable to consider staying. Then there were the pogroms last November, this Kristallnacht, that had prompted Hugo to write to his brother Ernst in Hagen, because family can never be strangers in such circumstances as these; he hadn't heard back. He would never know that Ernst was taken to Dachau and killed there, but he knew; oh, he knew. He had been overcome on reading that the German consulate in Melbourne had turned away a deputation from the Australian Aborigines' League protesting the treatment of Jewish people; he was knocked sideways by their gesture of solidarity, that this world could be so small and large, so beautiful and terrible, all at once. He and Jo had already given their assurances throughout the community that they stood ready to accept any families or children in need; Jo was on the committee of the National Jewish Women's Council, who were raising money to help those displaced right now. But he was sure Claire didn't really want to know any of this. She was showing off somehow in front of this Leon Kessler, who was, to judge by his accent, American. Hugo was sixty-six years old – too old for this, too old for war of any kind.

He told his daughter: 'Ask your mother about fundraising – perhaps you could make yourself useful while you're here.'

'I'm going to New York,' she said, tossing her chin in the air. 'Leon's parents are there. His father is an investment banker – the Kessler of Kessler Holtz Ledermann. Leon's been looking into the wool market here – not staying, obviously.'

Obviously, thought Hugo, as Leon himself lit a cigarette, uninvited, at the table – a damned rude American. Slick, suave, gilt buttons on his blazer, Hugo supposed he was paying this visit for one reason alone: to check that Claire's parents weren't too unacceptable. He said to Hugo: 'I hope you can come over for the wedding. We're planning it for April.'

That was impossible. Hugo couldn't pack up at such short notice, leave his patients for what would have been a lengthy absence – a round trip of at least six weeks for the travelling alone. This was as good as being told they weren't welcome.

They finished the meal in near silence but for incidental chat about the weather and Sydney's traffic congestion, with Leon managing to offend again by saying, 'That Harbour Bridge was half empty, though – rather a grand structure for your quaint little city, isn't it?' At which Hugo shot back: 'You call a city of a million people quaint? Not travelled much then, have you, boy?' Lucy wished she could slide under the table; or find something to say, for Jo's sake. That Jo could barely speak spoke volumes of the depth of her hurt. Lucy watched Claire, not caring about her mother or her father: how sad it must be to have so little gratitude, she thought, to live in such a state of want.

Jo retired to her room as soon as they left, and later that evening when her husband joined her, she let go the tears that needed to fall; she said to him, grasping at straws: 'Claire is only trying to impress – impress you most of all. She loves us, I know she does, really. She's still searching for herself, for a purpose.'

'She'd go a lot further with an apology for being so disrespectful to you,' Hugo replied, quite unmoved, for an apology was something Claire could never seem to give, never a backwards step.

'I don't like that man, that Leon.' Jo held the soft flannel of her husband's pyjama shirt against her cheek.

'Neither do I,' said Hugo. But Claire was twenty-six years old – old enough to make her own bed.

By twenty-six, Lucy had made thousands of beds, and happily – not that she was ever any Pollyanna about it. She'd crack jokes with the men as she went about her work because she took her job with the Australian Army Women's Medical Service at Prince of Wales Repatriation Hospital very seriously. She couldn't know her patients' experiences of the war, but she knew something of their pain, there on the orthopaedic ward. She flirted mercilessly, as required. She tried to make them feel good to be nearly home, to feel that things as they were had become manageable.

She began there in the January of 1943, after completion of her degree and the postgraduate diploma in physiotherapy – all of which she sailed through while helping and learning further at Aurora, as well as volunteering with the Red Cross. Hugo had said, 'But a few more years and you would be a doctor.' And she'd replied, 'There are hundreds of doctors. What I want to do is needed now.' And it was. There weren't enough physiotherapists to go around.

Hugo himself had found it hard on the heart watching the casualties from New Guinea begin to come home: terrible wounds and terrible destruction of flesh and bone by tropical infections, the likes of which he'd never seen before. Renowned as a surgeon who never amputated, he was forced to recommend it now; nine times in all, personally, and he was sick each time, sick with his own failure, and sick with the disgrace it was that an otherwise perfect young man should be crippled in this way. He was far, far too old for war. 'Not near as bad as the last one,' he was often told, and that made him sick, too. The powers that had locked him up back then, needed his expertise this time around, with the Japanese threatening to invade – quite literally, submarines sneaking into the harbour, a few shells landing a bit too close to home at Rose Bay, Woollahra, Bellevue Hill – not that he'd ever have refused to offer his assistance anyway. He'd first been called in to a case at the Prince of Wales Repat in mid-1942 and, after that experience, had thought he'd cure Lucy of her idealism by encouraging her to enlist with the Army Medical Service as soon as she could – he thought he'd have her running back to university. No, she didn't do that. She found her calling as soon as she walked through the doors of that ward.

He had her observe surgery as often as was practicable, whenever he was demonstrating a particular reconstructive technique for the army doctors, but that only seemed to reinforce her hesitance. She told him: 'I'll be a doctor on condition that I'm allowed to do what you do with hammer and chisel – and shout at registrars. You know I'm not interested in any other medicine.' He insisted: 'But surgery is changing, moving ahead all the time. We won't be glorified carpenters forever. I want to see you shout at a registrar one day.' She shrugged: 'Maybe.'

And then she met that lowlife thoracic prick, what was his name? Whitbourne. Captain Ken Whitbourne. Forgettable in every way except that he pushed her right off her track. He'd get in her ear, a worm in her heart, asking her in front of her colleagues why she observed surgery when it was a waste of time for her to do so, telling her she was too pretty, telling her to be careful she wasn't a distraction to the men doing more important work. He was thirty-five, too old for her. The irony that some might have said that about Hugo himself and Jo once upon a time was not lost on him, but this was different. Whitbourne didn't love her – he just knew how to make her jump.

He'd lusted after her, wanted to bed her, and she was so vulnerable, so thrilled to be working at her first real hospital job, she bought the swaggering fantasy he was offering; she believed she meant something to him. When Whitbourne snapped his fingers at her once in front of Hugo, he had a word with the chief medical officer there, and suggested the fellow had such a quick hand he should be sent overseas. He was. Never saw the prick again. Whitbourne had wanted to tame the way she had with men, be her only one. No-one could ever do that. No-one ever should.

Lucy was devoted to the men who mattered, those men she treated, each one having his loneliness and fear lifted a little by her compassion, having his body made a little more ready to meet the future. She saw through their anger and sadness; she saw that dazed look of long and complex shock on their faces when they arrived, and spoke instinctively in that language. Hugo was sure she treated them all with such care because she'd been unable to 'help her father, to rescue him, and he worried for her in this respect. But he needn't have been too concerned.

When faced with the most wretched of losses, having found a young fellow had hanged himself in the shower block at the Repat, she turned up on the doorstep at Darling Point that evening in an agony of self-recrimination: 'I should have paid more attention to him. He seemed fine – he was going to be. It was a dislocated elbow, nothing more. We'd been having a laugh this morning. I didn't see – I didn't see he wasn't all right.'

Hugo didn't sugar coat it: 'You can't see all and be all when you have thirty other patients, but this boy will stay with you forever. If you stick with a medical career, he won't be the last to bring you undone.'

'I know.' She nodded, wiping her eyes: 'His name was Rob, Robert Norton, I won't ever forget him. I'm going to write a letter to his mother and tell her so, once I've collected my thoughts.' She smiled then: 'Thanks, Old Hugh Shoe. Thanks for listening to me rattle on.'

She astounded him. She was a rare and precious thing: a force of kindness in the world.

She'd ask after Claire all the time, too, though it would never go the other way; she'd ask because it was important for Jo, to talk of her daughter in New York: a miscarriage suffered in May 1940; worries over Leon taking up a naval commission after Pearl Harbor – *I'm not certain his Harvard connections will mean much to the Emperor of Japan*, Claire had written. And the more time went on, the more she'd ask in her letters, *How's Papa?* A subtle shift, a softening that meant everything to Jo, even if it would remain that Hugo left all that correspondence up to her.

He knew it was some kind of anomaly, some quirk of the universe, but it seemed natural to him that he should think of Lucy as his daughter as well – not the one he wished he had, but the one he actually had. As a father would, he delighted in having her on his arm, accompanying her to a concert or to the pictures; he delighted in having them mistaken for kin, with her dark hair and her dark eyes. It was Lucy who dashed across the city to him at the war's end, bottle in hand, drinking too much with him on the terrace, dancing badly. He was proud, as a father would be proud, to put her forward for the position that was going at Sydney Hospital, as physio and assistant to the senior ortho registrar there – he'd heard good things about David Oxley, and hoped he'd see Lucy's potential, encourage her to stretch her wings, go on to greater things. It was good timing, too, as the AAWMS had been all but demobilised, and he very much wanted to discourage her from staying with the army permanently, signing up with the newly formed Women's Medical Specialist Corps, as she had been contemplating.

Anton had laughed at the idea of Lucy going to Sydney Hospital: 'That's under Slade, you old fool. What would you send her there for?'

Hugo laughed: 'Slade? Who? Lucy might show him a thing or two.'

'Show him the door.' Anton grunted as they walked along together, on their way to meet Lucy now, at the Lyceum Theatre, off to see whatever film was playing, which on this occasion happened to be *The Man I Love,* starring Ida Lupino and Robert Alda – it was supposed to be terrible but the Gershwins' music would be good.

Through the early evening crowd, she rushed towards them at a clip, running late.

Hugo nudged his stalwart friend. 'Look at that,' he said, like the long-seasoned orthopaedist he was: 'Look at that gait.'

Yes, this war, in its own way, had been more abominable than any other. Tens of millions were dead, among them innocent Jews murdered in numbers Hugo could not bring himself to imagine yet: men, women, children – *children* – six million or one brother, how could it ever make sense? Half of Germany had been flattened, all his places of fond memory had been destroyed, in Berlin, in Dresden; even Hagen had been smashed by the bombs. In a grotesque finale, two cities in Japan had been incinerated by radio-active blasts that would change the face of war forever. And victory, for Hugo, would only ever be celebrated in Lucy's perfect gait.

She looked perfect in every way that evening, cheeks flushed with excitement: 'I've got an interview at Sydney Hospital on Monday.'

'Excellent.' He'd be on the phone to Oxley first thing Monday morning, have a personal word to him. He also wished he could call a good man into her life, one who could meet her mind and her heart, but perhaps she didn't want any man – perhaps she'd seen too much of men.

He gave her a rib-crushing hug there on the street. He would hug her every time he saw her from this moment until the end. He knew he was slowing down; he didn't know for certain he was dying at this stage, but he knew something was wrong. In that embrace he thought: I don't want to say goodbye; never, never; what good does dying do a man? At least the Taxation Department would leave him alone then, he also supposed. What was that harassment all about? Was it because he was Jewish? There was always that suspicion. But he didn't know *anyone* who'd been subject to the scrutiny he had: *yearly* audits. He wondered if the department had a special office just for his accounts. He didn't care about that anymore, really, either. They never found a problem, no discrepancy larger than a few shillings. Marjorie Benson oversaw the entire shop – they were *never* going to find anything amiss.

Who could care about such triviality in any case? The door of the café they stood outside swung open and closed like a valve on the music of here and now: a band playing out the back, soft snare brushing the flicker of streetlights and a woman singing something wonderful he didn't know. It was Saturday night.

He grasped Lucy by her shoulders and kissed her on the cheek. He felt for this exquisite moment he truly held the future in his hands, a light and humming, restless force of peace.

ELIOT SLADE

What comes first, obsession or madness? Chicken or egg? No matter the answer, there's only ever a fine, brittle shell between them.

For twenty years, Slade insisted Aurora House would be found to be a front for some illegal activity. The story changed over time: from suspicions of tax fraud to money laundering, to financing guns for the Stern Gang terrorists in Palestine, and, most recently, for the persecution of good Christians in the newly formed state of Israel. Slade was always just convincing enough, and the Taxation Department just willing enough to believe there might be something in it, to give it another go. It didn't help that the woman in charge, Marjorie Benson, would deliver the paperwork in such deliberate disarray that it would take months for the auditor to get through it. The auditor himself became infected with the desire to find something – anything – to justify all this effort. To no avail.

And yet Slade remained convinced he'd land his knock-out blow if he continued to persist – despite the evidence of all his failures lying in pieces around him. These days, no-one in the medical establishment was listening to his diatribes on Winter's so-called quackery: the man and his outstanding record of results was too broadly known, too quietly respected; the case against him exhausted. It was true that no-one in the establishment particularly *liked* Winter; but no-one liked Slade, either, and for quite different reasons. Winter might have been an upstart from the wrong country and the wrong religion, but at least he'd made a worthy contribution, especially in volunteering his knowledge of limb-saving techniques for the benefit of returned soldiers. Where was Slade's record of service to the nation? Non-existent, and not unnoted. He had claimed loudly that his ever-slim teaching role at the university constituted a valuable passing on of wisdom to those doctors who would be next at the frontlines, but everyone knew that was more bullshit: not much call for last-resort and outdated hip-fusions among an army of battle-fit twenty-year-olds.

Rumours had already begun that Slade had lost his balls for surgery – if ever he'd had them to begin with. He was almost sixty-five now, but while Winter, ten years the elder, still worked a patient load that would overwhelm most younger men, Slade seemed to be doing little more than filling a chair, both at the hospital and as Sydney BMA president, a position he'd now held for an unprecedented thirty years: he dithered more and more, forgot his train of thought on occasion, and generally made less sense than usual. Sounds were being made that he should be delicately moved on, put out to pasture.

The wheels of change would turn slowly, though. Yes, it was 1948, Australia had been brutally blooded by two wars and a devastating depression in between, but a stubborn bloc within the medical establishment seemed not to have moved into the twentieth century at all. These men were so zealous in their efforts to hold back the tides of science, they were presently dismantling the work of the internationally famed orthopaedic therapist Sister Elizabeth Kenny, renowned for her successes with the young victims of polio, liberating them from the strictures of plaster casts and braces and instead rehabilitating their muscles and their movement through intensive massage. Despite all the evidence of *her* success, the BMA sought to sweep the lot of it under the carpet. To them, she was a woman, an unqualified, uneducated bush nurse, and her physical therapies were too expensive to administer. As soon as she'd become unwell herself and unable to fight the bastards any longer, it was announced that her specialist clinics were to be subsumed by the hospital system; the children were to be put back in plaster casts and braces – and their parents were outraged. A full-blown protest of these angry mums and dads had now erupted at Royal North Shore Hospital, but it would fall on deaf ears. The BMA was still a law unto itself.

'The children who suffer for the blustering of men,' Audrey Slade muttered at the report of this North Shore protest, as she sat in her sunroom with the evening paper.

'Ah, there you are.' Eliot appeared in the bedroom doorway behind her, aimless but always accusatory.

She could see his reflection in the window in front of her, overlaid across the dusk-teal harbour, dappled with boats; he was dressed for dinner, evening collar and tie. She could have asked him: why bother? It was Audrey alone he'd be dining with, as usual, and she had no intention of looking at him for any longer than it took to ask him to pass the salt. Their own children no longer dined here unless they had to; everyone else in their respective families had either passed on or had kept well away for years. Catherine, married now and to a decent chap, was careful to only visit with her own daughter, Louisa, during the day, when Eliot wouldn't be here to criticise their marvellous little grandchild for behaving like a two-year-old. Alasdair lived in bachelor's digs at the Empire Hotel, had done for the past seven years, slipping home from the hospital for lunch with his mother once or twice a week.

Working with his father was torment enough: Alasdair was almost thirty-two and so under the thumb it was obscene. When he had wanted to join the Army Medical Service, partly as a chance to get away, Eliot had said no, told him he wouldn't handle the pace. When Alasdair had then suggested he might take a registrar's position in general surgery, to improve his pace in Casualty, Eliot had said no, told him he was needed in orthopaedics at Sydney, twisting his good nature around on him: 'If every pretender wanting to be a hero left his post, what would the rest of society do – mend their own fractures with broomsticks and string?' So Alasdair stayed, and stayed. And Audrey could have slapped her son, if she'd thought that would do anything other than shrink him further. He was too sweet a boy, too decent; he always would be.

She muttered under her breath again at the bitter husk that stood behind her: 'You're terrified your son is the better doctor – and there is the first and only time you'll have ever been right about anything.'

'What did you say?' Her husband stepped into the sun-room, sensing a certain tone.

'Me?' She feigned ignorance. 'Nothing. Should you get your hearing checked?' She shook out the pages of the news-paper as if they had her full attention.

He stepped away; she mouthed at the newsprint swimming before her eyes: 'Shove it up your derrière.'

She'd heard the rumours, too, subtly conveyed through the Auxiliary: 'You won't know yourself when Dr Slade retires,' and, 'Has he set a date yet?' She knew what it meant: that Eliot had had his day – like his father before him, he was losing his marbles, and he'd soon be ushered out. Audrey prayed for that eventuality to speed its way to their door, as she'd prayed every day, all these years, that by some miracle he'd be taken down by a bus crossing Macquarie Street, for only then, with his father gone, would Alasdair finally be able to come into his own. And as soon as her son was altogether free of the professional influence of his father, she would finally follow through with a divorce. She'd let that dirty linen air for all it was worth: all his affairs, all his abuses – the lot. She was a youthful-looking fifty-six years old, still tall, still blonde: she'd make a life of whatever was left of it to live – the life her children had deserved from her all along.

EIGHT

LUCY BRYNNE

'Good to meet you at last, Miss Brynne.' George Zlotkowsky holds out his hand. 'I've heard so much about you, it seems I know you already.'

'Not too well, I hope.' That's supposed to be a joke, of course, but I'm not really joking. The mind-sharpening benefits of a good night's sleep combined with the reality of being too close to my patient have caused me to become so nervous about this morning's surgery I can barely register that a doctor is showing me the courtesy of shaking my hand. George Zlotkowsky is the junior ortho registrar at Royal South Sydney, here to assist Anton at this surprise, sunrise Küntscher nail emplacement; with an anaesthetist from St Luke's and Mrs B as theatre nurse, Jim couldn't be in better hands all round, but the stakes seem even higher than they were yesterday, for my skittering heart at least. What if it doesn't work? What if, once they're in there, they do find a reason for the delay in healing – what if it's a tumour that didn't show up on the x-ray? Shut up. 'Pleased to meet you, too.'

'Are you sure you don't want to join us?' Anton asks me again.

'No, I do not want to join you.'

He laughs at my face.

It's not funny. I look down to my left to say cheerio to Jim and see that my hand, by his shoulder, is grasping the bedsheet. Let it go. I only feel this way because I've never been in this position before; because Jim is most definitely not my patient anymore.

'See you soon.' He smiles at me; he doesn't look worried.

I'm sure he looks pale, but I manage to say, 'Yes. Let's have lunch at noon – don't stand me up.'

I squeeze his hand and leave, before I put him off, take myself away to the reception room to wait, like the loved one I am. It's not going to be a lengthy operation, an hour or so, probably, but within half a second of sitting down, I'm running through all worst-case scenarios. What if he gets an infection? Well, we have penicillin for that these days, don't we? What if he's allergic to penicillin? There's not even a newspaper or magazine here to distract me, with everything but the furniture having been packed up.

Memories clatter in over anxiety: Hugo holding me here on that longest, darkest night, as I told him what had happened to my father, pouring all my sadness into his strong, broad chest. I don't remember what I said, but I do remember that the sofa was a dark green leather then. It had been blue when I was little, when my poor daddy would have sat in this same spot, waiting to see me. It's blue again now, but a lighter shade. Memory plays the strangest games, doesn't it? But fact says I survived four surgeries in this place, and Jim is going to be completely fine, too.

Until the rasping whirr of the bone-drill travels up the stairwell – that'll be Anton testing it. *Reowww. Reowww. Reowww.* In this otherwise silent hospital, it sounds like a cat is being killed. And I'm not hanging about here a second longer.

I walk down around the oval and up along the eastern foreshore of the bay, where wide figs frame the city and, under this lilac-splashed dawn, the bridge looks as though it's been stitched across the horizon, fixing the sky to the earth.

Don't you want to be a doctor? I can feel Hugo holding my small hand as we walk and walk. And for the first time I feel myself give him the straight answer: yes, I do. Of course, I want to be a doctor. What have I got left to be scared of? I've stared down worse than any rejection the establishment might come up with for me – I'll make a better doctor than Eliot Slade, for one. I'll be a doctor not in spite of where I've come from, but because of it. I don't know what sort of doctor I'll be, what sort of patients might be mine, but, yes, it's time. Of course, it's time. Perhaps I'll go in and see about university enrolment next week – because I can. Because I've been unemployed for less than a day and no matter how much money I have in the bank, the idea of being jobless will always be more daunting than any other. I could laugh. But it's not funny, either.

Why would you waste faculty and hospital time? my thoracic heart-basher said to me when I confided in him that I was thinking about furthering my qualifications. *You'll only abandon medicine after five minutes to go and have your babies.* He informed me that, while women often top the class, it's only because they're good at rote learning; women don't have original thoughts, apparently. He also said that the minds of the lower classes are genetically less able to grasp complex ideas. I know that none of that is true, but … it gets absorbed. Like poison.

A gust whips up across the water, gulls play on the warm summer wind, and I look over my shoulder, back towards Aurora, across the empty early-morning park. What if Jim's not keen on being married to a doctor? We haven't discussed anything like that, never mind babies. What if I'm not a good mother? I wouldn't know the first thing about how to be one of them. What if we don't get along in real life? We don't really know each other. What if our marriage is a disaster?

Shut the hell up.

I just about run back to him as if I might get all the answers today.

But only laughter meets me through the doors – Anton's. In the echo, it sounds like Hugo's laughing along, too, and I run down the stairs to them, to see Anton shaking hands with George Zlotkowsky, here in the basement corridor, waving me over: 'Lucy!'

'You're finished?' I ask, stupidly.

'Why wouldn't we be?' He shrugs: 'George needs to get to his proper job by nine.' Don't look at the speckle of blood on the cuff of his gown. He laughs again: 'But seriously, it all went well. The bone is healthy – nothing wrong with it that I can see.'

'All the best, Miss Brynne – I'm sorry I do have to rush.' And off George goes into the day.

Anton is untying his gown, telling me: 'If progress is good, and I expect it will be, in six or maybe eight weeks, get him walking on it, another six weeks, we take the nail and the graft wire out – very easy business – and it's done. Get him out of bed tomorrow, if he's up to it.'

'Wow. I'm jealous.' I truly am. 'That's amazing.'

Anton grins with his own brilliance. 'Yes. It's a big difference. The advantage of this method is that the nail is able to support the bone from within. In ten years, no-one will think twice about doing things this way. Or maybe twenty years for Australia. You know, in New Zealand, they're already starting to bring this technique into public hospitals. *New Zealand.* But here?' Anton rolls his eyes, goes on with his explanation: 'There is one fault with a nail like this, however – it's not attached anywhere *to* the bone, no screws or pins. If he walks on it prematurely, the nail can move, which can cause the fracture to rotate out of alignment, or dislodge the graft, or at worst the nail itself can break inside. So, you make sure this young man of yours is careful and does exactly as he's told. I don't want to have to fix it again – I'm getting too old for this sort of thing.'

Anton Adinov doesn't look old at all – he looks twenty years younger – but I don't hesitate to promise on Jim's behalf: 'He'll do as he's told – of course, he will.'

'No – no chance,' is Jim's first reaction when I suggest he might sit up a little, to try to eat something. 'It's f— no.'

'I know it hurts,' I tell him. 'But the sooner you move, gently, the sooner it'll settle down. It's like when you've grazed your knee, you know, and ...' No, it's nothing like that. It feels like someone has rammed a chisel into your hip, because that is what has happened. Pain can be a bit of a lottery, but this graft-site round for Jim is so acute right now he hasn't even thought about the hammering in his leg. 'Do you want some more morphine?'

'No.' He's so wracked, I want to give him a shot against his will.

I check the dressing again, to make sure it's not bleeding or —

'Don't touch it.'

'I'm not touching it.'

'Come, come.' Mrs B returns with some pillows: she's going to be merciless with him. And with me: *Off you go*, says her glance. I'm not helping, no, because it's hurting me, too.

'I'd better go and call your mum,' I say, breezily as I can. 'She'll be waiting to hear how well it went.'

He looks at me as though I'm insane, but I go up to the office and call her anyway, because good news is its own tonic. 'Yes, Tess,' I squeak it out, 'he's great. The surgeon is very, very pleased.' And she sighs, shifting under her load of motherly worries: 'Oh, Lucy, thank you for calling. I'm so glad. I'm so relieved.'

But I'm not. Resisting the urge to return to him immediately, I go instead to the room next door, the room I'm staying in, and I sit down on the lonely chair by the lonely bed, trying to pretend this whole thing is not insane. That it isn't me who's hurt him. He's not my patient, and yet he is going to be when we leave here – how am I going to look after him? I'm going to look after him excellently well, because I am a professional. But as his wife? Deep breath, and another, and another. It's only that his pain has upset me: and that's normal. Absolutely unremarkable. Let time slip; not as though I haven't had to do that before within these walls. Watch a tiny spider crawling up into the cornice. Mrs B has put the wireless on for the mid-afternoon music hour: Mendelssohn's Violin Concerto in E minor. Hypnotic. Replenishing.

When it finishes, I'm ready to return to him, and I find he's sitting up, tapping the side of the mattress with that rhythm of his own; as though he's been watching the door, he says: 'Sorry about that.'

'Don't be sorry. How's it feeling now?'

'Fine.' It's not, but near enough. 'Pride's a lot sorer. Again.'

'Don't even think about it.' I tap my heart: 'I hold hundreds of state secrets in here – tears, tantrums, unchained profanity. Your effort hardly even rates.'

He grunts at himself; then he says: 'Why don't you go and stay at the house, at Maroubra – at home. It's your home now. You don't need to be here all the time. It's been suggested to me that a nurse can be called in for the evenings, and probably should be. Why don't you go and have a rest. Please.'

I shake my head with my own secret: 'I don't want to be in real life without you, not yet.' Not alone, not to stay overnight by myself; I'm too pathetically scared of that. 'Anyway, I don't want to miss being with you when you get out of bed tomorrow morning.'

He shakes his head: 'That's not happening.'

Yes, it is.

Mrs B comes in with a pair of crutches: 'I've made plans for the weekend. I need you out of here by Friday.' She's only teasing but she really has made plans: she and her friend, Mrs McLaren, Phyllis, are going birdwatching in the Mountains; they've been best friends forever, even live in the same block of flats. Regardless, Jim will be getting out of bed – approximately now.

He frowns down at the plate of fried eggs he's just demolished as if this might have been his last meal. Could well be. He won't be getting anything like that from me at home. I can't cook – there's another dreadful secret. I might have packed a lot of eggs when I was a kid, but I couldn't afford to buy any, too worried I'd break them the wrong way and waste money we didn't have. But I can get a man out of bed.

Mrs B hands me the crutches: 'You're the expert, Miss Brynne.' She knows this is my favourite part: there's nothing more wonderful than seeing someone you've looked after stand up for the first time, no matter who they are – it's like meeting that person all over again – but this time I might be a tiny bit more excited than usual.

Jim says: 'Lucy, I don't know, maybe later —'

'I won't be able to get you to sit back down in a minute,' I promise him. 'Before we go anywhere, though, there are a couple of rules. Rule one, you're not to put any weight on your left leg. Not at all, none. Don't even rest on it. Rule two, you won't be travelling far – to the bathroom and back, as necessary. That's it. At all other times it's bed or chair until further notice, no arguments, no cheating.' I help him move around so that he's sitting on the edge of the bed. 'Ready?'

'No.' He's looking at his knees: one he doesn't yet trust and the other that's flexed at thirty degrees of heavy and useless; a hip above that probably feels like it's going to split if he tries this, but it won't: Anton's incision is barely an inch long: he's that brilliant.

'You can do this,' I promise Jim. 'As I'm sure you've done it before. Take all the weight in your shoulders – there's nothing wrong with them. Right hand, crutches, left hand, bed, and then haul up. If you feel off balance, or the pain is too much, lean towards me and I'll sit you back down.'

Of course, he does it without any trouble, and here he is, on the vertical, the slightly surprised smile on his face reminding me why I love this work so very much. I can't ever not do this work. But this job here … James Julian Cleary. My hand is still on his chest, a token of assurance, and I'm looking up at him for the first time. I know he's six-two – I've seen that written on half a dozen forms – but they're just numbers, meaningless measures, replaced by the word: 'Wow.'

He laughs: 'Hello, shortie.'

'First and last time you ever say that,' I warn him, and don't kiss him or I might not stop there. I tell him: 'That's enough. You can sit back down again now.'

'I'm all right,' he says, pleased with himself – so predictable, you could set your watch by it.

'No. Really.' A sterner warning: for the time being, this actually is my job. 'Sit back down. Don't overdo it.'

'Be careful of your foot on the steps,' I say, following him up to the house, pack-muling his bag and dragging wheelchair backwards, waving Anton off into the dusk.

'I'm not going to hit my foot on a step,' he says.

'A reminder never hurts.' There are nine steps altogether, six to go, up to the front patio.

'I don't need a reminder every five minutes, Lucy – don't do this, don't do that.'

I'm not going to have a spat with you on the threshold of real life. 'I only want things to work out well for you.' For us.

'Yeah, well, I know it can be difficult at times to tell, but I'm not a child.'

'I know you're not a child – I'm not treating you like a child.'

'Yes, you are – every time you tell me not to hit my foot, not to hit my knee, not to walk too fast, watching me all the time. You need to get another job.'

Ouch. Perhaps a watch could have been set by this, too. I know he's tired, and it's steaming hot, and going upstairs on crutches is unpleasant enough without being harassed, but I'm stung. Yes, I've replaced professional and competent with overbearing and neurotic faster than his quadriceps is putting on muscle, and he's had enough of me. Already. Disaster.

I don't reply; I'm juggling keys and bag and Jim and chair through the door when a crowd erupts inside:

'Surprise!'

Faces everywhere, half of them I don't know; Tess is holding mine in her hands: 'Welcome home.'

The dog – Mate – crashes straight into his leg in the hall; Jim doesn't flinch. It's fine. Two steps later, he almost trips on my suitcase and box of Hugo that I left here, in the way, yesterday, because I didn't know where else to put them. And that's fine, too. There is music playing on the radiogram, a saxophone swing, a martini is pressed into my hand, as Mrs Nichol's children run in and out from the back yard. A glass smashes in the kitchen: laughing, laughing.

I don't ask Jim to sit down, as he's doing it all on his own; ask him instead: 'Is this a quiet Friday night at home?'

'On occasion.' He laughs, at home: 'Except Mum and Aunt Betty aren't usually here.'

This is the party I want to be inside.

'When can you play, Jimmy?'

'Not tonight.'

They play without him; this little house jumps to the sound, a double-bass throbbing under my toes; three girls sing 'Don't Sit Under the Apple Tree' and they're so good I think it's a record on the radiogram.

Aunt Betty says: 'You young people, you're all too much for me.' As Rory grabs her for another dance.

This is real life. I'm so happy.

And hours and hours later, when everyone's gone home, somewhere near midnight, with the surf pounding into the rocks below, he says: 'Don't clean up. Come to bed.'

I had had vague notions of waiting until we were married, as if that might truly remake my own innocence; I had certainly thought it would be best to wait until those couple of stitches in his hip were snipped out next week. No: we're not waiting. To kiss him fully at last, to kiss him with my whole body, remakes me as something else altogether: a wild, bright pulse; a new form of energy, a new ray; a warm current moving through the cooling air.

And, afterwards, in his arms, another craving is fulfilled: I am safe here.

He holds me tight and kisses the top of my head: 'I'm sorry I snapped at you, earlier on. That won't happen again.'

'Bet it does.' I can feel the faint ridge of his splenectomy scar under my hand; all the things we've each endured: maybe our madnesses fit together as our bodies do. 'Bet I nag you, too.'

'Well, I won't mind,' he says. 'It's not too bad being cared for by you. I just had the shits this afternoon – my problem, not yours.'

'You're allowed to have the shits.' Amazing that he hasn't had more of them; but more amazing that he apologises for it. I don't think too many men take responsibility for themselves in this way, and I'm thrilled all over again that it seems I've got one that does.

We listen to the surf for a while before he tells me: 'I'm going back to work Monday week, the seventeenth.'

What? 'At risk of instant nagging, that's not a wise idea, Jim.' Returning to work is at least five weeks away, and only if Anton is happy with the x-ray.

'I'm not going to do much,' he says, with a reassuring squeeze, 'but I have to be there. Rory might be the best mechanic I know but he's hopeless with organisation – the accounts, the scheduling of jobs, pretty much instructions of any kind. He's teed up a meeting for that day, too, with a bloke from a dairy company, who wants to talk about his fleet of sixteen refrigerator lorries. Fascinating stuff, but I'm not letting Rory handle any client negotiations without adult guidance – he'll get too keen, cut the price because he hasn't worked on refrigerator lorries before. I've got to make sure there's a business for me to return to when I can do the work again. It's important, to me.'

'How are you going to get there and back?' I sound like he's suggested a trek across Antarctica.

'Rory will pick me up and bring me home.'

'Oh.' Of course; and there's a strange, cartwheeling blow. 'Goodo.'

'What are you going to do?' He kisses the top of my head again.

I want to tell him: darling, I'm going to re-enrol at university, in medicine. But I can't get the words out. Why? What on earth am I afraid of? That he'll say no? As if that is at all likely.

I mumble into his shoulder: 'I'll look for another job, I suppose.'

'You mean you're not going to keep house for me?' He grabs one whole cheek of my arse in his large, long-fingered hand: 'You're not going to keep yourself barefoot and pregnant for me?'

'Probably not.' It's enough to admit this at least, one small truth at a time: 'While I could go and invest in a cookbook or two, I think I'll be popping up to the chemist in the morning for a contraceptive diaphragm as a first priority.'

'Good idea.' He starts kissing my neck again, and wonderful doesn't begin to describe it.

Sex should be a recognised therapy in its own right. It's almost all we do for the rest of this first weekend alone together, and it's a revelation. I had no idea that a man could be so intent on my pleasure; but then, I've never had a man make love to me, have I. What's he going to be like when he doesn't have a broken leg to hold him back? As it is, I've never found it such a challenge to get out of bed.

But I have to, on Sunday morning, when Tess comes around to discuss wedding plans before she returns to Canowindra. My eyes are so glazed as I answer the door, I'm sure I must look drunk.

'Lucy dear ...' She smiles so approvingly into my love-drunkenness, I giggle, and she does, too. She cranes her head around the bedroom door and says to Jim: 'Please don't get up – I haven't come to talk to you.'

'What a shame,' he says, rolling over to go back to sleep; Mate thumps his tail from his mat on the floor beside him, not getting up, either.

I haven't got the kettle on before Tess says to me: 'I hope you don't mind, but I've already spoken to our reverend at home, at St Paul's, and suggested July the ninth, as it falls exactly between your birthdays, yours being on June the twenty-fifth, and Jim's on the twenty-second of July. I thought it might be nice that you'd then have a whole celebration month, every year, just for the two of you to share. Do you like that idea?'

For a moment I can't see to light the stove. 'That's the loveliest thing I've ever heard of.' I find a smile for her as I turn away to stare at the tea caddy, emotions whirling too fast for me to grab any one of them.

'I'm glad you think so.' She sits down at the kitchen table: 'I didn't want to be presumptuous. Now, you know this family you're marrying into is more for the spirit of things than any gospel or creed, but just to be sure, you wouldn't find issue with the Presbyterian Church of Ireland, would you?'

I think she's asking me if I'm Catholic, and a laugh flies out at the thought: 'No. My birth certificate says I'm Methodist.' So said my parents, whose lives taught me long ago that faith isn't much chop at delivering anything; and my only other influence has been Hugo, whose Judaism existed in his service to others, his work, not words or ceremony. 'All in all, I'm not religious.'

'Ah, good.' Tess sighs, hand to heart. 'Well, that's that out of the road, sectarian conflict avoided.' She's funny, in her quiet, ladylike way; I'm spooning tea into pot as she goes on: 'There is one other more amusing detail you might want to consider. It's become something of a Cleary tradition to go a little overboard with the music at our weddings – pipes and drums and all sorts of Ulster Scots racketing. It all started when I married John. I was alone, you see, just a girl of nineteen – I'd come out from Derry as a schoolteacher, as there was a shortage here and there wasn't much going on at home. I'd wanted a bit of adventure, but I got more than I'd bargained for, ending up at this little school in Eugowra, thinking I'd gone to the other side of the moon. Then, a handful of lonely Sundays later, I met this fellow called John Cleary at a church fete, and where was his mother from? Derry. I fell madly in love with him before I'd finished my cup of tea, but I was terribly homesick at the same time, so all his family made a big fuss of me, especially with the music, knowing how I love it. It's a fuss that seems to get bigger with every celebration these days. But if you don't like the sound of all that, we'll tone it down. We'll have whatever music you'd prefer.'

I look at Tess Cleary, her pearls and all her trim neatness, and try to imagine her as a girl crossing the world before the wars: what a leap of faith that must have been. What courage. You really can't pick people, can you? I tell her: 'I want every kind of celebration and music you want. Thank you.'

'No. Thank *you*, Lucy.' She tells me: 'You've brought the light back into Jimmy's eyes. You've brought my boy home.' But she's not one to rest on sentiment; she narrows her pretty deep blues and adds: 'If he ever gives you a moment of trouble, you come and talk to me.'

Must be the frisky mood I'm in, but I can't help thinking trouble with Jimmy sounds like it could be quite a ride.

Monday brings a wistful shift. It's the tenth of January, time to say goodbye to Jo, before she leaves on her journey to New

York. I don't want to say goodbye, but I can't not go to her farewell morning tea – my last opportunity to see her for who knows how long?

'You all right, Lucy?' Jim asks as I'm getting ready, pinning up my hair.

'Yeah.' But no. I can hardly say goodbye to him as I leave for the tram into town.

The city shimmers through a humid, gritty glare, over-heated business suits and shoppers scurrying everywhere, but it's all slow-cello sophistication inside the Moorish Lounge of the Australia Hotel, Sydney's premier den of wealth and privilege. Must be a hundred and fifty or two hundred people here, and I can't see Jo anywhere at first, nor Anton. I feel instantly out of place, always do with this crowd of mostly medical specialists and socialites, always feel like that little scrap of nothing off the street; and so I do what I always do in these circumstances: loiter aimlessly, like a little scrap of nothing off the street.

A tall, blonde woman smiles at me, over the rim of her teacup; she seems solo, too, half-hiding behind the fronds of a potted palm, and somehow familiar; I smile back a hello, although I'm sure I don't know her; just another effortlessly elegant woman twice my age, making me feel about as lovely as a stubbed toe. I'm wearing my most chic blouse: perennially fashionable harlequin pattern of navy and gold, but it's three years old and has faint sweat stains under the arms. I really should invest in some clothes, a new frock or several. Jim owns thirty-seven ties: there's a discrepancy.

And now I see Jo.

Oh, this one is hard; I see in her eyes that it's hard for her as well.

I dash to her, and promise: 'I won't stay. Only wanted to give you a quick hug and my new address.' I hand her the piece of notepaper I've scribbled it on. 'Can't wait to find out the flavour of Claire's baby.'

'New address?' Jo asks me inside this embrace.

'Long story,' I say. 'I'll write and tell you all about it. It's a good story, too.'

'Oh good.' She smiles and makes one of her funny faces, pretending she'll be shocked by whatever it is. 'Oh dear,' she says, 'I never thought I'd see this day. I never thought I'd leave Sydney. How strange and long all our stories are.'

And that's about as much as I can cope with. Jo's never been my mother, we've never been close in the way Hugo and I were, but Jo was the one who looked after me in ways no-one but a woman could: she helped me when my first period came, helped me choose underwear, took me into town to choose party frocks as required, bought me jars of Venetian Healing Cream for my teenage pimples; she made me feel pretty when I wasn't – when I was the scrappy little crippled girl at school, and the even scrappier mess stuck in bed. She made me feel better, simply by her grace.

'I'd better go.'

She nods; her eyes are full, too. She says: 'Please, yes – please write.'

'I will.' And I will.

But for now, I nearly run from the hotel, back to the tram, back to Maroubra: home. The sandy footpath under my sandals: home. The sea is a misty sheet feeding clouds along the horizon; two surfers sit out there on their long boards behind the breakers, waiting to take a wave; I want to go for a swim, but I wouldn't do anything so cruel to Jim. I buy two random vanilla slices from the bakery instead, to take home to him, to share. Yes: this really is home.

But when I get there, on the front stairs, I think this surge of grief and the shrieking of the gulls are playing tricks: I think I can hear a clarinet winding through the ocean breeze. It's not Hugo's; it's someone who can play: a lyrical riff; liquid – jazz.

It's not a trick, though, I see when I get in: it's Jim, sitting in the lounge room, out of bed, dressed, in the chair, holding a clarinet: 'Hello.'

'Were you just playing that clarinet?'

'Yes.' He looks like I've caught him at a secret and not very seemly habit; Mate looks at me, too, from the floor, head on his paws, a thwack of the tail on timber, assuring that nothing is wrong with this picture. Jim says: 'You weren't very long.'

'I didn't know you played the clarinet,' I say.

'I don't often,' he replies: 'I was just, um. Thought I'd get up and do something … achievable …'

'How …?' I'm not sure what I mean to ask. What greater force of love, or mystery, puts us together here? Right *here*. You and me; a dog; a clarinet. Some pattern of time and space and matter I can't quite see.

He bites his lip, smiles his embarrassed smile: 'Mum – she insisted we all learned an instrument through school.' He taps at the keys: 'Goes with Julian. Better than bagpipes.'

'That's hilarious.' I begin to laugh but I'm caught in such a storm of gratitude, I let go of everything else at once. Every last tether, every last rope of sadness, shame and fear, and every tear I've held inside – years and years of them. It all snaps free.

'Lucy – what's happened? Was it a tough goodbye?'

These aren't goodbye tears.

'Come here, please,' he says, hauling himself from chair to sofa.

'Oh …' I sit down beside him, and let him hold me as I cry, and cry.

JIM CLEARY

'Please, Lucy, tell me – what's happened?' I ask her again, and I'm thinking the worst: she's having second thoughts: she doesn't love me anymore. She's never outright said she does love me, has she? She's never said, I love you, Jim. She's crying so hard, I might be crying a bit, too. 'Please, tell me, what's wrong.'

'I'm all right,' she says, but she sounds a long way from it. 'My mind just gets so full of every wrong thing, and now it's all coming out.'

'What do you mean?' I'm thinking, here it comes for me. She's going to break it off. Because it would happen today: I'm having a shithouse day today. I woke up thinking I could smell sauerkraut, not knowing where I was except inside a nightmare where I can't move my leg, and that hasn't happened for weeks.

'I mean stupid things,' she says. 'Like I'm not worth anything. I've always felt I'm not worth anything, but I've even been worried about telling you I want to go back to university, that I want to be a doctor, avoiding it, hiding it, because deep inside me, I don't think I'm worth it.'

Jesus. How wrong is that? I tell her: 'I'll always want you to be what you want to be – I couldn't be happier you want to be a doctor. You're worth everything to me, and you know well enough I can think some stupid things, too – up until a minute ago, I was thinking you were going to say you didn't want to get married.'

She looks up at me as though I'm the one with the more serious mental issues, then she tucks her head back under my chin.

I hold her closer. I wish I knew all the shapes and extents of why she would think she was worthless: I know she's an orphan; I know she hasn't always had an easy go; I know she pushes herself to punishing lengths to do the right thing – it's exhausting to watch sometimes. But she doesn't give much away, only ever says as much as she wants to say.

She's stopped crying, but I keep holding her, with everything I keep from her, too, such as the fact that I'm counting the diamonds printed on the fabric of her blouse right now to calm myself down. The portion of her blouse that I can see, along the side of her back has twenty-four total full diamonds, eleven blue, thirteen yellow; eighteen partially obscured diamonds, seven blue, eleven yellow. No-one needs to know I do this sort of thing.

Counting, all the time: in music, running, dancing, engines. Counting the number of strokes it took for Lucy to brush her hair this morning; the number of pins she used. Keeping a completely worthless tally of my own blood pressure statistics. Arithmetic, geometry, mechanics, the simple logic of numbers: it all keeps my crap contained. Whatever works. Counting the waves in the sound or the sight of the surf, making me aware I'm here, home, alive. Flying over the southeast coastline of England, especially in the dawn, I'd be that euphoric we'd made it, it was a drug all its own, early on. No-one will ever know the quantities of real drugs I consumed, the amphetamines we were given: you're told by an RAF doctor to take a pill at this time and that time, and you take it. Most blokes just got keyed up and more focussed with it; some got aggressive; one or two got the shakes so badly they had to be pulled out of their crews; it got me counting – counting and constantly terrified. I don't smoke because somewhere I still think I'm carrying thirteen tons in explosives and fuel. How people take benzedrine for fun these days, I'll never know, but they do: up at the Cross of an evening it's everywhere. I've never needed assistance to party all night.

That drug was a little piece of evil for me: every operation, it'd come on right when I'd be making my final check through of the plane. It'd have me obsessively calculating loss-rate statistics, counting the number of sorties I'd been on and working out what percentage of dead I already was based on the personal log in my head, not only of combat casualties but accidents in training, parachute failure, engine failure, instrument failure, suspected pilot error, inexplicable fuckups, all of it: Easter 1942, I was 26.5 percent dead; 1943, 51.9 percent dead; 1944, 77.5 percent dead. In the end, I was 105.7 percent dead – that's how lucky I was, in a squadron that was entirely wiped out more than four times over the three years I was with them. I don't know what the official statistics were – I don't want to know – and no-one needs to know the ones I worked out for myself. Especially not Dad. *It'll be safer up there, son.* A conversation that will never be had.

Some truths can never be told, no matter how much they need to be. Like the one about the inexplicable fuckup that brought down my plane. Our pilot, let's call him Jack, was having a harder time than me, which was mostly why I couldn't bring myself to leave the crew after Dresden. He was twitchy, hiding it in his clenched fists, and practically non-verbal except for the essentials; he was also English – Australian but Cambridge Aero Club more English than the English – and wouldn't have bailed out if he was on fire. He was a good bloke, but not one who could have admitted to that kind of shame. No matter what drugs you give a man, you can't have him risk his life for the mass destruction of civilians and expect there'll be no dire consequence. There was nothing wrong with the plane – I was too unscrewed meticulous for there to be anything wrong with those engines, and if there ever was a problem, I would report it to the squadron leader because I never trusted any pilot to pay attention to any concern I might have. Jack was the type to ignore me, the type who'd say, 'Don't panic, Nanna,' at anything, so as not to let the side down. He was a risk-taker, a bit full of himself, and then he was suddenly white-knuckled and quiet. He took that plane down himself, I know he did. I'll never know if it was guilt or the drug or wanting to die on his own terms, or all three that made him do it, but it's the only reasonable explanation.

One I couldn't report, not even to Rory very quietly. I couldn't do that to Jack's family: I do believe your son wilfully murdered himself and his crew. Because he didn't do it wilfully. I don't know if I really heard it or dreamt it afterwards, but somewhere I'm sure he said, 'Sorry chaps,' on the way down; his voice so clear through the earphones, I can hear it now. I can't begin to think what state he must have been in to take that action, make that choice. I had to say I didn't remember anything, but that wasn't difficult to believe, considering for quite a while I couldn't remember much anyway, except the taste of endless sauerkraut and my own disbelief that the German standing over me was a doctor, and he didn't want to kill me; Schneider, he'd said he was called, but it was a false name, so the Red Cross told me later – he'd been worried about consequences, too. There were no consequences for me officially; except for my conscience: I should never have left the cockpit; I should never have got up to take that piss.

I'd been so keen on my chances at the start, putting on that uniform for the first time – it was a good-looking uniform, too – I can see myself straightening that dark blue tie, smiling at myself, like a permanent studio photograph in my mind called 'Portrait of a Young Man with No Idea'. I can see it in precise detail: I had a shaving graze on the left side of my chin – too keen – I brushed some lint from my sleeve, checked the angle of my cap was just right, before I stepped onto the parade ground. I'm still working out what happened after that; I'll always be trying to make sense of what happened after that.

But if it hadn't happened, if I hadn't done any of it, there's no chance I would be here with Lucy Brynne in my arms, and not counting anything but the diamonds on her blouse as I hold her because I love her like I'll never get to the end of that, either. I want to help her make possible whatever it is she wants to do, so I can be part of putting something good in the world. She's the best person I've ever met.

'Right then, unscheduled sobbing under control.' She wipes her nose, kisses my cheek, stands up, and swipes a paper bag from the coffee table. 'I got some vanilla slice at the bakery. Do you want a piece?'

Not really; I'm fat enough from lying about, but: 'Yeah. Why not.'

She frowns over her shoulder at me as she goes: 'Your foot shouldn't be on the floor like that – put it up on the sofa or get back in the chair.' Mate follows her out: he doesn't mind vanilla slice; he's fat, too.

I count her footsteps up the hall just because they're hers: 'I can't wait to take you dancing, Lucinda Jane.'

'Ha!' she calls back: 'Another secret to divulge – I can't dance to save myself.'

'You're going to have to,' I tell her: 'It's a condition of this marriage.'

HUGO WINTER

He bought a generous wedge of Emmenthal cheese and some black olives from the delicatessen on Bayswater Road on his way home; he stopped at the pub next for a bottle of merlot.

Jo was at a vase of flowers in the lounge when she heard his key in the door.

He said: 'You are the most beautiful woman to ever walk the earth.'

'Oh, you.' She batted away his exaggeration.

She took the bottle from him: 'Now or later?'

'Now,' he said, opening the lid of the radiogram, reaching for a favourite waltz – 'It's Time to Say Goodnight'.

She returned with glasses and platter, and he said: 'Dance with me.'

She did; she loved the evening roughness of his cheek against hers. 'What's brought this on, my darling?' she asked him, not that it was entirely unusual for Hugo to do this sort of thing. It had been a while, though; he'd been tired lately – not that she dared mention the 'r' word: retirement.

'I have to go back to the hospital tonight,' he said. 'I'm worried about our footballer's knee. He's in too much pain from the surgery, I think, but then, you know what men are like – babies. It's probably nothing, but I have to check on him.'

'Do you?' Jo was a little annoyed.

'Yes,' he said. 'But not for a few hours. Let's have that glass of wine.'

They did; they sat stretched out on the sofa and they enjoyed that wine and that cheese and those olives. They talked about all sorts and nothing much, and he slipped into the conversation, as he often did anyway, mention of Lucy: 'Perhaps we should give her the money now.'

Jo nodded but said: 'She's only really just started at Sydney. Perhaps let her find her feet there first – you know how independent she is.' Jo's face was made of affection and concern: 'Or how independent she'd *like* to be. There'll be a right time.'

'You'll know the right time.' He smiled: 'You always do.' He kissed her then: 'Don't stay up – there's some correspondence I need to attend to, and I might lose track of time.'

'All right, darling.' She'd already turned away to pick up their glasses.

He walked back to Aurora, rather than taking the car. There was nothing else left for him to do. He'd written to Claire, a few days ago, telling her how much he was looking forward to becoming a grandfather; a difficult letter to write, for many reasons. He'd written one last time to Ernst, too, via the Red Cross, just in case, though he knew the truth: that while two of his brothers had died for the Reich, one had been killed because of it: that mindless bigotry and its violence would know no end.

He reflected again on the use he'd made of his own life; threads of anger and regret at his dying spun through all his thoughts but not significantly. He'd done his best with what he had. Medically, the thorns were few: he still carried the guilt at what he'd put Lucy through – but the result, well, the result was so good. Other than that, he would have liked to have provided some orthopaedic care for Aboriginal children who'd been put in state homes, but his offers had been rebuffed by the authorities; he should have persisted; he guessed those kids must have been subject to an internment of sorts, but he'd run out of time and energy to press the point. What had he achieved as a doctor? He'd improved the physical capabilities of too many to count; he'd made children smile – and, yes, dance. As a man? He'd taken care of those in need wherever he could and changed their circumstances for the better: most recently, the refugees he and Jo had welcomed into Sydney, into the Jewish community here, into sunshine and safety. He'd felt more joy than sadness on balance across all the years. Far, far more joy. He was loved – by Lucy, by Anton, maybe by a few more. Most of all, he had been loved by Jo. And he was not going to die beside her in the bed. He would spare her that.

The night matron, Janet Taylor, waved from the office as she saw him pass by on his way up the stairs.

He sat down in his chair and looked out at the twinkling city lights on the harbour: a starless indigo sky; the branch of a leafy fig swaying as if it breathed. He opened the top drawer of his desk and took out an envelope he'd placed there some weeks ago now, waiting for this time; it contained one dozen medinal tablets, the ordinary but potent tranquilisers given to patients struggling with their nerves. Yes, it was the right time.

He poured a glass of water from the brass jug he'd kept on his desk here since 1921. It was the same age as Lucy. He smiled. He tipped the tablets into his hand, into his mouth, and washed them down.

His failing heart wouldn't survive the overdose of sodium diethylbarbiturate; his body would show only that his heart had stopped, that he'd succumbed to previously diagnosed coronary disease. Anton would confirm it, and Jo would never know of his suicide. She'd click her tongue, unsurprised he'd kept his heart problem from her, and Anton would hold her hand through it all. She might wonder over the years to come at the coincidences; she might suspect he'd have been that careful in his planning; but she would understand.

He closed his eyes, rested his head upon his arm, upon the desk.

Of all people, Jo would understand.

Such was their love.

There was a taste of salt; of almonds.

Irma ran ahead of him up the hall.

And he was gone.

ELIOT SLADE

From the moment Alasdair realised his father was going to take over the case of that difficult spiral fracture himself, he had to do what he could to see that as little harm as possible was done. There wasn't much he could do in that regard to begin with, except offer to emplace the Steinmann pin and wire the break under his father's 'supervision'. The theatre sister and the anaesthetist each breathed a sigh of relief when the senior Slade agreed, but that was as far as any protest went.

The BMA might have been losing faith, too, but the power Eliot Slade still wielded inside that hospital was more than considerable. The board remained behind him; there was no-one for Alasdair to turn to, no-one he could have that quiet chat with, to say his father must be stopped – completely. Even David Oxley had given way to Slade the Greater, in the beginning, too fearful of losing his job and damaging his career to argue any further. Alasdair was merely the Lesser, the joke, and in so many ways. His own father had undermined him assiduously, too, letting it be known his son was weak willed, never correcting any insinuation that Alasdair was not on staff by his own merit.

But then two things happened to force Alasdair's hand at last.

The first was realising Jim Cleary wasn't any old chap, not just the fellow Lucy Brynne had decided was the more attractive lunch companion. It had been fifteen years since Alasdair had last seen him, but they'd attended the same school. Alasdair was three years older; James, as he was known on the roll then, had been a boarder, out at Randwick; and as Alasdair had been a day boy, their circles hadn't much crossed. At fourteen, James Cleary had been blonder, his blazer hung off him like it was still on its hanger, and Alasdair hadn't recognised him all these years on – not until he saw Rory Scott in the room with him a few days before Christmas. That character, Scott, was unmistakeable – lanky, loose-limbed, unwaveringly cheerful. At school, Scott and Cleary had been a somewhat notorious pair: painting the form master's chair with glue; hiding the band conductor's sheet music; getting caned regularly. Cleary, he now recalled, had been conspicuously gifted in every field; he was from an established farming family, and known through the old boy's network for distinguished RAAF service. When Alasdair put all the connections together, he saw that this wouldn't go well for the hospital, and not for himself or his father, either, if the Clearys were given cause to be unhappy with the standard of care and treatment.

The second and far more serious matter that changed all courses was Oxley's sudden suspension almost two weeks later. That was the point at which Alasdair realised his father was perverted enough to mistreat a patient in order to score against the better man. He went looking for his father, to finally demand an end to this game – but of course, at that moment, he was in with Jim Cleary, informing him that the better option was amputation.

'What made you say that to him?' Alasdair challenged his father, for the first time ever, there in his office in the Central Admin building, after Jim had left the hospital with Lucy. Professionally appalled and personally ashamed, Alasdair had done all he could to make sure they'd got away without any trouble – not against any law to decide to change your doctor, and thank God they did.

'It was my considered medical opinion,' Slade the father spat the words at his son. 'And it remains my considered medical opinion.' In truth, Eliot Slade was furious and humiliated that the bone was not healing, but he would never admit this to a soul – he couldn't. It was beyond the capabilities of his character to admit to any mistake. He raised his voice: 'Do you know how much those orthopaedic nails cost? Twenty-five shillings each, for a tibia – and they don't work. Read the literature, if you can.'

'I have read the literature,' Alasdair told his father. 'The nails require careful management for the first month or so – but they work. What are you afraid of?' He said the words that no-one else had dared to say: 'You're worried that one day we'll all work out you're a hack? A has-been that never was? That day came a long time ago. You might have the backing to stay propped up here, but you don't have the skills. You've never had any interest in developing them. You're a danger to any patient with the misfortune of calling you doctor.'

'Get out of my sight.' Eliot Slade slashed at the air with his hand, an action that was as foolish as it looked, for his son had already left.

Within another hour, Alasdair had packed up all his belongings from both the hospital and his room at the Empire; he took a taxi straight home to Point Piper, to his mother. He told her what had happened, and with all her pride and joy, she popped a bottle of champagne: 'Oh, good for you, my boy. Good for you.'

Audrey was on the phone to the solicitor that very afternoon: 'Yes, that's right, I must discuss a matter of divorce.' The new young fellow at Daleforth's wasn't sure he'd heard that correctly, so she made it even plainer: 'I want to sue him for every penny. I want you to put him through the works.'

The house of cards that Eliot Slade had built from his cowardice and hatred fell quickly then. He was forced by his son and his wife to leave the family home as soon as he returned at six o'clock that evening.

'I'll take you on.' He squared up to his son at the front door.

But Alasdair was unmoved: 'Don't make me call the police. Just pack a bag and go.'

Slade took a short lease on a gentleman's apartment in Rose Bay, thinking it would be a temporary arrangement, thinking this was a storm in a teacup. It wasn't. With Alasdair, Oxley and Miss Brynne gone, the orthopaedic department collapsed under the weight of his incompetence – patients were having to be ferried out north and south to other hospitals. The board was finally forced to act.

But the medical establishment was gentle with him all the same. Poor man, losing balls and wife in one, it was said, not only among the members of the board but his supporters that remained within the BMA and at the university. They banded together to recommend he be awarded an Order of the British Empire honour for his long and, so they told themselves, venerable service. There was no other sort of inducement that might make him disappear quietly.

'You'll be on the next King's Birthday list,' they promised.

'It's a time in every man's life,' they commiserated, patting him on the back.

'You were one of the greats in your day,' they bullshitted for all they were worth to get him out the door.

And while he made quite a convincing display of humble acquiescence, even Slade himself knew that last to be untrue. He was never one of the greats. He was no-one compared to Hugo Winter, whom he managed to blame for his own failings even now. If it hadn't been for Winter's death, he'd never have been pushed to take Jim Cleary as a patient at all. First, there'd been that outpouring of grief and plaudits from all quarters of the general public at that damned funeral he couldn't keep himself from attending, lurking up the back like a criminal returning to the scene of his misdeeds. And then, the following Monday, that journalist had telephoned him for a few official good words on the man's life and career, asking about the rumours of internment, forcing Slade to lie reflexively: 'No, no, don't make things up – the man was merely debarred from the military. He was an odd and antagonistic recluse, wouldn't even join the BMA. I doubt he would have been interested in any sort of service anyway.' It was a lie that had unnerved him, for it wouldn't have taken the journalist much detective work to discover what a whopper it was, if the journalist had bothered. But as it was, it had put Slade in an especially spiteful frame of mind, so that when that complex fracture had come in on the Tuesday evening, and they'd initially had difficulty getting hold of Oxley, Slade saw it as his chance to prove – what?

Prove himself to a rival who'd left him behind long, long ago? No-one, not even Slade, would ever know.

He was a fairly simple animal, shark-primitive in his predatory impulses, and now, alone in his Rose Bay apartment with more time than ever on his hands, he set about discrediting that little bitch – Lucy Brynne. He'd make a mighty effort to have her struck off the register of physiotherapists, but he'd never succeed in this, either. His dementia was too far advanced: the spelling of words eluded him, phrases slithered away like eels. Not that this stopped him from trying, or misinterpreting the polite replies he repeatedly received:

Thank you for your correspondence on the matter, Dr Slade. Your concerns have been duly noted.

Please, do us all a favour and go the hell away.

NINE

MEDICAL MAN HONOURED

Dr Eliot Alfred Slade, the eminent Sydney surgeon, has been made an Officer of the Most Excellent Order of the British Empire (Civil Division) (O.B.E.) in the King's Birthday Honours List.

Attending Sydney University, Dr Slade qualified as a medical practitioner in 1907, serving an unprecedented 30 years as President of this city's chapter of the BMA. He devoted his career to orthopaedics, retiring only in January this year from the position of chief of that specialty department at Sydney Hospital.

A dedicated teacher and scholar, Dr Slade trained many who would serve in the medical corps overseas during the war, but was prevented from serving himself due to a chronic condition of the lungs.

At the date of his retirement, he was regarded as one of the greats in his field.

Sydney
June 17, 1949

LUCY BRYNNE

'One of the greats'? I note there is no name game enough to go on the record as saying any of this rubbish. 'Chronic condition of the lungs'? Chronic condition of crap, I'll bet. How dare they give him an OBE. Where's Hugo's award? I crumple the newspaper closed and shove it into my satchel as the tram pulls up at the beach.

It's half past four and the light is winter-dim, hazy with surf spray, but I can see Jim, still in his overalls, running along the wet sand with Mate and a tennis ball. Where's Anton's OBE for that leg? He got the length discrepancy down under half an inch, as good as mine, just about precisely; I imagine Hugo telling him that the original measurements must have been wrong, needling for an argument over who did the better job. It's not perfect: there's some residual weakness of the fibularis muscles along the outside of the shin, some damage to the nerves that won't be undone. But it's perfect enough for Jim.

He sees me and waves; man and dog bound up the beach towards me. I fall in love with that big, broad smile a little bit more every day – Jim's is all right, too. He's got his Friday night smile on. It's time to party.

He's scrubbing axle grease from his fingernails, calling out from the bathroom: 'What jacket should I wear?'

And I laugh every time he asks me something like this, about clothes; he means well, trying to encourage me to take more of an interest in dressing up, in frivolity, but I'll never be the show-off he is. I don't know what tie goes with what shirt. His sense of style is so intimidatingly up to date, I take him shopping with me and let him choose my frocks. I'd let him choose my wedding gown, too, if Tess hadn't forbidden it. Obedient almost-wife, I open the wardrobe anyway, and as I do, I catch the sparkle of the engagement ring he chose for me: one big diamond surrounded by a square of smaller stones; I can't look at it without feeling surrounded by all the little things he does to care for me. I choose his blue jacket, because it's my favourite – it's outrageously blue – and I lay it on the bed.

When he sees it, he says: 'Why don't you wear your red dress then?'

Indeed: it's not only red but it has a leopard-print collar in velveteen. It makes me feel ridiculous – splendidly ridiculous.

Rory picks us up in his lairy new Mercury – the duco is iridescent bronze, he's that much of a lair – and the four of us, with Carol, cram together in the front seat, drums and the sax in the back, as we head off into the night. The club they play at is called the Old Theatre, because it's an old theatre, and it sits in the thick of the Cross, on the colourful, seedy sweep of Darlinghurst Road, where not too long ago hordes of American GIs roamed; now, it's teeming with under-age drinkers who don't know what happened five minutes ago, never mind five years, and many more who want to forget.

The other members of the band are all ex-services, too, air force and army, and they're already here among the dinner crowd: the double-bass, the trumpet, the trombone, the pianist, and the singers, Steph, Peg and Angie. Nine Pieces, they're called, because they're all smashed up in one way or another. They split their cut of the door takings between them, and while Jim tends to sling his to the Maroubra Surf Lifesavers, he would do this for free anyway – he'd probably pay to do it.

He opens the show bang on eight o'clock and it's the most exciting sound ever – a jumping, thumping explosion of joy at being here, now, alive. Just the drums. I'm biased, yes, but he's so good everyone in the room rushes to the dancefloor. Even I can't help tapping my toes, while hoping that no-one asks me to join them – not my forte by any stretch. It's wonderful enough to stand by the bar and listen. When the horns blare in, the boards beneath my feet shake. It's an exuberant, jubilant scream of gratitude. They play an extended version of the dance standard 'Sing, Sing, Sing', which goes on for as long as they care to indulge themselves. No-one ever wants them to stop.

Jim does, though: when he can't sit there behind the drums any longer, he throws the sticks to Angie, who takes over the tom-toms while he jumps right off the stage. It's not a very high stage, no more than three feet, but the first time he did it, four Friday nights ago, I screamed myself – as his physiotherapist. When Anton had said he could resume dancing, I don't think he meant this kind of dancing. Jim grabs Carol, who jitterbugs like there's no tomorrow, and they show the kids how it's done. It's not much wonder he used to roll that ankle, and the rest. Eye-watering thought of what he might have lost if he couldn't do this sort of thing anymore. He loves to move, he just loves to move, and the crowd goes mad for that, too.

Tonight, even Alasdair turns up: I see him checking his coat at the door, as the wooting and whistling subside into 'Blue, Turning Grey Over You', a take-a-breath tune.

'Good evening, Lucy.' He's smiling his handsome yacht-club smile as he saunters over. I'm always pleased to see him, but I do wonder if he blows in now and again only to check that Jim's really not going to sue him; and he wouldn't dream of doing any such thing. I wonder this time, though, if Alasdair is feeling a bit cheesed off about his father's undeserved award – not that I'm going to mention it. 'Drink?' he asks.

'Gin and tonic, thank you.' Why not go a third? It is my third, isn't it? I dare the glib question: 'Are we celebrating or commiserating?'

'Celebrating, I think,' he says, but his cheeks flush: 'I accepted a position at the Royal Alexandra today.'

'Oh!' That's the children's hospital, in Parramatta. I pinch his shoulder, so thrilled for him: 'Well done. You're going to be the best paediatric orthopaedist in the world.'

'Thanks for the hyperbole.' He blushes some more.

'No hyperbole – here's cheers to you.' I clink my glass against his whisky and sip, thinking that everything seems right in the world at this news: Alasdair at the Alexandra; Oxley now chief ortho at Sydney; Claire has had her baby, a little girl, and they called her Jacobina, for Hugo's middle name, Jacob, as there isn't any pretty name that can be made from Hugo; the sun shone out from Jo's every word: *She has that beautiful dark skin and those soulful eyes of his – he is looking at me through her*. Everyone dear to me is healthy and happy. I have no concerns, except maybe one: Jim's last head cold, in April, laid him right out. We'd just got back from Royal South Sydney after having his leg cut free of the last cast, and he was so floored, he went straight to bed – that's the bug festival of busy public hospitals for you. I must look into ways to boost his immunity: more fruit, citrus fruit, vitamin C. It is his spleen, isn't it? Or lack thereof.

'What are you pondering?' Alasdair asks me.

Don't mention whacky spleen theory; I laugh: 'Vitamin C.'

He laughs, too. 'How's the study going?'

'Good, I think.' Bit of a doddle, once you've been working in the practicalities for a while, and it's not as though I'm doing any other job. 'Devouring it.'

'Great stuff,' he says: 'If you need any help, call me, hm?'

'Thank you.' You big, lovely sweetheart. Wish I could find him a girl. I look about: probably won't find her in a nightclub at the Cross: he might only live five minutes away, but this is so not Alasdair's scene. Maybe at a wedding in Canowindra, though … a nice, peachy country girl. There'll be a full house at the church, apparently. Let's pretend I'm not terrified about all that. And the gin has me blurting: 'Would you like to come to our wedding? A bit short notice at three Saturdays away, but I'd love you to come.'

His eyebrows jump and then frown, though he's still smiling as he replies: 'Ah, no thanks. Perhaps not your wedding.'

'Oh?' I'm not sure what he means.

He laughs again, at himself: 'I'll get over it, eventually.'

'Oh.' Now I blush. How awful. Didn't think he was serious about me.

'What sort of medicine will you be looking at, eventually?' he changes the subject quickly.

And I tell him just as quickly: 'I'm not sure.' But then the gin has me blurting again: 'I want to work with veterans, I think, have a clinic of my own – not exclusively for them but mostly for them, you know? A place they can go, to sort things out. I'm not sure how to go about it, though. Long way off.'

'You'll work it out, I've no doubt.' He nods: 'Sadly, you'd never be short of patients, would you.'

'No.' I nod, too, with the melancholy reality for the world outside my near enough perfect one. For all Prime Minister Chifley's beautiful words of peace and togetherness and his dream of all-Australian made decency becoming a light on the hill for mankind, the Opposition is declaring him a communist because he wants to put a chain on the banks, never mind his nefarious plot to introduce national medical benefits. Communism, it's going to start another war very soon, or the likes of Opposition Leader Menzies will. Everyone can feel it coming. What will this one be? An atomic blasting competition with Russia? In the face of never-ending war, my small ambition seems too huge. The tangle of problems so many veterans have beneath the injuries and chronic pain: alcohol, anger, violence, isolation, poverty; problems that see some of them end up on the street or in gaol or lead them to kill themselves when what they need is care, someone to help untangle it all, fill out forms. Listen …

'You'll be brilliant at whatever you choose to do, Lucy Brynne.' Alasdair drains his glass, knocks his chest with a fist: 'Well, I must be off, only stopped in for the one. My mother is throwing a bit of a party tonight, and I needed the brace before showing up – she's been kicking up her heels lately. Quite bonkers.' Whatever that might mean, he seems glad.

'See you soon, I hope.' I watch him turn away for the door, and I gulp down the rest of my gin.

The double-bass boom-booms; Jim grabs me around the waist: 'Hello, Lucy.'

'No ...'

'Yes ...'

He makes me dance against my will.

He's drenched in sweat and the beery, salty taste of him is another level of intoxication. The band plays without him, and the girls sing: 'There ain't nobody here but us chickens, there ain't nobody here at all ...' as he dances me through the crowd, holding me so tight, my legs have to follow, and all I can do is laugh, and laugh. I'm just drunk enough to let go.

And to believe that my feet seem to have been following his beat for longer than we know. For all those years I wasn't allowed to dance, I never had the privilege of clasping the sweaty hands of any private school boy at any debutante ball, but I'm in the clutches of one now. I didn't realise he'd gone to Grammar, *the* Grammar, the city's principal academic factory five streets away from my own school – don't tell him, but I didn't pick him as quite that bright. In my first term, which was the final term of 1935, I even saw him in a musical, *The Pirates of Penzance* – he played Frederic, the Pirate Apprentice. I don't remember much of the performance, too small and wounded to be concerned with anything much other than checking that Hugo stayed sitting beside me, but I do seem to remember the next term, after the holidays, I saw a Grammar boy with a broken arm on the No.80 tram, a couple of times, getting off at the Cross, two stops before me. Was that Jim, going down to St Luke's to have his wrist seen to? I don't know, but Anton certainly remembered having seen him once he heard that story about the boy who backflipped off a grain silo. So, me and Jim, we're either the result of a very tricky trick of physics or Hugo and Anton stitched us up from the start. Woo, how drunk am I? That last gin has gone right to my head, and Jim's just said something in real life.

'Pardon? What?'

'I said, I think we should buy a car.'

'A car?' Buy an ocean liner if you like.

'Yeah. A car,' he says, 'unless you want me to double you to Canowindra on a motorcycle.'

'Motorcycle – no.' One thing I have actually discovered of late is that I'm not quite foolish enough to approve of his motorcycles. He only goes to and from work on one or the other of them, but I don't like the physics here at all. He took me for a ride out to Frenchman's Bay at La Perouse and back last Sunday: no, no, no. Seven miles of no. But now he's said we should buy a car, hasn't he. His eyes are laughing at me, loving me, holding me, as I say: 'Car – yes. Let's buy a shiny, deep blue car.'

JIM CLEARY

'They balance each other out,' I hear Mum say behind me in the church. 'Lucy is so sensible.'

Rory snorts into the sleeve of his jacket beside me. Lucy was so legless last Saturday night I had to carry her to the car – not because she's a drunk, but because she forgot to eat. She often forgets to eat or doesn't eat enough. *I don't seem to get hungry until I'm past ravenous*, she said, falling asleep. *Too busy in your head*, I suggested, and she yawned against my neck: *Yes. No. Sometimes I see the baked beans next to the kero stove and I can only think that Dad didn't get to eat them, and I don't want to eat anything without him.* I asked her in the morning, *What were you saying about your dad and baked beans by a kero stove?* She rubbed her eyes: *I don't know.* She knows; she was straight out of bed and at the books, studying, avoiding the question. She'll tell me one day, if she wants to, how tough things were – and she'll eat what I put in front of her from now on.

'They were made for each other,' Mum says, and I turn around to smile at her, at the truth of that. She's talking to one of Dad's other sisters, Joan. I look around at everyone here – the church is packed. This is a small church, but I've never seen so many people inside it. I asked Mum when she was putting this all together why she seemed to have invited half the town; she said, *We can't have any empty pews. Why? I don't want Lucy to think she doesn't have anyone here.*

Family: she's got plenty now. My sisters love her as if they invented her themselves; even my brother looks happy today, managed to shake my hand without saying one shitty-livered thing – probably still pleased I told our mother no at the first mention of kilts. No-one puts on a show like Mum and the Aunties do, but no-one needs to see these legs in a skirt, either. I'm wearing a white tux, and why not? It's my wedding, too.

Dad comes down the aisle, a hand on my shoulder, a quiet word as he passes behind me: 'They're getting out of the car. It'll be all over before you know it.'

I start counting: the flowers on the stand in front of me, a ratio of 5:3 sweet-peas to camelias; the number of cracked bricks I can see in the back wall, seventeen; people inside the church, 173, which, as a percentage of the town, is about 9.8, which, in metres per second squared, happens to be the acceleration of falling objects due to gravity. I don't know why I'm this nervous. Nothing has ever made more sense to me than marrying Lucy. That's why I'm this nervous.

The reverend smiles: 'You'll be fine, James.'

Who's James? Outside, a piper lets go his first G and I start counting the notes of Wagner's Bridal Chorus, too, before I turn around, to see my niece Wendy coming down the aisle with her basket of pink rose petals, my sister Lizzie behind her, with Fran and Maryanne.

And then Lucy. Lucinda Jane. She's on the arm of Dr Adinov, and I stop counting. Stop everything. All I can see is her smile through the fine, white film of her veil, and the dress Mum has made her that shows exactly who she is: nothing fancy: just the best.

It is over quickly, or that's how it seems; words are said, hymns are sung, we make our declarations and Lucy's slipping a ring on my finger, call me flashy for it, call me a girl, as she whispers, 'You're a real husband now.' My hand shakes as I sign the register, then I'm lifting that veil from her face and kissing her while most of my personal history applauds. Mum cries through the opening bars of 'Amazing Grace', audibly, as the band of ten pipes and six drums is too big to fit inside this church, and I'm sorry for everything I've put her through. The skirl shifts as we're sent out into the sun as Mr and Mrs and I can't find the melody at first, but then I hear it – 'I'll Walk Beside You'.

Lucy's hand is in mine, the young wheat is coming up green everywhere, all around the town, as we walk half a mile to the Memorial Hall, making this racket of pipes and drums the whole way, more people cheering from their front verandahs. We cut the cake and Rory makes a speech I'm glad no-one will ever have to hear a second time, while Mum goes around individually telling everyone, to make sure they're aware: 'She's going to be a doctor, our Lucy.'

We get changed and get into the car, into our Holden that's shiny and blue, and that's been strung with tin cans that make us laugh like idiots as we wave goodbye. We laugh all the way up into the Mountains, where we'll honeymoon at the most expensive hotel but only for one-night, as Lucy's got an exam on Monday morning. We go to bed listening to rain falling on the windows until it turns into sleet, and then into snow – and we run outside again.

Seven years later I'm still chasing her – around the house. Every morning, telling her: 'Sit down and eat breakfast, will you. Please.'

It's a different house – we've moved to a bigger place, up around the bend in every way, to accommodate Mistake One and Mistake Two, and soon to be Mistake Three – but it's the same weekday routine.

'I'm eating – I'm eating,' she says, stuffing a piece of vegemite toast in her mouth, plaiting five-year-old Felicity's hair – 'Mummy, it's too tight' – while her almost three-year-old sister Alison wipes my face with her piece of toast: 'You eat, too, Daddy.'

Then everyone's got to get out the door, and into the car.

'Get in the car, Felicity – get in the car, you're a big girl now.'

'No! I don't want to go.'

'You love school. Get in the car.' I throw her onto the backseat.

'Daddy hurt me.'

'Did he? That's no good,' says Mummy, wiping my face with her handkerchief, while Alison sings her favourite song, 'Daddy, Daddy, Daddy, Daddy, Daddy, Daddy,' that sounds like an ambulance.

We let Mummy out at the top of the hill, at her clinic; she kisses us all; I watch her until she gets in the door, and then just a few moments more. Every day's a challenge. I don't have time to count, except for teaching the kids its general usefulness and pulling out the clarinet at bedtime because it's about the only thing that will convince Alison to shut up and go to sleep. I don't have time to catch a cold – please, not another one this year. I don't have time for a haircut. How do you do it, Jimmy? I get asked. How do I cope with my family? I wouldn't wind back a second of this for anything. Won't Lucy working damage the children? I've heard too many say that, too, but there's worse damage, isn't there. Felicity really does love school; Alison was born to go to Kindy Tots, where I am treasurer of the Fathers Club and keeper of the barbeque tongs, thank you; both the girls love being looked after by Carol the rest of the time as needed, and 'helping' her with their new baby. When I'm at work, every afternoon Rory asks me: 'What's for tea, dear?' because I cook dinner most nights, too. And I do it happily, for every night Lucy didn't have a proper dinner when she was small; packing eggs all day for baked beans at thirteen; for how ashamed she was at finally telling me this. For how much our daughters look like tiny versions of her. For how much she's just not a very good cook, and if it was left to her, we'd live on vegemite and fruit juice.

I do it because she works harder than anyone I know. She's the 'physio girl' on Maroubra Road; she doesn't care if they don't call her 'doctor', or if they can't afford the fee. I pay the rent when necessary, but that's necessary less and less. She gets referrals through old army contacts, other doctors, and through talk at all the local returned servicemen's clubs: 'Go and see Lucy, she'll sort out your aches and pains.' Once she gets them in there, they get a lot more than physio. She's their doctor and their advocate through the rest of the medical system, making sure they get the care they need.

She's my wife.

THE PHYSIO GIRL

Mother of three and wife of ex-RAAF Flying Officer, James Cleary, Dr Lucinda Cleary is making a name for herself as a general medical practitioner in the seaside suburb of Maroubra.

With brand new baby Gareth in arms, it is a wonder Dr Cleary finds time for a career at all. 'I have plenty of help,' she assures with a ready smile, too modest to elaborate.

Her practice specialises in the physical therapies of massage, manipulation and exercise. Many of her patients are defence force veterans who endure permanent orthopaedic injuries, requiring ongoing treatment.

Asked why she works in this often challenging area of medicine, Dr Cleary said, 'I was trained by the brilliant surgeon, Dr Hugo Winter, so I was always going to have an interest in orthopaedics.'

Dr Cleary added pensively: 'My father was a returned serviceman and so is my husband. I hold all those who give service to others in the highest esteem, and I hold kindness to be our most valuable therapy. Perhaps we'll find a way to measure it one day, and make it a medical specialty, too.'

Sydney
September 21, 1956

AUTHOR NOTE

The inspiration for *Walking* grew from a snippet of story I came across fifteen years ago when I was researching early twentieth-century surgery for my first novel, *Black Diamonds*. I'd blown up my hero, Daniel Ackerman, during the First World War and had to work out how he might have been put back together again. In trawling through the *Australian Dictionary of Biography* for such doctors, I found an intriguing entry on a German-Australian surgeon by the name of Max Herz, a brilliant and innovative orthopaedist who was interned as an enemy alien during the war, not because he was a danger to Australia but because his British colleagues wanted him out of the game – for reasons of prejudice and professional jealousy.

My own family history is marked by similar, though less dramatic bigotries from that war, and so Max Herz's story struck a deep chord. But despite an excellent biography written on him by former patient Joan Clarke – *Dr Max Herz, Surgeon: The human price of civil and medical bigotry in Australia* (1976) – and despite tantalising newspaper trails detailing his wonderful deeds, especially as a surgeon dedicated to the welfare of disadvantaged children, it seemed there wasn't quite enough information available for me to be able to write a biographical fiction based on him specifically, to show who he really was.

Then one day at the end of 2016, Lucy Brynne began chatting to me, as my imaginary friends have a habit of doing, and *she* began to tell the story. I decided then that I would free up all narrative possibilities by fictionalising my surgeon completely. While Hugo Winter is very much inspired by Max Herz and many of the things that happened to him, Hugo's story is a work of the imagination. The intervention of Sir John Monash in his internment and deportation case is fanciful and included to show the depth of the Jewish contribution to the war effort. Billy Hughes' defence of him in the federal parliament does, however, reflect the truth, as do the general circumstances of Hugo's imprisonment, the BMA's long persecution of him, and his extraordinary medical career, including his generosity to and treatment of the children of Lithgow and New South Wales generally. It is important to stress that all of Hugo's personal relationships and the manner of his death do not bear relation to anyone but the fictional Hugo himself.

Likewise, I have changed the name of the real-life German prisoner who was killed at Liverpool Concentration Camp's Sing Sing compound to Paul Albrecht, as it's impossible to know what really happened to that boy and why.

It must be noted here as well that Eliot Slade is also an entirely fictional character: no such man ever existed at Sydney Hospital or was president of any chapter of the BMA. I created him to distil into one character the well-documented narrow-mindedness, snobbery and discrimination that existed in the medical establishment at the time. Apologies to the wonderful Sydney Hospital for using you as the backdrop to all this chicanery, but the location was too beautiful and too historically important to resist.

In this story, the unfolding developments of orthopaedics across the twentieth century also swept me along on an odyssey of research, showing me the often cruel relationship between the destructiveness of war and the marvels of medical progress. In real life, Max Herz was by no means the only surgeon to be disregarded for new ways of doing things. Gerhard Küntscher, too, was denied any respect or credibility for his revolutionary nail in Germany until war proved its efficacy; just as advances made in traction splinting by Welsh surgeon, Hugh Owen Thomas, had been ignored by the British not least because the man was Welsh. As a study, the obstinate, petty resistance of the establishment is both fascinating and frightening.

Of course, there are many more good doctors in the world than bad, and one of the best is my stalwart friend, Dr Elizabeth Hovey, a storyteller herself and an oncologist who is a constant inspiration to me, not least because of the depth of her compassion. Thank you, Liz, for believing I could write this thing, and that I should. And a very special thank you as well to an old RAF navigator, Fred Dennis, who's no longer with us but who lives large in my heart. This novel might have been buried under a mountain of self-doubt forever if not for the editorial care of champion word-wrangler Jody Lee and the loyal support of my agent, the one and only Selwa Anthony – colleagues and cherished friends. Thanks as well to Lucy Halliday for mopping up after the madness with an enthusiastic typo-hunt. And once again, this novel would not be in the world at all without the publishing prowess of Joel Naoum, and Alissa Dinallo's beautiful cover design.

Incalculable gratitude as always, too, to my ever-steady muse de bloke, my husband, Dean Brownlee, for demonstrating to me daily the courage and strength of kindness – not only in putting up with me, but in the way your respect for all creatures brings all manner of goodness into my world.

PS: For those unaware of the quirks of Australian placenames, Canowindra, Jim's hometown, is pronounced 'ca-nown-dra'.

Take a journey through time with Kim Kelly.
You've never seen Australia like this before...

SUNSHINE

Three wounded veterans of the Great War find themselves sharing a patch of farmland, and not much else – until one battle-hardened nurse changes everything. *Sunshine* is a tale of home, hope and healing, of growing life and love, and discovering that we are each other's greatest gifts.

LADY BIRD & THE FOX

At a breakneck gallop through the wild colonial Australian goldrush, *Lady Bird & The Fox* untangles a tale of true identity and blind bigotry, of two headstrong opposites thrown together by fate, bushranging, and the irresistible forces of love.

JEWEL SEA

Based on the true story of the loss of the luxury steamship *Koombana* to a vicious cyclone off the coast of North-Western Australia in 1912, *Jewel Sea* is a tale of fatal desire, theft and greed – of kindred spirits searching for each other, and for redemption.

WILD CHICORY

A journey from Ireland to Australia in the early 1900s, along threads of love, family, war and peace, *Wild Chicory* is a slice of ordinary life rich in history, folklore and fairy tale, and a portrait of the precious bond between a granddaughter, Brigid, and her grandmother, Nell.

PAPER DAISIES

A haunting tale of love, murder and misogyny. Unfolding at the dawn of 1901, as Australia at last becomes a nation and her women rally for the right to vote, *Paper Daisies* tells of the dangerous path one woman must tread to see justice done – and the man who lights her way.

THE BLUE MILE

Against the glittering backdrop of Sydney Harbour, *The Blue Mile* is a story of the cruelties of Great Depression poverty, the wild gamble a city took to build a bridge – a wonder of the world – and the risks only the brave will take for a chance to truly live and love.

THIS RED EARTH

It's 1939 and the girl next door wants adventure before she settles down – but war gives her more than she's asked for. From Australia's sparkling coastline to her dusty, desert heart, *This Red Earth* charts a fight for home, and a quest to tell the truth about love – before it's too late.

BLACK DIAMONDS

From the foothills of the Blue Mountains to the battlefields of France, comes a story of war and coal. Told with freshness, verve and wit, *Black Diamonds* is the tale of a fierce young nation – Australia – and two fierce hearts who dare to discover what courage really means.

*Available at all major online retailers worldwide,
in paperback, ebook and audio.*

KIM KELLY

Kim Kelly is the author of nine novels exploring Australia and its history. Her stories shine a bright light on some forgotten corners of the past and tell the tales of ordinary people living through extraordinary times.

An editor and literary consultant by trade, stories fill her everyday – most nights, too – and it's love that fuels her intellectual engine. In fact, she takes love so seriously she once donated a kidney to her husband to prove it, and also to save his life.

Originally from Sydney, today Kim lives on a small rural property in central New South Wales just outside the tiny gold-rush village of Millthorpe, where the ghosts are mostly friendly and her grown sons regularly come home to graze.

PRAISE FOR KIM KELLY

'deeply moving ... alive, full-hearted and shimmering with hope' – Belinda Castles, *Bluebottle*

'Kelly is a masterful creator of character and voice.' – Julian Leatherdale, *Palace of Tears*

'history that makes you think as well as feel' – Wendy James, *The Golden Child*

'an author who writes with such a striking sense of atmosphere and sublime instinct' – *Theresa Smith Writes*

'storytelling is clearly encoded in her DNA' – *Writerful Books*

'It is uplifting to know that there are people who can write like this, with clarity, a bit of devilment and a hint of a smile.' – *Canberra Times*

'marvellous depth and authenticity based on some impressive research, and her characters, plot and fluid prose draw the reader into this world' – *Daily Telegraph*

'colourful, evocative and energetic' – *Sydney Morning Herald*

'storytelling that breaks the rules so beautifully' – Jenn J McLeod, *A Place to Remember*

'Kim Kelly's writing is magnificent' – *With Love for Books*

'told with wit, warmth and courage' – Kylie Mason, *The Newtown Review of Books*